& Then They Wed

Ampersand Love Book 2

Riya Iyer

Copyright © 2024 by Riya Iyer

& Then They Wed, Ampersand Love Book 2

All rights reserved.

No part of this book may be reproduced in any form or by any electronic or mechanical means, including information storage and retrieval systems, without written permission from the author, except for the use of brief quotations in a book review.

This is a work of fiction. Names, characters, certain places and events are a product of the author's imagination. Any resemblance to actual persons, living or dead, is purely coincidental.

Published by Riya Iyer Books

Editing by Sarah Ward

First Edition, July 2024

E-book ISBN: 978-1-7381020-2-0

Paperback ISBN: 978-1-7381020-3-7

To those who can't decide what they want more - a man feeding them good food or a man calling them a good girl - the answer is both. Always, both.

And to the women who were told that being 'too much' was a bad thing - don't dull your light because someone else prefers you in the shadows.

Acknowledgements

First and foremost, a big thank you to YOU, the reader, for choosing to read an indie South Asian romance. I hope you see the representation I once wished for and that you finish this book with a smile and a full heart.

To my beautiful beta readers— Anna P, Layna, Zaylee, Aparajitha and Apoorva— your insights have been invaluable. Thank you for giving me your time, for being excited about Rian and Aditi with me, for showing me so much love with your feedback, and for simply being lovely humans who've brightened my days. Know that you have my deep respect, gratitude and friendship.

To my editor, Sarah— thank you for being so thorough and helping me elevate this book in a way I never expected.

To my incredible life partner who demanded that I draw him a timeline and a map to explain this story— thank you for saving me from the singular pain of grocery shopping and for keeping our pantry stocked. I guess it's ok that you shake your head tiredly when I chortle at jokes only I understand. Honestly, I'm hilarious, but you just don't see it. If you'd only let me explain the joke once more. . .

Finally, most importantly, my thanks to my little one who sacrifices so much of my time and attention and tells me that she's proud of me for being an 'otter'— Please don't read this book till you're eighteen. ILYSM.

Contents

Author's Note	XI
Glossary	XIII
Playlist	XVII
1. The Meet-Cute	1
2. A Boy and a Girl	8
3. The Truce	18
4. A Lonely Goddess	28
5. The Temple Visit	35
6. The Art of Saying No	43
7. Dreams	51
8. Dickhead Date Diaries	60
9. Narwahl Attack	70

10.	The Ex Hex	81
11.	No Time to Weep	88
12.	Food for the Soul	97
13.	A Proposal	105
14.	Counting Pi	113
15.	Safe Words	123
16.	Laughter and Light	133
17.	Friends Know Best	141
18.	Mother Dearest	147
19.	Mistakes	152
20.	A Grinch and his Who	158
21.	Rian, the Wrecking Ball	169
22.	Blurred Boundaries	180
23.	His Aditi	187
24.	Chota Bheem	191
25.	Tit for Tat	199
26.	Shelter	209
27.	A String of Flowers	221
28.	Triumph	229
29.	The Firefly	235
30.	Afterglow	244

31.	An Uninvited Guest	253
32.	Crescendo	261
33.	Trust	268
34.	Envy	280
35.	Bunny	293
36.	Respect	298
37.	Distance	309
38.	Catharsis	313
39.	Love Song	324
40.	The Krishnan Clan	333
41.	& Then They Wed	342
Before You Go…		354
About the Author		355

Author's Note

There are topics within this book that might be concerning to some. I have listed them below and have tried to maintain sensitivity regarding them, as best possible. Please put your mental health first, before delving into a fictional world. If you have questions, please contact me at riyaiyerwrites@gmail.com or DM me on instagram @authorriyai.

Triggers include:
- fat shaming (off and on page),

- body image issues (on page),

- eating disorder (mildly discussed on page),

- mention of attempted sexual assault (off page),

- physical and emotional abuse of children (off and on page),

- physical violence against an adult (on page),

- panic attack (on page),

- difficulties due to undiagnosed neurodivergence (dyslexia).

Glossary

Hindi terms

Food items

Gulab-jamun— dessert; fried doughnut holes, immersed in rose-scented syrup.

Jalebi— a sweet snack or dessert, popular across western Asia.

Pav Bhaji— literal translation, bread and vegetables. Though it sounds lacklustre, this is a highly sought after street food across the South Asian subcontinent, consisting of buttery soft buns eaten with a mashed vegetable gravy, lovingly cooked in a beautiful blend of spices.

Roti— Indian flatbread

Vada Pav— Mumbai's most popular street food—a potato fritter stuffed within a soft bun, accompanied with sweet and spicy chutneys. It is the Indian version of a cheat meal burger.

Haldi Doodh— turmeric milk (or latte), quite commonly consumed for its health benefits

Hindi dialogues (from famous Bollywood movies)
Pyar dosti hai—Love is friendship.
Dosti mein, no sorry, no thank you— Between friends, no sorry, no thank you
Naam toh suna hoga—you must be familiar with the name

Articles of clothing/ adornment
Dhoti— a loose, plain garment worn by males, similar to a Scottish kilt, but ankle length
Dupatta— a long scarf worn with a kurta and salwar
Gajra— A string of flowers sewn together to form a small garland; usually worn by women as a decorative element pinned in their hair
Kurta/Kurti— a long shirt often worn by men and women alike
Pallu— the tail end of a saree
Salwar— a traditional Indian pant, worn under a kurta or kurti
Saree— Traditional Indian wear for women

Misc
Bazaar—marketplace consisting of multiple stalls and shops
Bhabhi—sister-in-law (many times used to respectfully address the significant other of a male friend)
Bhaiyya—brother (also used to address a male friend of higher economic status as a sign of respect)
Chacha—uncle (also a generic term of respect for an older male)
Mehendi— also known as Henna, temporary tattoos using a paste made out of the leaves of the henna plant
Rangoli— a traditional art form using finely ground rice flour to draw designs (at the threshold of one's house) that are a combination of geometric lines, with various loops and circles, sometimes with added colour. Also called Kolam (Tamil) or Muggu (Telugu)

Saheb— Sir (used to respectfully address a person of higher economic status, or a customer)

Hanuman Chalisa— Hindu prayers to the monkey God, Hanuman, known for his strength and lack of fear

Tamil terms
Amma—Mother
Appa—Father
Arana Kayiru—traditionally, a black thread tied around the waist of young children to ward off bad mojo (specifically, better digestive health)
Ayappa Satyam— in the context within this book, similar to the English phrase 'I swear to god'
Idli— Steamed rice cakes (popular South Indian breakfast item)
Kanjeevaram—Silk Sarees that are famous in South India. For Saree, see Hindi terms
Kolam—see Rangoli (under Hindi terms)
Paati—grandmother (maternal or paternal)
Payasam—Rice pudding (popular South Indian dessert)
Porum— enough
Suprabhatam— Hindu morning prayers

Telugu terms
Kanna —dear child
Nanamma —grandmother (paternal)
Muggu —see Rangoli (under Hindi terms)

Playlist

Just The Way You Are | Bruno Mars
Crush | David Archuletta
Lover | Taylor Swift Ft. Shawn Mendes
Beautiful Soul | Jesse McCartney
Shape of You | Ed Sheeran
Girls like you | Maroon 5
Ishq Bulaava | Sanam Puri, Shipra Goyal
Manchala | Nupur Pant, Shafqat A.A. Khan
Zehnaseeb | Chinmayi S, Shekhar Ravjiani
Maan Meri Jaan | King, Nick Jonas
Kabhi Kabhi Aditi | Rashid Ali
Titli | Vishal - Shekhar
Jaaniye | Vishal Mishra, Rashmeet Kaur
Chaleya | Arijit Singh, Shilpa Rao

RIYA IYER

Tum Tum | Sri Vardhini
Mangalyam | KK, Shaan
Aasa kooda | Sai Abhyankkar

1

The Meet-Cute

RIAN

"*You're a curse to me.*"

"*No,*" the boy whimpered.

"*Everything you touch, you destroy. That is your legacy.*"

Eyes clenched shut, he tried harder to block the noises that refused to fade amidst the hum of an engine.

The annoyed honking of an overeager truck jolted him awake. He squinted, suddenly assailed by the bright headlights of a car on the opposite side of the signal just as his driver made a turn into a road he recognized well.

Rian Shetty took in a deep breath and sat up with a sigh, tiredly rubbing his eyes with the heel of his palm. Without noticing, he reached into his pocket for his phone and tapped the screen. Just past 1:00 a.m. No wonder he felt so sleepy.

His flight from Singapore had landed a short while ago. Raju, his driver, had been present to pick him up despite the last minute notice.

"Did anyone else get hurt except Ankit?" Rian asked, his eyes meeting Raju's in the rearview mirror.

"No, Bhaiyya. I took him to the hospital to get stitches immediately. I told them not to call you but they wouldn't listen to me."

"I'm responsible for the safety of my staff. I'm glad someone informed me."

"But you had to rush back like this in the middle of the renovations in Singapore."

"Singapore will be fine." Rian added another voice note reminder into his phone for the morning while he sorted through his calendar. He was diligent about tracking his tasks and deadlines—it was the only way he had gotten as far as he had. "It is late now, but did you find out Ankit's address? I want to go see him tomorrow before I get to the restaurant."

"Yes, Bhaiyya, I will take you there first. No problem."

Nodding, he sat back, trying hard not to doze off again. If he did, he was certain he would hear her voice again.

The words from his dream kept repeating in the recesses of his brain, taunting him to admit that he was bothered by them. That he was still disturbed by the hate and rage upon his mother's face when she had spat those words at him.

He'd been barely eight, mourning the loss of his father, and he'd not known it then, but he may as well have considered himself an orphan.

Leela Shetty, wife of Abhay Shetty, an ex-model and socialite extraordinaire, had been as motherly as a snake.

That was probably an insult to reptiles all around the world, he thought grimly, watching the buildings outside go by in a blur.

She had been his harshest critic, and not in a manner that made one long to do better. She had done everything to make him feel like he was not worthy of being her son.

That he was not worthy of being a Shetty.

That he was not worthy. Period.

One would have thought this meant that she would ignore his existence.

Unfortunately, in the last few years, Leela had decided that she was an integral part of Rian's adult life. Each visit felt like he was on the receiving end of an unwelcome enema.

She never failed to scratch at old wounds, ensuring he spent multiple days after her visits trying to talk himself out of committing matricide. No matter her trespasses against him, he'd been unable to stop her shameless need to use him as a social stepping stool, especially since he'd made a name for himself in the food industry.

He tolerated her behaviour because he knew that Leela was vindictive enough to try to disgrace him otherwise. With her penchant for spreading gossip and rumours, uncaring of the people she hurt in the process, she could very well turn around and damage his hard-earned respect.

Now, more than ever, he needed to protect his image so that he would be received favourably by the board of investors at the bank. He was planning to leverage his work to entice them into approving his proposal. With his passion project on the horizon, he could take no chances with letting a cannonball like Leela wreck his dreams. And this, by far, was his biggest dream—a culinary institute with a special access fund for those children who had talent, but were limited by finances.

When he died, he would leave this behind as his legacy.

He would leave behind something good, and finally shed the burden of having carried his mother's horrid words with him since he was a boy.

He would prove her wrong.

He just hoped that he didn't lose his patience before achieving this goal, because truly, Leela Shetty could drive a saint to murder.

While he may not have been present to suffer her tantrums and outrageous demands this time, his restaurant staff was.

An altercation between his mother and a waiter at the main branch of The Mumbai Map, his beloved restaurant, had Rian leaving his new Singaporean venture under the watchful eye of his project manager.

Rian would have loved to stay back longer. The Singapore Map had been in the works for over two years, and was finally on track for a winter opening. Had his mother not injured Ankit, a long-time employee of The Mumbai Map, Rian would have never thought to return early to his home city.

Though it was Ankit who had required stitches to his hand, Leela had been heard making threats of reporting him to the cops for trying to hurt her. What had Ankit done wrong, you ask? He'd held her hand when she'd waved a butter knife in their manager's face for not serving her the best bottles of wine, and for daring to charge her for her meal.

Which meant that Rian's presence became necessary to protect his employees from his entitled harpy of a parent.

He yawned once more.

The noise must have alerted Raju because he spoke up just as they pulled into the parking lot of his high-rise apartment building.

"We are home, Bhaiyya. You can rest soon. I didn't see Nanamma today, so I did not get a chance to tell her that you would be back."

"That's fine. I'll surprise her in the morning."

Rian grabbed his backpack and luggage from the trunk, waving off Raju's attempts to help.

Nanamma, he thought fondly, dragging his suitcase into the large elevator and pressing the button for his floor.

He'd been trying to get his grandmother to move in with him for years, but she'd refused. Despite her age, Chitra Shetty loved being independent and had not been ready to leave the home she had shared with her husband in the twilight years of his life.

Velas, the small beachside town that she still called home, had become a safe haven for his friend, Kaya Sharma, when she'd been estranged from her family.

Now that Kaya, known to everyone else as Kaveri, had moved back to Mumbai to live with her husband, Arjun Rathore, it seemed that Nanamma had finally begun to feel lonely.

Begrudgingly, she'd agreed to spend a few months at a time living with Rian, insisting that she would go back to Velas in the rainy months to get away from the infamous Mumbai floods. Contrary to her plans however, she'd ended up coming back earlier. And not alone.

A temporary houseguest.

When she had last spoken to him, she'd explained that the grandchild of an old friend had been accepted into a specialty medical program at a nearby hospital and needed a place to stay.

Rian hadn't questioned why this person couldn't rent an apartment or why Nanamma had to be here to chaperone him. He'd assumed that this 'Adi' that Nanamma had mentioned was a young man-child. The typical, spoiled son of an overprotective family who'd had everything done for him and was incapable of an existence independent of help.

Regardless, since his grandmother rarely asked him for anything, Rian had acquiesced and allowed the use of his home to house this boy.

He supposed the presence of this Adi would not impact him anyway. Rian would be busy with his work and would categorically decline babysitting said man-child.

He punched in the code to his apartment. The answering ping and whirr of the electronic lock announced his success. He wheeled in his suitcase, stepping into a wide entryway with a side closet where he dumped his shoes. Leaving his luggage behind, he walked to the end of the foyer, which opened into an enormous kitchen and living space. The far end of the wall was completely made up of floor-to-ceiling windows, which brought in enough brightness that he didn't need to switch the lights on. Beyond the windows was a sizable balcony that led to a sweeping view of the Bandra-Worli Sea Link—a 5.6 kilometre long, eight-lane-wide cable-stayed bridge that linked the busy Western Suburbs of Bandra with the upscale locality of Worli in South Mumbai, where he now lived. As busy as it was by day, the bridge was a breathtaking sight at night, lit up to dominate the dark Arabian Sea over which it stood.

He slid behind the white quartz-encased island, a massive twelve-foot structure that he had commissioned. He loved cooking here. It was a departure from the black cabinets and black stone counters that lined the rest of his kitchen, drawing one's eye to the true heart of his home. He grabbed a drink and took a look around him, his sights inevitably drawn to the outside again.

Rian had splurged on this apartment once he had made enough money. Something about being this high up, and seeing the city lights blinking constantly made him feel okay, if only for a short time. Like he wasn't alone.

He slapped the bottle back down on the counter and walked towards the massive sectional that dominated his living room. Tired and wanting to rest, he unthinkingly leaned over the back of the couch and dropped onto the seat, belly first.

"Amma!" He heard a shriek, just as he realised he'd made a mistake.

The next instant, it was chaos. Thrashing, kicking, squirming, and screaming ensued.

He felt a sharp jab on his side and with an oomph, he began to roll off the edge, his surprise and confusion robbing him of the ability to fight. As he fell, instinct kicked in and he grabbed at whatever he could to halt his descent. His hands connected with warm skin and despite not meaning to, he brought down the weight of whoever or whatever was on his couch.

This person could not be human with the sort of sounds they were emitting. He was wrestling an alligator, he was sure, one that was still cursing and screaming. Or at least was trying to, because the noise was muffled under the blanket that covered its face.

Fighting still, Rian managed to pull the sheet off, only to be assaulted by a curtain of thick hair that blocked the remnant light around him.

"What the hell?" *A girl?*

"Thieeeeeeeef!" said girl screeched, smacking his chest and swinging her fists. "I won't let you steal anything! I don't know where the money is kept but I won't let you take even a spoon!"

She swatted at him ineffectually while he tried to grab her arms, causing her to drop the pillow she was smacking him in the face with. She pulled at her wrists while Rian frustratedly jerked his head until the pillow fell sideways.

"Stop screaming!" he ordered, sputtering when more hair slapped his cheek.

"I'm a police officer! How dare you attack me! I have guns! And knives! Get out!"

"Just listen," Rian shouted, trying to capture her hands again. God, this woman was like a slippery eel. He hefted his chest up and swung an arm about her waist, rolling them over until he had her hands trapped beside her head.

"Help! Thief! Murderer!"

"Will you shut up? I'm not going to hurt you!" Rian bellowed.

Bright light flooded the room and Nanamma's surprised voice pierced through all the ruckus.

"What is going on here? Adi? Rian?"

Rian heard nothing, his eyes firmly on the woman he held under him as she blew strands of hair off her face with an angry huff. Beautiful brown eyes framed under thick lashes stared back, widening just as recognition hit them both.

"You!"

2

A Boy and a Girl

RIAN

What an annoying woman with her big eyes and matter-of-fact observation, as if she knew everything! As if she would unearth his problems even though they didn't know each other. How dare she make him feel like his vulnerabilities and heartbreak were accessible for her to dissect and judge?

"If I were in your place, I'd cut my losses and channel my energy elsewhere."

The sound of waves cresting at the nearby beach could not drown the spike of anger at her words. He leaned in, trapping her warm hands under his, hating that this woman had seen something in a few minutes that he had not allowed anyone else to see for years.

Fear for Kaya's safety, worry for Nanamma's health, and irritation post his altercation with Arjun had not yet abated. Rian lost the battle to be polite to this stranger. Doctor or not, she had no right to diagnose him when he had not asked for it.

"I didn't realise that gossip mongering, and conjecture were taught in medical school these days," he had caustically replied. *"No wonder the quality of care is dropping each year."*

"You!" Aditi exclaimed, jarring him out of his memories. "It's you."

"I don't know what you're talking about," he lied smoothly, belying the curious panic bubbling within him. What the hell was this woman doing in his house?

"Remember me? That night! Late at night. When you and I met!" she insisted, nodding her head at a dizzying speed.

"You met with my grandson late in the night?" They heard Nanamma's shocked question. Both Rian and Aditi looked towards the older lady, seemingly surprised that they had an audience.

Chitra stared at the two children on the floor, neither moving, both speechless. She pointedly glanced at her grandson and jerked her chin towards him, bringing his attention to the fact that he was still lying on top of a person.

Embarrassed, Rian scrambled to his feet, slapping his clothes to rectify them and praying that his grandmother didn't suspect him of doing anything indecent. He glanced to the side when Aditi stood up, the blanket falling off her body to reveal shapely legs in short pyjama pants with the most blindingly bright citrus print on them. She bent down to pick up the blanket and on her rounded posterior were the words 'squeeze me'. The nearly faded message glared back at him like a dare, and Rian's mouth dropped open.

Throwing the coverlet onto the couch, she spun to face him, blinking rapidly when she caught him staring.

"Do you know her, Rian?"

He shook his head, releasing a breath he hadn't realised he'd been holding in.

Keep looking at Nanamma. This is safe. Nanamma is safe, he coached himself, still a little taken aback by the coincidence of seeing a woman he had never expected to.

"Were you two in some type of relationship, meeting late at night?" Nanamma questioned, her features etched with suspicion.

"No!" they exclaimed simultaneously, shaking their heads in unison as though they were a pair of school-going children who had colluded together to lie to their parents about the same incident.

Chitra was confused by the rapid shift in the atmosphere. They'd gone from yelling to awkward staring and silence within seconds. The Aditi she knew was never silent. The Rian she knew was never awkward.

Aditi cleared her throat when the wait for someone to speak got too long. "I met him once, a few months ago. When I was in Velas. I was. . ."

"It was nothing," Rian interrupted. He strode towards his grandmother and put an arm over her shoulder, rounding out to look at the young woman again. "She was going down the wrong road and I corrected her. Isn't that right?" He raised a single brow, a quiet but clear indication that told her to keep the discussion of that night to herself.

Aditi's gaze darted between grandmother and grandson, no longer sure what she was allowed to say.

"So, you don't know each other?" Chitra clarified.

"We kinda know each other," Aditi admitted, at the same time as Rian said, "I don't know her at all."

"I'm Dr. Aditi Krishnan. See?" she replied with a little tilt of her head. "It's so easy. Now we can get to know each other."

Rian peered at her, not sure what to make of her offer. Either she was truly friendly or was pretending to be so. Regardless, getting to know each other was not part of his plan.

He spun towards Nanamma, questioning her instead. "What is she doing here?"

"I told you we're hosting a guest for a few months. How come you're back so soon?"

"Restaurant troubles," he answered carelessly, sliding a sideways glance at the woman who stood near the couches, listening to their conversation with an unabashedly curious gaze. He leaned in towards his grandmother, gesturing to Aditi with a jab of his thumb. "I thought it was a boy. You kept saying you're bringing home Adi."

Nanamma nodded. "That's her name. Aditi."

"No, you said Adi. Adi is a boy's name. This," he pointed to the person across from him, "is a girl."

"Not to put too fine a point on it, but I'm a woman," Aditi clarified, completely unfazed by the look of incredulity he shot her way. He wasn't sure that it was a relevant correction but apparently she thought differently. "My family and friends call me Adi," she continued, hoping that an explanation would resolve whatever frustration he had with her name. "Adi. Aditi. Same same."

"See?" Nanamma chimed in, smiling warmly at Aditi before turning towards him again. "Same same."

"No. Not same same," he mocked.

"The ending of that name makes a huge difference. Adi sounded like a chill dude whom I could have a beer with," he explained, feeling no shame for lying despite the fact that he had fully expected to avoid said chill dude. "Aditi is. . ." He trailed off, at a loss for words, waving one hand in the air uselessly when his eyes met hers. She smiled. The barest tilt of her lips and he lost track of whatever he'd wanted to say.

"I can have a beer with you," she offered sweetly. "I don't enjoy the taste, but I could do it if it's that important."

She glanced from Nanamma to him, shrugging delicately, as though to indicate that she was willing to make this sacrifice for the sake of the greater good.

"Excuse us," he bit out, holding Nanamma by her shoulders to manoeuvre her down the hall. His bedroom was closest.

"She's got to go," he announced as soon as they stepped in.

Nanamma frowned. "Why?"

"Because..." He opened his mouth, closing it ineffectually when he couldn't think of a reason.

Hands on his hips, he tried to maintain a look of surety when really, he had no clue why he was reacting this way. Just that something about her put all his senses on alert. Like it had that night in Velas.

He couldn't help but remember how easily she'd deduced that he had had unrequited feelings for his friend Kaya, a patient she had just treated, and that he had needed to let it go.

If I were in your place, I'd cut my losses and channel my energy elsewhere.

"Because?" Nanamma prodded, twisting her wrist, palm facing up in a commonly used gesture to form her question, waving it impatiently when he couldn't answer fast enough.

"Because!" he started, wishing for some brilliant reason to make itself available. "She's a girl. And I'm a boy."

He winced even as he said it, the voice in his head cackling at how lame he was being. He was tired. And the shock of finding Aditi under him hadn't worn off. That's why he couldn't form a better argument, he decided. This was not his fault, it was hers.

"She's a girl," Nanamma repeated, watching him with an impassive look.

He nodded.

"You're a boy," she deadpanned.

He nodded again.

Nanamma clicked her tongue.

"That's your reason?"

Rian felt his ears heat. He knew he sounded silly, but he couldn't take it back.

Nanamma's deep sigh was that of an old woman about to embark upon the uphill journey of trying to understand a fool.

"I didn't need gender lessons, kanna. It's almost 2:00 a.m. I'm an old woman and I need to sleep. Can you please tell me properly what the problem is?"

He scratched his head for a second, letting out a breath before trying again. He held her hand and brought her with him, sitting her down in an armchair before kneeling in front of her.

"Nanamma, how can you be okay with a girl living in the same house as me? I'm an unmarried man." He pointed to himself, widening his eyes in mock horror at their situation. "She's an unmarried woman. What will society say?"

He held his grandmother's gaze, trying not to cringe. If his friends saw him like this, they would lose all respect. Not that he was making himself proud right now, but at least his embarrassment was private.

He saw Nanamma's face scrunch in thought. Slowly, she brought a hand up to gently cup his cheek. He tilted his lips downwards in a small frown, a picture of troubled innocence. Without a warning, she smacked him lightly, surprising him.

He shot up, dramatically holding onto his cheek, the shock of her reaction having hurt more than the gentle tap.

"Did you eat one of those Korean dramas you like for dinner? I will slap these stupid dialogues out of you, Rian. What will society say?" she mocked, picking the edge of her pallu and wrapping it over herself like a shawl before sitting back and assuming a stance befitting a mob boss.

Dammit, he'd thought his reason was genius. He should have known Chitra Shetty was not cowed by society's wagging tongues. He pouted as he rubbed his cheek. The judgement on his K-dramas was a low blow.

Nanamma shook her head. "Kanna, I don't understand you. I'm not telling you to live in the same bedroom. I don't see a problem."

Rian's eyes narrowed at her nonchalance. "This is not an attempt to fix me up with a woman, right? It's taking it a bit far, bringing a girl to live under the same roof as me."

Nanamma tilted her head, pursing her lips thoughtfully. "It's not a bad idea. You *are* thirty."

"I'm *only* thirty."

"Perfect age gap with Adi. I'm not averse to setting it up if you're interested. She'd make a great granddaughter-in-law. I really like her."

"I don't," he cut in shortly, walking backwards towards his bed.

"Are you sure? She's a doctor."

"I can afford to pay for medical services without having to marry a doctor," he dryly stated, shucking his jacket off and throwing it carelessly atop his mattress.

"You seemed very friendly when I entered the room, or am I meant to forget that I found you on top of her?" Nanamma accused, holding back a snort at the way her grandson spun around to face her, jaw hanging.

"We were almost killing each other!" he insisted, pointing in a general outward direction. "I was surprised to find a girl in the house! And she thought I was a thief! I'm not interested in her. I'm not interested in marrying anyone!"

"I know, Rian," she accepted with a disgruntled sigh. When she stood up and glanced at him, he saw signs of sadness that made his guilt stir up once more. "Though I am still going to hope and pray that I get to see my great-grandchildren before I leave this earth," his grandmother continued, "I don't expect you to marry Adi."

"You don't?"

"No."

"Why don't I believe you?"

"Rian!"

"Don't be shocked, Nanamma. You know it is well within the realm of possibility when I think you've manoeuvred things to suit your goals. You're a scarily smart woman."

Chitra couldn't hold back a pleased smile at that.

"See!" he accused immediately, pointing at her as though he'd won a big argument. "You're smiling. I knew it!"

"Hush, child. You don't know anything."

"You've been after me for months. You've tricked me into blind dates. I wouldn't put it past you to plan something by bringing a girl to live two doors down from me just to tempt me to change my mind. Which I won't," he added sternly, lest she begin to read between the lines.

"Okay," Chitra shrugged, unbothered by his statement. "But you should know that she's in the room right next to you, not two doors down. The other bedroom has a vent issue that needs to be fixed. It is too stuffy for a person to stay there."

Grandmother and grandson stood there facing each other, both locked in a daring game of who would blink first.

Rian lost.

"Nanamma, whatever you are doing, just stop. Please."

"I am not doing anything," Chitra softly pleaded, her downturned lips pulling down even further. "Why would you hurt my feelings like this?"

"I won't fall for that pout," he scoffed. "I know you."

Having given up on trying to convince him of her innocence, Chitra rolled her eyes. "Is that so? Then do you know that I am setting up Adi to meet with other eligible bachelors too?"

That stopped him short.

"That's right," Nanamma revealed triumphantly, correctly guessing his reaction.

"Her family has selected a long list of marriageable men for her to meet while she is in town. And I've suggested a few myself," she added with a satisfied look. "So you can rest assured, you are definitely not in consideration."

Rian didn't know what else to say.

"Now that we have put this particular concern to rest, do you have any other objections to that sweet child living with us?"

Rian shook his head. Nanamma approached him, her gait slow. He recognized the signs of age on her, suddenly feeling terrible about having kept her up to have this discussion now. She took both his hands in hers and patted him.

"Aditi is a good girl," she said, all traces of humour gone. "I have promised her family that she will be safe with me in Mumbai. I hope you treat her with the same respect that you would give to your friends."

"Yes, Nanamma. But that's all I can give her, okay?"

"I am old, Rian. Not deaf. I heard you the first time you said you were not interested. Do not insult my intelligence by repeating it again."

"Sorry," he mumbled immediately, chastised. A moment later, Chitra hugged him, an awkward endeavour considering Rian stood towering over her by nearly two feet. Rian tensed for a moment before softening, standing straight, and letting his grandmother hold him as she wished.

"It's good to see you back, kanna," she said, patting his arm before leaning back to look up at him. "I missed you."

He relented at last, cracking a half-hearted smile.

"Missed you too, Nanamma."

With that, Chitra left Rian to himself. As she passed the room next door, she smiled at the sight of Aditi, who was slumped in exhaustion at the edge of her bed.

Sweet child, Chitra thought fondly as she closed Aditi's door for her. Many years ago, she had chosen to look after Kaya when the troubled girl was attempting to figure out her path in life. She had not expected to play guardian to yet another young lady after Kaya had reconciled with Arjun.

A serendipitous encounter in Velas many months ago had reunited Chitra with her childhood friend, Gomati, leading to an introduction to Aditi. Time spent with them revealed that Aditi was trying to convince her parents to let her live in Mumbai for an extended work rotation. Too fearful of letting their daughter stay alone in an unknown city, they had refused.

Until Chitra had offered them a solution.

She had not thought much more beyond helping a young girl whom she'd taken a liking to, which is why it surprised her to see her normally polite grandson react this way to someone he insisted he did not know.

Chitra settled into her pillow, recalling how Rian had immediately put his walls up, almost wary of Adi. She smirked in the dark, the memory of her grandson's gobsmacked face causing her to let out an involuntary snort. Attraction often began with fear and refusals.

Rian deserved someone good and kind, more so because her sweet grandson seemed to believe the opposite. Even today, when she showed him care, it took him a minute to accept it.

Perhaps Aditi, with her cheerful and open personality, would finally win Rian over.

Perhaps.

3

The Truce

Rian

Rian's eyes shot open, his forehead dotted with sweat and his chest tight. The cotton sheets he'd thrown on himself had bunched and twisted about his legs, constricting them. His hand hit his bedside table and he blindly tapped along the surface until he came upon a familiar switch. Dull light washed his room in a soft yellow glow, and he threw a glance about.

His bedroom. He was in his bedroom. He was okay. He wasn't eight anymore, lying on the cold and wet grounds of his childhood home, waiting in the dark.

He scanned the space around him, seeing nothing, the fear still fresh. His breathing was heavy and felt loud, even to his own ears. He hunched over and forced himself to close his eyes, focusing on counting his breaths. He willed his heart to slow down from hammering so painfully within his chest.

Slapping a hand over his forehead, he hissed in surprise when the sweat burned him. A peek at his palms revealed angry crescent marks in a series of perfect indents left behind by his nails, a reminder of having clenched his fists too tight while asleep.

Once again, without being physically present, Leela Shetty had managed to wound him.

Ever since he'd returned, his nightmares had gotten worse, and it likely had to do with the fact that he had been dealing with his mother more than he had wanted to. Vindictive as always, Leela had followed through on her threat to seek retribution and had lodged a complaint against Ankit. The poor man had been harassed while at the police station until Rian had managed to convince Leela to retract her grievance.

Rian recognized that it was a power play on his mother's part. Since he had not been responding to her calls or giving her the attention she liked to command from those around her, she had begun to resort to underhanded techniques like this to bring him to heel.

He was convinced that the closer he was to someone, the more sadistic pleasure she derived out of hurting them in order to hurt him too.

Rian gritted his teeth.

He had never been able to fully cut his toxic mother out of his life. She had an unexplainable influence over him. He didn't know why that was because he was as sure of it as his own name that he despised her and wanted nothing more than to end all relations with her.

Perhaps he would finally succeed once he had his school up and running.

Yes, that would shut her up. It would put these nightmares to rest, and then he could finally move on.

Rian lay back in his bed, counting minutes and wishing for sleep to return. Frustrated by the voices that tormented him, he shucked the covers off and swung his long legs over the side, striding out to get something to drink.

As he came to the end of the hallway, his gait slowed, eyes drawn to the figure on the couch.

Aditi.

He almost groaned. He didn't want to deal with her. Thankfully, her focus seemed to be on the show that was playing on TV.

He glanced at the flat screen, unable to hold back a disgusted frown before he turned away. DC? Ugh. Further proof that his decision not to befriend her was correct. Anyone with taste knew that Marvel was superior.

Shaking his head, he beelined for his kitchen, yanking open the refrigerator to pull out a bottle of milk. His gaze swung around, searching through the cabinets for the spices he kept handy.

She coughed, and for some reason, he stilled. It took effort for him to continue ignoring her presence. Rian had not thought it would be this hard. He had firmly believed that he could go days without seeing or talking to her. The duration of her program at the hospital would come to an end eventually, and life would go back to normal. His apartment would be his again, and he wouldn't feel so on edge in his own home.

Aditi had tried a few times to interact with him, but between his own need to maintain a distance, being busy with ensuring Ankit was okay, and keeping tabs on The Singapore Map, Rian had had his hands full, only coming home late at night to sleep and sometimes pick a change of clothes.

For nearly two weeks, this had been his life. Now that things were finally slowing down, he couldn't ignore the obvious.

Aditi Krishnan was *everywhere*.

When he walked into his house, her sensible shoes were lined neatly next to his collection of sneakers. When he grabbed himself a glass from his kitchen, he'd inevitably see one of her silly mugs with nonsensical jokes sitting in the sink. Sometimes, when he returned home late at night, he'd see her huddled form wrapped like a caterpillar and sleeping on his couch, a confusing array of items littered on the centre table while the TV ran on low volume. By the time he left the next morning, the space looked pristine, which meant that any complaint about her penchant to doze off in the living room and have stacks of books and papers on his table suddenly became invalid.

Even otherwise, he doubted he could crib about Aditi to Nanamma. Rian had observed them more than once on the way out to work, and the manner in which they interacted would have fooled anyone into thinking that it was Rian who was the houseguest.

Aditi had endeared herself to Nanamma so thoroughly in his time away that his obvious desire to remain aloof from her had had his grandmother shooting him disapproving looks anytime they were in the same room.

Additionally, he had been surprised to find that nearly everyone in the vicinity of his apartment building had met and fallen in unconditional love with Dr. Aditi Krishnan. From his newspaper boy to the maid, the shopkeeper across the street, the kids in the locality, and even the security guards, everyone asked him about Aditi when they saw him, often giving him something or the other to hand over to her.

Rian would promptly leave the gift on his kitchen counter in a silent ritual of passing the parcel. He assumed she received it because it was usually gone by the time he returned. Despite being curious about these parcels, Rian stayed away from Aditi as he had promised Nanamma.

Which brought him here. Still ignoring her, still feeling awkward in his own house, and still not understanding why.

He shut the fourth cupboard he checked, grunting in annoyance. Where the hell was his favourite mortar and pestle?

Assuming he'd just missed seeing it, he went back to the cabinet he usually stored it in, pulling out random objects to check behind, to no avail.

Perplexed, he stood back, staring at the cupboards as though doing so would make it magically reappear.

"Looking for something?"

Rian's head swung to the side, hiding his surprise when he realised that Aditi had entered the kitchen and was staring at the same shelves as him. How had he not heard her?

"You move quietly," he commented, unable to stop himself.

Aditi broke out into a lopsided grin.

"Occupational hazard. Working in ICUs got me used to treading very quietly, trying to not disturb the patients."

He didn't acknowledge the answer, simply turning away from her to begin searching anew.

"Are you searching for something?" she asked again. "Maybe I could help."

"Doubt it."

"You don't know that. Try me."

"Doc, this is my kitchen. If I cannot find something here, it is unlikely that you will."

"Let's assume I will fail," she easily agreed. "Would you care to tell me what it is I will be failing in searching for?"

Damn, she was tenacious. Rian blew out a quick breath, wishing for patience before he answered her.

"It's a marble pestle and mortar, about yea big," he gestured, holding his curved hands a few inches apart.

A moment later, she brushed past him and bent down towards a lower shelf, pulling out the very thing he'd been searching for. She placed it on the counter near him, grabbing a small green jar from a drawer as well.

"I figured you'll need the cardamom too," she said, nodding towards the bottle.

Rian peered at her, confused how she had known that. His curiosity must have shown because almost immediately, she offered an explanation.

"Looks like you're going to make a late night drink, so. . ."

"That was not where I usually store it," he said, pointing at the base drawer she'd just closed. "How did you know where my mortar and pestle was?"

He could almost hear her think before she admitted sheepishly, "I kept it there."

"I liked where it was kept before."

Did he sound petulant? Yes. Did he care? No.

"But I couldn't reach it," she explained in a rush, her head bobbing with an almost equal fervour. "See, Nanamma was missing you one night and telling me all about how the two of you often share warm haldi doodh at night. And then, we started doing the same, making masala milk in the evenings together— which she's so good at — and we needed to crush some of the spices. It just made sense to store it in a spot where we wouldn't need a ladder to get to it every time. You're so tall, it probably didn't occur to you that it isn't easy access for people like Nanamma. Or me."

She put one hand on her crown, measuring herself against him for emphasis. The edge of her palm hit his collarbone with a soft thump, just above the rounded neckline of his T-shirt.

Rian stared where her hand lay and then at her, their height difference somehow more pronounced by the fact that she was in her socks—a fuzzy atrocity with avocado prints—without the benefit of any heels or shoes.

"You're taking over my kitchen and you're blaming my height for it?" he asked, stepping back a little. God, when did he start sounding so uptight?

"Haven't you heard? Guests are like gods in our country. We get to take over the places we visit," she joked, her smile dimming when the stern lines on his face did not relax. She tapped one foot awkwardly in place, lips turned inwards. She chanced a single glance up at him, sighing when he still looked like he was holding back on giving her a piece of his mind. "Are you really that bothered about me moving a few things around?"

"Not the point," he said, heading to the counter to keep himself busy. "You can't move stuff without asking the owner of the house."

"You weren't here," she reasoned, handing him the spice box he'd been wanting without him having asked for it. This only irritated him further. "And you weren't even supposed to be here for a while longer."

"Seriously?" he griped, swiping the box from her hands with no effort to mask his displeasure anymore. "You're complaining that I came back too soon to my own house?"

Aditi's mouth dropped open. "That's not what I meant. You're twisting my words."

"Stop saying twisted things then," Rian shot back, turning his back to her. He pinched a few kernels of red peppercorn and began to pound it into a fine powder.

Rian could feel Aditi's gaze boring a hole into him, but he didn't acknowledge her. He heard her step away and assumed she would leave him alone. Instead, she walked around the island until she was standing across from him.

"All I meant to say," she continued, evidently hell-bent on debating this further, "was that I would have put everything back in its proper spot eventually."

"Maybe," he shrugged, still not looking at her. "But it was still inappropriate behaviour."

"Was it really?" Aditi's eyes narrowed, feeling quite like that barb was meant for a past transgression and not the one being presently discussed. "Or are you just trying to find a reason to dislike me and continue being mean?"

The unexpectedly frank question had the pestle slipping from his hand just as he hit the base of the mortar. He stopped, pushing it away and slapped his palms on the stone counter, facing her once more.

"Excuse me?" he bit out, feeling an uncomfortable heat climbing up the back of his neck. He had never been accused of being unfriendly, and though he had been exactly that, he had not expected to be confronted over it.

"You are nice to everyone. Except me."

Aditi didn't look away, meeting his gaze head on, daring him to contradict her.

"I haven't said *anything* to you."

"Exactly!" she snapped. "And when you do, it's in that clipped tone with a face that looks like you've smelt something bad."

"What?" he spat again, his own voice rising a few decibels.

"See? Exactly like this!" she said, pointing at him and making a scrunched face to presumably recreate his expression. It was not pretty.

"Okay. Listen," she barrelled on without giving him a chance to interrupt, gathering her hair and furiously wrapping it in a bun on top of her head. "I understand that I said something the night we met and you didn't like it. Maybe I misunderstood your relationship with those people, who I can't even remember anymore! I was coming off the end of an extra-long work shift, doing a health check because there were no other doctors available during the storm. I was exhausted, barely thinking straight, and I said something. You corrected me, quite rudely, might I add. Can't we just let it be?"

"You made a conjecture about my life after knowing me for barely two minutes and *I* was being rude?" Rian huffed, shaking his head in reproach before picking up his pestle again.

"I apologised then, and I'll do it again if that makes it better. I am sorry."

"Doesn't mean I have to be okay with it," he muttered.

"No. It doesn't," she replied, her shoulders lowering in defeat. "But, haven't you ever made a mistake?"

Rian stilled, but said nothing. He heard her release a sigh.

"I've moved on. It is up to you what you hold on to," she said quietly before walking back into the living room.

He watched her retreat from him, a little stumped at how boldly she'd brought up an embarrassing moment from the past and stated her feelings on the matter.

Haven't you ever made a mistake?

He didn't know why he was reacting like this to Aditi, but the way she'd lost that little spark of life, her attitude dulling given his brusque behaviour, troubled him. She'd turned away as if she didn't expect understanding or forgiveness, leaving him feeling like a complete asshole.

It is up to you what you hold on to.

Cut your losses.

Was she wrong? His conscience piped up this time, unwilling to remain quiet anymore.

She wasn't so terrible, he finally admitted to himself, watching the milk come to a boil. It's not as if she'd known he'd been emotionally volatile that evening. And she really had apologised, twice now.

He whisked some honey into the spiced milk and poured it through a sieve, his sights inevitably drawn once more to the woman on the couch who was staring outside the window instead of watching her TV show or reading the several books she had stacked on the centre table.

With a sigh, he picked up the mugs and strode into the living room, clearing his throat to grab her attention.

"I thought you might like some," he gruffed, extending a mug out to her. He felt a twinge of guilt at the way she stared at him, wary of his sudden approach.

Her eyes flickered from the mug to his face and back. Her full lips parted, curving ever so slowly, as the stiffness in her receded. She reached for the cup, accepting it without a word. Eyes on the screen, she scooted towards one end of the sofa, making space for him. It was an unnecessary move given the massive size of the sectional, but as an invitation, it drove the point home.

He hesitated for a second before taking a seat, quietly leaning back against the cushions. For multiple minutes neither said anything, letting the dialogues filtering through the speakers fill the silence between them.

Aditi took a sip of the warm drink, her murmur of appreciation making him breathe easier.

"So, is this how you usually apologise for being mean? Gifts of food?"

"You just had to bring it up, didn't you?" he grumbled. Unlike before, his tone was light, sheepish even.

She giggled, an inherently happy sound, and turned towards him. As he watched her talk, holding no ill will towards him despite him having given her no reason to be so friendly, Rian marvelled at her ability to let go of the uncomfortable moments. Just as she'd advised him.

As she asked him question after question, offering up her own answers without the reservations he'd come to expect in people he newly met, Rian realised that for all his planning on staying away from his temporary housemate, he had not accounted for one thing.

Her.

4

A Lonely Goddess

ADITI

Aditi carefully slid her jewellery onto her lobe and screwed on the backing, giving her head a slight shake, happy to see her earrings dangle about prettily. Picking up the packet of *bindi*, she selected a simple round one in a dark maroon colour and applied it onto her forehead, bringing it to the centre of her brows.

"Is that so? And then what did Appa say?" she asked, listening to her sister's voice trickling through the speaker on her phone. Her younger sister, Anika, was catching her up on all that she had missed with her family. This was their usual Sunday morning ritual, and despite being in different cities, they had refused to give up on the joys of sisterly gossip.

She laughed as Anika imitated their father's irritated grunting when cornered by *Paati*, their maternal grandmother who also resided with them. The suburbs of Bangalore had been home to Aditi and her family since she was a young child. With nearly all their extended relatives also living in the same city or nearby, she had never had a dearth of company while she'd been growing up.

This was the first time she'd been away from her family members for an extended period of time. As much as she missed them, sometimes she found herself breathing a little easier at the lack of constant focus on her and her life.

"I miss you," came Anika's small voice, cutting into her thoughts, and immediately, Aditi's guilt ramped up.

"I miss you, too, Anu," she said softly, smiling at her sister on video. "I'll see you in a couple months for *Amma* and *Appa's* anniversary party."

"Are you sure you won't forget me by then? You weren't even paying attention before," Anu grumbled.

"I'm trying to get ready for the temple. I promised Nanamma I'd join her. It's some auspicious day today."

Anu nodded. "Paati is making us all go also. I just hope we don't run into the Hebbar family again. I cannot stand Mrs. Hebbar."

Aditi stopped midway in the application of her lip balm. "You met her recently?" she asked, her focus now on her sister.

"Yes." Anu frowned, looking like thunder. "Amma and I saw her at the market a couple days ago. She was boasting about all the proposals she is getting for her son and Amma was fuming. I don't know why you ever dated that fool."

"I know you don't like Harish," she started, only to be interrupted by her annoyed sister.

"Even street dogs don't like Harish. Other people named Harish don't like Harish!"

"Anu!" she admonished, unable to hold back a chuckle. "No matter how mad you are, please don't mention to Amma and Appa that Harish is in Mumbai too, okay? They'll make me come home otherwise."

"I cannot believe that he got into the same program as you."

Aditi grimaced, nodding in agreement. She'd been delighted at her acceptance into the rotation at Sanjog Hospital with the mentor she had wanted. It had come as an unpleasant surprise to see that she would have to work alongside Harish Hebbar, her ex.

Aditi and Harish had dated each other in medical college. Young and naively in love, she had hoped to marry him once they graduated, planning on working on their post-graduate doctoral degrees together. Nearly three years into dating, she had finally admitted this to her parents who, despite their conservative outlook, had agreed to meet with the Hebbars to finalise a proposal. They were all part of the same social circle, and Aditi had been hopeful that despite the differences in their language and background, both families would find a way to come together for the sake of their kids.

In the end, it was Harish who had broken that dream and blown it to smithereens.

Aditi looked back on that outcome with relief.

She had no doubts whatsoever that marriage to Harish would have given her only two things—mental health issues, and an ugly divorce.

She supposed she should be thankful that the only side effect she was still experiencing from that embarrassing episode in her life was the pressure to get married soon, and well.

Both families had been in silent competition ever since the break up. The mothers would inevitably exchange barbed comments when they met in any social setting, gloating over which of their children was more in demand on the marriage market.

For that reason alone, Aditi was glad to be living away from home for a few months. She didn't like feeling like she was about to be auctioned off to the highest bidder at any given moment. Not that she had much respite from thinking about grooms even here, she accepted grimly, brushing her hair as she absentmindedly nodded at something Anika said.

Meeting more suitable men that her parents had picked had been one of the conditions she'd agreed to in order to be allowed to come to Mumbai alone.

It seemed silly that as a twenty-six-year-old educated woman, she still required her parent's approval for this. But in a culture that discouraged girls from leaving their homes unless their destination was their husband's house, she knew it was a reality that thousands of other women like her dealt with every day. At least her family loved her immensely. It made it a little easier to put up with the many restrictions she still operated under, knowing that these limitations came from a place of sincere care.

"Adi?" Anika called, bringing her attention back.

"Hmm?" Aditi stood up, adjusting her dupatta along her shoulder before picking up her phone once more.

"Are you okay with having to see Harish everyday?"

"I can't be bothered with him anymore, Anu," she replied, pulling a pair of matching sandals that she'd left at the foot of her bed. "Maybe extra prayers at the temple will work today and I'll find myself a good guy in Mumbai."

"You do that, and don't let Harish stress you out! You're eating well, aren't you?" She heard the worry in Anu's query.

"Yes, yes, I'm eating. I won't forget." Aditi pacified her sister, listening to the same lines that she'd been told to repeat as a mantra if ever she was tempted to skip her meals.

"Remember, your body is your temple!" Anika chirped.

"Okay, if my body is a temple then where is the devotee who's supposed to worship at my altar? I'm a lonely goddess, wilting away," Aditi grumbled, pushing her foot into her sandals, letting out a frustrated grunt when it slipped off again.

In a hurry, she picked up her phone and shoe both, irritatedly thrusting the phone under her chin, keeping it held against her collar while she fumbled with the strap. "It's been so long since I've been worshipped, I'm forgetting what sex feels like."

Just as she said this, she turned and gasped, finding Rian standing stock still at the doorway to her bedroom. She straightened immediately, uncaring that her phone slipped down her front and toppled onto the floor, face down, the video on it hidden from her view.

Aditi barely registered her sister's dull hellos after that, nor the click of the call ending, her entire attention on this man who had appeared out of nowhere.

"Nanamma's waiting in the car," he said, his expression indecipherable.

Aditi had no idea what to do with that information.

Why was Rian here? Did he hear her say that she can't remember sex?

MOTHER EARTH SWALLOW ME WHOLE!

Rian stared at Aditi for a second, and then, as though having made up his mind, walked into her bedroom instead of walking away. Without a word, he reached for the shoe.

"May I?" he asked, his voice low.

Aditi nodded mutely.

Rian bent down on one knee and wrapped his long fingers about her ankle, lifting it to slide her naked foot into her sandal. Bracing her hand on his shoulder automatically for support, Aditi felt a strange shiver pass through her at the feel of his roughened fingers against the delicate arch of her foot. It was a gentle graze, and suddenly, instead of the gurgle of embarrassment, there was an uncomfortable clench of desire swirling at the pit of her belly.

It was no great effort for her to accept that Rian was a prime specimen of masculine beauty. Tall, broad shouldered, and handsome beyond measure with equal parts charm and broodiness. He was like a character who'd escaped the pages of the romantic novels she devoured in her free time.

This was before they'd even made peace.

Now that he'd stopped avoiding her existence altogether, she'd begun to see flashes of his dimpled grin and it never failed to spark a flutter within her gut, like a butterfly had been let loose.

They'd developed an oddly teasing relationship over the last couple weeks since their truce. Not a friendship quite yet, but no longer the awkward tension of before. They shared meals if they were both around with Nanamma, spoke about random things, and often found themselves watching TV together late at night to wind down.

She'd thought the initial spark she had experienced with him—primarily physical—would fade. He was a nice man, but obviously not interested in her.

It took just this light touch, this unexpected moment, for attraction to come knocking at her door again. When did wearing shoes start feeling so intimate? She wondered dazedly, trying to recollect her wits. She gaped at his dark head as he delicately wrapped the flimsy strap around her ankle and straightened the tassels.

A man like Rian, at her feet, worshipping her. Like she'd just been wishing.

The butterfly turned into a swarm and her stomach lurched.

Rian glanced up, and it was all Aditi could do to remain standing. From this viewpoint, he was easily imaginable as a fallen angel, waiting for her to command his services.

Aditi's chest grew tight as he held her gaze, slowly unfolding to his full height, and she had to tilt her head back to meet his eyes. Fuck, the height difference made him hotter.

Yep, she was definitely starved for sex if the simple touch of a very good-looking man made her hormones go on a rampage. Either that, or she was getting close to her cycle. Her sexual cravings usually ramped up in the days leading to her periods.

Breath stuck, she waited, wondering what he was thinking.

Probably not about periods, the imp in her head chimed.

"Let's go," he said after a moment, breaking into her silent spiral.

Demurely, she followed him out of the apartment and into the elevator, hating the fact that she felt so tongue tied.

The entire way down to the parking lot, Aditi kept sneaking glances at Rian, wanting to ask him but also dreading his response. Annoyed by the impossibility of her position, she whipped towards him as they neared his car.

"You heard me, didn't you?" she accused, knowing she was right when his nostrils flared. One edge of his mouth trembled, as if itching to laugh openly.

"It's like riding a bike, Doc," he said instead. Light-grey eyes stared down at her, brimming with ill-concealed mirth, the slightest smirk on his lips.

Confused by the seemingly unrelated comment, she scrunched her nose. "What is?"

"Sex," he answered simply, opening the car door for her.

5

The Temple Visit

RIAN

Rian watched keenly as the flush on Aditi's very pretty face bloomed everywhere, her eyes growing round at his admission.

He also knew very well that had Nanamma not been right there, Aditi would have continued this discussion. Her sights flitted between him and his grandmother, shooting him a look that promised retribution somehow. Unapologetic, he tilted his head to the side, smiling insolently as she got into the car with a huff.

Her agitation only served to amuse him. He bit the inside of his cheek to stop himself from snorting at the memory of her concerned rambling. He rather thought if he laughed now, he wouldn't be able to stop Aditi from attacking him.

He shut the car door once she was settled, sliding his sunglasses on as he directed his driver, Raju, towards the temple.

She was going to chastise him for eavesdropping at the first available opportunity, he was sure. But he couldn't bring himself to regret it.

Her frustration had been comical, only because it seemed so out of the ordinary for her to be annoyed. In the weeks since his return to India, the only time he had seen Aditi not being her charmingly bubbly self was when she had confronted him about his standoffish behaviour.

Since that flimsy shield of caution had been shed, Rian found that he rather enjoyed her company.

The fact that she had all but announced that she wanted sex had not done any favours to his hyperactive mind, however.

He had no reason to deny that Aditi was an attractive woman. He caught sight of her in the rearview mirror, observing her without her knowledge.

Beautiful thick hair, classically Indian features, large doe eyes that were lined with kohl today, and a pouty mouth that begged to be kissed. With her medium height, honeyed skin, and plentiful curves, she had an inherently sensual image, which contrasted with her sweet and friendly aura.

It was for this reason that Rian often found himself watching her, trying to figure out who she truly was. Because she seemed to change very quickly from goofy to kind to serious to silly once more with almost no effort.

If she was pretending—conscious of being his guest—Rian suspected the act would drop eventually, and her true personality would come through with more frequency. He wondered what that would be, hoping that it wasn't too different than the Aditi he'd seen so far.

He had not expected to join Nanamma today, but it had been a long time since he'd prayed. She'd caught him on the way out to the gym and had all but demanded his presence at their outing. He didn't mind. Rian usually made it a point to come visit the temple with his grandmother anyway, but had been relieved of that duty of late. Aditi had been keeping Nanamma company, he'd learned. The more he found out about things that she did to make people around her happy, the more he felt terrible about judging her unnecessarily before.

He climbed the steps of the temple beside his grandmother with a chattering Aditi who was helping her on the other side, and he couldn't hold back a small smile. *It was no wonder that she'd made friends everywhere*, he thought, watching her turn to Raju to include him in the conversation. She was almost always happy, exuding a warmth that drew people in.

While the ladies were waiting outside the main entry, Rian approached his usual shop for the prayer plate that he knew Nanamma liked to offer inside the temple. He reached for his wallet, handing over a large orange note to the vendor who set about looking for change. While waiting, he noticed Aditi browsing the flower garlands at the stall nearby where rows upon rows of strung jasmine and crossandra were being displayed.

He saw the female vendor ask her a question, and Aditi shook her head regretfully, gesturing in a manner that indicated that she hadn't brought her purse. With an apologetic smile, she waved at the seller and walked away, throwing one last glance at the flowers.

"I don't have the exact change, Saheb."

Before he could think twice about it, he pointed at the stall next door. "Keep the money. Get me a string of those flowers instead and add it to the prayer plate."

As Rian approached the two women, he couldn't help but feel silly. He had no idea what possessed him to purchase these flowers for Aditi. He supposed he wanted to do something nice for someone who was so kind to others.

But Nanamma was there, right next to her.

And there was no way Rian could give Aditi something as simple as a string of jasmine to wear in her hair without Nanamma thinking that it was an indication of interest. Knowing his grandmother's fervent wish for great-grandchildren, she'd probably ask the priest to get them married immediately.

"Ah Rian, *kanna,* did you find everything?" Chitra asked when he joined them.

"Yes, Nanamma." He handed the plate to her, unable to tamp down the sliver of disappointment at the thought of having to leave those flowers be. Maybe she had seen his preoccupation with the plate because she exclaimed in surprise, "You got flowers?"

Rian glanced up, startled. "The vendor must have added them by mistake. You can use it for the prayers."

"These are cut too short for that. But it's just as well," Chitra beamed, extending the jasmine to the young woman next to her. "Aditi was just telling me how her grandmother used to make flower garlands for her and her sister to wear for such occasions."

With a glad grin, Aditi accepted the flowers, promptly pinning them onto her hair in the back. It was such a simple pleasure, but it was clear that it had made her very happy.

"You got your heart's desire without even asking for it, *kanna,*" Chitra said, cupping Aditi's face in a loving gesture. "I will pray that all your wishes come true so that you keep smiling, just like this."

Aditi's smile widened at that blessing, her sights drawn to the man standing behind Nanamma. Twinkling brown eyes met his, and out of nowhere Rian had the most curious sensation of being pulled towards her by an unseen thread. His heart thumped awkwardly, and his palms got sweaty until he shook it off, spinning around to head inside.

For the next hour, he studiously avoided looking in Aditi's direction. It wasn't hard considering the massive crowds leading into the main dais. He had his hands full trying to herd the two women he was with, making sure the throng did not hurt or crush them.

By the time the three stood in front of the altar and handed over their offerings to the head priest, Aditi was exhausted. Her eyes swept the space around her, noting the beautiful carvings on the pillars that stretched to the ceiling. She realised upon closer inspection that they were depictions of different scenes from the mythological stories she'd heard as a child.

Wanting to share this with someone, she turned back, doing a double take at the sight that greeted her. There was Rian, eyes closed with his palms joined in supplication, a mask of calm upon his handsome face.

As though he felt her staring, his lids cracked open and met her curious gaze. He tipped his chin in question when she didn't look away.

"You pray?" she asked, unable to keep the surprise out of her tone.

"Occasionally. Why?"

"Didn't take you for the religious kind."

"I'm not, but I do enjoy some aspects of it," Rian explained. "I find it peaceful. Like meditation." He self-consciously shoved his hands into his pockets as she kept watching him.

"You're not at all how I thought you would be," she admitted after a moment.

"How did you think I would be?"

"Cold. Aloof. A jerk."

Rian's lips thinned at her reply.

"You're using this as an opportunity to call me names, aren't you?"

Caught, Aditi grinned unrepentantly, one hand coming up to tuck an errant strand of hair behind her ear. "In all seriousness, I think you're a genuinely nice guy," she said, trying to placate him. She followed a couple steps behind Nanamma as they performed their customary circumambulations.

"You don't even know me."

"Of course I do," she replied, her voice low so as to not disturb the prayers around them. He kept pace with her, wanting to hear what she had to say.

"You're Rian Shetty." She cast him a wink and kept walking. Just when he thought she had been teasing him, she continued, "You're a man who keeps his promises even if it inconveniences him. You put up with the presence of an unwanted stranger in your house because you'd given word to your grandmother. You apologise quickly when you realise your mistake, granted in a roundabout but charming way. I know that from experience. You're a big softie—a man who has a running tab at the store around the corner to make sure the children from the nearby slums get something to eat everyday. You're kind to the people around you, but especially to those who work for you. You're the sort of man who'll cook and pack meals for his driver all week when he lets it slip that his wife is visiting her hometown and he's all alone. You are surprised that I know all this, but I promise you, I am not a stalker. Simply observant."

They came to stop in front of the main dais but instead of looking at the Lord, Rian couldn't move his sights away from Aditi. Her insight into him felt personal, like she saw more of him in a short time than others had in years.

"You're also the kind of man who blushes when he gets complimented," she added with a tiny grin. "How cute."

Rian felt heat flood his face, completely and utterly silenced by this woman. Horrified, he almost touched a palm to his forehead, feeling faintly feverish.

Upon hearing their names being called, Aditi turned away and Rian finally let out a relieved breath. Never had he been more glad for someone to have interrupted a conversation. He couldn't remember if anyone had made him feel shy before. He'd been barely able to meet her gaze without feeling like he was stepping onto a hot pan.

Directed by Nanamma, Rian and Aditi received their blessings from the priest, humbly accepting the sugar candy that was being distributed to all devotees as *prasad*.

"It's so good to see you bring your young family members," the priest said, complimenting Nanamma and waving towards them both. "The temple needs the devotees as much as the devotees need the temple."

Aditi and Rian turned to see each other at once. Her eyes widened and his nostrils flared. Unable to hold back a snort, he raised a fist to cover his unholy grin as his shoulders began to tremble.

Pink and embarrassed, Aditi smacked his bicep as if she had every right over his person. Unthinkingly, she pulled him away from the line, walking towards the exit together. At his continued amusement, she threw him a dark look.

"Behave yourself! You're in a place of worship!" she hissed, the sheepishness in her tone ruining her effort to sound mad.

He snickered harder, his eyes crinkling at the edges as he gasped for breath. "You're the one who put the words in my head. Temple, devotees, and you being a lonely goddess."

"You heard what you weren't supposed to."

He spun to face her, walking backwards just so he could tease her. "You were being loud."

"Was not!" she shot back, swiping some sugar candy from his hands.

When she tried to steal some more, Rian held his closed fist high above his head, wordlessly taunting her for being shorter while she attempted to jump up and pull his arm down.

An almost giddy Nanamma shrewdly observed the natural ease between Rian and Aditi from a distance and smiled to herself. Pretending not to notice their playful flirting was the least she could do, hoping once more that Rian took the opportunity to grab a happiness that was quite literally walking alongside him.

As Rian drove the two women home, he couldn't help but glance in the rearview mirror once more, the jasmine flowers shining like a delicate crown on Aditi's bobbing head. She was speaking animatedly, engrossed in the story she was relaying to his entertained grandmother.

He forced his gaze away to focus on the road, but couldn't stop that small voice in his head from questioning him, daring him to figure out if the peace he felt at that moment was because of his visit to the temple, or because of the unlikely goddess sitting in his back seat.

Like a coward, Rian ignored the voice, unprepared for anything more.

After all, this wasn't part of his plan.

6

The Art of Saying No

RIAN

Rian walked into his kitchen on a bright weekday morning, surprised to find Aditi sitting on the bar stool. She was slumped over the island counter, her face resting sideways over folded arms.

He glanced at his watch, then back at her. It was nearly 9:00 a.m and while he was getting a late start today, Aditi was usually at the hospital by now.

He shuffled a bit closer, moving quietly despite his size, and peered at her. A small huff of amusement escaped him when he realised she was sleeping with her mouth open, a thin line of drool glistening down the side of her squished cheek. Lips twitching, he focused his phone on her face, feeling only the slightest bit guilty for taking a picture at such a vulnerable moment. He couldn't wait to tease her with this. He stared into his phone, setting it as her contact profile, knowing that each time she called or texted would make him laugh just a little bit more.

"Rian?"

Groggy, she sat up, rubbing her eyes tiredly before swiping at her mouth. His amusement dwindled into a fond warmth at her gesture, looking more like a young girl than the busy doctor he knew her to be.

He slipped his phone into his pocket and strode around the kitchen island, heading to his coffee machine.

He lifted his usual mug out of the cabinet, picking up one of her atrocious ones at the same time. He waved it at her, placing it under the machine while he waited for it to come up to temperature. "What's up, Doc?"

"Not me, Bugs," she answered, slapping her cheeks lightly to awaken herself.

Brows clashing, Rian turned around and faced her. "What did I do to piss you off?"

"What?"

"Why are you calling me a bug?"

At that, her scrunched nose relaxed and she chuckled. "I'm not calling you a bug. I am calling you 'Bugs'. Like you call me 'Doc'. I thought we'd gotten far along enough in our relationship that I should give you a nickname, too."

Rian crossed his arms over his chest and leaned back against the counter, still not convinced that she wasn't finding a new way to pull his leg.

Since their truce, Rian had come to understand a few things about Aditi.

She was a dedicated medical professional and very involved with her patients. Nanamma told him that she'd graduated top of her class, and Rian could believe it. The tomes of medical books that she pulled up to reference when she studied each evening looked intimidating to him, but obviously did not phase her.

On the other side was her laid-back persona. The one who liked to roam about in her colourful pyjamas, drink copious amounts of coffee out of equally colourful mugs, watch TV as if she were in a competition, and read, as he had discovered one evening by mistake, romance novels that some might categorise as porn. Those people would be incorrect and narrow-minded, judgemental assholes, he'd been informed immediately by a flustered Aditi. He still had scratch marks from the speed with which she'd ripped her Kindle from his hands. The suggestive cover had intrigued him but she'd refused to look him in the eye after that *or* tell him was the book was about.

Obviously, it meant that he'd teased her about reading it out loud and finding out for himself. Only he knew it was a false threat. A childhood filled with tutors, teachers and his mother making him feel stupid for not reading or writing well, never to realise that he was dyslexic, had turned him off the activity altogether. Just as he never spoke about his learning challenges, he would never willingly put himself through the trauma of reading any book, even if it came with the added benefit of annoying Aditi.

Perhaps she was also trying to annoy him with this ridiculous nickname.

"I call you Doc because you're a doctor," he explained, reaching over to press the button for fresh coffee beans to be ground perfectly.

"And I call you Bugs because Bugs Bunny always greets his friend with '*what's up, Doc?*' Just like you greet me!" She yawned.

He should have known she would have a reason. A convoluted one, but a reason nonetheless. Shaking his head, he tamped the coffee grounds into the basket until the surface was flat.

"Did you have a night shift?" he asked, taking her tired hum as a 'yes'. He watched the fresh brew pour into their mugs while he swirled the frothed milk in his pitcher, readying it for the latte he knew she preferred.

"No wonder your brain isn't working," he grumbled, picking up her mug and angling it to begin pouring the milk. "Once you're less tired, we're coming back to how Bugs is not a good nickname."

"Too bad. I like it. It's cute and it suits you. You don't hear me complaining about your uncreative nickname for me, do you?"

Rian glanced towards her just as she yawned again, stretching long such that her back arched and her scrubs tightened over her upper body.

Distracted, he didn't realise he was staring until he felt hot milk splash over his hand, causing his mug to slip. With a little curse, he looked down to see brown liquid spreading across the counter, dripping onto the floor.

"Aww, crap," he mumbled, dabbing the counter with a nearby towel.

"You okay?" Aditi came up to him, face twisted in concern. Her eyes fell on the reddened patch of skin and she pushed him towards the sink, forcing his hand under cold running water.

"Stay here until the sting reduces," she ordered, spinning around to begin cleaning up the mess he'd made. "I'll put more coffee on."

"Maybe you should hold off on caffeine until after you sleep."

"Who says I'm going to sleep?"

"Aren't you?" He'd seen her passed out until early afternoon after the last two night shifts she'd been on, emerging from her room looking like an ogre until that first sip of coffee. It never failed to amuse him that for such a happy person, she had terrible morning moods.

"No sleep for me today," she yawned, walking past him to throw the wad of paper towels into the trash can. "I need to run errands for my family."

Rian turned off the tap, reaching for the towel Aditi held out. He had seen her on calls with her family many times. He knew she was close to them. He had also seen her send multiple packages home in the weeks since he'd been back.

"What kind of errands?"

"My aunt wants to wear this particular colour saree for my parent's anniversary party. I have been tasked with finding something at the cloth markets here because her usual shops were a bust."

His reaction must have shown on his face because she sheepishly scratched her ear.

"I know that sounds like a silly thing. I'm usually the planner for all the big events in the house but since I am not there, I offered to pitch in from Mumbai as much as I can."

"That's why you keep sending boxes home?"

She nodded. "Decorations, invites, gifts, jewellery. I'm getting a lot of it sent directly—thank god for online shopping. Those boxes you've seen hold just the items I've picked up from the markets here."

"Why do you take so much on? Tell them to do it themselves. You're in a whole different city. I'm sure it's okay if you take a step back."

Aditi's nose scrunched in an odd expression, a defeated sort of smile gracing her face as she considered that option. She waved him over so that he could help her fit the portafilter into his machine properly.

"You don't have a large family, do you?" she asked, focusing on getting the coffee basket in.

"No."

"Pros and cons to it," she said after a moment, stepping back to take a seat at the counter once more. Her chest expanded as she breathed in, clearly about to explain further. "Almost my entire family is in Bangalore so we are all very close—physically, and emotionally. I have four uncles and an aunt on my dad's side and two aunts and an uncle on my mom's."

Rian tipped his head, wondering where she was going with this.

"The younger generation has me, the eldest child," she pointed to herself, tapping her fingers in a silent count, "and fifteen younger siblings and cousins. I have always been the one to lead the way. Whether it was studying, or extracurriculars, or being the dutiful daughter, I was expected to set the proper example. Now, it's simply become my place to get things done."

Finished with her explanation, Aditi watched Rian, his expression hard to read. Had she confused him or was he just thinking?

"You can be a role model without letting people walk over you," Rian told her quietly.

"It's not easy to say no when it's family. I feel like I'm letting them down."

He could understand that. He had been manipulated to feel that way for a good part of his life. Leela had only bothered to pay attention to him when she required him to play the part of a perfect son. And when he failed to meet those expectations. . . Even now, recalling those moments made him anxious—the yelling, the rage, the loneliness which inevitably followed each punishment.

His eyes focused on the woman in front of him. By all means, she didn't look like she shared the kind of tumultuous relationship with her family that he did with his mother. Unfortunately that did not mean that she was not being taken advantage of.

"Do you *want* to run these errands today?" he asked instead, handing her a cup of coffee.

"I usually don't mind."

"But?"

"I'm tired. I want to sleep. And this doesn't seem important. But if I don't do it. . ." Her voice tapered off and she tiredly closed her eyes. With a shake of her head, she lifted her mug and took a tentative sip, annoyed when he pulled it back to grab her attention.

"If you don't do it, then someone else will learn to get off their ass and figure shit out. Don't do it. Go sleep."

"I can sleep later."

"When? After you drop down from exhaustion? You look like you are five seconds away from doing a faceplant."

She patted her cheeks self-consciously, wondering if she looked that terrible. She hadn't had time to change out of her scrubs yet. She glanced at herself, a little embarrassed.

"I'll be fine," she muttered, picking up her phone to begin scrolling for the closest fabric markets.

Engrossed in her task, she did not notice Rian's annoyance. His brows clashed at her refusal to put her own needs ahead of others. He wished he could demand that she go to bed and take care of herself first, but recognized that he had no right.

What he did have, however, was an alternative. He plucked the phone out of her hand, shushing her protests.

"I have a proposition for you. Call your aunt and say you can't go right now."

Aditi's face cleared, surprise etched across her features. Wide eyes met his and she blinked, waiting for him to say something more.

"It doesn't have to be a call," Rian caved, her obvious shock and stunned silence prompting him to explain further. "Text her. You do that, and I'll take you shopping after you rest."

"You will?" she asked, unable to hide her scepticism. "*You*? In person?"

"No, my spirit will accompany you," he snapped, rolling his eyes. "Yes, me. In person."

Her phone rang, interrupting them. The caller ID flashed, and Aditi cast him a discomfited look.

"It's my aunt," she explained. "She probably wants to know if I'm on the way to the shop yet."

Feeling weirdly like she was doing something wrong, she reached for her phone, her sights snapping to his face when he placed his hand over hers to hold her still.

"Don't pick it up," Rian requested again. "If you can't say no, at least ignore the call. And I'll take you to the market later tonight."

His face was serious, and Aditi couldn't understand why. She tried to lighten the moment.

"I am looking for a very particular shade of saree. This isn't the kind of shopping anyone would like."

"I'll deal with it. Don't pick it up," he said again, nary a smile on his face, his eyes never straying from hers. She gulped, feeling the phone vibrate under her hand, but Rian did not let go.

"But..."

"At most, she'll be waiting a few hours. Not the end of the world."

"Rian."

"Listen to me."

Aditi waited for the urge to rush to her family member's aid come calling, the guilt that was part and parcel of an elder daughter's life when she was unable to jump to do their bidding.

However, for the first time in a long time, none of those emotions hounded her. Rian seemed so certain that it would be okay for her to pick her own timeline to help them, his request—nay, order—so clear, she felt a calmness leach into her. The compulsion to obey him felt like a relief rather than cause for alarm, because it was clear he was concerned for her.

The phone went silent and she still couldn't look away, his ash-grey eyes pinning her in place.

"Good girl," he said quietly, giving her hand a soft squeeze of approval before he let go.

Good girl? Did Rian Shetty just call me a good fucking girl? Heat bloomed across her body and all she could do was stare at him like a mute fool while he entered a voice note reminder for himself on his cell.

"Go sleep. I'm off to the restaurant. I'll be there to pick you up later."

7

Dreams

ADITI

Listen to me, she heard his deep voice murmur. Roughened fingers glided over her skin, brushing up and down her body. Aditi turned towards him, searching for his warmth. She gasped when his weight held her down, keeping her still.

His touch turned teasing, soft then hard, never quite long enough to give her relief. Warm lips followed where his fingers left a trail, scorching a path lower and lower. Her body twisted, need blazing through her as her legs splayed open.

Please, she begged, her back arching when his lips found their destination. Pleasure crashed over her, immediate and intense.

Rian! she screamed.

Aditi awakened, her eyelids fluttering as consciousness rushed in like an uninvited guest.

Rolling onto her back, she stared up at the ceiling fan that was circling above, failing to cool her down from the searing heat of her dream.

She raised a shaking hand to her chest, feeling her heart beat like a bass drum. Her thighs rubbed together when she recollected the reason for her increased heart rate, the dampness between her legs and the pulsing ache—a clear reminder of unfulfilled desires and incomplete cravings.

Good girl. His warm baritone washed over her once more and she almost moaned when her pussy clenched automatically. She touched one hand to her cheek, certain that she was red.

Aditi had sat at the kitchen counter for a good ten minutes after Rian had left that morning, trying to coax circulation back into her shaky legs. His touch, his words, and his authoritative behaviour had sent her mind into overdrive.

Well, crap. Clearly, the attraction she'd previously felt for him had turned into a full-blown crush, which was awful because that was all it could be.

A crush.

That first night after he'd returned, she'd heard Rian's vehement insistence on remaining unwed. Despite liking him far more than any of the other men she'd met so far, she wasn't foolish enough to assume she could change his mind.

She had been fine with the slowly budding friendship between them, but the more she got to know him, the harder it was to ignore his allure.

"It's just a crush. A stupid, silly crush," she muttered to herself, trying to forget the heat of his hand when he held hers, the scent of his cologne invading her senses. "It'll go away, Adi. Just focus on finding a man to marry instead of letting Rian distract you."

Mind made, she rolled into a burrito within her soft sheets and valiantly attempted to fall asleep once more, praying that this time she would not be interrupted by frisky dreams of hunky men who had no business making her want things she couldn't have.

Aditi slapped a hand over her mouth, stifling a yawn as she walked beside Rian, the noise of the evening market surrounding them.

"Did you not listen to me and go to sleep?" Rian frowned at her.

"I tried," she grumbled, silently blaming him for her predicament. "Had some dreams."

"Bad ones?" he asked sympathetically, directing her down a crowded path.

Her lips twisted in the semblance of a rueful grin. "Worse. Unattainable ones."

At his curious look, she shrugged, not wanting to delve further into the topic. She turned in a slow spin, her eyes skimming over the crowds, noticing vendors calling for passing customers and people perusing the many items out on display. It was loud, colourful, and chaotic, and Aditi loved it. She adored the buzzing energy of outdoor shopping markets in India. For a curious woman like her, a bazaar such as this one was a veritable treasure pool of new discoveries.

A tap on her shoulder had her looking at Rian, who pointed at a stall. "Should we try here?"

Nodding, she followed him. True to his word, Rian had taken the time to bring her to a massive fabric market in one of the busiest parts of Mumbai, and was exhibiting incredible patience when one after the other, her aunt rejected the saree pictures she sent, extending their search well past dinner time.

She sifted through a few more options at this new shop as Rian called for the vendor to bring more inventory out for her. With permission, she snapped a few photos and sent them off to her aunt, waiting for a reply.

"Mohan Chacha was asking me if you liked his gift," she heard Rian say at one point, speaking of the night watchman at his building.

"Yes. I need to go thank him. It was so sweet of him to remember that I was looking for those pickles. I hope he doesn't send more though. That one jar can feed my entire family for a year."

"I can't believe he brought you homemade pickles. He's known me for years and he's only ever scolded me for parking in the wrong spot."

Aditi snickered, running her hand over the beaded designs on a mannequin.

"He's a sweet old man. I like the folks around where we live. It's a nice community."

He believed her. And it was clear that they returned the sentiment. The parcels she'd been receiving, as he had recently found out, were gifts of gratitude.

Aditi had been helping people with medical queries in his locality. As word of mouth about her spread, so had the number of people who'd approached her.

"It feels like you operate a free clinic everywhere you go," he said, handing her a sample piece that the vendor pulled down. "Aren't you a gynaecologist, not a family doctor?"

"OB/GYN," she corrected. "But, it doesn't matter to them. They hear that I am a doctor, and they want a solution. Why would I hurt their feelings by turning them away when a sympathetic ear is really all they require? It costs me nothing to help them address a cold or fever," she explained, sending him a soft smile before walking past him to inspect the saree.

Rian stood behind her and watched her interact with the vendor, charming him into holding the saree up so she could take a photo. The more time he spent with her, the more things he saw to admire. Still, he struggled between appreciating her kindness and disapproving her inability to stop people from imposing on her.

She spun towards him suddenly, her face bright. She held up the phone, showing him the screen with a toothy grin. "Success! She liked this one," she said, pointing to the saree that the vendor was holding.

"How much for this?"

"This is a special piece, sister. Only one of its kind," the seller began, causing Rian to stifle a snort. He wondered if all the shopkeepers in India read the same manual. This particular dialogue was used before every purchase, no matter the product.

"For you, I will even add a discount. Only Rs. 12,849." He smiled widely, unaware that his betel-nut-stained teeth made him look like a vampire about to attack an unsuspecting victim.

"That's *with* the discount?" Aditi asked, gulping at the price tag.

"Okay, for you, sister, just because I want you to be happy," the vendor added, as if he hadn't deliberately named a high price at first, "give me only Rs. 12,800. It is a nice round number."

Rian almost burst out laughing when Aditi's polite smile twisted into a look of bewilderment, unsure if she was being pranked. He watched her attempt to lower the price, only to have the man regale her with a well-practised sob story of how he would make no profit on this, how his children would not have any new clothes for the upcoming festivals if he let his customers steal from him, how this saree was made by blind nuns in the midst of the Sahara with only water to fill their bellies.

Okay, that last one was his own frustration talking, but Rian couldn't hold himself back from interrupting when he saw Aditi reach for her purse.

"8,000 rupees. Not a single paisa more."

Aditi's eyes grew comically wide at the number he threw out, her head whipping around to see if he was serious. He blinked once, reassuringly, telling her without words to not interfere.

The vendor blustered, emphatically refusing to accept a price that was less than five figures.

Aditi watched in awe as Rian steadily wore the man down, going as far as asking her to move on to the next shop to look for a similar saree before the seller finally caved.

A short while later, sitting at the outdoor stall of a nearby restaurant with the saree safely tucked into her bag, Aditi couldn't help but stare at the broad back of the man who was picking up their orders, as at ease in this hot and dusty roadside eatery as in his posh apartment. Rian seemed to surprise her at every turn.

"I can't believe he agreed to your final offer," she said yet again, accepting the plate he passed to her. "Why wouldn't he listen to me?"

"He probably figured that you were not from here and attempted to stick you with an expensive tag. Your Hindi is far more polite than Mumbai's street language." He ripped open a packet of ketchup and squirted some onto her plate for her.

"Thank you for stepping in."

"I had to. It's obvious that you can't say no to people easily. First the sick folks, now the vendor. How do you get through life without being taken advantage of?"

Aditi puffed out her cheeks in irritation, looking like a chipmunk. "I'm not being taken advantage of. And I don't like to disappoint people when I can help them. My Amma always says that good deeds earn good karma."

Rian snorted softly, wishing he could be as idealistic as her. He picked up his food and took a bite, enjoying the flavours that the famous Vada Pav packed in each morsel. A delicious layered concoction of golden bun, spicy cilantro chutney, dry garlic spread, and a hot ball of potato fritter stuffed within, there was no doubt that this was one of the most popular snacks amongst Mumbaiites on the go. He glanced at Aditi momentarily, glad to see that she was enjoying her food as well.

"You're close to your parents?" he asked, munching quietly.

"Yes. You?"

"My father. Towards the end of his life."

Aditi watched him for a half a second before she inquired, "And your mother?"

"Not so much."

Maybe she saw something in his face because she didn't push for more answers.

"How did you learn to haggle like that?" She sipped on the cool drink he'd paired with their meal, no indication given that she'd diverted the conversation for his sake.

"Had to save money when I was starting the restaurant so I'd go haggle at the docks for cheap veggies." His lips tilted up in the barest hint of a smile, memories of those early mornings still fresh in his mind. "Money was tight. Taught me things."

"I wouldn't have guessed that," she said. "I thought you came from old money."

"All that belonged to my father. And it's passed to my mother. But I'll admit, I was able to get loans because of my name. And I had a trust fund to lean on in case something went awry. Thankfully, I haven't had to touch it."

"So, you are self-made."

He tipped his chin, saying nothing else. He popped the last piece of his sandwich into his mouth, licking the sauce of his thumb. He knew that most people assumed he had generational wealth to fall back on if his business failed, or worse still, that his success had been purchased because he had connections.

Rian had worked independently—and very hard—to earn every bit of the life he enjoyed today. Somehow, letting Aditi think otherwise felt unacceptable to him, which was odd because he had long since stopped wanting people to acknowledge his efforts.

Aditi pushed her plate away, done with her meal. She wiped her hands on her napkin as Rian placed a few fresh bills out as a tip for the server.

"You know," she said as they began the trek back towards their parked car, "I was pleasantly surprised by your apartment when I first came to this city."

He raised a brow, saying nothing.

"It is beautiful. You must be very successful if you managed to purchase that without family money."

"I still have debts to pay off, but yes," Rian admitted, "I've done well."

"I fully thought I'd be coming to one of those crazy rich mansions facing the sea," she said, settling into the passenger seat. They pulled onto the road, the traffic ever-present.

"Disappointed?"

Aditi chuckled, shaking her head. "No. Your home feels comfortable. Like a pair of pyjamas that I've worn many times but still reach for instead of something new."

Of all the compliments he had received, he couldn't place a finger on why this felt so right.

"What's next for Iron Chef Shetty, then?" she prodded.

"I'm not an Iron Chef."

"Is that what you want to be?"

"I want to start a culinary school." Rian surprised himself by admitting this. He hadn't told anyone. Not Nanamma, not Kaya, not Arjun, nor Vihaan, whom he'd grown to have good friendships with.

But for some reason, he wanted to tell Aditi. It was easy to tell her things.

"A school?"

"Yeah. Maybe fund some of the underprivileged. Give them a path for a career, a stable future."

"Sounds like a lot of work," she commented, her eyes tracing Rian's side profile.

"I'm not afraid of hard work," he said. The look of approval on her face warmed him.

"Well, if you need help. . ."

He couldn't hold back a soft laugh. This woman had a problem, he decided. She was too nice.

"Are you really offering me help when you already have the entire population of your extended family waiting for you to do things for them?"

"As long as I'm in Mumbai, I'll always make time for you," she said nonchalantly, turning to look outside the window as they drove across the sea link bridge, a gentle smile upon her lips.

When they reached home, Rian observed her rush towards Nanamma, sharing the treats she'd insisted on purchasing for his grandmother. Despite the chatter, her words echoed in the recesses of his mind.

I'll always make time for you.

For a man who had learnt not to rely on others, to have someone he barely knew say this to him shouldn't have mattered so much.

Then why did it?

More importantly, he asked himself, why did he want to believe her?

8

Dickhead Date Diaries

ADITI

A DITI STOOD IN LINE with her close friend and colleague, Dr. Nina Jaiswal, waiting patiently for her turn to be served. The busy cafe that operated within their hospital was the most popular spot for doctors and visitors alike to grab their favourite cup of joe.

Nina and Aditi had joined the same specialisation group, hand-picked by their supervisor to work at Sanjog General while they completed their postgrad degrees. As much as she had hated seeing Harish as part of the program, she had found an immediate friend in Nina.

She usually looked forward to their morning coffee break together, but right now it was an unwelcome reminder that she still had a long work day ahead. Just the thought of it made her groan out loud.

"Rough morning?" Nina asked, following Aditi to pick up their drinks as the two ladies headed to one of the open tables, ready to rest their feet for a short while.

"Awkward morning," Aditi replied, letting her head loll back while she closed her eyes. "Everyday I'm at the clinic, I find new cases that surprise me."

"What happened?" Nina sipping on her drink, watching the passers-by before turning to her friend. "Did you detect a complicated pregnancy? That's always tough on me."

Aditi shook her head, sitting up before she reached for her cup. "Nothing that serious. It was a bit funny actually. I had this couple come in asking for a full evaluation on the lady's health. They've been trying for a child for over a year with no luck, so I ordered every test possible, even genetic. The pathology reports came back clean. Today, I finally diagnosed the problem." She sighed into her coffee.

"What was it? Don't build the suspense, Adi. Spill it!"

Aditi's nostrils flared as she tried to control her reaction to the memory of sitting with her patients, the reality of their situation finally dawning upon her.

"It turns out that they come from conservative, orthodox families," she started.

"So?"

"So," Aditi drawled, waving one dainty hand in the air. "Sex education was negligible for them both."

"Wait. They weren't having sex?"

"Oh, they were definitely having sex."

"Then?"

"He's been ejaculating into her belly button."

Nina spluttered as she tried to take a sip, some of her drink spilling onto the table. With a defeated laugh, Aditi pulled out a few tissues and handed it to her.

"He didn't!"

"He did. According to him, babies grow in the belly so he figured the belly button would be the most direct route. He couldn't believe his process kept failing."

"Oh my god!" Nina gasped, snorting when Aditi started to chuckle softly as well. "How did you keep a straight face?"

"I had to!" Aditi insisted as she sat back, her tiredness receding slowly. "The poor lady had been through so many medical tests already. You know how it can be for some of them. The pressure they face from the families, the immediate judgement that something must be wrong with only the woman. I couldn't bear to laugh at her misery."

"Did the husband finally understand what he was doing wrong?"

Aditi nodded.

"I felt a little like a sex ed instructor at one point. But the silly man was so glad that his wife was healthy, he promised her that he'd get her pregnant immediately."

"And what did you say?"

"I asked him to please wait until he got home!" Aditi quipped, causing Nina to burst out laughing once more, her eyes bright with mirth.

"Adi, I don't think I've ever laughed this much while working on rotations. If I was a boy, I'd have married you just for that."

"I'll take you as you are, Nina. I'm not sure any boy is going to like me anyway," she muttered, picking her phone up when it buzzed.

"The last date didn't work out either?"

Aditi pouted, shaking her head as she swiped on her messages.

"How many is that?"

"Eleven," she admitted dully, her lower lip jutting out further when Nina's eyes grew big at that number.

"I can't believe you've crashed and burned through eleven different men," Nina said, not unkindly. "Your double-D count keeps increasing."

"Double-D?"

"Dickhead dates," Nina explained with a single shoulder shrug, as if it had been perfectly clear.

"It wasn't all my fault," Aditi sniffed. "Some of them didn't like me, which is fine. I'm not everyone's type. But some of them were absolute jerks who should never procreate."

"Like DD number 2. The silencer."

Aditi grumbled under her breath, taken back to one of the early dates she'd been set up on when she'd first landed in Mumbai. DD number two had been Ananth Sivakumar, age twenty-nine, a Sanskrit professor who had been so annoyed at her asking him questions during their date that he'd put his spoon down, looked her in the eye, and announced, "You talk a lot."

His tone made it clear it wasn't a compliment and she'd spent the rest of her very short dinner in silence. While he had suggested a second meeting, she had refused. Little did she know then that she'd eventually consider it one of her better dates.

"Who was the guy who stalked you on Instagram?" Nina asked after a bit.

"Oh him!" Aditi recalled, shuddering when she remembered Rahul Ayyar, the twenty-eight-year-old IT expert.

"I'm Rahul. Naam toh suna hoga." *He'd grinned, shaking her hand for a lot longer than she'd have liked.*

The overused dialogue wouldn't have bothered her, considering she loved Shahrukh Khan. She would have probably quipped back with a dialogue of her own, except he spent the entirety of the evening talking to her breasts. Eventually she'd had enough, and had slammed the table hard enough to startle him.

"What? What's wrong?"

"My eyes are about ten inches north of where you've been staring, asshole."

Just as she was about to leave, he'd called her back.

"Do you think I could take a picture of you? Just for the memories?" he'd asked, reaching for his phone.

"You touch that phone and I'll make you eat it!"

"Tell me you blocked him after that!" Nina exclaimed, creeped out on Aditi's behalf.

"I reported his profile as suspicious and got it suspended." Aditi bared her teeth in a gremlin-esque smile. Who said revenge didn't feel good? Liars. All of them.

"Did you ever look up the underwear model on social media?" Nina asked, leaning in when Aditi flashed her phone to show her a feed full of a half-naked man.

Nikhil Pillai, age thirty, had strode into the restaurant she'd been waiting in with all the confidence of a man who knew how good he looked. Despite being late, he had neither offered an explanation, nor an apology, ordering the staff about for fast service like he was owed their complete attention.

Aditi had grinned and borne it, trying to be polite, but after the third time he'd insulted their server, she'd cut in, unable to curb her irritation.

"You're being unnecessarily rude."

Nikhil had cast her a critical glance, his smug half-smile not faltering one bit.

"This is the most basic job there is. If he can't bring me my order fast enough, he's an idiot."

"You've changed your mind three times. That's not his fault."

"I'm trying to be careful of what I put in my body," he had reasoned, his smirk taking on a superior look when he nodded at the cream-covered pasta she'd been about to eat. *"You could be careful too."*

Aditi had stilled at the insinuation.

"Meaning?" she'd asked, a dare more than a question, something that Nikhil had been too obtuse to pick up on.

"You're healthier than your profile picture on the matrimonial website."

Healthy. The polite word for fat in India.

"That's disappointing to you?"

"A little."

"I understand." She'd nodded, seemingly sympathetic to his plight. "I'm disappointed, too."

This had confused him.

"What about? I have a six pack."

With a careless wave of her fork, she swirled her pasta carbonara and slurped it, making him wait for an answer.

"You might have abs," she told him between bites, "but not enough brain cells. I was expecting someone a bit smarter so I guess a photo only tells you so much."

Not used to having women treat him with derision, he'd stared at her. "Are you insulting me?"

"If I have to confirm what is obvious, then you are proving my point."

With a long-suffering sigh, she'd shaken her head at him, tutting like he was a silly child. His reaction was worsened by the fact that the server he'd insulted had overheard her, and had snorted out loud. She'd winked at him deliberately, grinning. At that, Nikhil's colour changed to an alarming crimson.

"Oh look, you can turn red." She'd pointed with the tines of her fork, delivering the final blow. "Another thing the picture didn't tell me."

Nina hid her snorts behind her coffee cup when Aditi finished re-telling her story.

"But what happened to your date last night?" she inquired, coming back to the reason why she'd started this discussion in the first place.

"It was worse than Nikhil Underpants."

"Why?"

"He asked me if I was a virgin. I didn't even have the energy to say anything after that. I got up and left," Aditi lamented, tossing her cup in a trashcan.

"And still, you're planning another date tonight?" Nina asked, catching up to her as they began to walk towards the elevators.

"I've been through eleven. Maybe twelve is my lucky number." Aditi swiped at her phone. "Or maybe not."

"What's wrong?"

"I can't seem to book a decent spot for dinner tonight."

"Who needs dinner, kanna?"

Aditi spun around in surprise, gasping in delight when the friendly face of Chitra Shetty stared back at her.

"Nanamma! What are you doing here?"

"I came for some routine blood work," Chitra explained, pulling a little tiffin out of her bag. "I saw you so I thought I'd say hello. I also made fresh tamarind rice. I was going to ask the front desk to give it to you. Eat this for lunch. You have been working too hard lately."

Aditi swiped the lunch box, taking a whiff of it. She pounced on Nanamma, hugging her like a kid who'd been given dessert before a meal.

"Now what is this about dinner?" Chitra asked, laughing when Aditi refused to end the hug.

"Oh! I can't seem to find an open table anywhere good for that matrimonial date tonight."

Chitra nodded, stopping when she saw Nina. Aditi stepped back, belatedly remembering her manners. "Nina, meet my Nanamma. Nanamma, this is my friend and colleague, Nina."

"Hello Nanamma, I have heard so much about you," Nina held a hand out, letting out a small squeak when Nanamma pulled her closer for inspection.

"What a beautiful young lady you are. Are you single?" Chitra asked, taking both women by surprise. "I know a young man who is also unmarried."

"Are you trying to get rid of me again, Nanamma?"

Aditi whipped back to see Rian approaching them, struck anew by how good-looking he was, his long legs eating the distance between them easily. She watched Nanamma make introductions, obviously pushing Nina and Rian together, and Aditi couldn't curb the tendril of irritation she experienced at the situation.

"We need to get back to doing our rounds," Aditi interrupted, shooting an apologetic glance at Chitra. "Bugs, you should take Nanamma home."

As Aditi manoeuvred Nina away from the conversation, she felt a bizarre chill rush up her spine. She entered the elevator and turned, catching sight of Rian, who was watching her with an indeterminate look.

Unable to help herself, her lips tilted and the tightness in his expression faded slowly. She lifted her hand in a singular wave goodbye, watching him finally glance and nod at Nanamma who was, oddly enough, pointing at Aditi as well.

Or maybe she was talking to Rian about Nina, she conceded, unable to hold back a frown as the two ladies stepped out. The open layout on the second floor allowed them a clear view of the lower-level entrance of the hospital.

When her phone buzzed suddenly in her pocket, Aditi pulled it out, her brows shooting up in surprise.

Table for Aditi Krishnan reserved at The Mumbai Map for 7 pm.
Nanamma's reason for gesturing suddenly became clear.

She looked down, scanning the message to confirm that she hadn't misread it.

She'd never visited Rian's restaurant before. She took a few steps towards the indoor railing, catching sight of him ushering Nanamma out the spinning doors.

Should I follow him and thank him in person? Aditi wondered as she chewed the inside of her lower lip.

"So, who was that?" Nina's curious voice cut into her thoughts.

"Rian."

"He is delicious."

Aditi chuckled. "He's a chef so that line is appropriate in more ways than one."

Nina bumped shoulders with Aditi playfully. "Why aren't you eating him up, girlie?"

"He's not interested."

Nina snorted. "Oh honey, he's interested."

"No." She shook her head with a breathy laugh, pushing away from the railing. "He's just a nice guy."

"So, you don't mind if I go on a date with him? His grandma gave me his number."

Aditi's smile dropped. "Delete it."

Nina gasped, mischievously cackling as she watched Aditi grow flustered at her own reaction.

"You have a girlfriend. What are you doing even taking his number?" Aditi asked, spinning away to begin walking towards the wing that housed her patients. She heard the click of heels, knowing that Nina had hurried to catch up.

"I play for both teams. She's not my girlfriend, and I'm keeping my options open."

"He's not interested in a relationship."

"But you still like him," Nina guessed in a sing-songy voice. Aditi knew there was no hiding it from her. She was a tenacious woman and would needle her until she spilled the truth.

"Okay, yes," Aditi admitted, stopping to turn and look at her friend. "He's hot, and really sweet under all the grump and silence. And I'm attracted to him. That's all. I'll get over it soon."

Nina's eyes narrowed, as if gauging her truthfulness.

"Best way to get over it is to get under him," she said after a moment.

"Nina!" Aditi's mouth dropped open. "I just told you he doesn't want a relationship."

"So? Have a fling." She pulled her notepad out and began flipping through the patient charts. "No strings attached."

Oh.

Aditi quietened for several seconds as she signed release orders.

"I've never done that."

"Doesn't mean you can't, dollface," Nina didn't bother to look at her, busy with her own forms.

A casual fling with Rian? Seemed inconceivable.

"No." Aditi wiped her clammy palms on her white lab coat. But the thought had taken root regardless.

Maybe Nina heard the indecision in her friend's voice because she finally glanced up from her paperwork. Checking to see that the nurses weren't eavesdropping, she beckoned Aditi closer.

"Adi, ten years from now when you're herding your two and a half kids from school and a million extracurricular activities, the most anticipated thing of your day being uninterrupted sleep, at least you will have the memory of that sinfully gorgeous man doing incredibly naughty things to you to keep your mind occupied while you have missionary sex that feels as exciting as brushing teeth with with your family-approved, straight-laced, mommy-loving husband."

Aditi blinked at the bored, matter-of-fact tone in which Nina had delivered that monologue.

"Wow," she croaked. "Way to paint a bleak picture for my future. Kill my imaginary dog too while you're at it."

Nina laughed, tapping her temple and pointing towards Aditi. "You're thinking about this casual sex thing with your head."

"And you suggest that I think with my heart?"

"Hell no." She grinned before making a circle in the air with one long nail pointed below Aditi's waist.

"With your libido."

9
Narwahl Attack

RIAN

Far be it from him to judge anyone on their chosen attire, Rian thought, standing at the edge of his living room and staring at the young woman on his couch. When one spent as long as he had hobnobbing with the rich and famous, one got used to seeing outrageous clothing being passed off as fashionable. He had become proficient in not letting his real opinion reflect on his face. Today though, he was failing.

He thought he'd gotten used to Aditi in her cheeky, bright-coloured pyjamas that ranged from cute to funny to (and he would deny it until his last breath) sexy. Which is why, when he came home barely a minute ago and saw movement on the sofa, he knew it was her. He had not expected this avatar, however.

"What are you wearing?"

Her eyes swivelled towards him before zooming back to the TV screen, one end of her lip tugging up in the mischievous smile he'd come to associate with her.

"If you're going to come on to me as soon as you step foot in the house, at least buy me dinner first."

"Do you always like to talk nonsense?" His deadpan expression did not give away his inclination to laugh. Aditi's quick wit never failed to amuse him.

"Yes, I find life is more fun that way."

"Where's Nanamma?"

"Out."

"Weren't you supposed to be on a date?" he asked, remembering clearly that he'd reserved her a table upon Nanamma's insistence. The fact that his restaurants tended to be booked months in advance had not stopped Nanamma from demanding he clear up a spot for her precious Adi.

"Cancelled."

With a nod, he checked the time, wondering if he could get a workout in before sleeping.

"It's a narwhal," he heard her say, just as he was turning away.

"What?"

Aditi glanced up at him and in a slick move, flipped the hood onto her head. She pointed to a little horn on the top, holding up a matching mug with a cartoon sea animal on it. "It's a narwhal onesie. I'm a unicorn of the seas."

The straight face with which she said this did not douse the teasing twinkle in her eyes.

"You're. . .something," he said wryly, chuckling when she threw a pillow at him in mock-outrage.

"Be nice!"

"Not tonight," Rian snorted, tossing the pillow back onto the couch.

He headed in to change into his nightwear with every intention of going to bed, but he was distracted by an enthusiastic cheer. He strode back into his living room and all he could see was a shark thrashing about on the couch, fin waving in the air. Giggling.

Correction. It was a Narwhal. Narwhaling. If that was a word.

"What the hell, Doc? Are you having a seizure?"

Aditi's red face emerged from the pillow behind which she'd been muffling her laughter. "It's this movie. I can't get over it," she gushed, eyes bright. "Shahrukh puts everyone to shame." She sat up, pointed at the screen and sighed. "I love him."

Rian didn't even realise when he sat down, but he found himself watching the hero fight off a horde of angry villains in an overly dramatic sequence.

"He can't be the standard," he said after a minute. "You need to watch Captain Jack Sparrow for a good fight scene."

This was offensive enough for Aditi to pause the movie. She shuffled and turned towards him.

"Pirates of the Caribbean?"

"Do you know any other Jack Sparrow?" Rian asked dryly.

"Shahrukh fights all the bad guys. Even the big ones. Look at Tangaballi." She waved, gesturing to the giant villain on screen.

"Captain Jack Sparrow fought entire leagues," he argued immediately.

"Shahrukh saves the girl. Always."

"Captain saved the Black Pearl."

"I thought all he did was steal ships and search for treasure."

"The term is *commandeered*," he corrected, looking so affronted that Aditi sniggered.

"Fine, stick with your Captain. I'm happy with Shahrukh." She hit play, only to stop immediately with a gasp. "I just had an epiphany," she began, almost vibrating with excitement.

"You look like you're going to pass out if you keep it in. So spill."

"I love Sharukh Khan. You love Jack Sparrow." She held one hand up for each. "If you bring them together," she drawled, her palms meeting with a loud smack, "what do you get?"

Nose scrunched, he sat back, watching her bounce in place as a way to get him to hurry and answer. "Shahrukh Sparrow? Jack Khan?"

"No, Bugs!" She rolled her eyes. "Shahrukh Khan *as* Jack Sparrow! Ugh, you have no imagination."

She huffed and plunked back into the cushions, snapping her hood to partly cover her face, obviously annoyed with him not being as excited as her about the possibility of her favourite actor playing his favourite character.

Rian hid his smile at her childishness. He liked teasing her. Their dynamics had developed naturally, and he had no intention of changing anything about it. It felt too good to mess up.

As Aditi guffawed and openly enjoyed the theatrics of the movie, Rian found himself watching her instead. He'd been in a terrible mood when he'd returned home today. His mother had unexpectedly shown up to the party he'd attended at the behest of one of his industry colleagues. He'd thought to expand his contacts as he gathered intel on those who might be interested in investing in his school.

Seeing Leela Shetty there however, had thrown his plans for a loop. She had inserted herself in every conversation, forcing introductions with wealthy families. Specifically, wealthy families with daughters of marriageable age.

She'd pushed him ahead as if he were a trophy that she could use to discuss a merger instead of a marriage, until finally, put off by her behaviour, Rian had abandoned the party and returned home.

Had he been alone, he would have stewed in annoyance or worked out in the gym to release his anger until he was tired. Not today.

A few minutes with Aditi had improved his mental state significantly. He was used to coming to an empty house but right now, his frustration dwindling steadily, he was glad she had been here to serve as a distraction.

He wondered if any of the girls his mother had so eagerly introduced to him would have been able to hold such a ridiculous conversation just for fun. Aditi was everything they were not. It wasn't that she wasn't sophisticated or beautiful. She was all that, and more.

There was something real and refreshingly honest about her. She was unabashedly silly when she was in the mood for it, inherently helpful and considering how often he found himself checking her out, definitely attractive.

The multitude of facets to her personality simply added to her physical appeal. The best part was that she didn't seem to have a clue how intriguing he found her.

He sat up straight.

Aditi was everything the girls from the party were not. She was everything his mother wouldn't want.

He picked up the remote and hit pause.

"Hey! We're getting to the good part!" Aditi protested, reaching towards him, making grabby hands.

"I have something to ask you, Doc. Listen." He held the remote out of reach. "I have an event to attend and I'm expected to bring a plus one. Will you go with me?"

She stopped, stunned.

"It's for one evening," he explained. "Go with me and...pretend to be my girlfriend."

She blinked, trying to absorb his request. She was embarrassed to admit how quickly she'd assumed he was asking her on a date.

"My mother has been taking every opportunity to introduce me to women she wants me to marry. I can't deal with it at this event, too. I need you to run interference."

"You want to use me as a shield?" she asked, finally finding her voice again. "Why me?"

Rian shrugged. "You won't try to turn it into a relationship."

He couldn't have been clearer that he didn't want more. Aditi tried to brush off the sinking feeling in her gut, knowing there was no reason to take personal offence to that comment. Despite that, the little pinch in her heart felt uncomfortably close to regret.

"Why do you need to go? Wouldn't it be easier to say you're busy than to bring along a fake girlfriend?"

"There will be people at this event who I need to meet. Investors."

"Oh." Aditi nodded understandingly. "Sounds important."

"It is. The only other girl I would have trusted to go with me happens to not be in the country. And her husband is a possessive idiot."

It was at the tip of Aditi's tongue to ask who that was. *None of your business*, she reprimanded herself. "One night?" she confirmed, her mind running a furious pros and cons list when he nodded.

One night to pretend that she was in a relationship with this man who made her stomach churn and her libido come alive with a single look. One night of make believe where she could behave like she had the right to hold his hand, to hug him whenever she wanted, to kiss him if the opportunity presented itself. One night to look back on, to make memories that might cause her to wonder in the future—what if it had been more?

She glanced surreptitiously at him, searching for an appropriate response. It was clear that he had no idea the multitude of emotions she'd undergone in the last minute alone. He was oblivious to her feelings towards him. No wonder he'd asked her for this as a favour.

With how she'd been feeling lately and Nina's suggestion ringing in her ear, just one night seemed like it would open doors to something more. Which did her no good if he remained unaware.

"Thanks for asking, Bugs." She swallowed the bitter knot that had begun to form in her throat. "But, no."

It was Rian's turn to be surprised. "No?"

Lower lip trapped under her teeth, she shook her head apologetically before turning away.

For the next minute, Aditi tried hard to ignore the burning gaze of the man seated two feet away. She tried to focus on a sweaty Shahrukh climbing a million stairs while carrying the woman he loved, a scene she had watched and gushed over before.

"Doc?"

She sighed and paused the movie once more. She drew in a deep breath before turning towards him, meeting his gaze head on. "I don't want it to be just one night."

"What?"

"Date me," she said, sounding calmer than she felt.

Rian let out a breathy laugh, waiting for the punchline, but turning wary when the silence stretched and her seriousness became evident.

Aditi watched Rian's face transform, his disbelief almost comical. She knew well that he was firmly against a long-term alliance, but she had not felt this way about a man since her break up with Harish. Two years of being single and getting over what she'd assumed would be a life-long relationship had left her with shaky confidence and multiple regrets.

She didn't want regrets with Rian. She didn't want to live her life wondering what would have happened if she'd been brave enough to act on this attraction. Hence, despite believing that Nina's suggestion of a casual fling was outrageous, she found that it was also the most logical course of action for her. Maybe once she'd indulged in this madness, she would stop comparing other men with Rian. Maybe once she'd satiated this lust he induced in her, she would find him less compelling.

"Well?" she prodded, trying to sound nonchalant when internally, her organs were twisting like spaghetti on a fork.

Rian had expected Aditi to yell '*April Fool's!*' It didn't matter that April was long gone. But she said nothing, only watching him with that look on her face as if she was standing in front of a firing squad but too stubborn to move to safety.

His skin grew cold. "I can't date you." Rian thought he saw something akin to discomfort flicker in her eyes, the deep brown orbs holding his attention while he tried to get his bearings again.

"Then I can't go as your fake girlfriend," she firmly responded.

She had never indicated a romantic interest in him before. She'd been going on arranged dates the entire time he'd been back, for heaven's sake. "You said you'll help me," he pushed, still not certain what she was after. "You said if I needed help, I could ask you."

Caught, Aditi bit back an annoyed growl. "Fine. As a friend, I'll do it. But I still want you to consider what I said about dating."

"Doc," he pleaded.

She combed a hand through her hair, flipping it over one shoulder. The action caught his eye, and despite himself, he couldn't help but appreciate how effortlessly alluring she looked.

"I'm not asking for a relationship," she clarified, trying to placate him. "I'm suggesting a casual. . .situationship." She couldn't hold back a grimace at her use of that word, but calling it anything else seemed too serious.

"A w-what?" Rian gulped, unable to believe his ears.

"You heard me."

"Nothing more?"

"Of course not! I'm not an idiot. It's like I'm at a pet store. I know what I'm there for: to pet the rabbit, not buy it."

"A Bugs Bunny reference? Really?" Rian griped, trying to squash his irritation. Her vehement dismissal of wanting more than a fling should have made him feel safe. It didn't. "Doc, be honest. Why are you asking for this?"

Aditi drew her feet up, wrapping her arms about her shins before resting her chin on her knee. Her usually friendly face was devoid of a smile, all traces of mischief gone.

"Have you been in a serious relationship with anyone?" she asked, her voice barely audible above the drumming in his ear.

Rian shook his head.

He saw her throat working hard, her shoulders stiff. She had never looked so uncomfortable before.

"I was in one a few years ago," she said, looking down at her clasped hands. She hadn't expected to discuss her past today, least of all with Rian. He'd asked her for honesty, and she would give him exactly that. "I thought all was good, until it came crashing down around my ears. I don't have any experience outside of it and I haven't felt comfortable with another man since then to attempt it again."

She turned her head to find Rian watching her, his expression devoid of judgement or pity. This gave Aditi the courage to continue.

"The closer I am to getting married, the more I'm worried about what I don't know. My dates haven't been working in my favour and I doubt the next one will be any different. I might be on an unexpected break from meeting other men. I figured, I may as well find a different way to experience what I've missed out on."

"So, this *situationship* you're proposing is...what? A memorabilia of your unmarried days?"

"Yes!" Aditi exclaimed, almost relieved with his input. "That's the perfect way to explain it. You are so good at figuring me out."

Was he? Rian wondered if he looked as conflicted as he felt. He had no fucking clue why he wanted to run from her at the same time as run into her.

"See, I'm fairly confident about most things. But the intimacy stuff...I would like to be better at that." Aditi tried not to let her embarrassment show. "I don't want my inhibitions to affect whatever relationship I would have with my future husband. And I don't want to go around kissing or hooking up with random guys. My schedule and own sense of safety wouldn't allow it. But you're here, I'm living in your house, I feel comfortable with you, and I know you won't take advantage of me. It's convenient."

Hearing himself get described as convenient did nothing for his ego. Or temper. What the fuck was wrong with him? Most men would kill for a no-strings-attached deal handed to them by a gorgeous woman like Aditi. And here he was, acting like a goddamn virgin who was complaining about commitment. Or lack thereof.

"And I'm not asking for exclusivity. I know you don't want to get married."

"You do?" he asked dubiously.

She nodded.

"How?"

"I may have heard what you said to Nanamma the night you returned from Singapore."

"You eavesdropped?"

Her eyes grew round, her face taking on that innocent look she employed every time he caught her being mischievous. It was a look he had grown accustomed to seeing. She shot him a strained smile, scratching lightly behind her ear.

"In my defence, you weren't very quiet. All I did was stand outside my room and I could hear you."

At his frown, she folded, not bothering to justify her actions anymore.

"Okay fine," she admitted. "I was standing outside your room. But I was curious. And I was also the topic of discussion."

Rian sighed, rubbing his eyes, a sudden tiredness settling into his bones.

"You are absolutely free to continue dating whoever you fancy," Aditi continued softly, watching this mammoth of a man slump back, his hands covering his face. "If you get serious with someone, we stop. If I get serious with someone, we stop. It's that simple."

"Do you realise how messed up this sounds?" he interjected.

Aditi watched him with a wry smile, waiting until his hands fell away and he was looking at her once more.

"Bugs, I have had time to think about this. I've never had a friend-with-benefits before. But I like you. I've been attracted to you for a while and this is just my way of experiencing something without committing to it."

Honesty, Rian realised, had nothing on Aditi Krishnan. She had admitted to so many things in a single conversation that could overturn any male-female relationship. Somehow, despite this, she had made it sound enticingly straightforward.

"This won't work," Rian whispered, the voice in his head warning him while the curious tug below his waist pushed him to take a chance that may never come again. Being with Aditi, without commitment.

He could never have imagined a time when the possibility of this existed. Yet, here he was, at the threshold of exactly such an opportunity, terrified of accepting it.

"It won't work," he said again, wondering who he was trying to convince because his brain was screaming something while his body and heart were clamouring for the exact opposite.

"Maybe," she said, turning back to the TV screen and letting the movie resume. "But if you want to find out, you know where I live."

10

The Ex Hex

Aditi

Aditi glanced around The Mumbai Map, patiently waiting for her date to show up. How did she score yet another reservation? Nanamma. The old lady apparently yielded more power than she knew. This time, Nanamma hadn't even bothered to inform Rian before calling the restaurant manager and asking them to clear a table for Aditi and her date.

Aditi would have had to be a fool to refuse. So, she'd shown up on time, dressed to impress in a peach-pink wrap dress that showed off her flawless brown skin and accentuated her curvy figure. Aditi felt quite confident that today, she would finally pull off a successful date.

She made herself comfortable in her booth, sipping her spritzer, Kindle in hand; simply enjoying the anticipation of meeting someone new.

She'd caught sight of Rian briefly when he'd passed by her table, a leggy woman with cherry lips hanging onto him like he was her safety net against gravity.

Aditi had had to control herself from scoffing.

He was obviously on a date as well. And unless this woman was the love of his life, it was sure to be a casual one. Like the kind she'd asked from him.

Except, he'd behaved as if she'd demanded his kidney.

Rian's rejection had chafed at her pride. Seeing him out with another woman, dressed in that powder blue that made his eyes seem like clear skies on sunny days, made her gnash her teeth.

No matter how peeved she was, it seemed like her body was entirely attuned to him if he were in the vicinity. She wanted to throw her complimentary Naan chips at him for having such an effect on her.

Which made the stakes for this evening to be a good one that much higher.

She'd caught him frowning at her, but she chalked it up to the intense discussion he seemed to be having with his lady friend. Fine, she'd decided then, determinedly ignoring his gaze when he'd looked in her direction. She was going to forget that she'd asked him for a fling, and forge ahead with the hope that candidate number twelve would be the man of her dreams.

"Hi."

Aditi glanced up, the ready smile on her face transforming into a scowl almost immediately. Faced with the man she loathed instead of her date, she wondered if she was praying to the wrong gods. Why else would her ex-boyfriend be standing in front of her, looking for all intents like he'd come prepared to stay?

"What are you doing here?" Aditi asked, surprised when he slid into the seat across from her.

"We're both here. May as well get dinner. I'll order."

"Harish, stop," she commanded, her voice sharp. "How did you know where I was?"

"I heard you tell Nina," Harish replied, raising his hand to snap his finger at a passing waiter and ordering a drink for himself. "The nurses have been talking about how you've been on a dating spree. Eager to get married, are you?"

"You're one to talk. Aren't you engaged?"

"I broke it off."

"That's not what I heard," Aditi muttered. Her sister had regaled her with gossip around Harish's broken engagement, apparently caused by his interfering mother and his own inability to take a stand for himself. The touch of unease in his expression told her that the gossip was probably true.

"Forget that," he said, obviously wanting to move on from the topic. "Are you getting married?"

"How is that any of your concern?"

"We were together for a long time. I have a right to be concerned."

She couldn't hold back an incredulous huff. "No, you don't. We broke up. It's been almost two years."

"Time won't erase our memories."

Aditi sat back, watching Harish put on his best impression of a docile, loving man. It was this version of him that had had her fooled for too long. She released a breath, finding thankfully that he had no effect on her anymore.

"Did you bring your wallet?" she inquired, her tone flat and even.

Confusion flickered in his eyes. "Yes, why?"

"Because I think you're stealing terrible dialogues from a B-rated movie and if I have to listen to your bullshit, you're going to have to pay for my drink."

Immediately, his nostrils flared. All pretence of softness fled his face. "You've turned into a bitch."

"Ah, there's the asshole I knew and loved." Aditi insolently raised her cup to him, taking a sip. "I could pretend that I missed you but if I were that good at acting, we would still be in a relationship."

"You'd be tolerable if you didn't have so much to say." Harish clenched his teeth tight enough that his jaw looked like it would splinter. She hoped it would. "You're impossible to love, Aditi."

Despite herself, those words caused a dull ache in her chest.

"Considering the only one you love is yourself, Harish, that was the first correct thing you've said since you got here. You could never have loved me."

"Me? It was your behaviour that ruined it." The vicious gleam in his eyes was hardly hidden anymore. Aditi knew Harish's personality. The fact that she had not immediately fallen over herself to speak with him meant that he would use every opportunity to belittle her and wear her down until he could get her to do her bidding.

It was a tactic she was well acquainted with.

"You got drunk and missed coming to a planned meeting with my family. I sat there, dressed to the nines, waiting for you and your parents to come discuss our engagement," she said, her voice devoid of any feeling.

"You avoided me for days after that," she recounted, remembering the numbness and confusion of not knowing what had gone wrong. The paralysing doubts that had surrounded her when she couldn't contact him. Worse yet, she'd been responsible for the embarrassment her parents had faced when they'd been stood up by the Hebbars.

She had cried for months, the loss of her first love weighing as heavily on her as the guilt of letting her parents down with her choices.

"I called you numerous times, left you countless messages. You didn't even bother texting me back once. I was devastated."

Instead of discomfort at being reminded of his ungentlemanly behaviour, Aditi saw a hint of sadistic pride at her confession. Disgust swirled in her, hating that she had never recognized this side of him before.

"I was busy," he said, as if it was sufficient enough excuse for his callousness.

"Yes," Aditi laughed sarcastically. "You were busy getting drunk and partying with your friends. And I remember clearly what happened after that, don't you?"

The sly smile on his face dropped.

"You tried to force yourself on me. You insulted me in front of everyone because I refused to sleep with you in your friends' house after you called me fat and stupid. And *my* behaviour ruined it?"

"Let it go, Aditi," he replied, not the least bit bothered by how horribly he'd treated her in their final moments together. "Here. Let me make it better. I'm willing to give you another chance as long as you can work on being the woman I want you to be."

"Are you delusional?" she spluttered, completely lost as to how Harish thought this was the concession she was seeking for her heartbreak.

"You don't have to pretend," he smirked.

Slowly, deliberately, he dragged a gaze over the parts of her that were visible above the table. His sights lingered at her chest, his appreciation making her feel unclean.

"Obviously you've put effort into your body and how you look after what I said to you. You wanted my attention by doing this and now, you have it. But you can do more. Work on your attitude, too."

"Or, you can go fuck yourself," she spat, her fists clenching into tight balls, uncaring that his demeanour changed instantly at her defiance.

He straightened, leaning forward in a threatening manner meant to intimidate her. "Don't be foolish, Aditi. I'm not asking you for something unimaginable. We had good times before. We can have them again."

An angry Harish would have previously cowed her into submission, playing hot and cold until she'd feel like their problems were because she'd overreacted. Today however, she would throw hands if that meant saving herself from repeating her mistakes. So, despite knowing that his temper was fraying, Aditi held back no punches.

"What makes you think, after witnessing your disgraceful behaviour, that I would ever want to be with you? That I would ever consider giving you another chance?"

"If you hadn't been such a ball-buster, I wouldn't have gone off on you. I was a little drunk but you should take accountability for what you did to make me react that way. You could have been more mature."

"Too bad your maturity does not compensate for your insufferable personality," Aditi declared, slipping her phone and Kindle into her handbag. "You should consider a lobotomy. It would be a vast improvement over what you are."

"You'll be sorry if you don't shut up," Harish warned.

"I must have been blind," she continued, pretending as if he'd never spoken. "How did I never see what a spineless, toxic, piece of shit you are?" Aditi stood up, having had enough. She'd only just taken a step away when her wrist was grabbed.

"You're disrespecting me in public." Harish spun her around, looming over her. His grip on her tightened, causing her to wince. Physically, he was stronger, and it was obvious that he wouldn't stop at using this to get his way. "Sit down," he ordered, shaking her a little like she was a silly child who was throwing a tantrum.

"Let. Me. Go," Aditi hissed, struggling to get herself released.

She was seconds away from smacking her purse across his face when she saw a shadow fall across them both.

The scent of cinnamon and soap surrounded her, her gut recognizing him even before his furious growl reverberated in her ear.

"Take your fucking hands off her!"

11

No Time to Weep

Aditi

Aditi didn't have to turn to know that Rian was behind her. The bubble of fear in her chest popped, relief slowly seeping in.

"Listen to her," she heard him say as he came to stand beside her. "Unless you don't like having fingers."

Harish's grip loosened, but stubborn rat that he was, he didn't let go.

"I can handle this," Aditi declared boldly, glancing sideways at Rian. He looked relaxed, but the tight line of his mouth, the patently false smile, and the icy chill in his gaze told her that he was furious.

"I'm certain you can, Doc. I still don't enjoy seeing him put his hand on you."

Unable to keep up the appearance of being self-sufficient against a man much stronger than her, she confessed, "I'm not enjoying it either."

"You heard the lady." Rian pointedly glared at the hand that was still wrapped around her wrist. "Drop it before there is bloodshed."

"Are you threatening me?" Harish huffed, puffing his chest. His ego would never let him back away from a challenge.

"It's not a threat," Rian corrected, his tone deceivingly polite. "I'm promising you that when Aditi jabs your hand with this fork," he explained, picking one from their table and handing it to her for emphasis, "I will hold your wrist just like you've held hers, and push it in harder until all you feel is gut-wrenching pain. No one will help you, unless I allow it. Which, I won't. This is my restaurant, my turf."

Aditi wasn't sure if it was the possibility of a fork injury or the revelation of who Rian was that finally made Harish let her go.

"You're the owner?"

"Not quick on the uptake, are you?" Rian drawled, very much wanting to rip this man limb from limb. Aditi had not wanted him to interfere, and it was only this knowledge which had quelled the blood lust he'd experienced, seeing her get pushed around by this asshole.

Harish reddened at the insult. "How do you know this guy?" he demanded, too intimidated by Rian to continue a direct conversation with him.

Aditi ignored him, allowing Rian to place a hand on her back, ready to lead her out.

"Aditi, we're not done talking."

"Yes, we are," she shot back, turning away when she heard his footsteps behind her.

"I'll find you at the hospital."

Aditi didn't have time to react to this, because within the blink of an eye, Rian had stepped in between them, making it impossible for Harish to have direct access to her.

Perhaps he finally realised who he was up against, because Harish's previous bravado faltered when faced with a stronger, taller man who was looking at him with steely eyes that promised a future full of pain.

The tension was palpable and Aditi wondered if the two would come to blows. Rian's voice rumbled, low enough that perhaps only Harish and her could hear him speak.

"My camera's have caught you manhandling Aditi. You threatened to stalk her at the hospital, of which I am a witness, along with my employees. While I'm being nice, take my advice. Maintain your distance."

Harish gulped. "You can't talk to me like that."

"Just did."

"I work with her."

"Then work. But if she feels uncomfortable because of you, you'll find yourself regretting your life choices."

Aditi glanced at the sturdy back of the man she had been cursing for the last twenty-four hours. A man who had recognized from across the room that she was distressed and was even now shielding her from an unsavoury past.

Without meaning to, she stepped closer, needing his scent to feel calm and safe.

"Rian," she called, placing one hand at the centre of his back. He turned towards her, his concerned gaze giving her a once over.

"Ready to go?" he asked, glad to see her nod.

Aditi stayed silent as he made his excuses, instructing his staff to escort Harish out without drawing too much attention. At her behest, they chose to walk around the block first instead of heading directly home. Aditi didn't think she'd have been able to sit and stew inside a car anyway.

She glanced about, the crowds and lively chatter of people around her giving her something other than the argument to focus on. There was beauty in the chaos of Mumbai—always something to see and appreciate.

"Sorry," he said as he kept pace with her. "I didn't mean to interfere in your personal matters, but I couldn't stand back and watch when he started to get physical."

"Dosti mein, no sorry, no thank you." She chuckled darkly, her weird sense of humour being the only shield stopping her from crumbling. The fear from her confrontation with Harish still lingered. At his exasperated look, she added, "I'm glad you stepped in."

"You're not mad?"

Aditi's chest filled with the breath she took before she released it in a loud huff, trying to reduce the anxiety that had built in her.

"Dealing with Harish is always draining. It was nice to have back up."

"Who was he?"

"My ex."

Rian had to control himself from reacting to that piece of information. He found himself curious about her old relationship. She had mentioned to him last night that it had ended badly. Given the abominable behaviour he'd witnessed, Rian had no doubt that the break up would have been ugly as well.

"Are you going to cry?" he asked, watching her pinched expression as she pretended to check the goods at a roadside hawker selling salted peanuts. She was hurt. Probably embarrassed. He hoped she knew that he wouldn't judge her for feeling low. That she could lean on him if she needed to.

Before he could say anything further, her control snapped into place.

"I don't cry," she confessed, chewing the inside of her lips in consternation. She would rather shave her eyebrows than cry over Harish-fucking-Hebbar. She'd been there, done that, and buried it with a circle of salt around the grave so that even the ghost of that ugly relationship couldn't be revived.

"You don't cry. *You*?" Rian found that hard to believe. Aditi was one of the most expressive people he had ever met.

"Over fictional characters? Sure. Over real people? Rarely. A person has to matter a lot for me to cry over them."

He let that sink in, saying nothing as he paid for a cone of the salted peanuts before she could object. He handed some to Aditi as they each began their stroll towards the restaurant once more.

"I'm sorry your date was ruined because of me," she sniffed.

Rian's forehead creased at her apology. "That wasn't a date. It was a business meeting," he clarified, on the verge of admitting that even a date wouldn't have stopped him from standing up for her.

Oddly enough, the seriousness of his thought was juxtaposed by her snorting, a dry look on her face when she twisted her neck to see him.

"I might not be so great at this whole dating thing," she accepted with a sideways nod, "but even I know a date when I see one."

"If it was a date, I wouldn't have brought her to my restaurant at the busiest time of the evening."

"Does she know that?"

Rian frowned.

"Bugs, she was interested in a lot more than just business," Aditi said, taking undue pleasure in the crunchy texture of the nuts she was consuming. "She looked downright pissed when you excused yourself to leave with me. If she is still around, I can explain to her that we're just temporary housemates. I don't want to be a cockblocker."

Rian almost got a peanut stuck in his throat, choking in surprise. He looked about him to see if anyone else had heard her. Thankfully, not.

"Do you ever listen to yourself when you speak?" He had never before met anyone who was the living definition of an open book. Rian was equal parts in awe of her ability to be forthright and candid as he was envious of it. One required a lot of conviction and self-love to be like Aditi.

"I have to be very careful about my bedside manners at work," she admitted, munching on her snack. "I don't bother holding back outside though."

He snorted. "Yeah, I can see that."

A moment later, he stopped, doing a double take when he realised that she was no longer walking beside him. Worried, he spun around, letting out a relieved breath when he found her an arm's distance away.

"Doc?"

"There were times I couldn't say anything," she confessed, watching him with that odd look. "I had to stay quiet and provide care for a girl who was impregnated a month after her marriage. She was fourteen."

Rian's heart dropped to his stomach, but he didn't interrupt her.

"I had to release a lady and her child back into the care of her abusive in-laws. I had no power to speak up against it. I had to bite my tongue when my patient's husband wouldn't look at their newborn and told her she could only die after she bore him a son. She was barely two days postpartum with their third daughter. I have had to say nothing despite wanting to because that is part of the work I do. So yes, in my personal life, I say what is on my mind. Do not mistake my choice to speak freely as an inability to understand when to remain silent. I'm not stupid."

This was the first glimpse of vulnerability he'd seen in her. Rian couldn't help but feel that if he didn't pick the correct response, he would damage something integral to the woman she was. To the woman he admired.

He took one step closer, just enough that he could respond without having to be loud, but far enough away that it was still considered respectable in public.

"Doc," he said, choosing the simplest words possible. "The only one who is stupid is someone who thinks you are."

Instantly, the tightness in her chest eased. Her lips curved up in a bashful smile, and no other words were exchanged. When his sincerity was so evident, no other words were needed.

It was some time after they'd returned to his apartment, sitting around his kitchen island while they split dessert, when Aditi spoke up again.

"The offer is still open," she began, stabbing a fork through the gulab-jamun cheesecake they'd acquired after their stroll. "I can talk to your date and. . ."

"Not a date," Rian interrupted, trapping her fork with his to bring her attention to him. "I am not interested in her."

"Are you interested in anyone, Bugs?" Aditi asked instead, using her free hand to steal the last piece. Triumphant, she beamed in happiness as she popped the last piece into her mouth, licking the remnants off her fingers with gusto.

Rian couldn't look away even if he tried, each dart of her tongue painting tortuously erotic pictures of things he could experience if he found the courage to accept her offer of a fling. He gulped. He'd thought of little else since she'd admitted to being attracted to him. If only he was as comfortable accepting his desires as she was.

"I've been so focused on finding a guy, I never asked if you like someone too?"

Considering all he'd been able to think of was her, that was not an answer he was willing to share. Aditi snapped her fingers in his face, bringing clarity back to him. "No. I don't like anyone. Don't have time."

Aditi peered at him, amused. "Love doesn't need time. It only needs a moment."

"Careful, Doc. Your medical licence might get revoked if you keep talking like this," he teased, watching her pick up the plate when he made a move to collect their forks. "You studied science. You're supposed to rely on facts, not feelings."

"Love can be a fact and a feeling," she glibly replied, gesturing to him to sit back down. She proceeded to rinse the dishes in the sink, loading them meticulously into the dishwasher.

Rian watched Aditi move about his kitchen, at ease with where things were kept, needing no direction from him. The domesticity of the moment held him in its thrall, an intense longing blooming in him for something he couldn't recognize.

"Fact or not," he cleared his throat, trying to avoid feeling overcome by this new emotion, "I'm not going to go down that path again."

"Again?" She glided up to him, wiping her hands on the dish towel. "Bad experience?"

He shrugged. "It's not for me, Doc. Love is uncomfortable and all-consuming."

"Isn't that the point of love? To be so consumed by how you feel for someone that everything else just feels. . . less."

Her words tickled some sleeping part of his heart to a mild wakefulness.

"Well, I should call it a night. My date was a bust but at least I had good dessert." Aditi grinned, sounding mostly recovered from the stress of the evening. "Now, if only I could manage a good dessert, a good date and a good kiss—all in one evening—that would be tremendous."

She turned towards him, smiling still. With him being seated, the difference in their heights was no longer as pronounced. She cocked her head, only now realising how close they were. Her eyes grew warm, deepening to a dark brown. Without a warning, she leaned in.

Rian stilled, his breath hitching when her nose bumped against his skin. His entire being stood at attention when her soft lips brushed against the hollows of his cheek. It was a delicate graze, but held him arrested. He blinked rapidly, his body awash in goosebumps as she pulled away.

"Thank you." Her voice was a bare murmur above the blood rushing to his ears.

"For?"

"For stepping in when I needed help. For trying to cheer me up, and for turning a bad evening into a good one. You're a pretty good friend to have."

Friend. It was quite possibly the most hated word in his dictionary as of this moment. What a ridiculous and unnecessary addition to any language.

"We're. . ." He gulped, needing to take a breath. "We're not friends."

She didn't argue, smiling at him indulgently. Like she accepted his need to maintain this farce of a distance between them.

"Good night, Bugs." She sashayed down the hall and into her room, unaware that Rian still hadn't recovered.

It had been a chaste kiss, but had left his gut twisting with need. "Good night, Doc," he whispered, well after the lights under her door dimmed, wondering how the feel of her pillowy lips on his skin hadn't worn off yet.

And dreading the moment it would.

12

Food for the Soul

Rian

"You have a motorbike."

"Umm, yes."

Rian watched Aditi process this fact like he'd just opened a trunk full of drugs. Why she would behave this way was a mystery to him. He was having a hard time figuring out what Aditi was suffering from, because one thing was certain—she was not her usual self.

He'd only just returned from work when he'd found her trying to slip out, muttering furiously under her breath.

She was hungry, she'd explained, but his offer to cook for her had been declined with disconcerting politeness. Worried to let her roam about by herself, he'd proposed that they all go out together. Nanamma had suddenly announced that she was far too exhausted to join them, practically shooing them out the door before either could try and convince her to change her mind.

Which brought them here, in his underground garage, with Aditi staring at his BMW Roadster like it was a three-headed dog she'd been asked to harness.

"He has a bike," she mumbled, not realising that he could hear her.

"It'll be faster to weave through traffic with this."

She barely heard him. She'd woken up that morning after yet another raunchy dream featuring her oblivious housemate, frustrated that she was unable to find anything about him that would turn her off. His immediate support of her at his restaurant had only amped up whatever she'd already been feeling. Now, with the image of his strong, jean-clad thighs straddling a motorcycle, his defined biceps flexing as he adjusted his black jacket on himself, he'd just gotten exponentially sexier. How was she supposed to get over her crush like this?

A sudden thought struck her, a mischievous little cackle resounding in her brain.

"Will you let me drive?" she asked. *Say no, say no, say no. Be mean. Let me find one reason to dislike you just a little, please!*

Rian extended his keys towards her and the indetectable smile she'd sported dropped.

Well, fuck you very much.

"You're just going to give it to me?" Her dull reaction caused his brows to knit, confusion flickering across his handsome face.

"Is this a trick question?"

"Aren't you scared I'm going to crash your expensive bike?" she asked, almost hoping he'd change his mind.

"You were riding one when we met in Velas. If you have problems with mine, I'm right here to help you." He shuffled back, making space for her in the front.

To his consternation, Aditi declined. "Some other day. Besides, I don't know where we are going."

She tossed him the keys, her feelings regarding the man she now sat behind ranging from disbelief over his sweetness to utter annoyance over the exact same thing. It was like someone had read the book-boyfriend manual and created Rian Shetty in that image.

It was impossible to remain vexed with him, she ruefully accepted. She observed him joke and tease the owner of the beachside stall he'd brought her to, throwing a friendly arm over one of the server boys as he introduced her to them. The joy with which these people had greeted Rian told her that he was a dear friend.

It never failed to impress her that despite being an heir to millions, Rian had the most normal life imaginable. It made him approachable in ways she had not expected.

His modest life, his behaviour, and commitment to his work had made more sense once he'd divulged that he'd not accepted his inheritance. It had been clear enough that there were familial tensions making it imperative for him to find his own path in life. Aditi recalled reading that the Shettys held major market shares in multiple businesses, the value of which kept them listed amongst the wealthiest families in India.

No one seeing him thus would have guessed that he came from such opulence.

She watched him engage with Chandan Lal, the owner of the most visited Pav Bhaji stall on this strip of Juhu Beach. The scent of seawater and spices made her mouth water, her stomach grumbling in anticipation of her meal. With the ocean waves swooshing on one side mixed with the sizzling sounds of vegetables being pan-fried nearby, she felt one with the energetic throng of hungry and happy beachgoers. Slowly, Aditi felt the tensions of her day beginning to fade away.

She giggled, good-naturedly joining Chandan Lal and Rian behind the counter, trying her hand at sauteing and mashing the vegetables on his massive cast-iron pan.

"You're going to come back here everyday, Bhabhi," Chandan joked, plating a generous portion for her. "Rian bhaiyya is always trying to steal my recipe but I will tell it to you for free."

Aditi bit her lower lip, looking at Rian for direction when his friend addressed her as bhabhi, obviously under the misconception that they were a couple. To her surprise, he didn't seem perturbed by this, busy forcing payment on a reluctant Chandan instead.

"Why did you not let me pay for our meal?" They took their plates and found seating outside, choosing to sit side by side so that they could watch the sunset while they ate.

"That's never going to happen. When you're with me, I pay. No arguments."

"I don't know if my feminism will survive you," she teased, chuckling when he grumbled under his breath like an old man. "What? Was I meant to say 'yes, Chef' and roll over?"

Rian almost choked on his tongue, his entire body reacting to her calling him chef.

"How did you meet Chandan?" Aditi asked, blessedly giving him something else to focus on.

"I ate here often when I was roaming Mumbai for inspiration for the restaurant. Became friends with Chandan over time." Rian motioned for her to take a bite.

Aditi pulled apart the fluffy buns that had been provided, a little sceptical about the copious amounts of butter that had been used to roast them. Maybe her misgivings showed on her face because Rian reached over and plucked the bread off her fingers, dipped it in the bhaji, and brought it to her lips.

Without a second thought, Aditi accepted the morsel of food, only realising how intimate the gesture was when her lips closed around his fingers. Her eyes darted to his, but all she saw in him was a curious excitement. A second later, his anticipation made sense. A world of flavours exploded in her mouth—spicy, salty, tangy, sharp. The soft bun made a perfect vehicle for the kaleidoscope of textures within the bhaji. The brightness of the cilantro and lime, and the heat of the chillis warred for recognition while butter enhanced the indulgence of the dish.

"Oh my god," she moaned, closing her eyes, one hand unknowingly resting upon her heart as she tried to make sense of what she was tasting.

Rian took a mental picture of how Aditi looked, riveted by her obvious pleasure. *You can put that look on her face without food involved,* the devil on his shoulder whispered in his ear, his cock beginning to stir at the thought. He adjusted himself in his seat, stuffing his mouth with food before unholy ideas took root.

"No wonder you wanted to steal his recipe." Aditi looked down in awe at her plate before she attacked it with a zeal akin to a hungry tiger hunting a deer.

"If you ever wonder why I've been taking you to these small, hole-in-the-wall restaurants, it's because they have the best food."

"I believe you," she mumbled, her mouth full. "This is incredible. Phenomenal. Stupendous. I'll never be the same."

Rian grinned at the theatrics, glad that Aditi was slowly starting to sound like herself again.

Happy to just be, they observed the slow descent of the sun flirting with the horizon that stretched ahead. The beauty of the golden glow infused a sense of calmness into the atmosphere, the comfortable silence punctuated by sounds of chewing and the occasional call of the crows overhead. There was a sense of contentment in that moment that wasn't often easy to find in their busy lives. Perhaps it was this that led Rian to admit, "I owe them everything."

At Aditi's look, he explained.

"The small-business owners, roadside cooks—they see the real Mumbai. When I was a young chef trying to understand the beat of this city, they were willing to teach me whatever they knew. No gatekeeping, no desire to make a buck off me. They represent the heart that makes Mumbai different. What I learnt from them is what makes The Mumbai Map resonate with people. I owe them my success."

Aditi took a moment to let that sink in before reaching her clean hand for his. If her action surprised him, he didn't show it, only waiting patiently for her to speak.

"I'm glad you're humble enough to remember their help. But don't discount your hard work. I can't let you be unfair to yourself."

Rian glanced down at her thumb rubbing the back of his hand, feeling a link snap into place every time Aditi spoke of him with such conviction.

"How are you so sure of me?"

"I told you I'm observant. I've seen how hard you work. Besides, you've given me no reason not to believe in you."

"In that case, believe in me that I'll help you and tell me what's been bothering you."

Aditi's hand slipped, not having expected the turn in their conversation.

"You were clearly not happy when I came home. What happened?"

"It's a long story."

"We have time."

A look of discomfort and unsurety settled on her otherwise happy face.

"I used to be...bigger," she began, somewhat uncomfortably. Her chest rose as she took in a deep breath, clearly preparing herself for what she had to say.

"I've struggled with fluctuating weight since my late teens," she confessed, looking outwards instead of at him. "I became conscious of how I looked when I began to date in medical school. I knew I was never going to be that beautiful, skinny girl who everyone envied. But I tried. Crash diets and intense exercises became my go-to. It worked for a while. I went from plump to fashionably thin. That's when I met Harish. The longer we were together, the more relaxed I became and the more I changed. Add to that the pressures of medical school and dieting dropped lower on my list of priorities. I was already too loud, too opinionated, too chaotic. When the weight gain happened, I also became too unattractive."

A tremulous, embarrassed smile graced her face, but the hurt in her eyes from the mere recollection of these memories couldn't be erased. The ache within him seemed to be a reflection of her pain. It felt like a travesty to have a day when Aditi Krishnan was not her joyous, confident self.

"Harish didn't say anything outright at first. But there was always a disapproving comment here and there about my food consumption, whether I could afford the extra calories that day, maybe I should eat a salad for lunch instead of whatever I liked. By the time we broke up, I had ruined my relationship with food. I had convinced myself that I don't like to eat."

"But you're a doctor!" Rian exclaimed, baffled that Aditi had struggled with this. "Of all people, you know why a good diet is important!"

"Bugs," she chided in a gentle tone, shaking her head once. "Being a doctor is my profession. My contentious relationship with food was the result of the insecurities of a young woman in love. Those two are not mutually exclusive."

Troubled by how much Aditi hid behind her happy-go-lucky facade, Rian asked, "But you're better now?"

"Yes, I'm better now, but sometimes, those insecurities come back. Like today. That's why I needed to eat something utterly delicious, even if it was late. To remind myself that I would miss out on things like this if I let that feeling win over me again."

"What happened today?"

Aditi grimaced. "Harish made a comment along the lines of how I would never find someone because of how I am. One line, and he targeted my personality and appearance both."

"That little fucker." Rian couldn't hold back the curse.

"He didn't approach me directly. I think he remembers your threat." She scoffed, her mouth tilted in a sardonic twist. "Just made the comment in passing loud enough for the cafeteria to hear and the gossip to spread. People like having someone to talk about to distract themselves from their own issues."

Rian wanted to say something to ease her pain. He wanted to admit that he thought she was amazing, that he was constantly in awe of her, that he saw her beautiful heart that competed with how beautiful he found her physically as well. But how did one say all this and still remain not-friends, as he so often insisted?

"I will never be with someone who will make me feel what Harish did, ever again. Like I need to be embarrassed of myself. Like I am not enough." This was a vow she'd made to herself and planned to stick by. At his sombre look, she reached out and patted his hand, her lips curving up for his benefit.

True to form, she was reassuring him instead of letting him make her feel better. Had she never learned to lean on someone else? He knew how isolating and tiring it could feel, always being the one providing support instead of reaching for it.

Rian watched her finish the rest of her meal with gusto, flitting from topic to topic, laughing, sharing anecdotes, forcing him to stay involved and engaged. Not for a moment did he see her wallow in self-pity.

And all he could think of was that Aditi, with her wide smile, kind heart, sunny disposition, and innate strength, deserved someone who believed she made the world go around.

Because she was Aditi. And that was reason enough.

13

A Proposal

RIAN

Rian assumed that Aditi had changed her mind.

Considering that in the week since her offer to have a no-strings-attached fling with him, she had not brought it up again, it was natural for him to conclude that she had decided against it.

There had been plenty of opportunities for her to broach the subject because Rian, out of an uncontrollable compulsion to see her eat, had been finding one excuse after another to drag her out of the house at random hours of the evening to visit different eateries around Mumbai. Aditi had called it her personal food tour across his city, and maybe it was exactly that.

While the menu at his restaurant offered a range of gastronomical delights reminiscent of Mumbai and its spirit, somehow, sitting with her at a roadside eatery or inhaling seasonal treats from little known boutiques while they visited Mumbai's landmarks made for an immersive experience unlike any other. He had never had the opportunity to share this in the past. He'd never wanted to before.

With Aditi and her obvious delight every time he brought her to a new place and introduced her to new foods, he couldn't imagine having done anything else.

He'd driven Nanamma and Aditi to Gateway of India that evening, treating them to a lavish dinner at the heritage hotel across from it, the Taj. They'd passed by Haji Ali on the way home, another famous tourist spot near which was a small mom-and-pop shop that served one of the best desserts in the city—a custard apple pudding that rivalled the leading ice creams in the country. Watching his grandmother laugh and enjoy the evening with them had put him in a good mood, any niggling doubt about the reason for his solicitousness towards Aditi brushed aside in light of Nanamma's happiness.

Plus, he was being a good host, he told himself, unable to stop an indulgent smile from gracing his face when Aditi dug into another ice cold bowl of custard apple cream.

With Nanamma asleep and no longer available to shield him from the full force of Aditi's pull, he hoped he could continue reminding himself of why he'd refused a date with her. Sitting out on his massive balcony, music playing on the speakers, the cool breeze a welcome relief from the heat of the day, he was hard pressed to recall when last he felt this level of attraction for a woman. Everything about Aditi made him want her to a degree that felt irrational and illogical. And nothing seemed to stop that need from growing.

He sat back, trying not to stare at her smacking her lips. The happy shoulder jiggle after each bite and the little noises she made with each lick of her spoon were as adorable as they were torturous.

This woman should never be separated from food, he decided right then. As long as he was around, he would keep her fed and fed well.

Aditi's phone buzzed, interrupting his thoughts.

As she read her incoming message, the bliss on her face from the sugar rush dimmed. Her lips thinned before she began to type furiously, sitting up with a low curse when there was the ping of an immediate response. Huffing, she laid her phone facedown and sat back, her eyes glazed over.

"All okay?" he asked, watching her chew on her spoon instead of eating her dessert. Startled, she glanced at him, as if only now remembering that he was still there. She nodded at first and then let out a beleaguered sigh.

"It's nothing. Just my mother asking me if I liked anyone I've gone on a date with. Or if I'd given thought to Pratik."

"Who's Pratik?"

"Some guy my family has picked. He's perfect," she spat, scrunching her nose in distaste. "Perfect face, perfect family, perfect height, perfect age, perfect citizenship, and. . ."

"Wait. Citizenship?"

She rolled her eyes.

"He's an NRI so people think he lays golden eggs." Rian snorted, but Aditi kept talking. "He's my father's best friend's son. He's also filthy rich. He's the right caste, the right sub-caste, the right lineage. Even our astrological charts have a decent match. How do I say no?"

"He sounds like an asshole," Rian muttered, feeling discomfited by how unnaturally flawless this new man seemed. "No one is that perfect."

"I don't want perfection," she said, and the knot in the centre of his chest loosened. He watched quietly as she stood up, stomping over to the railing. "I don't want to move to a different country. People think I'm crazy to complain. I'd have a lavish life and would need to do nothing except be a good little wife."

"Somehow, I don't see you as the do-nothing type."

Or be a good little anything. The woman was opinionated, mouthy, incredibly smart, and had the potential for destruction not unlike a Category 4 hurricane. She also had a fantastic ass and a body that should make men beg at her feet. But that was neither here nor there, he decided, irritated with his mind wandering where he'd not given it permission to.

"Exactly! I will go insane." She spun on her heel, swaying her hips as she stalked back and forth between him and the glass railing, giving him a view of the perfect peach of her posterior, lush, delectable and encased in pyjama shorts, this time with cherry prints all over. If he wasn't hungry before, he was certainly hungry now.

"I'd rather get married to someone I pick instead."

Right. He gulped, trying to settle the uncomfortable swirl of desire that seemed harder to ignore around Aditi each passing day.

She wanted marriage. And he was determined not to touch that time bomb with a hundred-foot pole. Besides, he'd promised Nanamma he'd treat Aditi with respect. That's the only reason he hadn't accepted her friends-with-benefits deal, he reminded himself, hard pressed to continue justifying it when she bit down on her lip. The urge for him to do the same thing spiked at the sight. He shook his head, stalking up to the railing, needing more air than he seemed to have while seated.

"Someone who lives here," he heard her mutter under her breath, their shoulders just barely touching as they both stared at the distant lights flickering. "Someone I could be friends with."

He nodded distractedly, uncorking the lid of his water bottle slowly, trying to calm his hormones because his dick certainly seemed to be a little too eager to make its presence known.

"Bugs?" She waited until he faced her. He took a sip, humming at her to continue. "Would you like to marry me?"

Rian choked on his water, spraying it right into her face.

Aditi jerked back, closing her eyes upon impact. Liquid droplets clung to her thick lashes and dripped down her cheeks in tiny rivulets. Her mouth tightened in irritation.

"I didn't need a second shower today, but thanks." She peevishly grabbed the edge of his shirt and pulled it up, involuntarily reducing the gap between them. Childishly, she wiped her face dry, leaving a dark, damp spot on his blue tee. He couldn't even protest, his mind stuck, replaying her question over and over again.

"What the fuck did you just say?" he croaked, his throat still burning.

"What?" She tilted her head back to see him, finally registering his shock.

"Oh! Oh yes! Will you marry me?" She bounced on her feet like a happy little penguin who'd just successfully found a fish.

Was it crazy that her smile made him want to say yes? She had such a pretty smile, the kind which was reflected in her eyes. It made him want to do things that would keep her smiling at him. His eyes widened, determinedly pushing the thought away. His heart hammered in a furious rhythm, refusing to calm itself.

"Doc, I think the heat has gotten to you."

Actually, the heat had gotten to him. He tried to run. He needed to run. His feet wouldn't move.

He stared down at the little woman who had thrown his world for a loop with a simple question, her eyes impossibly brown in the dim lights that illuminated her face. He felt like he was drowning in a pool of luscious cream and chocolate with no intention of saving himself. How the hell had she made him want to say yes?

"Bugs, listen!" she exclaimed, placing a hand on his arm. He should have worn long sleeves. Her bare skin touching his felt like he was being branded.

"I like you," Aditi continued, looking at him earnestly. "Whatever I know of you, I really like. You're a nice guy. And I'm a pretty nice girl. I think you could like me too. What do you say we make a go of it?"

"You're a nice girl and I'm a nice guy? That's your basis for marriage?"

She pursed her lips in a fishy pout, shrugging like she'd just asked him to share a bite of his food instead of his entire life.

Fuck, he needed a drink. And all he had was this goddamn water bottle. He lifted it high, chugging it down in a single breath, one eye still on the mad woman who had just proposed marriage to him.

"You've gone crazy. Good luck." He turned, feeling like he would cave and do something stupid if he didn't put some distance between them.

"Wait!" She tugged him back, one hand on her hip. "You're just going to leave? You're not going to offer to help?"

"Why should I?"

"Because we're friends."

"No, we are not!" he snapped, unable to keep calm.

"Oh my god, relax. What is with the overreaction, Bugs? It's not like I said *pyaar dosti hai*."

Rian pinched the bridge of his nose, head tilted heavenwards in a bid for grace. He took two breaths in, releasing it in short puffs before he spoke once more.

"You did not just quote *Kuch Kuch Hota Hai* to me," he grumbled, his eyes closed, praying for strength.

"I saw an opportunity and I took it." She giggled, his frustration only adding to her merriment. "But see? We get each other. Help me out, hmm?"

"I'm not going to help you by marrying you." *Yet*, that annoying voice in his head added. Rian had to work hard at maintaining an unaffected visage. His mind and heart had not been so torn over a person since he'd caused an upheaval in his friend Kaya's life. And that was thirteen years ago.

To face such a confusing array of feelings over a woman again made Rian wary of getting too close to Aditi. Not that he'd been the least bit successful in staying away from her either. It was as if she was a giant magnet and he wore an iron suit.

"Are you certain? I'd make a fun wife. And," she snapped her finger, gesturing to herself, "you get free healthcare for life!"

"I don't plan to get pregnant so I don't need a gynaecologist," he sullenly argued. How was she so unbothered? She'd just issued a proposal. A PROPOSAL!

"Semantics," Aditi waved, as if it was a trivial detail. "I can treat other things. Unofficially."

"Then I hope you know how to unofficially treat an aneurysm because I think you might be giving me one."

His glare told her that if she laughed, she would pay. Aditi had to physically wipe the mischievous smile off her face. Bothering Rian and seeing him get twisted up in knots had to be the best part of her day.

"Killjoy," she needled him. "Help me in a different way then."
"How?"
"Find me a nice guy. Maybe you know people."
"You're mistaken. I don't own a marriage bureau."

"No, you own a restaurant." She rapped his chest, walking off towards the flowering plants that spilled over the baskets on the railing. She played with the fronds on one end, adjusting them until they lay prettily on the side. "I can bring my future dates there. You can observe, and coach me. Be my love guru."

There were crickets. She turned to face him, his stupefaction telling her that he was on the verge of stomping off.

"You don't believe I need help? I got anxious at one of my previous dates and had to go to the washroom. Guess how I excused myself."

"How?"

Her cheeks turned a dull red, intriguing Rian.

"I waved at him and said 'don't Barry, I'll be back in a Flash.'"

Rian's nostrils flared. He didn't know whether to laugh or cry.

"Because, you know," she continued, taking a step towards him. "Flash is that DC comic character who super speeds everywhere?"

"Doc, stop."

"And his real name is Barry Allen."

"Doc," he groaned.

"And Barry sounds like hurry..."

"Quit explaining the joke," he begged, his mirth clashing with fear for what this was leading towards.

"I thought it was kind of funny," she said in a small voice, head low, kicking an invisible stone with one foot in an embarrassed move. "So, you see. I need help. And you can help me."

"You don't see potential problems?" Her surety provided him no relief. This plan was insane. It was like the beginning of a bad romantic drama.

Aditi shrugged.

"Would be a problem if you were attracted to me. But you're not."

I'm not? Rian watched as she paced back and forth, the escaped curls from her top knot framing her sweet face, her lips pouting in annoyance, her skin pink and luscious. She crossed her legs and leaned back, her shorts revealing fleshy thighs that looked like they'd fit his large hands perfectly. Nothing bony or sharp about her.

His eyes tracked her well-rounded calves, down the line of her shin ending in dainty feet. She had cute toes, he couldn't help but think, seeing them curl inwards as they stepped closer to him, as if nervous.

"So, what do you think?"

His gaze swung up to hers. "Huh, what?"

With a sigh of an old woman, Aditi explained once more, "I was saying that you not being attracted to me makes it easier."

"Makes what easier?" he asked warily.

"Kissing, of course."

14

Counting Pi

RIAN

Rian reared back, eyes wide.

"W-what?" he squeaked in an undignified manner. Kissing? Who was kissing who?

"It'll be like research. Cold and clinical," Aditi said, thankfully not noticing anything amiss. "You can tell me what I'm doing wrong."

"D-d-doing?"

She stepped closer. If Aditi was the predator, his fight or flight response was non-existent. He was going to die. He just knew it. She was too close and he couldn't breathe.

"What the hell are you doing?" he rasped, his feet locked in place.

"Getting into position." She placed one hand on his shoulder.

"What position!" His mind conjured images of positions. Many many positions that Aditi could assume. Starting with her on her knees, her mouth full of him. Or bent over the kitchen counter. Or riding him on the couch. His pants were getting too tight and he still couldn't breathe.

Fuck my life, is this what a panic attack feels like?

"For the kiss," she frowned. "Haven't you been listening?"

He hadn't. His mind had been painting vividly erotic images that had caused him temporary deafness and permanent brain damage.

Then, as if she'd realised something shocking, she backed away.

"Oh no. I'm so sorry. I shouldn't have assumed."

What now? Rian had no energy to ask the question.

"You look like you would have kissed scores already. I didn't realise you've never been kissed."

That broke through the haze that had clouded him for the last multiple minutes.

"Stop talking," he ordered, aghast that this had been her conclusion to his obvious shock.

"I'm sorry if I made you uncomfortable, Bugs. Forget I said anything. I'll find someone else."

The fuck? Someone else? The acid in his stomach rose at the thought, observing her as she turned away.

"Doc. Wait."

Before he could talk himself out of it, his fingers gripped her chin, tipping her face up. He bent low and pressed his lips against hers, gentle, soft, noting that she'd gone still. When he straightened, his focus was on her. He had no idea what her reaction was going to be.

"There you go," he awkwardly said, as though he'd just survived a chore. Aditi blinked, air filling her cheeks as she clamped her lips together, swallowing back a response. Rian had kissed her and it had been...underwhelming. Not that it was a bad kiss. For a sister. And she would wade through a vat of cow dung before she allowed him to think of her as a sister.

"Nice." Her voice pitched high as it usually did when she lied. She cleared her throat. "For your first kiss, it was fine."

His eyes narrowed. "That wasn't my first kiss."

"Sure," she agreed, wincing when her soprano gave her away.

"You don't believe me."

"No offence, but when my ex kissed me, I could count to fifteen decimal places for pi. What you did, I didn't have time to think of the word much less start counting. It ended before it began."

"That was deliberate. You asked me for a kiss. I gave you one. Duration was not a factor."

Suddenly, she didn't feel too well. A kiss from Rian, as unexpected as it had been, had possibly been the nicest thing to happen to her in a while. To hear that he couldn't bear to mash lips with her for longer than a few seconds made her feel like she'd been pushed out of a moving train.

Rian couldn't hold back a frown, watching Aditi retreat from him in a way he had not expected. "What?"

"Nothing, it's fine."

"Aditi!" he barked, his patience wearing thin, worry and lust creating a frustratingly confusing mix of emotions within him.

"I just expected more," she admitted sadly, no longer looking at him.

More?

"Maybe it's me. Maybe I don't inspire the kind of passion I read about in books or see on screen." She sighed, staring outwards again, leaning her elbows on the railing. Her stance reeked of defeat. He had never expected to witness this touch of melancholy in her, and it didn't sit right with him. Her uncertainty regarding her sexual appeal boggled his mind.

"I hadn't considered that Harish could be right," she said, her wistful smile curling like a thorny tendril about his errant heart, squeezing it so painfully that it ached.

"He's not right."

A quiet *ha* puffed out of her. "You don't even know him. He was –"

"An idiot," Rian firmly said. Her profile was illuminated by the lights around them, the golden glow making her look like a goddess bathed in honey. Anyone foolish enough to make her believe that she was less was definitely of questionable intelligence. Thankfully, his grumpy frown hid his thoughts well.

"Your ex didn't know what he was doing if you were counting numbers while kissing him."

"Hmm?"

"You won't be thinking when I kiss you."

If you kiss me, she wanted to snap, still annoyed with his non-smooch. All that build-up and it had ended before she could blink.

"I don't believe you. Not that I think you can't kiss well. Maybe you can—"

The 'maybe' was starting to get more irritating by the second. He wanted to kiss her until she had no breath left in her body to doubt him again. But that would be a mistake. Truly, kissing this woman would start something that he wasn't prepared for.

". . .but my brain is too loud."

That stopped him short.

"Your *brain* is the problem?" he asked, incredulously.

She nodded.

"Harish was not half bad in bed. But I could never stop thinking enough to be what he needed."

"Let me guess. Your idiot ex told you that," he griped, judgement dripping from every word.

"Yes. But I don't think he was wrong. My mind is just always. . .running. Thinking about the things that need to be done. Or that I could do." Aditi rubbed her arms up and down, the chill slowly getting to her. "That's why I rewatch old movies before I sleep. So I can stop in the middle without wondering about the plot. I tend to read books only with happy endings, because at least I know what to expect." She paused. "I think I've lost you."

"You haven't," he said, startling her when he wrapped a blanket around her, turning her towards him to adjust it. "You find comfort in what is known to you."

She blinked. "You understood all of what I said?"

"Perfectly. Was I not supposed to?"

"I'm just surprised. By now, Harish would have rolled his eyes and told me I'd stopped making sense a long time ago."

Harish is a real fucking tool, Rian almost spat, his dislike growing every time Aditi mentioned the guy. He wished he'd given in to his impulse to sucker punch Harish's face at the restaurant. He could only guess that her ex, intimidated by her intelligence, had attempted to maintain his superiority by making her feel bad about herself.

"If someone doesn't understand you, it's because they were too lazy to pay attention. You make perfect sense to me. Continue."

The sound of crickets grew louder.

"What was I saying?"

She looked so adorably concerned, Rian couldn't help it. Laughter bubbled within him, bursting out in a rough bark once, then again, until he was chortling in earnest.

When she glared at him, god help him, he actually did want to kiss the pout off her face.

"Don't laugh," she almost cried, her feelings still teetering on the edge of hurt. "Help me out of this situation."

"By immersing myself in your situation? Correction, situationship?" Rian joked, still wheezing.

"Yes!"

"No."

"Ugh, fine," she grumbled, thoroughly annoyed. She pushed off the railing to head back inside. "Dr. Sameer is a nice guy. He might agree. He doesn't want anything serious anyway," she muttered to herself, missing the murderous shadow that darkened his face. "Might even kiss me like he means it."

Rian didn't know what possessed him. His tightly reined control snapped and his screaming practical brain was subdued by the calculative and ruthless side of him who had but one aim.

To conquer. To pillage. To own.

He spun her around and hauled her against him. "Just remember that *you* wanted this."

"Wha..."

His fingers slid into her hair, cupping the back of her head just as his mouth landed on hers, drowning out her exclamation. His arm encircled her waist as he bent over her, his lips drawing hers, suckling one and then the other, going back again and again until her shock receded. Aditi felt a jolt of awareness drum through her when the tip of his tongue traced the seam of her mouth.

Her lips parted automatically, a tacit encouragement for him to deepen the kiss, one which he accepted without delay. His fingers curled into her scalp, pulling slightly to tilt her face so he could have unhindered access. His tongue swept into her warmth, tasting the sweetness of the cream she'd devoured, adding to a flavour that was innately her.

Her hands moved up his arms, gently tracing the flex of his biceps under the cotton he wore, finding their path up until her fingers met the exposed skin of his throat. She tried to rise up on her toes, gasping when he helped her by grabbing her ass and lifting her upwards. Her breasts grew heavy and her nipples puckered under her nightshirt, fueled by the feel of his muscular body against hers, all hardness and heat in contrast to her lush curves.

The unintentional scrape of her nail against his collarbone caused him to shudder. With a needy growl, he tightened his hold, squeezing her derriere in approval. Her little sounds enchanted him, his ears attuned to her whimpers, his hands full of the woman he'd been lusting after for weeks. The heady feeling of finally giving in to at least this one kiss only fueled the fire. He wanted more of her than he already had.

Aditi gave in to Rian's demands, letting him kiss her like she was the only tether he had left to life itself. Just when she thought her chest would burst for need of air, he pulled away.

Eyes closed, she leaned her forehead against his cheek, needing multiple moments to simply catch her breath. She didn't know what to think. Her body was trembling, her knees felt like jelly. The only reason she hadn't melted into a puddle was because she was in his arms.

She was still having trouble recollecting normal words. Given the fact that his hands were still squarely on her ass, she didn't think she could get her brain working anytime soon.

She was so confused that her first attempt at speaking was a singular squeak. Nothing more. She gulped and tried again, "What was that?"

The heated look he shot her was one she felt all the way to her core and back.

"A kiss."

His husky voice threatened to obliterate any remaining brain cells she had. She supposed it was some consolation that he sounded as out of breath as her.

"Why?" She had to claw back the urge to pull him towards her again when he stepped away. He didn't speak for what felt like an eternity, observing her like he'd found an unsolvable puzzle that intrigued him as equally as it vexed him. The sound of heavy breathing punctuated the space between them.

"If I say yes," he started, still panting like he'd not recovered from kissing her, "I lead this."

It took a moment for Aditi to realise what he was referring to. "Are you saying yes?"

Rian nodded. It seemed obvious that Aditi was set on following through with her plan to experiment romantically. If not him, she'd find someone else. By agreeing to this fling, Rian could keep her safe from unscrupulous men. And keeping her safe would be the most *respectful* thing he could do, which is what he'd promised Nanamma.

Maybe Aditi had rubbed off on him because despite the serpentine reasoning, things finally made sense. Suddenly, his mind was on board with something his heart had wanted for a long time. He could finally justify giving in to his base urges.

"I set the pace here, not you," Rian instructed, still cautious.

"Deal!" With unexpected enthusiasm, Aditi jumped and threw her arms about his neck. The kiss already had him on edge and with her full breasts pressing into him, Rian could no more control his body's reaction than he could the phases of the moon. She jumped back, her gaze dropping to his crotch, the result of their liplock and her exuberant hug now evident.

"You're attracted to me." He hadn't rejected her many days ago because he thought she was a loathsome toad? He hadn't just agreed to a fling because he pitied her? She raised her eyes to his, needing an answer that wouldn't hurt her pride. "Are you?"

Why she sounded so surprised, he would never understand.

"Only a blind man or a fool wouldn't be," Rian admitted with a snort. "And I am neither."

Her nose twitched. "What a roundabout way to say yes."

"Fine, yes. I am attracted to you."

The smile that grew on her face made his heart pound harder. Like it was ready to burst out of his chest, yodel like Tarzan, and swing right into her arms.

"So you do want to kiss me?" she confirmed.

"Yes."

"Okay," she beamed. "I'm all yours."

Something else pounded just as hard as his heart. How he didn't just bend her over the railing right then and fuck her until her body knew what it was to truly become his, he'd never know. Goddamnit, he needed a cold shower pronto.

"Don't say stuff like that," he snapped.

"Why?"

Because I liked it too much.

"Because I am not ready," he gritted out, pride be damned. He was afraid of pouncing on her like an ill-bred animal. He was plain afraid of her.

"Will you be ready tomorrow?"

Rian dropped his head into his hands, hoping she didn't test his patience anymore. "Good night, Doc," he muttered, spinning on his heel, ready to head to bed where he knew he was condemned to spending a night cursing himself over his inability to stay away from her.

"At least answer me this." He glanced behind to see that she had followed him into the hallway.

"What made you change your mind?"

He tilted his head, turning fully to face her.

"Why did you kiss me right now?" she asked, her voice dropping so that she didn't wake up Nanamma.

Because the thought of her kissing someone else while he was right next to her made him irrationally enraged. Even now, the mere idea of it left a bitter taste in his mouth.

"You've been begging me for a kiss," he gruffed, trying to make it seem insignificant. "I felt charitable today."

"I do not beg!" she hissed, fire flashing in her eyes. Her anger only served to arouse him, wanting to see what else he could do to make her lose composure.

"You would."

"Don't be so sure of yourself."

"How many decimals of pi did you count when I kissed you?" he asked, his slow smirk growing when her ire turned to surprise.

Aditi realised, stupefied, that her overactive brain had not been working while kissing Rian. Pi? She probably couldn't have told him her name if he'd asked her thirty seconds ago.

Rian placed both palms on the wall beside her face, trapping her between his arms. The cool wall dug into her back, her heart flapping around like a caged bird in anticipation of what he would do next. Her eyes closed involuntarily when he leaned down, his breath warming her face. He traced the curve of her cheek with the tip of his nose, deliberately going slow until he licked one earlobe, flicking it teasingly, causing her breath to hitch.

"R-Rian," she gasped, feeling woozy, his scent seeping into her.

"This is how I know, Aditi Krishnan," he whispered, his breath hot against her skin. "If I wanted you to beg, you would."

Her eyes opened to the rush of cool air as he backed away and walked off. She wanted to stalk after him and smack him for daring to tease her. But the embarrassing heat in her underbelly told her that despite her denial, Rian was right.

For him, she would beg.

15

Safe Words

RIAN

"Pick a safe word."

Aditi stopped halfway to taking a bite of her toast, blinking at the suddenness with which Rian had declared this. She sent a panicked glance where Nanamma had just disappeared, the sound of her morning prayers floating down the hallway.

The serene chanting of *Suprabhatam* as a backdrop to discuss safe words for sexual exploration felt morally unsafe. It was also the crack of dawn and she had not slept the night, reliving his kiss over and over again until her body and mind had been so aroused that she'd had to indulge in some self-love.

She'd never orgasmed that quickly to the memory of just a kiss. So, if Rian wanted to discuss safe words at 6:30 a.m. on a Thursday while his grandmother prayed to all the lords of the Hindu pantheon, then Aditi would find a way to live with that.

When she didn't reply fast enough, Rian spoke again. "A safe word is—"

"I know what a safe word is!" she furiously whispered, crunching down on her toast for emphasis.

"You do?" Rian hated the idea of a dickwad like Harish ever having touched Aditi. He didn't deserve to lick dust off her feet, and knowing all the ways in which he'd offended her, Rian was certain he must have been a selfish bastard in bed as well. He passed Aditi her latte, unable to help himself from adding another diss. "Your ex didn't seem adventurous enough to need one."

"He wasn't. But I'm a woman in my prime."

Rian's brow lifted.

"And I've read books," she added, a becoming blush gracing her skin. He adored that she couldn't lie well. It fit her personality.

He leaned over the counter so that he was face to face with her. "One of these days, I want you to read these books to me."

Her blush deepened.

"Read them yourself," she suggested, trying to sound annoyed. She looked away, and that was the only reason she didn't see the momentary loss of his teasing smile before he shook it off.

"No. I'd rather have you do the honours. Or we could listen to the audiobook together."

She raised her half-eaten toast and waved it at him. "That's not part of this deal we have going on here."

"It could be. The rules are whatever you want it to be, Doc. I set the pace but you have all the control."

Aditi watched the veins in the back of his hand pop with each motion as he cleared the coffee grounds, thick biceps flexing under his skin-tight T-shirt as he tapped the filter against the knockbox. Barely ten hours ago, she was being crushed by those strong arms. Those large hands had touched her body and to her disappointment, had not left a mark. Rules? What rules? Left up to her, the rules wouldn't exist and Aditi was most afraid of letting her emotions run rampant with this man, like her hormones already did.

"Pick a safe word." His long fingers drummed the countertop, bringing her attention back to him.

Feeling like she needed to regain control of the situation, her crooked mind landed on the one word that might irritate him. "Bunny," she announced, barely holding back an impulse to cackle at the way he stiffened. She waited for him to call her out on her choice, but to her consternation, he simply nodded.

"Okay. Bunny then. If you are uncomfortable at any point when we are together, say your safe word and I will stop. Then we'll reassess."

"Okay. And the same safe word applies to you."

This surprised him. "It does?"

Aditi stood up, dropping her plate into the sink before swiping up her mug. She walked over to stand next to him in the farthest corner of the kitchen, both keeping an eye out in case Nanamma returned.

"Yes. You use the safe word too. It'll help me understand when I'm being too much. I would like not to scare you away by being too. . ." *me*. She grimaced hating that Harish had managed to leave this bit of insecurity in her.

"Too?"

She found herself under keen observation, his light eyes glinting with interest.

"I want to be able to keep a person interested. In this case, you."

"You don't have to do anything more to generate interest. Trust me."

Aditi let out a guffaw. "Sure. That's why I've had thirteen unsuccessful matrimonial dates in three months. I'm not perfect, Bugs, so don't try to make it sound like I am."

The damndest thing was that she was pretty close to perfection in his eyes. Rian was hard pressed to think of one single thing he didn't find charming about Aditi Krishnan. Even her penchant for overextending herself when being helpful only told him that she was a kind human. Her ability to be honest with herself and the people around her was refreshing. How much more perfect could she get?

"Hello? Bugs? You okay?" She snapped her fingers in front of him, calling him back to their conversation.

"Yeah. Fine," he mumbled, sipping his black coffee. "Where were we?"

"You were about to kiss me."

His hand shook and he stopped short of dropping his cup. "What? No, I wasn't."

"You certainly were," she insisted, grinning at him in that open, happy way that made his mind go blank. "You're going to knock my socks off with an expert kiss. That's what this whole discussion is leading towards. I'm just jumping a few steps ahead."

She placed her mug down and stood with her arms on either side, as though ready for him to make good on her expectation of a fiery smooch. He would have done it had it not been for Nanamma being some twenty-odd feet away. She'd either catch them in the act and get a coronary, or she'd jump around for joy and thrust them both down the aisle in the next minute. Probably, the latter.

He couldn't risk it.

"Doc, you said you'd listen to me and let me set the pace."

As expected, her luscious lips turned down into a pout. Fuck, had her lips always been this irresistible shade of berries?

"Is the pace pacing towards kissing?" she asked, her mournful tone wanting him to throw caution to the wind.

"Not yet," he gritted out.

"Then I don't like it."

"Bunny!"

"Ugh, fine," she huffed, stepping away to place her mug in the sink. "I bet you just want me to shut the fuck up and double teedeelag."

Nose scrunched, he peered at her. "What the hell is that? Some medical terminology?"

When she turned back to face him, she had that familiar mischief dancing in her eyes. She bit her lower lip, thinking, and then sauntered towards him slowly, deliberately swaying her hips in a way that had his cock starting to strain against the zipper on his jeans.

He felt the cold countertop dig into his butt when she stepped closer, her chest brushing lightly against his as she raised a hand and jerked him down by his collar.

"If you figure it out," she husked, his body reacting to her sultry voice, the teasing trail of her fingers against his jaw making him gulp audibly, "I'll listen to whatever you say."

His throat worked hard, barely listening to her, wondering if he had time to sneak in a kiss before Nanamma returned.

"I might even double teedeelag for you."

She tapped his lip playfully, breaking him out of the trance she'd put him under. With what could only be described as an evil grin, she swung her backpack on her shoulders and winked at him before leaving him alone and aroused with no hope of relief. The sound of the front door clicking to a close cut through his disbelief. Siren that she was, she'd just taken revenge for how he'd teased her last night. And he'd fallen for it—hook, line and sinker.

Rian couldn't stop thinking about Aditi and her challenge all morning. Which meant that he'd spent nearly every break he'd had to look up *teedeelag* and its variants, to no avail.

Now, sitting across from his best friend who'd come to visit him for lunch, his mind was still stuck on winning.

Kaya watched Rian pretend to be interested in listening to her talk about her honeymoon while his eyes kept darting towards his phone.

"Rian?"

"Hmm." He clicked a link, scrunching his nose at the small font. He took a deep breath and tried again, zooming in and using his finger as a guide to check the glossary index. Nope, he decided, switching his Bluetooth on, hearing the beep on the single earbud that he still had on. A few clicks later, he was running the script through his text-to-speech software.

He looked up to find Kaya staring at him. He smiled.

"I'm pregnant."

"Good."

He tapped on another site that looked promising, letting a very monotonous voice list out the words and their definitions from the live page. A moment later, Kaya's words finally struck him and his head whipped up.

"Wait, what?" he yelped, eyes wide.

To his surprise, she rolled her eyes and took an aggressive bite of her meal instead.

"That took you way too long to react. And I was testing you to see if you were paying attention."

"So, you're not pregnant?"

Kaya shook her head.

"If I was, Arjun would be here with me to tell you the news also. I'm seeing you after nearly two months and you have been occupied with something else."

At her chastising tone, Rian shot her an apologetic glance, finally putting his phone away and taking his earbud out.

"Sorry. I'll be good, I promise. How was New Zealand?" he asked, finally paying attention to everything Kaya had to say. Kaya and Arjun had been married for nearly six years, but had been estranged up until a few months ago. Eager to spend time with his wife, Arjun had whisked her away to a different country altogether. They'd just returned a couple days ago.

Rian observed the glow of a woman well loved on Kaya's face. The air of anxiety and sadness that seemed to hover about her had lifted. She was clearly happier, and Rian knew that Arjun had everything to do with it.

He listened indulgently to Kaya gush about her newborn nephew, leaning in to see pictures of him on her phone. One after another, he was presented with beautiful family photos.

Six months ago, this family was broken. Today, they were united, glad to be part of each other's lives again. His eyes roved over the elder Mr. Sharma.

The Sharmas had been publicly shamed by his hateful mother at a party where a teenaged Rian and Kaya were found together, alone, about to get intimate. It had resulted in an exile that had lasted eleven years for the young girl, and had cost Kaya her family, her confidence, and the love of a good man.

In a twist of fate, she had recovered all three in a single stroke.

Kaya's relationship with her father had been contentious, much like his with his mother. The only difference was that Shubham Sharma had come to a realisation that his behaviour would drive away his daughter forever.

"Are you and your father still going to therapy?"

"Yes, why? Considering it for you and your mother?"

A puff of air escaped him, a laugh laced with bitterness. "Leela Shetty is beyond help. You know that as well as I do."

Kaya reached across the table for Rian's hand, holding on with a friendly squeeze. He smiled reassuringly at her. He didn't hope for reconciliation with his mother. He simply wanted to be able to reach a point when the thought of her wouldn't leave this fragment of misery in him. Maybe *he* needed therapy.

"I'm glad you made up with your father. You seem happier for it."

"I'm glad, too. But. . ."

Rian caught the fleeting look of discomfort in her eyes. He tilted his chin up, encouraging her to speak without hesitation.

She sighed. "I am happier than I have ever been. But that's because of Arjun, more than anyone else. Therapy with Dadda has only given me closure. I'm glad we don't have that bitterness between us anymore. But I am no longer the Kaya who yearned for his approval," she admitted. "He tries, but our relationship cannot be what it used to be thirteen years ago. That time is long gone and the person it would have made a difference to no longer exists."

Her acceptance was bittersweet. The young girl who had craved her father's love had been forced to grow up without it. When change finally came about, she was an adult with a different support system. Clearly, she had made her peace with that, and Rian couldn't be more proud.

"Enough about me." She tossed her curls up into a messy bun when she got too annoyed with them flying into her face. "What were you searching for?" One dainty finger tapped the case of his cell.

Rian's eyes landed on his phone, then back at her. If anyone was good with research, it was Kaya. She was an author and had a penchant for spending hours creating elaborate backgrounds for her characters. She may well have come across this while writing. So, in the hopes that he was right, Rian asked her.

"Double teedeelag?" Kaya repeated with a frown, her face a close replica of a child who'd been asked to solve astrophysics. "I've never heard of that."

Rian almost groaned. "I wouldn't put it past her to send me on a wild goose chase. The woman is a menace."

"Woman?" Kaya perked up immediately. "Who?"

"My house guest."

"You have a guest I don't know about?" She smacked his arm in mock outrage. "How could you not tell me?"

"You've been playing house for the last forty-three days straight. In another continent. When would I have told you this?"

Kaya sat back, crossing her arms as she considered Rian's odd behaviour throughout lunch. "She's gotten under your skin if you're calling her a menace. Will I like her?"

"Most definitely." Except for idiots and psychopaths, everyone liked Aditi.

"When will I get to meet her?"

"Not anytime soon if I can help it," Rian brattily replied, picking up his phone to begin his search anew, his voice assistant rapidly firing off new words in quick succession.

"You're being so lazy! Just read it yourself. Why do you need it read out loud?" Kaya asked, taking another bite of her meal.

He shrugged, not looking her in the eye. "It's easier."

"Why medical lingo? Is your houseguest a doctor?"

Rian nodded, busy listening intently, mumbling to himself. "Teela? Tila? Double t's?"

He looked up. "Is there a word that starts with two Ts? The only one I know is tteokbokki and I am pretty sure she isn't talking about spicy Korean rice cakes."

Kaya grinned at his guess, teasingly sticking her tongue against the inside of her cheek. "Are you still justifying your K-drama phase as research into new foods?"

Rian huffed, pasting a supercilious expression on his face. "It is. You liked the kimchi-flavoured pancakes I made before."

"I also liked seeing you pretend like that TV show about the North and South Korean couple was something more than a love story. What was it called? Crashing Into You?"

Rian tried hard not to take the bait, but he couldn't resist correcting her.

"Crash Landing On You. If you're going to rag on me about my Netflix choices, the least you can do is remember the right name."

"And," he continued, deliberately ignoring Kaya's trembling lips as she held back her laughter, "that TV show brought to light political tensions between North and South Korea and its impact on the general public. Where is your heart?"

"With Arjun," she shot back immediately with a moony smile.

Rian made a gagging sound, pretending to want to throw up. With a shake of his head, he shifted his attention to the screen of his phone when Kaya gasped, drawing a look from him.

"Ri, is it maybe T-T-D-L-A-G-G? An acronym, not an actual word?"

Rian shrugged, neither the word nor the acronym familiar to him.

"Does your guest, by any chance, read romance novels?" Kaya asked, a peculiar gleam in her eyes.

"Yes! How'd you know that?"

She burst out laughing, confusing him further.

"What? Do you know what that word means?"

Between snorts, Kaya nodded. Every time he thought she was done, she would begin laughing anew, until her face was pink and her eyes teary.

"Kaya, for fuck's sake, tell me!"

"First," she gasped, wiping the edge of one eye, "promise me that you'll bring her out to meet us all tomorrow. Arjun, Vihaan, me, you, and your guest."

"But..."

"I'm not budging on this. And trust me," she added, curiosity building in her about the woman who had gotten her normally unflappable friend to pay singular attention to such a silly exercise. "You want to know what this means."

16

Laughter and Light

ADITI

"**Y**OU'VE BEEN ASKED TO come to dinner with my friends tomorrow," Rian informed a surprised Aditi that evening.

Passing him the ladle to load into the dishwasher, Nanamma beamed at him. "Kaya called me today to tell me this, too. I am glad she's back. Adi will enjoy meeting her."

Aditi, curious about this girl she'd not heard of before, piped in. "Kaya is?"

"She's like my granddaughter. Very sweet child. And she's an author! You might have seen her books being promoted everywhere," Nanamma added, evidently proud.

Aditi nodded, wiping the kitchen counter clean. All three had been at home that evening to enjoy a family dinner together and were now cleaning up as a unit. During moments like this, Aditi felt sad for the day she would have to leave them. She had not expected to settle into Rian's home this easily and this well.

It was hard to remind herself that while Rian and Nanamma felt like family, this was all temporary. The thought settled like a boulder in her chest as she watched Nanamma hobble off to her bedroom, searching for her medicines.

"What's the occasion?" Aditi asked Rian, trying to guess the reason behind the sudden invitation. At his direction, she stood near him, accepting the clean dishes he passed and stacking them neatly inside the cabinet.

"Nothing. Just us hanging out. If you don't want to join us, I can tell them you're busy."

"Why would you do that?" The clink of porcelain plates settling atop each other and the gurgle of the dishwasher starting were the only sounds around them. "I need to eat anyway. And I like meeting new people. I'll come."

"I'll let them know you'll," he paused, unable to hold back a choked laugh, "come."

She cast him a suspicious glance when he smirked, swiping the bowl he passed to her.

"What's so funny?" she asked, her brows knitting, her back to him.

"Nothing. I just knew that you'd," he snorted again, "come."

"Oh yeah? And how did you know that?"

"Because you promised to shut the fuck up and take that dick like a good girl."

With a loud gasp, Aditi spun around, forgetting that the upper cabinet door next to her was still open. A loud thunk sounded as her head smacked against the wood. She teetered from the impact, an involuntary cry escaping her as pain shot across her skull. Before she could do anything else, she was swept off her feet.

"Rian! Put me down," she hissed, worriedly glancing about for Nanamma.

"You almost fell backwards," he muttered, beelining for the couches.

"I'm too big to be carried!"

"If you mean too old, that's a no," he replied, his strides even. "If you mean too heavy, that's a fuck no. You could double in size and it wouldn't be an issue."

Silenced, she tried to maintain her dignity, only to squeak and grab him out of self-preservation when he bounced her once, adjusting her against his firm chest. He sat her down and kneeled beside her to inspect her bruise. A small red bump was the only evidence of her accident. Aditi irritatedly tried to slap his hands away, proving yet again that doctors made the worst patients.

"You don't need to hover," she grumbled.

Once he was certain that she was not seriously hurt, his worry receded and the devil on his shoulder came out to play. "I can't let a good girl like you get hurt on my watch, can I?" He winked, his grin widening when she skewered him with a deathly glare.

Nanamma walked to the living room to find Rian blowing cool air on Aditi's wound while she sulked.

"Rian? What happened?"

"Aditi ran into the open cabinet door. Could you stay with her, Nanamma? I'll get the ice pack."

When Rian returned, it was to a worried Chitra scolding Aditi for being careless.

"You should pay more attention, Adi. What will I tell your family if I send you back home with bruises all over?"

Rian nodded vigorously in agreement. "Exactly. She's so distracted all the time." He was just adding fuel to the fire. "What could have been so important that you couldn't watch where you were going, hmm?" He caught Aditi's eye, lifting one shoulder unapologetically for getting her in trouble and pretending like it wasn't his fault.

He held the ice pack to her reddened forehead, pressing back a smile when she swiped it from his hands in obvious ire.

Muttering about silly children and the dangers of being on the phone while walking, Nanamma ordered Aditi to stay put while she made warmed milk for her. No matter what the ailment, every Indian grandmother believed that warm turmeric milk would cure it all.

Left alone with Rian standing just behind, Aditi squirmed, feeling his gaze burning a hole into the back of her skull. She glanced at Nanamma puttering about in the large kitchen and attempted to follow her, shocked when he unceremoniously pulled her back down on the couch. His hands remained on her shoulders, holding her still and warning her from trying to escape.

"You should listen to Nanamma, Doc. Rest here. Be a double G. You know, good girl?"

His voice was low enough that Nanamma wouldn't hear them. Despite this, Aditi felt the tips of her ears burn in embarrassment. When she glanced at their reflection in the blank black screen of the TV across from her, their gazes locked.

"You're never going to let me live this down, are you?" she asked, watching as he bent down slowly, firm fingers kneading her tense muscles.

"Where would the fun in that be?" he whispered, bringing his mouth dangerously close to her ear.

She bit down a whimper when his breath warmed her neck. His thumb pressing into her nape caused a troublesome quiver within her core. She startled when he blew a puff of air into her ear before he retreated, walking off with the most devilish smirk she'd seen on him yet.

When Rian settled down in his massive bed a short while later, it was with no little satisfaction at having won their game. Kaya's revelation of what T-T-D-L-A-G-G meant had momentarily stunned him. Since then, he had alternated between wanting to laugh at Aditi's mischievousness and planning retribution.

Seeing her face when she'd gotten caught, her usual confidence swept under sudden embarrassment, had only made him want to tease her more. He could grow to adore this unexpectedly shy side of her, he realised. With Aditi around, he felt like being a little silly also. A sudden thought struck him, and he picked up his phone, talking into it, watching his words transform into texts.

Aditi lay herself down in bed, staring at the ceiling. She was unable to believe what had happened, mortification very much at the top of what she was feeling. She'd been confident that Rian would never figure out what that acronym meant. He disliked books. He didn't read at all, much less romance. She'd even cheated and made it sound like it was one word!

She had flirted outrageously with him, finding sadistic enjoyment in seeing him blush and get tongue-tied. Karma had really wasted no time to come knocking today because the only one who had turned beet red had been her. And the only one who had been rendered speechless had also been, to her lasting shame, her.

She looked beside her when her phone lit up, swiping open to see a new message from Rian.

Bugs Bunny (9:57 p.m.)

> We should discuss when and how you plan to keep your promise

Chaos Doc (9:57 p.m.)

What promise?

> **Bugs Bunny (9:58 p.m.)**
> You said you'd TTDLAGG if I figured out what it meant.
>
> And I did.

Her mouth dropped open. She couldn't help it. She sat up immediately, her fingers flying furiously over her keyboard.

> **Chaos Doc (9:58 p.m.)**
> Did you? Or did you ask someone?
>
> Because that's cheating!

> **Bugs Bunny (9:58 p.m.)**
> And making me believe it was one word wasn't?
>
> Let's talk tomorrow.
>
> Unless you want me to come over to your room tonight?

Her stomach clenched at his offer and she glared at her body. *Traitorous pussy!* She scolded herself, shaking off the part of her that wanted to throw her door wide open to welcome him.

> **Bugs Bunny (10:00 p.m.)**
> Since I said yes to your situationship offer, would you really be a good girl for me?

> **Chaos Doc (10:00 p.m.)**
> I'm moving out! Or to China.
>
> Wherever has cheaper rent.

All Aditi heard after that was a roar of laughter coming from the other side of the wall. Before she knew it, she was smiling too. Maybe her embarrassment was worth it after all. She'd made him laugh in a way she hadn't heard from him yet, like it came from somewhere deep within.

She just wished she could see him too.

If any one of her cousins witnessed how she routinely embarrassed herself in front of Rian, they'd be hard pressed to believe it was her. She had always been the serious and reliable elder child of the house. Not that she hadn't been carefree around them, but she'd always felt the need to exercise some restraint due to the expectations placed on her.

Being in Mumbai had freed her from that constraint. She'd been the most unfiltered version of herself and instead of judging her for it, Rian seemed to welcome it.

There was a sadness that lingered in his eyes sometimes that she wished she could drive away. He made her feel good and she wanted to return the favour. If that meant he had to laugh at her to find relief, then it seemed like a small price to pay. The sound of his laughter, she decided—warmth spreading through her at his happiness—was by far the best thing she'd heard in her entire life.

Her phone lit up again.

Bugs Bunny (10:18 p.m.)

> Good night, good girl. Don't go to China, okay?

Grinning, Rian lay back against his bed frame, trying to bring his focus back on the updates his project manager had sent him on The Singapore Map. He had a laundry list of to-dos that his PA had sent to him via voice note, but he couldn't stop thinking about Aditi. He couldn't remember when he had last laughed this consistently or this hard.

When was the last time he'd looked forward to seeing someone who wasn't Nanamma or Kaya? Honestly, even that didn't compare with the anticipation he felt when he returned home and saw Aditi on his couch.

His phone buzzed.

Chaos Doc (10:18 p.m.)

> Good night, bad Bugs. China plan on hold indefinitely.

When Rian turned the lights off later, the smile lingered. He had been sleeping better than he had in years, laughing a little more, feeling lighter than before.

Maybe it had to do with the girl on the other side of the wall. Maybe he was learning from her to focus on a happy present. Maybe, with Kaya's life finally settled, he was learning to let go of old burdens.

Rian dozed off, never realising that the nightmares that used to hound his dark nights had slowly been phased out, replaced by dreams of a woman with twinkling chocolate eyes and a smile that felt like home.

17

Friends Know Best

ADITI

If Aditi had had any apprehensions about meeting Kaya Rathore, they vanished the moment she came face to face with the curly-haired beauty.

Warm and inviting, Kaya had shyly introduced herself before turning to the two men who'd been waiting with her.

Arjun Rathore and Vihaan Oberoi.

Men blessed with good looks, manners and evidently, a lot of money. Arjun was one of the most sought after businessmen in Asia, with his company recently going public. Vihaan, on the other hand, was on track to becoming the next media mogul, having recently acquired a new broadcasting channel in addition to the print press work his publishing house already excelled at.

Speaking with them should have been a daunting experience, but neither seemed to show any awareness of how important they were.

Seated between Rian and Vihaan at the circular table they were sharing, Aditi was forced to accept that Mumbai's water contained something special. Not only had this city produced three beautiful odes to masculine beauty, but had also blessed her with the opportunity to be seated with all of them at the same time.

She watched the four friends bring each other up to speed, each ensuring that Aditi felt included in their discussions.

Arjun, she noted, was a gentleman who was clearly besotted with his wife, Kaya, and vice versa. Vihaan in contrast was a complete rascal who'd begun flirting with her immediately, much to her amusement. He was charming, and she was flattered. She'd laughed at his dramatics when he complained about having to work when there was so much life to enjoy, half wondering if this lazy persona was a front that hid something deeper.

Out of nowhere, she felt a strange sensation creep up her neck. She glanced beside her to find Rian watching her, a small smile playing on his lips. That was all it took for any flicker of curiosity about someone else to switch into an awareness of him.

With his piercing eyes—sometimes silver, sometimes stormy—his wavy hair, his chiselled jawline that looked like it would cut her if she ran a finger along it, Rian was breathtaking.

Yes, Arjun and Vihaan were distractingly handsome. For Aditi however, it was only Rian who caused her body temperature to rise and her panties to dampen at the mere thought of kissing him again. His height made her feel like a delicate doll, and there was not much about her that could be considered delicate. The recollection of how easily he'd lifted her, her weight no barrier, had her bringing a hand to her cheek.

She let out a quick breath, warning her brain and her body to behave through dinner.

"Doc, how long are you in town for?" Vihaan asked her, continuing their conversation.

Before she could answer, Rian interrupted them.

"Her name is Aditi."

"So?" Vihaan grouched. "She's a doctor, isn't she?" Without waiting for Rian to respond, Vihaan looked at her, tilting his chin in question. "I can call you, Doc, right?"

"She has a name. Call her Aditi. Not Doc," Rian stubbornly demanded.

Aditi and Kaya stared at Rian, both women blinking at him in confusion. Hadn't he himself called her 'Doc' multiple times already?

"I can give her a nickname. Friends give friends nicknames. You can call me V," he told Aditi. "These fools do."

"Hey!" Kaya protested sadly, her lower lip jutting out in a pout.

"Not you, Kaya." Vihaan immediately consoled her, a hand on his heart in apology. "Never you. You're my star. You're the best thing in—"

"Careful," Arjun warned, a single brow raised. "She's my wife."

Arjun's serious remark confused Aditi. Weren't these men friends? Rian must have been watching her because he leaned towards her just as she looked to him for help.

"He's possessive because Vihaan once had a crush on Kaya," Rian teased.

Aditi's jaw dropped open. "What? Really?"

That's when Aditi noticed that in contrast to his tone, Arjun's eyes were twinkling with mischief.

"Yep," Rian nodded. "Flirted with her and everything. Of course, he also is the reason why they found each other so I guess Arjun can't hate him too much."

Vihaan puffed his chest up with pride, tugging on his own collar. "I was instrumental in bringing these two together."

"Oh yeah?" Arjun drawled, taking a sip of his drink. "That's why you planned to ask Kaya out on a date?"

Aditi couldn't hold back her reaction. She turned towards Vihaan, asking for confirmation, watching him scratch the back of his neck in an endearingly embarrassed move. "I didn't know Kaya was Arjun's wife."

"That's the only reason I didn't knock you on your ass," Arjun barked from across the table.

"Stop that!" Kaya swatted her husband on his arm. She turned to Vihaan, addressing him in a sorrowful tone.

"V, I'm so sorry you had to deal with my husband and his mood swings when I wasn't around. If it is any consolation, it was you I wanted to work with. You were so sweet compared to this guy." She threw a sassy look at her husband, squealing and giggling uncontrollably when Arjun threw his arm around her and crushed her to him, pretending to be annoyed. His smile told everyone how much he enjoyed being teased by his wife.

"Get a room, the two of you," Rian grumbled, shaking his head.

"Tell us where. I'd rather not see your ugly mug anyway," Arjun shot back.

"You're just sore because I beat you at basketball this morning. You're out of touch. Honeymooning for forty-five days straight will do that to you."

Arjun sniffed the air loudly. "I smell the jealous stench of a single man, Shetty."

"See what I have to deal with?" Vihaan sighed, turning to Aditi and then Kaya. "We have beautiful women with us and these two buttheads are talking about basketball. No wonder I don't have a decent wingman."

Aditi giggled, patting the back of his hand with mock sympathy. "It's okay. You can talk to us, V. We're listening."

He held her hand, all desolation lost in moments.

"So, if I feel unwell, can I come to you? Like my heart, that's been extra active since you stepped into this restaurant." He winked, shooting her a grin that she was certain had had women throwing themselves at him. She blinked, blinded momentary by his prettiness.

"I'm not that kind of doctor, V, but if you're hurting, I will hear you out."

Something shifted in his expressions, his overly flirtatious grin gentling into a genuine smile.

"I like you, Doc. Where did you say you were from again?"

Aditi felt a heavy arm land across the back of her chair.

"She's from none-of-your-goddamn-business. Stop calling her Doc!" Rian clenched his teeth, reaching over to break their hands apart.

Aditi frowned at him, wondering if he'd gone crazy. He thrust a glass of juice into the hand that Vihaan had held, rendering it occupied for the near future.

She looked down at the glass and back at him, confused.

"Drink," he instructed, clearing his throat. "You'll like it. It's pomegranate and orange."

"What's with you, today?" Vihaan snorted after a long pause.

"Yeah, Rian. What's with you today?" Kaya asked in a low voice, leaning towards him. Their eyes met, and she slowly slid an inquiring gaze towards a distracted Aditi, before looking back at him.

Caught, Rian glanced away immediately, thankful for his staff having shown up with their meal just then. But try as he might, he couldn't stop his ears from turning red.

Kaya almost screamed in glee. She had never seen Rian look at a woman like this, ever. Like he was afraid, in awe and completely enthralled by her, all at once.

Having met her now, she could see the allure. Aditi was vivacious, friendly, and sweet-natured; perfect for Rian, who was so soft at heart and lonelier than he'd ever admit. She could smell a love story brewing and the only thing better than writing romance was witnessing it.

With dinner drawing to a close, and a popular night club just down the block from his restaurant, the group of friends made plans to continue their evening out with a change in venue. They made their way to the exit when Rian was stopped by his manager. Whispered words were exchanged, and Rian's smile dropped.

"Everything okay?" Aditi inquired. She could sense the tension rolling off him, but had no idea why.

"Yeah, just business," Rian answered. "Why don't all of you go ahead?" he said, opening the door for them as if he couldn't wait to usher them out. "I'll join you in a bit."

Before anyone could protest, he turned and stalked away, steeling himself for what was to come.

18

Mother Dearest

RIAN

Rian had been having the best evening in a very long time. The thought had come to him, and he'd acknowledged it.

He shouldn't have, because now he was certain that he'd jinxed himself.

He should have been with the people who had made him smile and laugh all evening.

Instead, for the good part of an hour, he'd been stuck in the VIP room of his restaurant with Leela Shetty and her friends, enduring a mind-numbing discussion about their wealth and connections. It was no different than a dick measuring contest and nowhere near as subtle as they hoped.

Worse still, this dinner was clearly a matchmaking attempt. He cringed, unable to smile at the young woman that Leela pushed to sit closer to him.

Sonia Dasavi, the only daughter of construction magnate Madhav Dasavi, was stunning. If one liked pouty lips pumped with fillers, a sharpened nose, and boobs that had magically changed sizes thrice in that many years, then Sonia would fulfil that fantasy.

Her purchased perfection in addition to her daddy's name made her a catch in their social circles. She was exactly the kind of woman he tried to avoid however, having witnessed an unattractive personality behind that picture-perfect face. Unfortunately, she'd decided that she was enamoured with him. When Rian had proved too evasive, Madhav Dasavi, unable to deny his precious daughter her wishes, had approached Leela.

Which led to him being paraded by his mother like this relationship was all but certain. Mr. Dasavi had commented multiple times about everything that Sonia would inherit from him. Her husband would be a lucky man, he'd announced, giving Rian a meaningful glance.

It was rich people talk for dowry, he realised. Mr. Dasavi was leveraging his wealth to buy his daughter a husband of her choice, and his mother was salivating at the thought.

He may as well have been a product for her to sell, he scoffed internally, shifting away when Sonia leaned in to surreptitiously brush her chest against his arm. She shot him a coy look from under her lashes, one end of her mouth tilted suggestively. It was all Rian could do to suppress the shudder of repulsion that zipped through him.

With a murmured apology, he got up from his seat, only to have his hand held by his mother.

"Ah, my wonderful son! Look at him, ladies." Leela smiled, her lips stretched wide over bright teeth. She winked at Mrs. Dasavi and nodded at Sonia, putting on the usual act of a good mother who adored her offspring. "He gets his looks from me, doesn't he?"

Mrs. Dasavi giggled while Sonia gave him a once over like he wasn't wearing clothes. Ignoring them, he leaned down to speak to his mother in a low tone.

"That's enough. You're drunk."

"That would require you to have something decent in this shitty little place," she murmured, her smile belying the contempt in her words.

"You have had your chance to show off. I will get on with my evening," he said, unwilling to take the bait and get into an argument in front of the Dasavis. He straightened and wished everyone a good night, making an expedient exit. He was halfway across the rooftop of his restaurant when he heard the furious clacking of heels behind him.

"Rian!"

Knowing that she would make a scene if he escaped without facing her, he turned, waiting until his mother reached him.

"You can't leave! I brought them here to meet you! Go, entertain them," she demanded, her features twisted in annoyance. "Show them how charming you can be!"

"No," he hissed, refusing to be led back inside and be bartered for a few million rupees. He'd be expected to live his life like a pet dog if he married a woman like Sonia. "I'm not your fucking show pony."

"Language! Ugh, you have no manners. This is why we can't talk."

A snort of disbelief escaped him. "Sure, my language is the cause of problems between us."

"Do this for me," Leela tried again, coaxing him. "Be an obedient son. Don't embarrass me in front of my friends."

"Why would I care what you want? You seem to forget that we hate each other."

"You can't hate me. I'm your mother."

"Biologically, yes. Unfortunately," he added, watching a familiar look of loathing overtake her expressions.

"You were always a thankless little prick," she spat, her face contorting in fury. No amount of fillers and makeup would hide the ugliness of Leela Shetty for him.

"Me?"

"I brought you under the notice of that family. Do you think they would want their daughter to be married to you if I hadn't built you up?"

"I do not want your help finding a wife."

"But you will take your grandmother's help, won't you?" she jeered, her mask finally dropping. "I am your mother. You should be listening to me, not her!"

Rian shook his head, unable to hold back from responding to her hateful comments. "Whatever sick competition you are in with Nanamma is in your head. Leave her out of this."

"You will marry the woman I pick for you," Leela ordered, a manic look in her eyes. "That family will bring us more wealth and fame. Did you hear Mr. Dasavi mention how much is in his daughter's name? All that will be mine if you just marry her."

"Yours?"

"What is yours belongs to me. You think you would have this success if it wasn't for me?"

Rian took a step back, feeling his throat close in disgust. There was no point in arguing with a belligerent drunk.

"Go back inside and spend time with people who pretend to like you. I am not one of them."

He strode away, feeling claustrophobic in Leela's presence. Descending the stairs swiftly, he slipped into the back kitchen, weaving through his employees. The clang of dishes, barked orders, and chaos of a busy dinner service surrounded him. Unfortunately, Leela had followed right behind.

"I pushed you to achieve something in your life!" she cried, her voice rising despite having an audience. "You would have stayed a worthless little shit, whoring your way through cheap trash if I hadn't demanded you to be better! You owe me!" When he still showed no sign of acceding to her, she picked up a glass nearby and launched it at him.

Pain exploded between his shoulder blades, the sound of glass shattering near his feet bringing the entire kitchen to a standstill. Two of his employees immediately approached him, the worry on their faces clear.

Before they could check him for injuries Rian turned and charged at his mother, his vision red.

Perhaps Leela realised the depth of his fury because she stepped back, apprehension flickering across her face. He stopped an arm's length away, unbridled disdain for this woman who called herself his mother spiking within him. The pressure behind his eyes built, every bad memory of her callous treatment of him crashing upon him over and over again, threatening to submerge him in a tsunami of hate he had worked hard to claw his way out of.

"All I owe you," he informed her, his fists clenched as he held back the urge to smash it into the wall next to her face, "is the last name that you married into and the same blood that you have drawn many times. I put up with you in public because I don't want to feed gossip. If you ever get physically violent with me or my staff again, especially in my place of work, I will forget every consideration I have shown you, public perception be damned."

Leela glared at him, her stubborn expression showing no regret for her behaviour.

He spoke softly, a deathly chill in his voice as he moved past her towards the exit. "This is my final warning, Mother. Don't test me. You won't like the results."

19
Mistakes

RIAN

I SHOULD HAVE GONE home, Rian thought, sitting in the dark upper balcony of the posh club he was in, watching people around him have fun and make merry. The episode with his mother had brought back memories he wished he could forget. Despite his friends trying to involve him in their fun, his altercation with Leela had put him in a terrible mood.

He was struggling. Worse, no one truly knew how bad things were with him and Leela. How hard he worked to come out from the shadows she'd thrust him under.

Those shadows had slithered out of the dungeon today and despite trying his best to fight them off, he couldn't lock them away. The pressure within his chest increased, and the pounding ache between his eyes made their presence known. With each breath, his childhood flashed in front of his eyes. He relived the episodes that formed his nightmares even today.

The revelry around him only served to increase his anger because their carefree happiness seemed to mock him for his inability to break free of his burdens. His resentment grew. Had he been in his right mind, he would have known the futility of such feelings.

He barely acknowledged Arjun and Kaya as they left their private booth to head to the bar. Vihaan had been strangely tense as well, but it was Aditi whose gaze he wanted to avoid. He sipped his drink, refusing the alcohol in case it tipped him over the edge. He was wound too tightly anyway. Better to leave, he decided.

"Where are you going?" Aditi looked up at him, surprised when he stood up and shrugged his jacket on.

"Home. I'll send the car for you later."

His voice was gruff, his mouth thin. Aditi took a step after him, holding his arm. She searched his face for answers, wondering what had happened that had put Rian in such an unsettling mood. The relaxed, sweet man she'd come out to dinner with had been replaced with someone who looked like he was locked in a battle with demons no one could see.

"Do you want to dance? They'll be starting up the music soon."

"No. I'm fine. I should go."

"How about karaoke?" she offered, pointing to the side room that had been set up for private entertainment.

He stiffened at the offer, shaking his head once, but all Aditi could see was that he needed a change of scenario. She felt his tension leach into her and she hated it. Pasting on a bright smile, she leaned in.

"Come on, Bugs, let's go sing a duet."

"I don't like singing, Aditi. Leave me be."

"Please, it'll be fun! They have good songs to choose from."

"I don't want to," came his answer once again, the vein in his forehead ticking dangerously.

Unfortunately for her, her determination to lead Rian out of his bad mood meant that she disregarded the signs of danger.

"Bugs." She tugged at him playfully. "Let's go."

"I said no!" he burst out, his voice louder than she'd expected.

The fury with which he jerked off her hold had her gasping. She saw Vihaan frown, stepping closer to her just as Arjun and Kaya returned, their relaxed smiles waning when they registered the tense atmosphere.

Rian, in the throes of anger, couldn't hold back.

"How many fucking times do I need to say no? If you want to make a fool of yourself for someone's entertainment, go right ahead. Leave me the hell alone!"

Aditi stared at him, her face turning white with shock, and then red.

"S-sorry," she croaked, embarrassed. She bit down on the inside of her lip, unable to utter another word. She clutched the side of her dress to hide her shaky hands. "I. . .I think I need a drink." Avoiding all eye contact, she slipped away before anyone could stop her.

The silence that surrounded him after Aditi's footsteps faded felt like a judgement in and of itself. His eyes remained stuck on the empty space she'd left, his wrath now twisting and flowing inwards, the object of his disgust morphing from Leela Shetty to himself.

"How could you be so rude to her?" Kaya chastised him.

"She was being pushy." One part of him wanted to hold on to any reason to justify his outburst, the fear of hating himself stopping him from admitting that he had royally fucked up.

"She was being fun," Vihaan snapped. "We can all see you're pissed about something. Her only mistake was that she tried to help you."

"Who pushed a stick up your ass tonight?" Arjun asked, clearly unhappy with Rian as well.

"You should apologise to her," Kaya suggested.

"Right after all of you get the fuck off my case," he snarled, his ego buckling down hard.

"What the hell is your problem, Rian?" Vihaan argued, taking an agitated step towards him. Kaya held him back.

"Shut up, Vihaan."

"Or what? I met her just tonight and even I know she didn't deserve this shit attitude."

Rian said nothing, stalking towards the railing that allowed him to look down into the busy club. His eyes fell upon a familiar green dress, the shapely figure of the woman he'd wounded walking along the periphery of the dance floor. His hand clenched over the metal bar, needing something to hold back this violence within him. The vision of her joy dimming, her face etched with painful embarrassment at his scolding now joined the multitude of other memories that already tortured him.

"Get your head out of your ass before I beat the shit out of you," Vihaan hissed, his patience gone. "I'm going to go look for her. I'd rather hang out with her than with you right now."

Rian said nothing, inspecting Aditi as best he could. Even from a distance, he could tell that she was tense— no longer the same smile or cheer on her face. He'd taken that away. Acid burned his stomach.

"Whatever your reason for acting like this, you know as well as I do that Aditi didn't deserve to be insulted." Kaya linked her arm with Arjun, shaking her head in disappointment when her friend didn't acknowledge them. "I'm going to go make sure she's okay, too. You can stay here and sulk or you can do the right thing and explain yourself to her."

With that, Rian was left alone with emotions that threatened to overwhelm him, and a sinking feeling that he may have damaged the opinions of the only people in the world who mattered to him.

Aditi stood at the counter, her mind in a daze. The bartender asked her something. She saw his lips move, but she heard nothing. The shock of Rian's reaction hadn't worn off. The joy of new friends and a fun outing had been obliterated when he'd yelled at her. In the time she'd known him, he'd only ever been kind and indulgent. Even when he'd not wanted her around, he had never been outright rude.

She stood there, her heart murmuring uncomfortably, until a gentle hand shook her out of her reverie. She glanced beside her, coming face to face with a lady she didn't know. Tall and svelte, she was possibly one of the most stunning women Aditi had ever seen. The kind who would be an artist's muse, a man's desire, and a woman's envy.

Her confidence was obvious given her demeanour as she coolly dismissed the men nearby who were trying to gain her attention.

This was a woman who would never have let someone's rudeness affect her.

"Are you okay?" she asked, her kindness making Aditi's eyes burn and her nostrils flare. Perhaps her dismay was clear because she turned to the bartender and ordered two drinks, handing her one. Aditi accepted it numbly, gulping it down without thought.

"If it's a man who has you looking like you're going to cry, it's not worth it." Her tone was devoid of judgement. Her gaze flickered to behind Aditi and almost instantly, the tiny turn of her lips tightened into a firm line, the kindness in her cat eyes all but lost.

"You," Aditi heard her hiss like it was a curse word, just as Vihaan reached her.

Unlike the playful, flirtatious man he'd been all through dinner, he looked like he was preparing for war with this mystery woman.

"What the hell are you doing here, Vera?"

The lady watched him for a long moment before shifting her gaze to Aditi, as though trying to assess their relationship.

"If it's because of him," Vera told Aditi, her smile no different than a sneer, "it's definitely not worth it."

With that, she left, her blood-red dress disappearing into the throng of people who were crowding the dance floor.

Aditi turned towards Vihaan, the unmistakable tightness of his jaw and the glimmer in his eyes telling her those words had affected him. Just like Rian's words had affected her.

With a sigh, she turned to the bartender and ordered another drink, hoping that this one would be strong enough to dull the ache and bury the fear that had developed in her.

Rian could hurt her.

And tonight, it had become clear that if he did, she would cry.

20

A Grinch and his Who

RIAN

Rian sat the clear plastic box on his gleaming countertop, the overhead light making the mango coulis shine atop the cheesecake.

His intention had been to surprise Aditi with something to indulge in, listening to her exuberantly express her adoration for all things mango. He had wanted to make her happy.

He'd failed.

The drive home had been excruciatingly silent. Every time he'd tried to speak, he'd lost his guts, the stiffness in her posture dissuading him from breaching the wall she'd erected.

Aditi had greeted Nanamma at home with a cheerfulness that was forced, drawing her into a conversation until both ladies had retired to their respective rooms.

The entire time, she had not spared him a glance. If this was an indication of her behaviour with him in future, Rian wasn't sure he would survive it.

He checked his phone. The read notification told him she'd seen his message, but confirmed his fear. She was avoiding him.

He walked on leaded feet towards the hallway, noticing the lights under her door. He approached her room, apprehension and fear twisting his gut. What if she refused to speak with him? He rapped his knuckles against the wooden panel before he could change his mind. A moment later, the door cracked open to reveal her in her old, now familiar, pyjamas.

Aditi watched Rian open his mouth before closing it, evidently unsure of himself.

"I brought you dessert," he said, wincing at his lame opening line.

She didn't respond, and his wavering confidence plunged even lower.

"Doc, I..."

She turned away, heading for the armchair in the corner of her room. She turned on the small TV on her side wall, flipping through the channels. Rian stepped in and cleared his throat.

"You can watch whatever you want on the big screen in the living room. You don't have to stay here."

She didn't acknowledge him.

"I'm sorry," he said, fighting the urge to rip the stupid TV off the wall. He hated this awkwardness. "Will you please say something?"

"Okay," she tossed out, eyes glued to the screen.

"That's it?"

"Hmm."

He left the room, confused. A moment later, he barged back in, standing directly in her line of vision.

"You won't ask why I acted like a jerk?" The idea that she might not care enough to know his reason for behaving out of the ordinary bothered him. His restlessness was turning into a desperation for Aditi's forgiveness.

Brown eyes pinned him for a moment, and he almost stopped breathing. Hurt and fear swirled in those chocolatey depths. Her chin trembled, the small flare of her nostrils telling him that she was reining in her feelings.

She was hiding from him. He knew instinctively that she would not ask him for clarification. The freedom she'd thought she had before—questioning him, teasing him, being silly with him—he'd snatched that away in one cruel moment.

Regret and shame washed over him, the weight of his actions unbearable. If he wanted her to feel free around him again, he would have to take the first step. He'd have to lay himself open and let her see the scars he'd always kept hidden.

Aditi fought hard not to rear back when Rian approached her and held his hand out. "Please."

She didn't know what made her do it, but she allowed him to lead her out to the kitchen. She stood silently, trepidation and anxiety filling her when he pulled out a spoon and scooped a piece of the cake, holding it out for her.

The look of incredulity she shot him had him feeling like a fool. Rian sighed, his hand dropping to the counter.

"I know you have no reason to do as I ask, but please, can you give me a chance?"

Just when he thought she would refuse, Aditi picked up the spoon and took a bite. The stirring of relief he felt boosted his courage. He pulled out his phone and tapped on a music app.

"Pick a song."

Her expression turned mulish. Accepting defeat, he pressed play on something he hoped she would like.

"Dance?"

Apparently this was her limit because Aditi whipped around, fully intending to walk away.

Rian rushed to block her path. "Please, Doc." His hands itched to hold her so that she wouldn't leave. She glared at him.

"What do you think you're doing? Dance? Really? Are you having fun at my expense?" Her voice wavered, unable to hide how upsetting she found his behaviour.

"No!" He ran a hand over his face, drawing it down to rub his jaw. This was going to be uncomfortable, but he owed Aditi an explanation. He felt helpless when she watched him with such wariness. "I'm not making fun of you. I am trying to correct all the things I did wrong this evening and all I ask is that you give me a little time. If, after you hear me out, you're still angry, I'll leave you alone."

His honesty worked in his favour. Her forehead creased when he stepped closer, but she didn't stop him from taking her hand in his and bringing her closer, assuming the most common slow-dancing stance known to the world.

One large palm pressed into the low of her back as their feet began to move, matching the gentle tempo of the tune he'd played. Despite the tension between them, Aditi sighed when Rian's chin settled on her crown. It was ridiculous that this simple gesture made her want to wail. Why could she not resist the comfort of him when it was also him who'd caused her discomfort? How was he both the source of pain and the solution for it?

For what felt like a long time, all they did was sway together in the middle of the kitchen, the music and each other's touch having a calming effect on them both.

"Growing up, I liked music." His words were soft and carefully measured. "I was told I had a good voice, but I didn't like to sing in front of people. Stage fear, perhaps. My parents used to host massive parties at our family home. Even after my father fell ill, my mother continued to throw these galas that were the talk of town for days. She craved the attention she garnered as the hostess. One evening, she forced me on stage, announcing to everyone I would entertain them. I froze. I couldn't get a sound out."

His chest rose in a deep breath, and she felt the soft shudder with which he released it.

"She was spitting mad at me for making her look bad."

His eyes stung, old wounds reopening, Leela's venomous declaration that night clear despite the passage of time.

You're a curse to me. Instead of making me proud, you made me look like an idiot for having such a stupid son. Others boast of how accomplished their children are but you've been nothing but a disappointment to me. My image, my happiness, my pride—damaged because of you and your failures! You're a stupid, worthless fool. Everything you touch, you destroy. That is your legacy. I wish I'd never given birth to you.

"She dragged me out onto the grounds beside our house, berating me for embarrassing her in front of her guests. My apologies did not matter. She left me there with a warning not to step back in the house until she forgave me."

His eyes glazed over, remembering the chill of the night, the wetness of the ground as it drizzled on and off around him. He'd huddled under a tree, beyond afraid of the deep darkness around him, but terrified of his mother's wrath if he sought safety inside the massive structure that was meant to be his home. Exhausted from crying, he'd eventually fallen asleep in the dirt and had been found in the wee hours of the morning by a security guard patrolling their gardens. His mother, drunk and in her own world, had never bothered to return for him.

"I couldn't stand to talk in public forums, much less sing, after that," he admitted, his throat hoarse.

Sensing his torment, Aditi's hand on his chest moved in a soft arc, back and forth, right over his heart. "Thank you for telling me. I understand why you reacted the way you did. I should have known you had a reason."

Her easy acceptance astounded him.

"She was there at the restaurant today. That's why I had to stay back. And she managed to make me feel like shit again. I wasn't in my right mind at the club and I took it out on you." His voice cracked, laced with regret. "I'm so sorry. I wish I could take it back."

"I know I can be too much. That's why I said you needed a safe word, too. I should have backed off when you said no once. I won't do it again."

The understanding that this condemnation of herself was a reflection of his behaviour wounded him far more than she'd ever know. Repentant, he held her a little closer, hoping that he could convince her of his true feelings.

"Too much? Yes, I suppose you are."

Aditi stilled, nose prickling at his agreement.

"You're too nice," he continued. "Too understanding. Too friendly, honest, and forgiving in a world that isn't any of that. But that's your strength."

Aditi drew away from him, clearly unwilling to give credence to his words. Their eyes met, and whatever Rian saw caused him to bridge the gap between them once more. He cupped her cheeks, lifting her face such that she was forced to meet his gaze.

"What happened today was my fault. If anyone should feel shame, it's me. You did nothing wrong." Some of the hurt receded from her eyes. "Promise me you won't change the way you are with me. Promise me you won't hold yourself back because of what I did."

She nodded, her hesitation slowly ebbing. She had no armour strong enough to deny Rian what he asked after he'd laid himself bare. She had never realised how much he'd hidden behind his sweet and silent exterior.

"Did I make you cry?" he asked.

"Almost," she whispered.

Under the soft glow of the lamps around them, it was impossible to hide anything. Her gaze flitted over features that had become so familiar to her in a short time, recognizing now the source of his unhappiness. The melancholy he'd become proficient at concealing had emerged today, and Aditi was left stunned at the revelation.

"My mother is not a good person, Doc. I hope your paths never cross. I wouldn't want her shadow to touch you."

Her inability to console him appropriately frustrated her. How did one find words to dull the cut left behind on a young child by his mother's meaningless hatred?

"Did she hit you?" she questioned, her instinct warning her of the possibility.

He hesitated for a second before he loosened his hold on her. He'd never revealed this to anyone else. He was finally speaking honestly about his struggles, and if he stopped now, he may never find it in him to discuss this again.

"She threw a tantrum at breakfast once because her friend's son scored better at school than I did. Swiped the entire table of food in anger before throwing a crystal glass at me." He extended his arm, folding his sleeves to reveal a tattoo on his lower bicep. It was a solid line that covered the circumference of his muscle, interrupted by two open arrowheads pointing up. Upon closer inspection, she saw the scar along which the tattoo was set. "It's the only time she left a mark."

Aditi traced the jagged edge of his wound with the gentlest of touches, as though fearful of causing him pain again.

"I couldn't read properly for a long time so school was tough. Unable to focus, unable to stay organised. I wasn't a good son, I wasn't a good student, I wasn't good enough—plain and simple."

"That seems like a terrible criteria to judge a child."

He let out a disappointed breath, wishing everyone thought like her. "She believed I was a lazy brat who brought her shame by not being a beacon of perfection. The older I got, the worse her reaction to my failures. I think she only stopped because I grew bigger than her. She couldn't intimidate me with her size after a certain point."

It had been why he'd obsessively worked out as a teen, wanting to be stronger outside so he could feel stronger inside.

"You didn't have an easy childhood, did you?"

He shrugged, unwilling to linger on it longer than necessary. He wasn't certain he deserved Aditi's understanding. That she was empathising with him instead of tearing him apart for his mistake was unsettling.

"I had money. A big house. Staff who cared for me as much as they were allowed to. I suspect one of them finally told Nanamma. She did her best to protect me after she found out. I was fourteen by then."

"Sounds lonely for a young boy." Her fingers left his skin, making him wish for contact again. Somehow, it was easy to confess to the hard things when she was touching him.

"If it is any consolation," she finally said, "you did an admirable job of growing up."

"Even after how I behaved today?" he asked bitterly, unable to hold back a self-deprecating laugh.

"You're a good person, Bugs. One argument doesn't change that. One mistake doesn't define who you are for me."

"You only say that because you don't know what I've done."

Aditi rolled her eyes and stood back, arms crossed. "Unless you murdered someone in cold blood, I'm sticking to what I said. Rian Shetty is a pretty nice guy and I don't mind him one bit."

The sudden return of her sass made it feel like there was air in his lungs again. Unable to help it, he laughed, just once, but it was enough for the edges of her mouth to tip up. "Talk about damning with faint praise."

"Don't want you to get a big head, do we?" she teased.

Finally, his world was righting itself. He would have spiralled into anger and self-hate if she hadn't been around. "Thanks," he said, glad for who she was.

"See?" she clucked, readily moving on from their fight. "Again with the nice guy behaviour. Can I tell you a secret? It's more fun when you're grumpy and I can be the sunshine girl."

Bantering with her brought with it a happiness he'd feared he'd lost. He almost kissed her in relief.

"Isn't that a book trope you keep harping about?" he asked, smiling softly.

"Yeah. Sometimes, I wonder if I got into the wrong profession. I should have done something with books."

No, he thought. She was a healer, through and through. She made people feel safe and cared for. No wonder her family and cousins turned to her for everything. He felt that way more and more. Like she could fix things for him. And what she couldn't fix, she would hold together so he didn't fall apart.

"Come on. Let's change our mood."

She dragged him towards the living room, and he followed mutely, no more able to resist her than he could gravity. She fell onto the couch, flicking the remote until she settled on a movie.

She patted the space nearby. "Sit. Watch this with me. I need something to calm myself before I can sleep."

He took a seat next to her, automatically sliding one arm along the back of the couch to tuck her into him.

At her questioning glance, he shrugged. "This is allowed in a situationship, isn't it?"

She pinkened adorably.

"Nanamma?" she asked, clearly worried about the practicality of cuddling on the couch even though it was getting close to midnight.

"She's deep asleep. Won't be up until the morning." He cupped the side of her head and directed it to lean on his shoulder, unwilling to hear more excuses.

"Bugs?" he heard her mumble after a moment.

"Hmm?"

"Please don't embarrass me in public again. Harish did that too, and I hated it. I hated it tonight even more than before."

Nose buried in her hair, he breathed her in, the gentle request hurting him anew. "Never again," he vowed in a whisper. "Not in public, not in private."

Her body loosened considerably with his promise, her weight resting against him. If he thought to say anything else, it was lost to confusion when the first scenes of the movie played on screen.

"It's a Christmas movie," Rian complained.

"So?"

"We're in the middle of October, Doc."

"I love Christmassy things," she declared.

His brows rose. She came from a fairly traditional Hindu South Indian family so this new piece of information surprised him.

"You celebrate Christmas?"

"Never had the opportunity, but look how pretty!" she whined, pointing towards the TV. She sighed, a content sort of sound. "I love all festivals. It's just another reason to be happy. When I have my own home someday, I'll put up a tree, decorations, the works. I'll celebrate Christmas just like Diwali or Eid or Navratri."

Rian's eyes swept his apartment, picturing Christmas lights everywhere, a lit up tree in the corner near the windows, and him on the couch, dressed in a silly Christmas pyjama, cuddled with a woman wearing a matching set.

He glanced down just as Aditi looked up. Warm brown eyes met steel grey ones, setting his heart galloping within his chest.

Aditi. Christmas. With him. Together.

"In the meantime," Aditi grinned, utterly oblivious that he was close to fainting from pure shock, "I figure there is never a bad time to watch the villain learn his lesson and become a hero."

So, somewhere between the Grinch making his plan to steal Christmas and standing atop the snowy cliff, watching the village of Whos singing, Aditi fell asleep.

As the Grinch's heart grew three sizes bigger, Rian pulled the thick blanket over the woman next to him and stroked her hair, understanding just how powerful one sweet girl could be to thaw the ice around a grumpy Grinch's heart.

21

Rian, the Wrecking Ball

ADITI

"Are you done yet?"

Aditi glanced up from her conversation, startled to find Rian standing next to her table, his lips drawn in a severe line. Granted it was his restaurant, and his presence wasn't entirely a surprise. And she *had* been thinking about him all evening. She simply couldn't figure out why he looked like she'd taken his favourite toy away.

"Rian?"

"We should go home. Nanamma sounds ill."

Her gaze swung across towards her date, her surprise turning into an awkward embarrassment when Rian continued to ignore his presence.

If someone had told Aditi that she'd be on a date with a man who had stood her up once, and would be enjoying herself, she'd have called them crazy. But when Tarun Nair had messaged her that afternoon, apologising for having missed their matrimonial meet and asking for another chance, she had agreed.

Nina had been there with her judgy eyes, shaking her head when Aditi had stubbornly insisted upon continuing with the arranged dates. After all, one kiss with Rian and a situationship that sometimes felt real did not mean anything in the long run.

A kiss, a situationship, and a blissful night spent sleeping in his arms.

She had woken up draped over him in the wee hours of the morning, horny and grinding against his thigh. When she'd fallen asleep with him on the couch, she didn't know. But it was clear that the two of them had spent the night with their limbs tangled and their bodies pressed against the other. In her sleep-induced haze, she'd arched and rubbed against him, gasping awake when the pressure between her legs had built up too much to allow her to remain in that liminal space between sleep and wakefulness. Her shocked sound had woken him up as well. Under the dull pre-dawn light, his eyes had locked with hers, widening at the realisation that his hands were caressing her naked back and his arousal was stiff against her stomach.

His head had lowered just an inch, until the sound of Nanamma cluttering about had broken the moment. Fearing discovery, they'd rushed to their respective rooms and Aditi had been left with a lingering fear that despite her denial, Rian had gotten too close for comfort.

Aditi had always been fiercely protective of the people she was close to, and overnight, she found that she felt that way about him as well. But that was all it could be, she told herself. Lust was okay. Friendship was fine. Protective instincts were natural, especially when she remembered that he was a young child when he'd suffered abuse at the hands of someone who should have protected him.

Beyond that, she needed to remember her goals.

The medical camp she had proposed leading looked like it would come to fruition in the near future. Her supervisor and mentor had made enough indications to that effect, asking if she would consider shifting base to Mumbai if required.

Working with her mentor long term would mean that Aditi could assist on the toughest and most rare gynaecological cases in Asia while learning from the best. She would be given a team to command, and enough budget to make multiple medical camps available for pregnant women in remote villages across India. She'd meticulously planned for this. She simply had to find the right person to fit into said plans– someone to marry so she could stay in India, progress in her chosen career, have a family, and keep her parents happy at the same time.

At the end of the day, Rian did not want to be that person and she wouldn't force him to be.

So, despite Nina's disapproval, she'd given Tarun another chance.

Their conversation had been easy, both making the other laugh and showing an interest in taking it further. He'd been jovial and chivalrous, and while Aditi had had to work hard to keep thoughts of stormy grey eyes from hogging her attention, she'd been mostly enjoying herself.

Until Rian had unceremoniously interrupted them.

"So? Are you done?"

Aditi was sure her confusion wasn't hidden anymore.

"What? I don't think—"

"I can escort her," Tarun offered, staking his claim. "Hold on, let me finish paying for the meal."

"That's not needed. It's on the house," Rian said smoothly, his tone not the least bit friendly.

"It is?" Aditi asked, her voice sharper than Tarun's.

To her horror and surprise, Rian loomed over her, gracing her with a look that was borderline intimate. He lifted a hand to her face, drawing a finger down from her temple to her cheek, tucking a strand of hair behind her ear.

She couldn't move, goosebumps erupting everywhere at his touch. What the hell was he doing?

"I've told you before," he murmured, his eyes boring into her. "When you're with me, I pay for your food. No arguments."

Her mouth dropped open.

"What's going on?" Tarun demanded, clearly irritated.

She would have answered, but that would mean having to look away from Rian, something she seemed incapable of doing.

"You ready to leave, Doc?"

"But I can drop her off." Tarun's continued protest seemed to annoy Rian.

"That'd be out of the way for you," he informed her date, his smile looking like a snarl.

Either Tarun was clueless or he really liked Aditi because he dared to question Rian anyway.

"Wouldn't it be out of the way for you?"

"Of course not," Rian replied, a supercilious glint in his eyes. "We live together."

Aditi gasped, knowing that this truth sounded worse out of context. "Wait, I can explain," she said, hoping to salvage the train wreck that Rian was causing.

"Later. Remember Nanamma's waiting?" Before she could clarify Tarun's doubts, Rian took her hand and led her out.

Given that he'd driven his bike to the restaurant, she was forced to stew in silence during the ride home. The minute they stepped foot into his apartment, Aditi stormed towards Nanamma's bedroom to talk to her about what a massive idiot her grandson was being.

"Nanamma?" she called, confused when she was nowhere to be found.

She stomped into the living room to find Rian lounging like a massive panther on the sofa, scrolling through the watch list he'd made with her.

"Where's Nanamma?"

"At some group prayer meet. She'll be back later."

Aditi blinked. "You said she was sick."

"Yes," he answered, without looking away from the screen. "She coughed on the phone. You should call and check on her."

"You made it seem like she's at home and needed us immediately."

"Whoops. Sorry." He could feel her glare from across the room, one which he pointedly ignored.

"You're kidding me, right?" The words barely made it through her clenched teeth.

"What?" he asked, adopting his most innocent look. "You don't want to watch this? It was next on our list," Rian said, pointing to the movie he'd picked.

Aditi exploded, her voice thinning out into a shriek. "No! I don't want to watch a goddamn movie! I was finally on a date with a good guy and you wrecked it!"

To her utter frustration, all he did was place one arm along the back of the sofa, and raise an insolent brow at her. "I didn't realise you were on a date."

"What the hell else could it have looked like?" she snarked, her fists balling.

"I don't know. I didn't bother looking at him."

Her lips wobbled when her anger peaked. "How could you?"

The change in tone did not go unnoticed. Rian watched Aditi's shoulder droop and he finally sat straight, no longer wanting to antagonise her with glib comments. Despite feeling bad for hurting her, Rian couldn't bring himself to feel guilty about the failed date.

The moment Aditi had stepped into The Mumbai Map, his senses had gone on high alert. He'd been beyond pleased to see her from his office and had immediately stepped out to go receive her.

He'd long since given his staff instructions to always make space available for Aditi, and he'd been happy to see her drop by for meals every so often. Today was no different.

He'd sauntered down the hall towards the main reception, taking his time to appreciate the way her dress had clung to her body, outlining every beautiful curve.

She'd glanced behind and he'd been mesmerised by the long column of her throat, tracing her profile all the way down to the lush swell of her breasts. Her neckline had been low enough to provide an enticing view of the top curve of her chest, leaving him feeling hot under his collar. Her hair had been left open in waves, her lips glossy and pink. Her satin brown skin had glowed under the bistro lights, and her white dress had made her seem like an angel who'd lead a man to sin.

She'd always been beautiful, but tonight, she'd looked ethereal.

And then she'd smiled. Not at him, but at the man who'd followed her in. She'd let him place a hand on her back when they'd walked to their table, the thigh-high slit of her dress revealing teasing glimpses of a smooth leg ending in strappy heels. The fact that she had dressed so alluringly for another man had left his hands shaking with an unfamiliar rage. It was nothing like the anger his mother had ever induced. This felt personal on a whole new level.

He'd tried to let her be. Throughout her dinner, he'd tried his damndest to ignore the sick feeling in his stomach. Eventually, his rational mind had been left exhausted battling indecipherable emotions.

"Why are you going on these dates?" he asked, instead of answering her question. "I thought you were going to take a break."

Her eyes narrowed suspiciously. "Did you ruin my date on purpose?"

He should have known she'd be direct. There was no point in lying.

"Yes."

"Why? Do you want to date me?"

"N-no," he replied uneasily.

"Then you had no right," she scolded him, her disappointment no longer hidden.

"I don't want you to force yourself into a relationship. I can't watch you make that mistake."

"How fucking arrogant of you!"

That took him aback.

"What qualifies you to determine if I am making a mistake or not? I don't recall asking you for your input!" She stormed off towards the kitchen and Rian leapt up to follow her.

"You keep saying we are friends," he argued. "This is how I protect my friends."

She ignored him, swiping through her contact list. "I'm going to call Tarun and hope to god he lets me explain myself."

Rian lost the last bits of his patience.

"No, you are not!" he barked, snatching the phone from her hand before she could resist. He was aware that he was behaving like an overbearing oaf, but logic and him were not occupying the same room today.

"I need my phone back," Aditi ordered, a deathly chill in her voice. Her palm open, she extended her hand out. "Now, Rian."

Given the disparity in their sizes, her attempt to intimidate him should have been amusing. It wasn't.

An angry Aditi terrified him as equally as she aroused him. It was the darndest feeling, not knowing if he wanted to apologise to her or lay her flat on the ground and fuck her thoroughly, until they both forgot what they were fighting about.

He slid the phone in his back pocket, a single brow rising in defiance, hoping that his size was a deterrent to her attacking him.

The murderous gaze she shot him had him changing his mind immediately. With a grunt of frustration, he dropped the phone on the counter nearby.

"I don't like being at odds with you, Doc. I still don't understand this whole arranged marriage business but if you feel so strongly about it, I'll apologise to your date."

His offer bowled her clean, unexpectedly diffusing her ire. She poured herself a glass of water and gulped it, perturbed by the sudden highs and lows of her emotions. Rian's interruption of her date had annoyed her. His offer to smooth things over with Tarun, to her consternation, annoyed her more. She could have avoided him altogether by going to a different restaurant tonight. She knew that. Mumbai only had several *thousand* options to choose from. Still, she'd insisted on meeting Tarun at The Mumbai Map. Was it even Rian's fault when she'd all but dared him to react?

She'd lost her mind, she decided, gulping a second glass just to have something to do.

"Why are you so hell bent on meeting someone this quickly?" Rian asked. "It's like you're working on a find-a-groom deadline."

"I may as well be. When I go back for my parent's anniversary party next month, I'll inevitably be asked about my future. If I don't have a good answer, I'll have to meet their choice of men again."

"Just say no."

"That's not an option."

"You are a strong, independent woman! Why are you letting others decide the course of your life?"

"I'm not!" she insisted. He scoffed and Aditi wanted to tear her hair out, or better—his.

"Of course you are," he condescended to her. "You don't need to marry to have a satisfying life. Focus on your career."

Her forehead creased and she frowned, as if he had missed a very crucial point. "I love being a doctor. But what makes you think that I don't want a family, too?"

Her simple question instantly extinguished even the most minimal feeling of righteousness he'd retained to justify his actions.

"I want a family, Bugs. I want a husband, kids, the works. Call me traditional and maybe I am, but I want it all. Career, love, a house with people who want to be with each other, chatter around the dining table, festivals with friends and family crowding into my home. . .and a life partner to hold me at night. I *want* that."

Her voice grew emotional and with each word, her longing spun a silver web around him, invisible to the naked eye but there nonetheless. In the centre, hidden away until now, were dreams he'd never known existed.

A slowly ageing Aditi whose laugh lines only made her more beautiful, playing the perfect hostess to a crowd of guests. Children who cuddled into her motherly embrace for her warmth. And a partner who hugged her possessively, playfully demanding her time and attention when those children ran to join their friends. A partner. Her partner. Him?

His vision superimposed with reality. The little children faded away, the crowds disappeared, the lively chatter dulled to a hum, until it was just him and her.

It could be their world.

It could be their future.

It could be real.

The thought was powerful enough to knock the wind out of him. Without a warning, she'd opened chambers of his heart where the echoes of lost companionship and family had tormented him, until he'd decided one day that he did not need them to survive. Vehemently, he shook his head, willing those echoes to remain silent.

"I understand that you don't feel the same way," Aditi said, mistaking his action to be a response to her. "You don't need marriage. But I do."

"Have you considered that this is the story you've been fed by your family, just so they can get you hitched to the NRI asshole?" he swore, desperate to keep from unravelling in front of her.

"Do not bring my family into this!" She smacked her hand against the counter, irritatedly blowing a strand of hair out of her face. "I love them. And they love me."

"Using love as an excuse to justify their emotional manipulation is pathetic."

She paused, pinning him with a look that made him squirm.

"Did you steal that line from one of your Korean dramas you pretend you're not watching?" she spat coolly.

"No, from one of your smut-filled romance books that you leave littered everywhere," he sneered, no more holding back his shots than her.

A low growl emanated from her, his comment enraging her more than it should. "Do *not* judge me for finding fictional men more satisfying than real ones," she hissed, chest heaving, struggling to hold back her anger. "Present company included!"

Jealousy roiled in his stomach, even the thought of fictional men in her life suddenly abhorrent. "Doc, you haven't been satisfied by me, so keep that mouth shut before I do it for you."

Unafraid, she walked right up to him, her head tilting back to glare into his face. "Big talk, Bugs. I dare you to try."

His jaw tightened, brows drawing low in warning.

"Go on," she goaded, hands on her hips, one foot tapping the ground.

His eyes flashed dangerously. The air hummed with tension from their argument, their skin prickling in awareness. Their agitation had no other outlet besides each other. The pull between them grew stronger with each passing second, overtaking any and all sensibilities.

"Can't do it, can you?" she taunted, unable to see that Rian's control was fraying. "See, that's what I thought. You're full of sh. . ."

His lips came crashing down on hers, muffling whatever colourful insult she was about to spit at him. Her back hit the wall near the switchboard, the accidental brushing of her hand dowsing the apartment in darkness. Crowded against his sturdy frame with his mouth hot on hers, Aditi had one final realisation before everything was lost to the fog of desire.

This was precisely the outcome she had wanted today.

22

Blurred Boundaries

RIAN

R IAN HADN'T MEANT TO pounce upon Aditi like a barbarian bent on marking his woman. But the glimpse of wildness in her, her defiance and flush of anger made him want to plunge headlong into the pool of flames from which she'd arisen.

If she was an inferno, he would gladly burn.

If she was a storm, he'd be the leaf that got swept away in her.

Whatever she was, whoever she would be, he would become a part of her.

It could be no other way.

He bit down on her lip, pulling it out, prying her mouth apart. She responded immediately, opening for him, meeting every rough thrust of his tongue with hers, revelling in his domination.

The tenor of their kiss changed almost instantly, as if Rian had realised that she wouldn't protest, going from a harsh punishment to a slow and tender exploration. He traced her lower lip with the tip of his tongue, flicking the edges, teasing her before deepening their kiss again.

Aditi moaned softly, almost fusing herself to Rian in pleasure. It was the kind of kiss that made one despise the need to breathe, where one's body disavowed all ownership over itself, giving full authority to the person who was robbing them of the ability to function normally.

With his lips moving against hers, and his touch branding her skin, she remembered no one. Not her family. Not Tarun. Not her reasons for trying to find a man to marry.

All she could think of, all that she could feel, was Rian.

His scent, his aura, his need consumed her and she grew damp, unconsciously rubbing her thighs together to ease the growing tension between them.

"Hands or mouth?" Rian gruffed when they broke off.

"What?" she asked, her voice barely audible, nearly out of breath.

"Do you want to be satisfied by my hands, or my mouth?" he asked clearly, said mouth latching onto the strip of skin just under the curve of her jaw. He suckled her right there and she was sure she was going to faint. She couldn't have heard him right. "Cat got your tongue?" he taunted softly, placing nibbling kisses down her neck. "Or are you just all big talk?"

Somewhere, from the final vestiges of her rapidly departing sense, she gripped his collar and brought him to face her. He thought she would back down? Hell no.

"Both," she answered, watching his eyes darken. "Hands and mouth."

"As you wish. Get on the counter."

"Here?" She gasped when his hands slipped under the slit of her dress, cupping her ass and squeezing. Her white lace thong offered no protection from the heat of his palm. She felt the edge of the countertop against her lower back, mumbling against his mouth as he continued to rain kisses on her. "What if someone sees?"

"No one else is home," he grunted, lifting her onto the countertop. A shiver raced through her at the feel of cold stone against the warm back of her thighs.

"What's your safe word?" His lips teased the outer whorls of one ear, causing her to grab one solid bicep. He nipped at her, distracting her from his hands which were steadily pushing her dress up, sliding along her silken leg. She moaned when his tongue pressed against a particularly sensitive spot right below her ear, flicking it before drawing it in between his lips, the sting pleasurable in its own right.

"Safe. Word," he repeated, kissing the fluttering pulse at the base of her throat, nudging her until she was lying down.

"Bunny," she croaked, unable to believe that his mouth was tracking down her body, hating that her clothes were in the way.

"Good. Use it. I will not stop otherwise. Understood?" He lifted his head to stare down at her.

The moment she nodded, his hands gripped her bottom and pulled her to the edge. He settled himself on the stool, as if ready for an evening meal.

Warm palms curved about her calves, pressing and massaging her muscles, moving up to hold her knees before spreading them apart. His lips never left her skin, tracing a path halfway up one thigh before switching to the other side. Her stomach clenched, the anticipation of when he'd reach his destination causing her need to surge.

Her dress slid up, cool air washing over her thighs and she had to fight herself from screaming to end it there. It had been far too long since she'd let a man see her and she hadn't expected to feel so vulnerable.

A second later, his finger hooked into the gusset of her damp panties. She felt him run his knuckle up and down her slit before exposing her. The few seconds of wait felt excruciating, making her lift her neck up. Her eyes locked with his. She was given no time to second guess if he'd been waiting for her approval because he bent down and his warm mouth covered the most intimate part of her.

Her head fell back with a gasp as his tongue searched her, flicking up, stopping just before he reached the little peak that needed his caress. He licked her slowly, gently, teasing her until her reservations ebbed and her breath transformed into needy sounds. Her hips tilted up, searching for more pressure in the one spot he kept avoiding, groaning his name when he didn't oblige.

He shifted instead to hook one leg over his shoulder, giving himself better access. He brushed his thumb over her slit, spreading her arousal. Under the dim moonlight streaming into his apartment, her pussy gleamed with evidence of her desire. He didn't dare speak for fear of breaking through her haze. He could hardly believe that she was letting him play out this fantasy. Whatever spell she was under, he felt it too. He wanted this. He needed at least this to survive tonight.

Aditi felt firm fingers spread her sex open, her breath coming out in a broken cry when his tongue thrust into her without warning. He tasted her deeply, his murmur of approval vibrating against her sensitive skin. His finger replaced his tongue, stroking in and out of her, curling it until he was pressing into a spot that made her eyesight go blurry. Her body twisted, chest heaving as she strained to take a breath.

"Rian," she sobbed when he slid a second finger in, clenching him immediately. Repeatedly, he sunk his fingers into her while he licked and laved her swollen folds, never letting her guess at his pace. He played with her until she was trembling, chanting, "Please, oh my god, please."

"Do you want me to make you come?" he hummed, his breath wafting across her in tense puffs.

Her hips moved up in an answer, pushing herself against his hand, aching for a release.

"Say the words. Tell me exactly what you want."

"I want you to fuck me with your fingers," she panted, wiggling her hips. He thrust his index in, knuckles deep, causing her to slap a hand over her mouth.

"And?" Rian asked, his voice hoarse, unable to see beyond the erotic vision of Aditi laid atop his kitchen counter, writhing for him, the smell of her arousal in the air. Her tight pussy sucked him in as he moved his fingers with deliberate precision.

"Kiss me again," she begged, her voice catching as he broke rhythm, making her wait for his touch.

"Where?"

"I...th..."

"Where, Aditi?" he growled.

"My pussy!" she cried, her desperation greater than her shame.

Any other time, he'd have made her beg more as payback for her sass, but he'd gotten so hard already, he was about to burst in his jeans without ever having touched himself. If he didn't end this soon, his fingers would be replaced with a much larger part of his anatomy.

His hot mouth closed over her clit and he suckled hard, his rough tongue repeatedly flicking against it.

"Yes, please don't stop," Aditi urged, her body tensing when his fingers picked up speed, thrusting in perfect counteraction to the torment his mouth was wreaking upon her. Her hand found its way into his hair, clutching him, crying out as he licked, flicked, and sucked her into an orgasm that had her arching her back. Blistering pleasure washed over her like a fiery shroud, enveloping her in its cocoon. Momentarily, she felt weightless, propelled into a space where the rush from her freefall held her, cradling her until she could gently land on her feet once more.

Rian couldn't stop kissing her still. His palm curved under one thigh to hold her open, letting her release coat his chin. The feel of his fingers leaving her, replaced by his tongue set off yet another tremor within her. No longer able to remain lying down, she propped herself up on her elbows, unprepared for the sight that greeted her.

Some twenty odd feet across from her, reflected on the wall of windows beyond which were millions of city lights glittering in the night, she saw what she looked like. Chest heaving, her breasts straining against the sweetheart neckline of her dress, messy hair, swollen lips and her hand gripping the head of a broad-shouldered man who had his face buried between her naked thighs.

It was an image she would never forget.

Her shocked breath had him looking up.

The pressure on his skull released instantly. She let go of his thick hair, the strands slipping between her fingers in a sensually soft movement. She felt him press his mouth against her skin, like he couldn't bear to stop. His stubble scratched her when he moved, giving her fleshy thigh a soft squeeze before lowering her leg off his shoulder.

The scrape of the stool legs broke through the fog she was in. She gasped when he wrapped an arm around her waist to help her sit up fully. They held each other's gaze, wonder and fear of the unknown clashing between them.

His eyes dropped to her lips, red and swollen, looking like she had bit down hard on them to keep from making a sound. She'd failed because even now, her delirious cries of ecstasy rang in his ears.

Despite the fact that his lips had just been between her legs, kissing her on the mouth immediately after felt like it would be far too intimate a gesture. Like it would obliterate every boundary between them.

Aditi's gut clenched when Rian licked his lips, her attention drawn to them. She'd never gotten off on a man's tongue before, but she finally saw the appeal. His mouth had driven her to the brink of satisfaction within minutes and pushed her over the summit more than once in quick succession. With an almost reverent touch, she wiped the remnants of her desire off the edge of his lower lip.

For the first time since he'd met her, Aditi had no smart aleck comment, and he didn't know if that was a good thing. He needed something to distract him from her flushed face, her kissable mouth, and the soft body that had shuddered under him.

The flavour of her release, like saltwater taffy, was still on his tongue, and he was hard pressed to think of anything he wanted more than to taste her again.

With a control he didn't know he possessed, he adjusted the open edges of her dress over her limbs, covering her. He stepped aside, allowing her to shuffle off the counter. Silently, he followed her down the hall, all the way to her bedroom.

He inspected her side profile for any indications of distress, thankful that apart from the heightened colour of her skin, she did not look disturbed. Gone was the anger she'd displayed at knowing he'd blown her date on purpose, or the dismay in her eyes when he'd refused to understand her reasons for pursuing an arranged marriage. In its place was a woman who glowed with the flush of sexual satisfaction, and perhaps, the anticipation of more.

Aditi reached for the knob and pushed her door ajar. She stepped in, walking ahead, her heart hammering at the thought of continuing what had begun in the kitchen. She turned around, finding that he'd stopped just outside the threshold.

"Rian?" she called softly, unable to say anything else to break the tension between them.

"Go to sleep," he ordered, his voice rough.

Aditi nodded, turning away to hide her disappointment.

"Doc?"

She glanced back expectantly. Their eyes met, and the proof of lingering desire almost brought him to his knees.

"Lock your door tonight."

23

His Aditi

RIAN

A WEEK LATER, RIAN sat in the courtyard of The Singapore Map, overlooking the calm waters of the Marina Bay. He sipped on his beetroot juice, staring at an absurdly adorable picture of the very person he had run from.

Aditi.

A day after their first intimate experience, he had left the country. Sure, one part of it had been the requirement of his presence for work to continue at The Singapore Map. But he'd also needed the space. He didn't know what fear had possessed him because despite indicating that she'd been willing, he'd not been able to take their intimacies any further that night.

Years of random sexual encounters had not prepared him for the same thing with Aditi Krishnan. His pathetic attempt to put some distance between them so he could clear his mind and figure out why he had these reservations had only made one thing certain.

He liked Aditi. Far more than he had expected to.

He abhorred the way he'd behaved when she'd been on her date. The jealousy he'd experienced at seeing her smile at that moron had nearly maimed him.

Aditi had been right to be angry. Bloody hell, he was angry with himself too. He had pushed his own views on her because it had suited him. He hadn't thought about the repercussions of his immaturity on the goal she'd wanted to achieve.

But he had not been lying about his motivations. He truly couldn't watch her enter a relationship out of some ridiculous compulsion to meet her family's expectations.

Her admittance that she had planned her life around having a family had floored him, however.

For the rest of the week, her words had weighed on him and her absence tormented him. Every trip he'd made to Singapore's famous food stalls or tourist spots felt a little less magical than before. He couldn't help but think that it would be better if he'd been able to bring Aditi with him, just like their late-night jaunts around Mumbai.

On a whim, he'd parcelled her a traditional Singaporean dessert, waiting eagerly for a reply. Today, after forty-eight hours, he'd been rewarded with a picture of her gorging on the sweets, looking like an endearing chipmunk and wearing the pyjamas he'd also included as an apology gift. The sushi cartoon print had reminded him of her and he'd been unable to ignore his impulse to purchase something he knew would make her eyes crinkle, exactly like in this photo.

Sitting on their couch, she looked comfortable, happy, and at home.

Their couch? His lips tipped up, his sights raking over her again. Somehow, it seemed weird to say *his* couch anymore. His apartment, something he'd taken pride in, had become Aditi's in a short time.

He closed his eyes, trying to recall the way his house looked before she had moved in, and he couldn't. In his mind's eye, he toured his home, noting her backpack in the front closet, the navy and beige canvas decidedly dull for a woman as lively as her. He canvassed the space, remembering the many books on the centre table, at least three different highlighters strewn about. He recalled his kitchen with her sitting on the counter top instead of the stool, swinging her shapely legs while she regaled him and Nanamma with her many stories, hands flying everywhere. Beside her, her colourful mug bumped up against his clean white one, infusing life into his orderly and staid home.

Aditi.

Like a call that came from his soul, her name reverberated within him. A jolt of longing more intense than anything he'd felt before shot through his senses.

He felt comfortable with her. He wanted to share the mundane moments with her as much as the exciting ones. Such feelings spoke of the kind of connection he had ached to have once.

A friendship, a situationship, or a relationship—Rian no longer knew the right term for what they had. Only one thing was certain.

She was his.

He needed exclusivity with her for his own peace of mind. Because he liked her. Truly, deeply, madly. He'd been afraid to admit it and it had held him back from taking her to bed that night after their argument. He'd been done with one night stands and flings for a long time already.

Sex with Aditi would never be something meaningless and non-committal. Whether they got serious enough for marriage, how soon they did, if she'd even accept him as a permanent option—these were not questions to which he had answers. He'd never had a girlfriend who'd lasted longer than a couple months. He didn't know how relationships worked. But he'd figure it out eventually.

In the meantime, he was going to focus on what was most important.

Aditi. His Aditi.

As bright as the sun, as lovely as the moon, and as chaotic and mesmerising as the Milky Way.

With this in mind, he sent her a message.

Bugs Bunny (1:02 p.m.)

> I'm ready to level up the benefits in our friend-situation-(callitwhateveryouwant)-ship

Chaos Doc (1:03 p.m.)

> Was it the new PJs that did it for you or the mouth full of food?

The dull text narration on his phone only made Aditi's response funnier. Rian laughed. And he laughed and laughed, planning all the ways in which he would rip those exact PJs off of her delectable body, counting down the minutes until he could make her laugh, sigh, and cry his name like he'd been wanting to for a very long time.

24

Chota Bheem

ADITI

A DITI HAD ALWAYS KNOWN that going to the gym had benefits, both on a person's physical and mental health. It was one of the reasons she'd often dragged herself to exercise at either the local women's club or, if she was being lazy, the rooftop gym in Rian's building.

The facility was well equipped, but lacked on-site trainers. However, when the benefits included being able to ogle a sweaty Rian Shetty deep in the midst of his own workout routine, she wasn't sure she could find a single reason to berate the quality of this gym centre anymore.

This had to qualify as some kind of live porn, she decided.

Rian could sell pictures of just his biceps curving or his quads tightening, and he'd easily be able to fund another three restaurants in this city. He could market GIFs of that sweat trickling down his neck, slowly dripping past his clavicle and teasing its way down his uncovered chest, and it would cause the internet to crash.

On second thought, he probably shouldn't.

Women's ovaries might spontaneously combust at the image of his glistening abs and those sexy hip bones dipping into his workout shorts. Said shorts slid just a little lower when he performed another pull up, revealing the top curve of his rounded ass as he made it to the highest bar.

Call her Felicity because holy Smoaks, the man was on a salmon ladder!

Aditi let out an audible whimper.

"What the. . .what are you doing here?" he questioned, surprised by her presence. He jumped down from a height, his muscles flexing with each movement, the power in them no longer hidden by the barrier of clothes.

Her entire body tightened, feeling very much like a peeping tom for enjoying this so much. "Gym. Working out." Was she drooling? She patted around the edges of her mouth, just to be certain.

"I didn't realise anyone else was using the facility this early."

"Just you and me. I couldn't sleep. I'm not used to being home alone."

"Alone?" Rian asked, surprised.

"Nanamma stayed back in Velas yesterday for some community event. She'll be back in the afternoon, in time for the Diwali party tonight."

Rian nodded in understanding. He'd himself only come back a few hours ago, so to learn that he had alone time with Aditi before his grandmother returned was the best news he could hope for.

"You're back," he heard her say.

He smiled. "Yeah. I'm back."

She blinked. "You're naked."

"Yeah, I'm. . .what?" He glanced down at his uncovered chest and rolled his eyes. Snagging the towel he'd hung on a seat nearby, he wiped his face.

Aditi could swear she felt her uterus clench.

The tattoo, the veins, the damp hair, the light eyes, the barely-there smattering of chest hair on tan skin that only made him look more masculine—he was a walking blueprint of things that turned her on, encompassed in one breathtaking form. It was no wonder he triggered something in her brain that was borderline primitive & deeply sexual. She was afraid she'd go feral on him one day and he'd be scarred for life.

"How do you look like this?" Aditi asked, somehow sounding like she was in shock.

Rian tilted his head, staring at her in confusion.

"Chefs are supposed to be fat and jolly," she continued, looking like she couldn't wrap her head around something very important.

"I think you're mistaking chefs for Santa Claus," he said, slinging the towel around his neck.

If Santa looked like him, no wonder he got all the ho ho hos, the impish voice in her head cackled. The terrible pun didn't even phase her, too occupied with drinking in every detail of him. Like she'd been parched from walking in the desert and he was her oasis.

He turned and the sight of his back muscles contracting as he set the weight bar back on the lowest rung had her feeling lightheaded.

"You work with food all day long but look like you came from Asgard."

"Whose ass?" he asked, sure he hadn't heard her right.

"Thor!" she exclaimed. "You're an Indian Thor. Or Superman. Take your pick."

He snorted. "Please, no. I don't think I can carry the underwear-over-my-pants look."

All that did was give Aditi images of Rian in his underwear. Did he wear tighty whities or boxers? She gulped, unable to stop picturing him in both.

Definitely boxers.

"That would be better for his *chota bheem*," she muttered under her breath. She recalled the feel of his arousal pressed against her the times they'd kissed.

Okay, maybe not chota, she corrected herself right then. There was nothing small about him from what she could tell. Her attention shifted, only to find that he had a gobsmacked look on his face. His lips quivered for a moment before he bit down on it.

"Ch-chota Bheem?" he finally asked, his voice oddly choked.

She blinked, trying to control her internal panic. How had he heard that? She racked her brain for a response that wouldn't involve her having to admit that she'd inadvertently nicknamed his dick after a cartoon with superhuman strength.

"Umm, you didn't like Superman's dressing sense so I figured Chota Bheem is a better option."

Goddamnit, her voice was too shrill. Did he believe her?

"Ah, a dhoti?" He pursed his lips like he was giving it real thought.

She let out a relieved breath.

"Wouldn't it be too airy?" he wondered out loud.

"You can pull it off."

A mischievous glint shined in his eyes. "Are you asking me to strip for you? At least buy me dinner first."

Aditi's jaw dropped open, recognizing those words as hers!

"Rian Bugs Shetty!" she gasped, sounding like a scandalised matron. "Put a lid on that confidence for a minute. Just because you look like you were carved by Michaelangelo is no reason to forget humility."

He leaned a shoulder against the metal edge of the workout machine next to him, crossing his hands across his wide chest in an unreasonably sexy pose. "Are you trying to say that I have a good body?"

Body, face, hair, eyes, mind. The man was a twelve-course meal and she was starving.

"I plead the fifth."

The look of amusement on his face grew.

"That only works in the US, Doc. We live in India."

"The sentiment is the same," she sniffed, refusing to give him any quarter. It really was his own fault for being so inhumanly gorgeous that her brains melted into her knees every time she looked at him.

He leaned in, taunting her in a quiet voice. "Coward."

"I love myself with all my flaws," she piously stated, glancing past him. "You just did a salmon ladder."

The speed with which she changed subjects gave him whiplash.

"Umm, yes. I did. How do you know that?"

"I'm an Oliver Queen fangirl." She threw her palms open with a look that told him he should have guessed at the reason.

"The Green Arrow? Really?"

"He's hot. I can't even do a pull up. I need to hit the gym more often."

Subtle lines of worry marked his forehead.

"You know, apart from the gym, diet is important. Like eating enough greens. And protein. And good fats," he listed, trying to sound as unbothered as possible. "The number on the scale is just that. A number."

Shrewd eyes narrowed at him.

"Have you been talking to my sister?"

"What?" he spluttered. "No."

"You sound exactly like her when she's fishing for information."

He ruffled his hair with one hand and scratched his scalp, groaning when he saw no other way to ask his question. "What is your motivation to go to the gym? Is it your health or. . .?"

"I want to get fit," she explained.

"No crash diets? No extreme weight-loss solutions?"

She shook her head.

"You won't do what you did to yourself before, will you?"

"I won't," she promised, unable to hold back her silly heart from skipping a beat at his sweet concern.

"Good. Because you're not...you shouldn't lose anything. I mean...you're very..." He gestured to her, tracing her shape in the air, awkward, out of words.

Aditi bit back a smile. If this had been anyone else, she would have been offended.

"Are you trying to say that I have a good boooody?" she teasingly sing-songed, leaning back in a way that laid her out for his perusal.

Rian blatantly let his gaze roam about her body, lingering on the way her thigh dimpled in her sport shorts when she crossed one foot over the other, how her workout top hugged her breasts as she put her weight back on her elbows, her back arching just slightly.

Hell yes, she had a fantastic body. All soft and womanly with curves that went on and on. He could spend days tracing her lines. With his hands, with his mouth, with his dick.

"I plead the fifth," he mumbled, grinning sheepishly when she outright laughed. Her full lips spread into a stunning smile, revealing a straight set of teeth. Her chestnut eyes crinkled at the edges and when she met his gaze, she glowed.

Rian's heart thumped like a deranged rabbit on steroids, unable to withstand the force of nature that was Aditi Krishnan's smile. Beyond enamoured, he couldn't stop himself from placing a hand over his heart when he sighed, "Fuck, you're so pretty."

Her eyes grew round, but Rian did not take his words back or hide them under sarcasm and teasing. Being around her made him want to speak his mind with the same forthrightness and innocence as her.

Not that he was the least bit innocent.

Nothing about what he wanted to do to that smiling mouth or lush body was innocent. Nothing about what he had done to her before he'd run off to Singapore was innocent.

Maybe his thoughts showed on his face because her giggles ebbed, and she straightened, staring longingly at him instead.

The next instant, their bodies crashed together, their mouths eagerly seeking each other. It was messy and urgent, but neither cared. Aditi's hands looped around his neck, her chest pressing into his like she couldn't get close enough. With a groan of excitement, his fingers gripped her ponytail, holding her at the perfect angle as his mouth shaped the curve of her lips. His tongue swiped into her warmth, tangling with hers in a familiar yet tantalising dance.

His hands roved over her body possessively, shaping each part with a deliberateness that had her clutching his hair. He cupped and squeezed her lush ass, making her moan and greedily suck his lower lip in response.

He bent, drifting lower, nibbling her chin and the soft skin of her neck, appreciating the buttery smoothness under his mouth. He couldn't get enough. His hands slipped under her shirt, his thumb rubbing the naked skin on her waist, a string of warm metal breaking his touch.

Her stomach grumbled just as he squeezed her hips, causing him to lift his head. "Maybe we should get you fed first," he proposed, cocking a brow.

Aditi shook her head vehemently. "Nope. Forget you heard that." She curved her hand about his nape and pulled him down for another kiss, whining frustratedly when he ended it.

Rian grinned at her eagerness. "We're in a public place," he reminded her. She must have lost her mind along with her shame because the look she gave him told him she didn't care. "Shower first. Then, I'll make you breakfast." He kissed her cheek. "Then," he promised, a wicked glint in his eyes, "I'll introduce you to my chota bheem."

Her brows practically flew off her forehead, eyes comically wide. Cheeks aflame, she hid her face in his chest, mumbling something that sounded a lot like 'China plan back on.'

His body began to shake uncontrollably. His laughter rang in her ears, drawing a defeated giggle from her as well. When she raised her head, she saw what she had missed seeing all week.

A happy man.

The sight of a joyful Rian was like eating warm, pillowy idlis on a cold morning and drinking filter coffee out of her paati's steel tumbler. Comforting, like home, filling her with an unexplainable sense of belonging.

His dimples deepened when their eyes met.

Yes, she accepted, their laughter mingling together to form the sweetest melody. Coming to the gym was a good thing indeed.

25

Tit for Tat

ADITI

"Thank you for the pyjamas. I love them."

Rian glanced sideways from the eggs he was scrambling, his smile at hearing her voice turning into a frown.

"You're not wearing them."

The complaint and disappointment was not hidden.

Aditi scrunched her nose in apology, gesturing to her scrub uniform which she stuffed into her backpack. "I'll have to head to the hospital after breakfast. No point in lounging in my PJs."

With a grunt of acknowledgement, he switched the stove off, dividing the eggs into two plates.

When he went to pour the coffee, Aditi jumped up from her stool and rushed to the cabinet near him.

"Wait! I got you something too!" She spun around and thrust a mug that looked a lot like his usual ones towards him.

"It's a new mug," she declared.

Not wanting to be rude, he very kindly pointed. "Doc, that's my old one."

"No, it isn't."

"It's okay. You don't have to buy me anything."

In response, she blew a raspberry, clearly not impressed with his understanding nature.

"Look," she gestured, turning the mug around. "It says, 3.14% of sailors are pi-rates!" That's when he saw the writing on it. And the symbol of pi, with a crooked pirate hat. She began to chortle, clearly amused with her choice. Her happiness spread through the room, leaching into him. "Isn't it funny?"

"You're the funniest," he replied, dropping a kiss on her forehead in thanks.

"Are you laughing at me or with me?" she demanded, frowning suspiciously at his response. Chuckling, Rian poured the coffee into his new mug, handing her one as well.

Aditi stood beside him while he efficiently chopped and tossed fruits for their breakfast salad, occasionally popping a small piece into her mouth as he worked quickly to get their plates set. Watching Rian work in the kitchen was a pleasure and to her immense delight, he'd forgone wearing his shirt today. The man certainly wasn't subtle about indicating that he was ready for more from her, and she loved that she didn't have to guess with him.

He turned and walked towards the fridge, picking out milk for their coffee. His back muscles rippled when he moved, the single crease down his spine highlighting the perfect symmetry of his body.

She sighed. Now, this was a view she could get used to with each meal, she thought, the spark deep within her igniting when he came closer, a smile on his face. He leaned in, and her heart began to patter like heavy rain on the windshield of a car.

With a murmur of apology, he reached beside her for the pepper grinder, focusing on putting the finishing touches on their food.

That he hadn't grabbed her in a mind-melting kiss confused and bothered her. How was it that she felt so restless next to him and he didn't seem at all affected? But he was standing so close, she could bend forward a couple inches and her lips would meet his bicep. It was right there. She had to do it. There was no good reason why she shouldn't.

"The fuck?" Rian yelped. The pepper mill fell on the counter with a loud thunk, dusty black powder spraying atop the pristine white surface.

He spun towards the woman next to him, rubbing his upper arm furiously. "Did you just bite me?!"

Clearly flustered with her undomesticated behaviour, she shook her head, looking adorably like a young girl who'd been caught filching sweets from the candy jar.

"I. . . no. I was. . .smelling you," she declared, taking an involuntary step back before she was tempted to bite him again.

"You were smelling me?" he repeated incredulously.

"Yes."

"With your teeth?" His disbelief caused his voice to rise in pitch at the end of the question.

"I might have scraped you by mistake," she admitted, trying to remain nonchalant. "But I only wanted a whiff of your cologne."

He blinked once. "I'm not wearing cologne."

Giving up on excuses, she smacked her mug down on the counter near her.

"Okay. Alright. Look here. I have no idea what came over me. It was your fault!" She pointed at him, waving a finger towards his face and then dragging it all the way down. "You were just standing there, with your broad shoulders, your perfect abs, flexing those biceps I could swing on, wearing these indecently hot sweatpants, looking like an entire buffet for someone experiencing a famine. You were asking for it. Grey sweatpants are an invitation."

"Wow. You're gaslighting me," he accused, his tone giving away nothing.

Aditi caved. "I'm a terrible human being," she cried, having no will to continue with her denial.

"You need to apologise."

"I'm so sorry," she immediately offered, truly contrite.

"Sorry enough to let me bite you, too?"

"Of co...What?"

Rian shrugged, mirth dancing in his eyes like bubbling mercury.

"Tit for tat," he explained, laughter gurgling up when her sights dropped to her chest and then his crotch. God, she was a delight.

"I didn't mean that kind of tat, but glad that's an option," he teased, applauding himself for keeping a straight face.

He curled his pointer inwards, beckoning her to him.

He must be a piper, because she was powerless to stop herself from obeying him. She stepped closer, then again until, impatient with her speed, he reached forward, hooked two fingers in the belt loop of her pants and tugged her into him.

"Holy shit," she croaked, her hands gripping his forearms to steady herself. "That was hot."

"You're hot. Very very hot," he muttered, bending towards her. He trapped her lower lip between his teeth before diving in, kissing her with a hunger that made her entire being buzz with the heady feeling only he ever induced.

Breakfast forgotten, Aditi gave in, eagerly meeting his kisses with her own. She tickled his tongue with hers, testing his restraint, humming naughtily when he clutched her harder.

"Aren't you going to say sorry?" he rasped, taking her hand and placing it right over his crotch, gripping her palm over his rapidly hardening cock.

He waited, not pressing for an answer, letting her decide if she wanted to take it further.

"Hands or mouth?" she questioned, her face heating up when his brow rose, clearly impressed.

"Both."

"Yes, Chef." Her whispered response almost had him ready to fuck her against the fridge. But she was leading this, and he was going to let her.

Aditi dropped to her knees, looking up at him the whole time. She didn't know what she was doing anymore except that she had taken Nina's advice. She was thinking with her libido and her currently wet and aching pussy was evidence enough that she was ready for this man to fuck her into the next week.

Harish had affected her confidence when it came to sex. Seeing Rian's response however filled her with an assurance that was bone deep, making her far less self-conscious about what she was going to do than she otherwise would have been.

Teasingly, she ran her nail over the jutting hip bones on either side of him, kissing along the diagonal V until she reached his waistband. Her grip firm, she pulled it down slowly, unprepared for what she found.

Commando? That was one question put to rest. She would have sassed him about it, except what she was looking at had her needing a moment.

Rian's nakedness confirmed one thing. Every physical part of this man was beautiful.

Was it odd to find a penis beautiful? Long, thick, with a prominent vein that seemed to wrap itself from the base, leading right up to his purple crown.

Curiously, she dragged a single finger along the pulsing vein, feeling it throb in response. His velvety skin felt warm, and she inadvertently licked her lips when his cock twitched in her palm. She could barely clasp his girth when she tightened her hold around his base, feeling him grow harder under her touch.

She drew her free palm back and forth a few times, petting him, growing bolder when he let out a sound of encouragement that told her that he was enjoying it. She stroked him until she saw the white bead of precum form a pearl at his head, brushing her thumb over his slit to spread the thick cream around.

"Sunshine," she heard him groan, surprising her with the new endearment. "Put me out of my misery and open up."

Obediently, Aditi parted her lips, wanting to give him the same kind of pleasure he had given her.

"Wider," he ordered, tapping her cheek once before slipping just his tip in, causing her to suck him immediately. "Fuck. Relax your jaw. Let me into your pretty mouth."

Rian gathered her hair into a ponytail, using the grip to guide her head back and forth as Aditi adjusted to his girth, her tongue swirling and flicking his head each time he pulled away. He fed her his length slowly, thrusting little by little until she gagged. He was only a couple inches in, but he waited to see if she wanted to stop, if she was uncomfortable. Instead, she hummed around him, dragging her teeth gently along the underside of his cock. Sparks exploded at the edge of his vision, pleasure and pain building within him rapidly, the erotic view of her sucking him off arousing him to no end. One palm moved to cradle her cheek, drawing her eyes to his. Their gazes held each other while he unabashedly fucked her mouth with shallow thrusts, his firm grip forcing her to keep looking at him as he did.

"Shit, you look like a dream with your lips around me. Can you take more?"

Her hands curled around his thigh, holding him, feeling his muscles tremble in excitement when she anchored herself. Taking that as an agreement, he pushed deeper still, pulling out slightly before he resumed his rhythm, moaning every time his tip hit the back of her throat.

Aditi tried to breathe through Rian commanding her mouth, using her for his pleasure. His hands were gentle on her, caressing her cheek and brushing her hair away from her face even as he continued to fill her again and again.

"Yes, baby, like that," he rasped when she took as much of him in as she could. His palm curved about her throat, feeling his length pulsate within her. His tattooed arm flexed as his grip tightened on her hair, his eyes darkening at the sight of his cock moving in and out of her pink lips. His arousal and her spit made his turgid skin gleam.

He groaned at the carnality of the sight, his hips beginning to move erratically. "You're so good at sucking my cock."

His obvious enjoyment and his dirty praise set Aditi's senses on fire, his excitement streaming into her and making her body come alive with need. With renewed enthusiasm, she wrapped one hand around the base of his shaft, dipping down until her mouth brushed against the edge of her fist, gagging at his tip hitting the back of her throat. She pumped him a few times before letting him take control again. Her eyes watered, the burn in her throat warring with the growing heat in her belly.

"If you don't want me to come in your mouth, tap out," Rian warned her. Perhaps Aditi didn't hear, or maybe she simply didn't care. When he twitched and groaned in relief, his essence flooding her taste buds, Aditi began to gulp, some of it spilling onto her chin.

"Fuck, yes. What a good girl you are. Swallow what you can," he raggedly ordered, the last of his sanity draining with his release. Watching her struggle to keep her lips wrapped around him, her cheeks hollowing out after each gulp, had him jerking yet again, shooting jets of come down her throat. Out of breath, he loosened his hold on her head and used his palm to find support on the counter next to him.

Holy fuck, he silently swore when she released him with a pop. His body thrummed with the glory of a fantastic orgasm. She may have been on her knees for him, but he was definitely the one who had been begging towards the end of it.

Aditi sat back on her haunches with a satisfied smirk, wiping her chin with the back of her hand. "Well, that was something I didn't think I'd be doing this morning."

Chuckling, Rian pulled his joggers back up, extending a hand to help her stand once more.

He wasted no time in bringing his lips to hers, kissing her deeply and tasting his release on her tongue. With one hand under her ass and the other on her waist, he lifted her. Automatically, she wrapped her legs around his hips while he walked them into the living room, clearly intent on doing more of what had begun in the kitchen. He dropped her onto the couch, immediately settling himself between her legs before kissing her amorously.

In no time, she felt the telltale nudge of his arousal hardening, rubbing against the inside of her thigh.

"What brought about this change in you since last week?" she gasped, her nails digging into him when the gentle peck he dropped on her nose was contrasted with one hand cupping her breast, kneading it firmly.

"I missed you, Doc," he admitted, unable to stop himself. Surprise lit her features, the tops of her cheeks turning a ruddy brown. Suddenly, she couldn't meet his eyes.

He slipped his fingers under her chin, turning her face towards him and watching her like he would never fully understand her.

"I fucked your throat raw not moments ago and you're blushing because I told you I missed you?"

"Shut up," she mumbled, looking anywhere except at him. "I'm not blushing."

"Tell me you missed me too," he demanded, his thumb searching for the peak of her breast under the light padding of her bra. She arched up into him, the touch nowhere near satisfactory.

"Why would I miss you?" She nipped his chin. "I had my fictional boyfriends keeping me company."

"Tell me," he insisted as he pressed into her, moving lightly against her throbbing clit. His fingers flirted with the skin at her waist, slipping under her shirt as she mumbled a happy encouragement for him to keep going.

Their moment was broken when her pager buzzed in her pocket, causing them to groan in unison.

"I have to go to the hospital," she informed him, gently trying to push him off but having no success in moving the mountainous human who lay atop her.

"Now?"

She nodded, looking just as regretful as he felt.

"Breakfast?" he asked, pointing his thumb backwards in the general direction of his kitchen.

"Don't have time. Besides," she added, slyly watching him for his reaction. "I just had a banana milkshake."

Rian stared down at her, torn between laughter and disbelief. "You did not just say that."

"I definitely did," she giggled, looking very proud of herself for having slipped in a dirty pun in their conversation. "But now, I do have to leave. I have patients in labour. One of them might be ready for delivery."

He looked so disappointed, she lifted her neck up to kiss the tip of his nose. "I'm sorry, Handsome."

He sat up, helping her as well. "Flattery isn't enough. Say sorry to me later tonight. I have so many ideas for good apologies."

"Well, if you're a really good boy, I might find it in me to make more mistakes to apologise for." She winked, kissing him soundly before sashaying away.

He would not melt, he would not melt, he would not melt.

He kept chanting this in his head, holding on to the last bits of his reason.

"Bugs?" she called, halfway out the front door.

He raised his brows.

"I missed you, too."

He melted like a cube of ice thrown into an active volcano.

If only to avoid the temptation of running after her and hauling her to the nearest bed, he strode into his room, feeling an immense lightness in being.

He whistled one of his favourite tunes—an old Bruno Mars song, unconsciously mouthing the lyrics every so often. It was the closest he'd gotten to singing in over two decades. Unaware, yet inadvertently happier because of it, he stepped into his closet to get dressed for work. It was only when he caught sight of himself in the mirror did he realise what he looked like.

Flushed skin, messy hair, bright eyes.

And the goofiest grin that lit up his face.

26

Shelter

Rian

It was no surprise to him that he ended up standing outside Aditi's clinic at Sanjog General a few hours later, watching the gorgeous woman inside deal with her patients. Rian would have been there earlier, but he had not wanted to seem like an obsessive stalker. He also had his restaurants to check in on. The minute a viable excuse had presented itself, he had wasted no time to rush to the hospital, work be damned.

With a packed lunch that he was sure she'd love, and a very good reason to meet, he had shown up at reception, glad to catch Nina there. He'd wanted to surprise Aditi, and Nina had readily agreed to sign him in as her guest.

Which had led him to this moment, where finally, after months of knowing what she did, he was getting a little glimpse of her professional life.

He caught sight of pictures on the wall, outlining the results of an outreach program on the west coast of India. His lips curved automatically when his eyes landed on a photo of Aditi in her doctor's coat, sitting with a group of local village women, teaching them something from a chart. Their faces were rapt with attention, some watching her with the same awe he often felt himself.

He moved back, sighting yet another photo of her, her face dusty and serious as she spoke with a heavily pregnant woman, a hand of assurance draped over her patient.

This side of her never failed to leave him impressed. As carefree, silly, and vivacious she could be in her personal life, this truly was the part of her that people gravitated to. The part that showed care to another human, exuding confidence and humanity in equal measure. It made them want to rely on her for help and comfort. The longer he stayed with Aditi, the more it made sense why she had chosen this profession.

She was capable of empathy and kindness in a way that left him spellbound. Her intelligence and her drive to help people made her a good doctor but more importantly, a darn good human.

Eager to learn more of her, he stepped to the side and back, searching every corner of the massive board. He grinned when he spotted a picture of Aditi on her bike, in a place he recognized as Velas. From meeting her there to having her live in his home, he couldn't believe how far life had brought him. He recalled chastising her because of her honesty at their first meeting, wishing that he'd never cross paths with her again.

He was beyond thankful that this particular wish had not been fulfilled.

"Why won't you listen? You stupid moron."

Brows knit, Rian turned, his gaze falling immediately upon a man in a brown linen shirt struggling with a young boy. The child could not have been more than five, but was putting up a fight, unwilling to get up.

"We have to go, idiot!" the man yelled. The little child reached for some crayons on the table near him again, clearly not wanting to leave his colouring behind. "Listen to me! Leave that stupid paper alone, you good for nothing fool!" He yanked him by the arm, getting worked up by the boy's defiance.

The child made gurgling sounds, trying to get loose even as the man, presumably his father, shook his tiny body. He twisted with a wail, his small eyes meeting Rian's and it became clear. The child had Down syndrome.

The older man ripped the crayon from the boy's unwilling fingers with a force that made the other parents in the room wince. No one said a word however, unwilling to interact with someone who was so aggressive.

Rian broke out in a cold sweat, his peripheral vision dimming until all he could see was the child's distressed face. Suddenly, it was him there. No one to tend to his wounds. Huddling in the cold. Feeling disgraced and unwanted.

"Leave him alone," Rian called out, unable to stop himself. The father looked up, bristling at the unwelcome order.

"Whoever you are, stay out of this," he snarled, throwing a look of disgust at his son. "My bad luck that I have a stupid child to deal with."

"Don't insult him like that," Rian warned, taking a step towards them both.

"What's it to you? Shut up and mind your business. When you have a mentally retarded son yourself, give me your advice then." His grip visibly tightened over bony arms when the little guy tried to wiggle away, his one pointed attention still upon the art supplies he was being forced to desert.

With an impatient curse, the man unceremoniously smacked the back of the boy's head. A thump resounded across the waiting room. Rian's stomach lurched at the child's cry when he fell, huddling into himself, expecting another blow.

The defensive stance was enough for Rian to guess that this boy had known abuse before. He couldn't recollect when he'd moved towards them but within the next few seconds, he'd thrown a sideways punch at the father, knocking him into the row of chairs behind.

The commotion around them grew; children crying, someone screeching in fear of the impending fight. The blood rushing through his veins pounded in his ears, drowning out every other sound except the pitiful whimpers of the little child beside him. Furious, Rian grabbed the man and hurled him against the wall before he could escape.

Collar held in large firsts, Rian pulled him up, higher and higher until the man's toes barely grazed the floor, pinning him in place like a wayward pup.

"Did you feel powerful using your strength against a kid?" he snarled, his eyes red, the rage in his belly screaming for justice. "Do you like being held by the cuff of your neck and thrown about like the worthless pig you are?"

His opponent's eyes bulged, fear evident in them. Desperate nails dug into Rian's wrist, clawing for release, but he barely felt the scratch.

He could count on one hand how many times in his adult life he'd been driven to physical violence. His size had always made him extra cautious of using it as an advantage against others. This worm deserved no such consideration.

"Why are you doing this?" said worm croaked, the bruise on his cheek turning a dull shade of purple.

Rian's grip tightened, his knuckles pushing into the man's throat where his pulse throbbed rapidly, making it harder for him to breath.

"Because you are a piece of shit who deserves to have his fingers cut off for hitting a defenceless child."

He leaned in, maintaining eye contact when he dropped his voice so that only the two of them would hear it.

"Listen to me and listen well. I've seen your face. Someone related to you must be a patient here. Finding out your identity and where you live will not be a problem for me. If you think I will not be sending the police to check on your family regularly after this, you are wrong. And if I ever find that you have raised your hand to this child, you will not be left in a capacity to raise your body off the hospital bed. Do you understand me?"

The man's nostrils flared, torn between false ego and pride.

"I asked, do you understand me?!" Rian thundered, shaking him hard enough that his skull connected with the wall.

"Yes. Yes," he groaned. "I won't hit him again."

The rush of feet behind them announced the arrival of security.

Rian thrust the man away, staggering back, unable to keep his hands from shaking now that he had nothing left to hold. Little tremors pulsed through him, spreading before he could stop them. His body trembled like it was going into shock. The beat of his heart transformed into a speedy gallop, threatening to rip right out of his chest. He turned, stiffening when saw Aditi watching him, her clear brown eyes muddied with emotions he was too afraid to guess.

His stomach plummeted. For a second, he wondered if she would hate him now that she'd seen how violent he could get. Would she fear him? Would she let him explain?

"Doc," he gulped, barely choking the word out.

"Come with me," she ordered, taking his hand in hers.

Rian didn't know whether she was going to show him the way out of the hospital or elsewhere. All he could do was follow her, each step heavier than the last. A minute or so later, he found himself being pulled into an empty hospital room. The click of the door felt absolute and he waited for judgement, like a criminal about to be sentenced for his crimes.

"Are you okay?" Aditi stepped closer, one hand brushing up his forearm and it took everything in him not to grab her.

His vision went blurry. "I couldn't help it, Doc. I didn't mean. . ."

He gasped, struggling to take another breath in. His voice was barely above a whisper but even that had been too trying an attempt.

"Hey," she cupped his face, bringing her attention to him. "Breathe, Rian."

"What you saw–," he tried again, unable to continue. To his horror, the burn in his throat shot up and the pressure behind his eyes increased. "Aditi," he whimpered, his wheezing loud and hollow in the otherwise silent room.

She directed him to sit on the clean bed nearby, standing between his spread knees.

"I saw, Rian. I know it must have been hard for you. I've had problems with that man before. I understand."

He raised a trembling hand to wipe the sweat that had collected above his lips. The air in his lungs seemed trapped, and he could feel his panic rising.

"Don't hate me," he choked out, the knot within him tightening with each passing moment.

A split second later, Aditi threw her arms about his shoulders, gathering him close.

Before he could hold it in, an agonised sob erupted from his throat, hot tears leaving a damp trail down his cheeks. Maybe he wept for five minutes, or perhaps it was fifteen. Eyes shut, he buried his face in her chest, letting her scent, the steady rhythm of her heart, and the gentle strokes of her hand against his head and back calm him.

"Feel better?" she asked kindly when his body finally stopped shuddering. She cupped his cheek to look at him. Her thumbs swiped in a delicate arc over his cheekbones, flicking away the remnant dampness.

"My chest hurts," he croaked, fisting her coat on either side of her waist. He wasn't ready to let her go.

Sensing his distress, Aditi adjusted his arms to loop around her waist, giving him full control of how close or far he allowed her to go. "Breathe for me," she coached him, blowing cool air on his forehead.

She glanced down into the tense face of the man she adored, her heart breaking for him. She knew the history of the little boy with Down syndrome very well. Seeing him being mistreated would have brought back a lot of unresolved trauma for Rian. His burst of violence, and his subsequent breakdown confirmed her suspicion. To keep him from dwelling on it, she asked him something that had been on her mind for a while.

"Bugs, why do you never speak about your dyslexia?"

As suspected, the change in topic and the unexpected question had him glancing up.

"How did you know?"

Aditi shrugged, letting her hands smooth the jacket at his shoulders. She brought one hand up and gently sifted through his hair, twirling a finger around a wavy lock. The action was as calming for her as it was for him.

"You said school was tough. I noticed that you take a lot of voice notes, tons of reminders also. You also asked me to read for you. You're constantly using speech apps. I saw you using a dyslexia font on the computer in your home office. Wasn't hard to put two and two together."

"Yeah."

Her brows met in the middle, confused by that answer. She peered down at him, lips pursed.

"Yeah? I want to know how you've coped."

Rian sighed, leaning into her palm in a quiet demand for her to continue stroking his hair, one with which she complied without delay.

He picked his words judiciously.

"There were a lot of attempts made to 'fix' me when I was young. Tutors came and gave up. I was angry for a lot of it because I felt stupid. I didn't know how to make my brain work. I felt like I wasn't capable of the most basic things for a long time. Nanamma started doing art with me to see if that would help me concentrate. Muggu. First with chalk, then with rice powder."

"Muggu?"

"Like, rangoli, but plain," he explained.

"Oh," Aditi exclaimed, nodding in understanding. "We have that too. Kolam, in Tamil. We have it on the ground, just outside the threshold of our house."

Rian acknowledged that with a tilt of his chin.

"The geometric nature of the designs helped me figure out patterns," he admitted, his mind going back to the days when, as a young boy, he would sit in the backyard with his grandmother for hours, drawing intricate motifs on the cool earth. It was the first time he had made something beautiful that had given him a sense of accomplishment. "That made it better. For a while."

"What happened after?"

"My mother happened. She sent Nanamma away."

Maybe it was just in his head, but he thought he felt Aditi stiffen. "Then?" she asked.

"I was left to fend for myself for long periods. Eventually, I found myself in the kitchen. Nanamma would give me instructions over the phone sometimes to get me started, but I didn't have to follow any specific rules. I could create things however I wanted. I'd watch our chef and retain things I didn't think I would. I felt free. Like being me wasn't so bad."

Aditi's thumb kept stroking his forehead, his nose, wherever she could reach, wordlessly comforting him.

"It took me a while to figure out how to work with dyslexia," he confessed. "But I did. I found people to help me as I got older, worked through what I could and found alternatives when possible. Technology helped. Having a PA who knows how particular I am about reminders, who understands my need to be obsessively organised with my schedule—that helped too. My mother was surprised that I amounted to anything at all."

"Let's not talk about your mother," Aditi requested, her smile tight. "I feel the urgent need to introduce my fist to her nose every time you mention her."

"I didn't think you were a violent person."

Small palms cradled his jaw, lifting his face to hers.

"When someone hurts the people I care about," she announced, her tone utterly serious, "I tend to not like them very much."

Rian couldn't think of a response, feeling the warmth of her words flush out the toxins from his altercation at the clinic.

"Do you know I admire you a lot?" Aditi said, one tiny finger casually tracing his eyebrows and pressing along pressure points that made him close his eyes in relief. "Especially after what you told me, my admiration has only grown."

The gentle ministrations of her fingers along the edges of his temple had him feeling like she was pouring a soothing balm over his hurt. "I hope you're not pitying me, Doc," he murmured, wanting her to never stop touching him.

"Of course not! Look at you. You have a flourishing career and a bright future. You're one of the most desirable men on this side of the country. I don't pity successful people. But I do appreciate how hard you must have worked to overcome the challenges you had."

His lips quirked automatically. "You called me desirable," he said, lashes fluttering open to see that she was smiling.

"I also called you successful."

"Good way to balance the compliment."

A huff of laughter escaped her. "It may seem silly, but I'm proud of you."

"That's not silly."

"No?" she confirmed, biting her lower lip, looking surprisingly unsure. "I didn't want to come across as patronising you."

His hold on her waist tightened. "It felt good to hear it."

"I'm glad. I meant it, by the way."

"So, it's not just because you've been trying to distract me from remembering that I almost broke a man's face?"

Aditi gasped loudly, looking about the room in an exaggerated action before glancing at him again.

"You did?" she asked in an affected voice, eyes glittering with mischief. "I didn't see that. I thought we were just hanging out. Like friends do."

If he hadn't been won over by her before, her charming attempt to make him smile, ignoring that he'd misbehaved in her place of work, had him wanting to go down on his knees for her.

"Why do you insist that we're friends?" he asked instead.

"Because I like you, of course."

It was that easy and she was unafraid to say it.

"Doc?" he called, his voice soft, his affection for her evident in the way he uttered her nickname.

"Hmm?"

"I like you, too."

It may have felt like a big step for him, but all she did was giggle.

"I suspected it," she teased him, shaking her head like he was silly to think this would remain hidden from her. Like *he* could remain hidden.

"Hug me a little longer? I think I need it to be calm."

The look she bestowed upon him, full of gentleness and understanding, had him leaning in and nuzzling into the nook of her neck.

"You don't ever need a reason to ask me for a hug," she whispered, embracing him. She stroked his head like he was a young boy she was protecting instead of an adult man who generally towered over her and outweighed her by at least thirty kilos.

He thought she would talk even more to occupy him, but apparently, she knew exactly when to say something to calm him, and when he needed the comfort of silence. The comfort of being held. The comfort of just. . .her. God, she was so easy to love.

His breath halted and his heart skipped a beat, the revelation hitting him with the force of an avalanche.

L. . .love?

The absolute shock that ripped through him had him breaking out of her embrace, shooting up to a standing position. He looked down into her concerned face, and he saw his future.

Every moment of every day belonged to her.

All of him belonged to Aditi.

She'd claimed him so thoroughly that he had no way of escaping it.

This was it, he realised, cupping her face so that his large hands covered her soft cheeks. His sights roamed over features like he was seeing her for the first time, the seed of hope within him germinating in her warmth.

This was what he'd thought he could avoid.

But how did one avoid the sun when it shone so brightly?

How did one avoid the rainbow that dominated their sky after a rainstorm?

How could Rian have ever avoided Aditi, when she was the shelter he'd been missing all his life?

In awe, he bent towards her. He wasn't certain if he kissed her or if she raised her lips to meet his. All he knew was that a pack of bloodthirsty wolves licking at his feet couldn't have pulled him away from her at that time. He brushed his lips against hers in a slow, long caress, going back again and again to place the sweetest kisses across her mouth, like she was the most delicate and precious thing he'd ever held.

For him, she was.

"What was that for?" Aditi murmured when they broke apart, bemused.

He said the only thing that came to mind. "That's how they say thanks in France."

"We're in India."

"I know. Just trying to broaden your horizon. Nothing wrong with adopting good things from different cultures." He kissed her again, as if giving her proof of the benefit of said culture. He felt her smile against his mouth.

"Bugs?"

"Hmm?"

"As much as I love being thanked by you, I need to get back to work. Do you know your way out?"

Rian gulped, nodding at her, his mind still whirling with the newness of his discovery.

"I'll see you at home?" he managed to ask, her hand clasped in his.

"Yes. I'll be back in time for the Diwali party."

"Good." He tried to smile. "I don't think Kaya will let me enter her house without you."

"You won't have to find out," she promised.

It was quiet once more, and all Rian could do was stare at her like a complete muttonhead. She probably chalked his weird behaviour up to his panic attack, because she was far more patient than he would have expected her to be.

"Rian?" she prompted eventually, when the silence got too long.

"Yeah?"

"Are you going to let go of my hand?"

Cheeks aflame, Rian dropped his hold on her.

"Bye, Doc," he replied, already counting down the minutes until he would see her again.

27

A String of Flowers

RIAN

Rian pinched his fingers together, picking up a small portion of the dried white rice powder from the container Nanamma always kept filled.

Holding his hand steady a few inches off the tiled floor, he carefully sprinkled some at the edges of the geometric design he'd been working on. The muggu he'd made was not his best. He was out of touch, but it gave him something to do while he waited for the two women within his house to finish getting dressed.

Every Hindu household across India today would have something similarly decorative to celebrate Diwali. Even as he'd driven home from the hospital, he'd seen massive crowds filling the markets with late shoppers, laughing men and women carrying bags of pretty new clothes to wear for the evening, children chattering excitedly about the multitude of firecrackers they would light at night.

The happy chaos around him had failed to replace the constant hum of his new reality.

He was in love with Aditi.

To accept this had taken him time, but now that he was here, there was no avoiding it. It was love. But it was unlike any love he'd experienced before.

Despite having never been in a relationship, Rian wasn't a stranger to love. He'd been in love with Kaya in the past. For years, his feelings had remained unrequited. He'd watched from the sidelines, unable to do anything except wait to see if Kaya changed her mind. Even then, he'd known it was futile.

Kaya loved him, but not romantically. So, he'd become what she had needed. A friend, a confidante, and a silent supporter of her attempt to break away from the confines she'd been placed under by an authoritarian father.

When she'd found love with her husband, Rian had felt relieved.

Sure, he'd had other emotions to work through before he'd fully handed Kaya's future to Arjun. He'd been protecting her for so many years, it had taken an unknown woman with pretty brown eyes and a filter-less mouth telling him to cut his losses, to truly let go. A wry grin graced his lips. From their very first meeting, Aditi had managed to get under his skin.

His track record of loving people was rife with issues, riddled with doubts and guilt.

He'd loved his father. His father died.

He'd loved his mother. She hated him.

He'd loved Nanamma. She'd suffered his mother's wrath and had been, along with her husband, forced to leave her own home to keep the peace.

He'd loved Kaya. But only he knew that he'd hurt Kaya in ways she was unaware of, even today.

Now, he loved Aditi. And he was terrified. How could he not be? This love was easy, and he was unused to it being simple. It made him want to question it. Reject it.

He'd been ready to live a life alone, because he'd been exhausted with the complications of love. His experiences had given him no reason to trust his ability to love well, and in a way that would be reciprocated. Then, unexpectedly, Aditi had burst onto the scene and pranced right into his chosen solitude, filling the silence with her laughter.

His life was forever changed, and he had to try to figure out how to move ahead.

With her.

No sooner had he thought this than he heard movement behind him. He glanced back, slowly turning as his eyes were drawn to pretty feet emerging first from around the corner, covered quickly by a flash of silky material. He spotted a dainty hand adjusting the folds of the skirt so it fell perfectly. His eyes travelled up the length of her, taking in the soft curve of her hip as it came into view and the dip in her waist before it was covered by the open end of her saree. Whatever he'd expected, he hadn't been prepared for this.

Focused on her saree, she walked towards him, her hair cascading down one side in a profusion of gentle waves, her footsteps accompanied by the sounds of the anklets he assumed she'd worn. She raised her head, her kohl-lined eyes catching his, and he was afraid she would know just by looking at him, what he felt.

How had he ever thought he could resist such a gorgeous human being?

How had he even entertained the idea that he could remain aloof from her?

He was an absolute idiot, he realised, unable to take his eyes off her for even a second. Months of effort and lying to himself about how he felt, when he should have given in at her first smile.

Perhaps the thought of her smile had etched one on his face too, because Aditi's gait slowed, her mouth tilting ever so slightly in response.

"Look at you being such a well-cultured boy," she teased, pointing to the design he'd just finished. She fixed her pallu over one forearm, gliding towards him. "You've been brought up so well. You cook, you clean, you pray, you make pretty kolams. Perfect husband material. Are you sure you don't want to marry me?" she joked, expecting him to react as he'd done many moons ago when she'd first brought it up.

All he did however was watch her with that disconcerting expression that made her nervous.

Assuming that he was still not fully recovered from his bout of panic, she struck a deliberately exaggerated pose like the ones she'd seen in magazines, with her elbows sticking out in awkward angles. When he still didn't laugh, she twirled once, asking him in a bright and breezy tone, "What do you think?"

"It's. . ." Rian cleared his throat, trying to get words out. "You look beautiful."

Surprised by his candor when she was trying to be silly, Aditi stared at him, unable to control the rush of blood to her face. She watched him pull out a small paper packet from the pocket of his kurta, and extend it to her.

Oddly nervous, she unwrapped the package to reveal thick strings of jasmine bunched together to form a heavy and luscious-looking gajra.

"For me?" she asked, glancing at him in surprise. Before she could take the flowers out, Rian held the garland on one end. "Rian?" she questioned when he gestured to her to turn.

Aditi felt his body close in behind her, his warmth engulfing her. She felt the weight of the gajra settle against the back of her head when he delicately adjusted her hairpin to keep the flowers in place.

For a man as big as him, his capacity to be so sweet and gentle with her made her heart clench. The pads of his fingers brushed against the naked skin where her neck met her shoulder, and her breath caught. Unable to help herself, she threw him a glance.

"Perfect," he murmured, running one knuckle down her cheek, utterly enchanted by her deep blush. "Now, you look perfect."

Her body broke out in goosebumps, his husky declaration causing her gut to develop knots and her nipples to harden. She turned towards him, placing a tentative hand upon his chest. Was it her or was his heart beating hard as well?

The sound of Nanamma calling them had him taking a step back, gulping audibly as he pulled out his phone to instruct his driver to bring the car around.

Aditi, however, couldn't move on from that moment.

She was wrapped in a feeling she couldn't recognize.

She'd expected the attraction between them to lead to something fun in the bedroom. While their encounters so far had certainly whetted her appetite for more, she hadn't expected his gifts and compliments to affect her so much.

There was something different about him today and try as she might, she couldn't explain why she felt that way. She made no progress in understanding his changed behaviour as they drove to the Diwali party. Even after the enthusiastic welcome they'd received at Kaya and Arjun's home, Rian remained silent and contemplative, leaving her with only Nanamma and her new friends for company.

Vihaan, glad to see her once more, seemed happy to entertain her when the others dispersed. She shot him a polite smile, walking alongside him in the garden and trying to focus on what he was saying instead of letting her mind remain mired in solving a puzzle she wasn't certain existed.

Unbeknownst to her, the man who'd jumbled her thoughts stood just inside the widescreen patio doors, watching her like he would never tire of the view. There were a hundred people at this party, but only one who could keep his attention riveted like this. Now that he'd understood why, there was no sense in denying that these emotions felt permanent.

Which is why her unserious proposal from earlier kept playing in his mind over and over again. He knew she'd meant it as a joke, because she'd asked him exactly this question before when she'd been frustrated after her many failed dates. He'd shut her down immediately that night. But today? He sighed, held by the invisible binds her question had wrapped around him. Binds that led to her. He was her captive, and she held the keys to his freedom.

No, he corrected himself. She *was* his freedom.

"There you are. I brought you your favourites." He turned to see Nanamma hobble towards him with a plate of snacks in her hand. She came to stand beside him, sighting Aditi strolling across the lawn with Vihaan beside her.

Chitra pointed towards Aditi with a jalebi in her hand. "She's a nice girl, isn't she?"

He nodded. "Yes, she is." *The best.*

Nanamma seemed pleased with that response. "I was afraid you wouldn't see that after how you reacted when you met her the first night."

He had to bring a fist up to his mouth, coughing behind it to hide his laugh. He'd very literally fallen head over heels. He would never forget it.

"I'm glad you two have become friends," his grandmother declared.

Friends? Sure. He could accept that. They were friends who had touched, hugged, kissed, and tasted each other's bodies. Rian felt his collar grow tight.

He declined the delicacies his grandmother offered to him. Picking up her weathered hand in his, he placed it on the crook of his arm and led her down the deck to get some fresh air.

"She hasn't had the best of luck on those arranged dates that her parents or I suggested," Nanamma piped up again. For some unknown reason, she seemed determined to continue discussing Aditi today. Rian had no clue what sort of input was expected from him. As far as he was concerned, he was fucking ecstatic that those dates had been terrible. "Maybe I haven't been searching in the right place. I should have been looking for a boy a lot closer to me."

Rian's pulse thumped eagerly. "Nanamma, I. . ."

"Vihaan and Aditi seem to be getting along well."

What the fuck? He whipped around to see his grandmother, not bothering to conceal his shock.

Nanamma pointed towards the two of them in the distance, laughing at something together. Rian felt the warmth drain from him.

"Look at them," she said, watching her grandson with a calculative look he missed due to his preoccupation. "They seem happy and make a good-looking couple."

No they don't! he wanted to yell, barely tamping down the urge to throw a fit at the mere suggestion.

"Vihaan is not interested in settling down right now."

Did he sound anxious? If he did, his grandmother didn't pick up on it.

"Nonsense," she guffawed, as if Vihaan's opinion wasn't worth a consideration. "I was talking to his mother just inside and she is desperate to see him get married soon. He's thirty-one already."

"So?" Rian argued. "I'm thirty."

"You're *only* thirty, and you don't *want* to be married," Nanamma volleyed right back, the smile on her face borderline sinister. "And you heard how happy Vihaan was to see Aditi, right? I'm sure if I bring her proposal to Mrs. Oberoi, something good will come out of it."

Rian was positive he was going to lose his mind. The world was conspiring against him to drive him insane. He should tell Nanamma. He should speak up now before he lost Aditi.

"Nan. . ." He fell quiet when a group of ladies hailed her.

He watched his grandmother walk away, possibly continuing to plan Aditi's wedding with his friend instead of him, and it felt like a cruel joke. He had only himself to blame, of course. He'd denied wanting to be in a relationship so many times, no wonder Nanamma had given up.

His mood dampened considerably when he caught sight of Aditi happily chattering away with Vihaan. Possessiveness threatened to rear its head once more, like it had the evening he'd crashed her date.

But he wouldn't make that mistake again.

A bottle of water in his hand, Rian stalked off to find a darkened corner to sulk in.

This time, he would wait until she came to him.

28

Triumph

RIAN

"**B**ugs?"

Rian looked up from the blue waters of the swimming pool that had kept him distracted, only to find the object of his turmoil strolling towards him, looking resplendent. The saree she'd worn hugged her body lovingly, showcasing every curve to perfection.

He had no doubt that she'd left a trail of victims in her wake tonight. He was one of them.

"What are you doing out here alone?"

Aditi had been searching for Rian for some time. The pool area where he stood was tucked away on the side of the house. The massive outdoor garden where the Diwali party was in full swing was behind her, far enough away that the music and games did not seem intrusive in this otherwise silent space.

He had been absent from the party for far too long for her not to notice.

With his breakdown fresh in her memory, the possibility that he might be silently suffering had worried her to no end.

"Are you okay?" she asked, coming to a halt beside him.

He tipped his chin once, the answer allowing her to breathe easily once more.

She reached for his hand. "Come with me."

"Where?"

"Back to the party. Everyone has been missing you."

"And you?" Maybe he was being needy, but he was beyond caring. "Did my absence make a difference to you?"

Her forehead creased in confusion. "I came out here to look for you, didn't I?"

She had. For now, that was enough hope for Rian to hold on to. When she tugged at his arm, trying to lead him back to the house, he held her still.

"Are you set on your plan?"

"What plan?" she questioned, feeling exasperated. She let go and turned to him, arms crossed. "Speak clearly, Rian. What is it that you're talking about?"

A look of frustration crossed his features and he groaned, rubbing his eyes with one hand as he turned to the side. Aditi tilted her head, leaning to see his face, which caused him to turn farther away. Her sharp ears picked up his agitated mumbling. *Wait. Hanuman Chalisa? Was he praying?*

With a sound of determination, he spun towards her, surprising her with his speed.

"You said you wanted to find someone to marry. Are you still—"

"Looking?" She lifted one shoulder in a shrug.

"Do you really think marriage is a good idea?"

She released a contemplative sound, distracted by the gentle murmur of the water near her, its fluid surface dancing in a hypnotic rhythm.

"I don't know, Rian," she finally replied. "I still want a family. I want children. In the society we live in, neither of those is possible without a husband."

"So, a husband is just an unfortunate requirement?"

"No." She laughed softly, shaking her head. "What I truly want is someone who is willing to work at navigating life with me. Marriage will be only as good an idea as the quality of partner I find. If he turns out to be a mismatch, then I'll have to deal with the fallout, too. But I can't give up the possibility of getting everything I want because I am scared of failure."

Hearing her talk, Rian was reminded of a poem Kaya had quoted to him once, a line from which he had never forgotten. It'd suggested that the existence of a mature mind and a romantic heart in the same body was a tragedy. Perhaps the poet had met a woman like Aditi to have written those words and maybe it was the reflection of this emotion that had drawn him to her and kept him invested. Because he saw the dichotomy in the person she was and though it might frustrate others, it fascinated him. Someone else might need her to fit into a mould that was easier to understand. He wouldn't.

He wanted her exactly as she was. Unequivocally.

As for what she wanted, he could give her that. Romance, and a life of responsibility—both.

He could wait until she fell in love with him also, seeing more to their relationship than a temporary fling. He wouldn't allow any experience in her life to fall under the category of a tragedy. As long as he was alive, Aditi would only know triumph.

"Doc?" he called, a sudden peace falling upon him when his path forward became clear.

"Hmm?"

"Do you remember the question you asked me earlier this evening?"

Brows furrowed, she turned to face him, the slight shake of her head indicating her confusion.

"You asked if I was sure I didn't want to marry you."

She straightened, goosebumps breaking out across her skin as he stepped closer.

"The answer is yes. I do." He clasped the tips of her fingers in his hand. "I want to marry you."

"Ha. Ha. Very funny."

"I'm not joking."

She tried to step back, needing space to stop herself from falling for his words, only for his grip to tighten.

"You don't want marriage," she reminded herself as much as him.

"But you do," he replied, tugging her into him, his arm encircling her waist so that she couldn't distance herself anymore. "And I," he emphasised, his voice dropping an octave, "want you."

Aditi opened her mouth, closing it ineffectually when her mind refused to cooperate. She felt like she'd been thrust into a vacuum where only Rian existed with her.

He was all she could see and hear. Him, his silver eyes stripping away her defences, his words building a world she'd been too afraid to imagine. She felt trapped with longing for what he could give her. Warm fingers slid under her chin, keeping her arrested.

"I don't know if I'll make a good husband but your standards seem so low, I might have a chance at making you happy. You want a partner who isn't perfect but willing to learn? I can be him. Whatever you need, ask me. So no more of those stupid matrimonial dates, okay?"

At her incredulous huff, he continued, determined to make her understand how serious he was.

"If I have to see another person sit across from you, looking at you like he has a shot at taking you home, I'll end up going insane from curbing my jealousy. For their sake and mine, stop going on dates with other men."

Aditi was certain she looked as dumbstruck as she felt. "You were jealous?"

"Unhinged, to be precise."

He brought her hand up and placed a soft kiss on her open palm, one that she felt in her bones.

"Say yes," he prompted, his eyes boring into her like he would see into her soul and mesmerise even those parts that weren't already under his spell.

"Yes," she heard herself breathlessly whisper.

The absolute feeling of victory that shook his being was unexplainable. Rian wanted to hide away from the world with just Aditi, rejoicing in her acceptance. He stepped back, knowing that if he kept touching her, he'd end up kissing her in public and giving the partygoers a live show.

"Let's go, Doc."

She pointed to the Diwali party behind them and he shook his head.

Ten minutes later, he was driving them home.

"What if someone saw us leave?" she asked, watching people crowding the side streets, the noise of fireworks interrupting the soft music from the stereo.

"Then they'll speculate that we're together."

Rian didn't seem bothered, but Aditi didn't want people to gossip unnecessarily.

"Maybe they won't notice."

"Then I'll make sure to tell them."

His declaration silenced her. He may as well have tattooed 'mine' in large, bold letters across her forehead.

"Keep talking to me," he added after a moment.

"Why?" she asked, scrunching her nose at the odd request.

"Because if you don't distract me, I might park this car on a random road and fuck you in the back seat."

Her eyes widened comically at his very honest response. Far from being scandalised however, his admittance only caused a familiar tug of desire in her gut. "Maybe not for our first time," she suggested, unable to think about anything other than Rian doing very naughty things to her now. "But I don't mind trying the back seat in the future."

The vein in his head bulged.

"Okay!" she panicked, racking her brain for another reason. "Umm...at least we're in a car and not on your bike. Imagine having to balance on a bike while we..."

"Not. Helping," Rian bit out, his jaw clenching so tightly that she thought it would splinter.

"Sorry," she mumbled, folding her hands one on top of the other in a prim pose.

"Show me your feet."

Confused but unwilling to torment him like she usually would, she pulled up her saree, exposing a little above her ankles.

Rian glanced over at her once, then twice, before his forehead crunched.

"You're not wearing anklets," he finally said, eyes on the road. "But I could have sworn I heard the sounds. Why?"

"Oh. I'm wearing something that has the same chimes as anklets do."

"What is it?"

"Well, you see," she started in that tone that told Rian he was in for story time. "When I started losing too much weight, my paati got an arana kayiru made for me to wear."

"A what?"

"An arana kayiru. It's usually a black thread to ward off bad energy, but the one I have is in gold with a protection charm from the temple. Paati also added the chimes on it to make it pretty. Hence, the sound."

"Doc, any chance this gold chain is around your waist? I think I felt it before."

"Of course it's around my waist. Where did you think it was?"

He didn't think. He drove faster.

29

The Firefly

ADITI

HOW THEY GOT HOME that night was something Aditi would never remember. What *would* stand out in her memory however was the nervousness she'd felt at Rian's silence, his pointed attention on the road ahead, and the increasing tension every time their eyes met.

It didn't help either of them that they were forced to huddle into the back of their elevator when a rush of visitors and children kept stepping in and out of every floor.

The slight touch of his fingers at her waist, the heat of his breath on her neck, and the unmistakeable feel of his anatomy when her back brushed his front threatened to knock her unconscious with the depth of want that it created.

Keeping his distance, Rian led her into the apartment, allowing her to enter first. She turned as the door clicked shut, only to be pushed up against the wall, his mouth searching for hers.

He kissed her like a rapacious conqueror, claiming every sigh and moan, his tongue tangling with hers in a delicious game that had him excited for what the night would bring. Breaking off, he bent down and hooked an arm behind her knees, scooping her up in his arms. Her heels clattered to the floor and her purse slipped from her hands when she wrapped her arms around his shoulders.

Aditi continued to place hungry kisses along the edge of his jaw, scraping her teeth along his neck before biting him, making him stumble once.

"You're trouble," he grumbled, pinching her waist where he held her, causing her to gasp. She arched up and nipped his ear, purring into it, "Then I guess you better punish me."

This time, he definitely did stumble. He made it to his room on shaky legs, kicking the door shut before letting her foot touch the ground again.

Aditi prepared herself to be taken by the storm he'd create, only to be left waiting when he took two steps back, watching her as though he was memorising her in that moment.

"Twirl for me," he asked, surprising her again.

He extended his open palm towards her, waiting until she placed her hand in his. His fingers tightened as he lifted their joined hands over her head, slowly spinning her once, then again, his sights drinking in the way her saree shimmered as it caught the light. She was like a firefly who had led him out of darkness, and tonight, she embodied it.

"You're so beautiful. I couldn't take my eyes off you all evening."

His admission felt like a drug. She'd never been a glutton for compliments before but with Rian, she wanted his attention. Even so, she couldn't keep her truth in. "I can't take my eyes off you at any time, Bugs. Even when I don't want to, I can't stop looking."

Rian hadn't realised how much he'd needed to hear that until she said it. He brought her close, allowing her to loop her arms over his neck. His hand slipped under her saree to caress the skin at her waist, his thumb brushing back and forth in an arc while he dropped soft kisses all along her arm, finally settling against her mouth.

"Undress me," he directed her, displaying remarkable patience while she unbuttoned his top with shaky fingers. Rian needed the time as much as she did. He didn't want to rush into this and screw things up like her ex-boyfriend. When she left his bed after tonight, it would be with the knowledge that he had made it impossible for her to stay away.

If that meant exercising restraint and planning each step with a precision he hadn't before used in the bedroom, then that was exactly what he would do.

The rustle of his silk kurta sliding onto the floor had Aditi glancing at him, almost asking for permission to touch him now. With his hand curled over hers, he pressed her palm into the centre of his chest, letting her feel the pounding within.

Just as quietly she mirrored his actions, holding his hand over her blouse, between her breasts, allowing him to understand that she was just as affected as him.

"Turn around," he instructed her, his voice low.

Without hesitation, she complied, allowing him to unfasten her necklace and unhook her earrings with a dexterity that surprised her. He shifted her hair to fall across her front. The deep back of her blouse exposed her skin, tempting him to lightly trace the delicate bumps of her spine. He delighted in her sharp intake of breath when he trailed his fingers up from her lower back all the way to her neck, curling about her nape. He gently forced her to look back at him, his thumb resting on the fluttering pulse in her throat that spoke of his effect on her.

"I haven't eaten a single Diwali snack today," he said, untying the knot that kept her blouse together. He tugged her top off until her breasts were exposed. "You'll be my first."

She let out a shaky laugh, wanting desperately to tease him for that cheesy line, to say something that would distract her from the reality that he would see her body today. Blessedly, all she could focus on was his hand slithering across her belly, pressing her back into his naked chest.

She felt him unclip the garland from her hair, running the cool ends along her collarbones. Her skin erupted in goosebumps at the sensual teasing, her nipples hardening immeasurably when he ran the the flowers against her breasts, sliding them over her engorged peak.

"What are you doing?" she whimpered, her body shaking though his touch was light.

"Worshipping you."

Rian stripped the flowers from the string, gathering them in his palm. He raised his hand over her head and showered her in snowy jasmine, letting the petals cascade down her skin and spread their saccharine scent.

The back of her head met his shoulder, her eyes fluttering to a close as every little action threatened to overwhelm her. Where she had expected only carnality, he was seducing her with moments that made her feel revered.

"Kiss me," she begged, her hand reaching up behind his head to hold him. She moaned into his mouth, arching against him when he cupped her breast, the heat of his palm searing her. He kneaded her slowly, thumbing her nipple into a fine point. Aditi, lost in the sensations he was evoking, didn't realise that he'd loosened her underskirt until it fell in a heap at her feet, taking the rest of her saree down. The feel of his roughened fingers sliding into her underwear had her clutching his hair, her chest tightening in anticipation.

"You're so wet already. Have you been thinking about me doing this?" he whispered through her kiss, using a hand on her hip to make her face him as he backed her towards the bed.

"I've thought about you doing this a lot," she admitted, licking his lower lip. Tired of him treating her like she was breakable, she said what she knew would garner a reaction. "I've thought about you when I touched myself, too."

Her words broke his control. With a growl that reverberated in his chest, he tackled her onto the bed, trapping her body under his. Before she could understand what was happening, a rip sounded through the room. Cool air rushed across her damp core, replaced immediately with his touch. He wasted no time in sliding two fingers into her.

"Is this what you wanted me to do to you?" he rumbled, his mouth tracing the column of her neck, his hands moving relentlessly between her legs. "Or was it this?" he asked, before he clamped down on her nipple, sucking her in deeply.

She let out a lusty moan, her back arching in rapture as she clung to him, the pressure within her building at a dizzying rate. "Yes. Yes!" she chanted, her hips undulating against him, her knees falling open in a blatant demand for more.

"You look like a fucking goddess riding my hand," Rian rasped, his eyes glued on her face, tracking every expression as he drew small circles over her clit. If he'd thought she was gorgeous before, a flushed and naked Aditi writhing in his bed was the stuff of erotic dreams. "Come for me. I want to feel you like this, falling apart on my fingers."

Her breath stuck in her lungs, every sound in the world reduced to a single ringing pitch. Her blood rushed down to exactly where Rian pleasured her, every intentional swipe and thrust designed to make her want more. He slithered down, placing open-mouthed kisses across her shoulders and leaving a trail of love bites that would be evidence of the path he followed.

He curled his finger in, touching a spot within her that made her scream his name, setting off a detonation which left her quivering. "Oh my. . .you're. . . that was. . ." She gave up, breathing hard. He kissed his way down her chest and lower, to where her waist chain lay glistening against her brown body.

Assuming it was in his way, she reached for the lock, trying to unhook it when he nudged her hand away.

"Leave it on."

"But. . ."

Her protest died when he thrust his tongue into her navel, running the tip of it along the jewellery, slowly flicking lower before changing direction.

"You're driving me mad," she complained, needing him to fill her, to cover her body with his, to soothe this craving within her. "Come up here and do what you promised to do to me in the back seat of your car!"

The damn man laughed at her desperation, continuing to press kisses and nibbles on her skin, before finally dipping down to taste her pussy until she was squirming against his mouth.

"I think I'm obsessed with this thing," he told her, hooking one finger into her waist chain. "I'm going to buy you one of every kind." He kissed the inside of her thigh before licking her swollen clit. "And you'll wear it for me when I fuck you. Only for me."

When she didn't reply, he nipped her where she was sensitive, making her yelp her agreement.

"Good girl," he said, causing her to shiver furiously at what those two simple words did for her. Just when she thought he'd tongue her again, he rolled to the side, searching for something within his drawer. He pulled a square packet out, ripping the edge of it with his teeth while simultaneously undressing himself.

"Aditi, before we go further, we need one thing sorted."

"Hmm?" The haze in her eyes cleared at his seriousness. She drew a pillow across her body and hugged it. "I'm clear. Haven't been with anyone in about two years. And I have an IUD."

"Okay, two things sorted," Rian corrected with a soft smile, sheathing himself with the condom regardless. "This is not a situationship," he declared, settling between her thighs and ripping the pillow away like it was offending him by covering her from his gaze. "It's a relationship. As real as it gets. Understood?"

The world around her faded as she observed him reiterate a commitment she'd never expected. She would have slept with him without the promise of a relationship. She'd offered him her body, and he'd turned around and offered her his life.

The realisation trickled through her slowly, like a creeper growing and searching for its anchor, and the thought rooted itself into her heart.

How was she to ever deny him anything? She thought, her fingers tracing his chest, drawing up slowly to cup his jaw.

"Yes, Chef." She lifted her neck to brush a kiss across his lips, making him growl in approval.

"Fuck, I love hearing you say that. Say it again," he ordered, stroking her slit a few times, coating his crown with her arousal before positioning himself at her core.

"Yes, Chef," Aditi teased, licking her lips when his eyes darkened.

"You're going to use that all the time to drive me crazy, aren't you?"

"Yes, Chef." She smiled coyly, her mouth falling open in a gasp at the feel of his cock nudging her entrance.

"Just so you know," he said, leaning down to rest his weight on his forearms, "I'm clear, too. There hasn't been anyone in over a year."

Rian pushed in, and her expression of surprise transformed into a shocked cry. Her fingers dug into his waist as she held on.

"There will be no one except you," he husked, kissing her earnestly as he pulled back a little before advancing again. Aditi hissed at the burn of stretching around his girth, the sensation of having him within her equal parts pain and pleasure. It was like someone was branding her with silk and steel from the inside, the heat of which was unbearable and inescapable. He stopped eventually, and she let out a breath. She felt full, but not uncomfortably so.

"Loosen up for me, Sunshine. Relax."

"Give me a moment. You're big." She wiggled her hips, trying to get used to the pressure within her.

"I'll try not to let that go to my head," he chuckled, nudging her nose with his. "You can take me."

"T. . .take you?" she stuttered, confused. "I already have!"

She felt, rather than heard his laugh.

"I meant *all* of me."

"Rian? Rian! Oh!" She groaned when he pushed all the way in, filling her to the hilt. Her head twisted to the side as her body arched, trying to accommodate him.

"Fuck, you feel so good," he rasped, his hands slipping under to cup her ass and squeeze her flesh, causing her to clench around him in response.

He pulsed into her slowly, and she felt her walls tighten as she tried to hold him in, despising the emptiness when he pulled out. Every re-entry felt like a smooth slide home, her body adjusting to his possession, demanding more of it until she was grabbing at him, running her hands up and down his back in encouragement. She reached down to grip his firm ass, her nails pressing into his glutes without care for the marks she'd leave behind. The pain only turned him on, wanting to drive her as crazy with want as she had him. The flex and feel of his muscles twitching under her touch as he pounded into her had her biting down on her lip to stop from screaming.

He reared over her, his fingers tightening about the column of her throat, his thumb firmly keeping her chin up. "Eyes on me, Sunshine. You don't look away, okay?"

He kept his movements smooth, taking his time to touch and fondle every part he could without breaking pace. He caught her nipple between his thumb and forefinger, rolling it until she felt delirium grip her once more. Her pulse drummed erratically as the possibility of combusting became more real with each thrust of his hips.

"Rian, please," she whimpered. "I need to come."

"Then come," he ordered, unwilling to let her turn her head and hide from his sight. "Show me what you look like when I make you come."

What she saw in his eyes set her heart racing. With a keening cry, she was propelled up to a peak, splintering into a million shards at the height of it. She clawed at him, shuddering into completion, her eyes clenching shut as her vision went stark white. Rian thrust into her harder, seating himself deeper within her than before, taking pleasure in the way her body had tightened around him. He slid one powerful arm under her leg, opening her wider before he began to move once more. Feminine hands drew his face to hers, kissing him with a wild abandon that captured his soul.

Over and over, he drove into her pliant body, his groans and kisses finding a landing spot on her forehead, her eyelid, the crook of her neck. Aditi's hands slipped around his shoulders, her fingers spearing his soft hair as she rubbed her cheek against his roughened jaw. She crooned her delight in his ear when a tertiary orgasm ripped through her without notice.

"Come for me, Rian. Please," she breathlessly requested, unable to hold on any longer, sore and drained.

With a tortured moan, his body went impossibly taut as his release rushed up his spine and burst across his being, fiery flames licking him from end to end. Tremors shook him as he dropped into Aditi, finally replete with a satisfaction that had everything to do with the woman under him.

30

Afterglow

RIAN

"How do you feel?"

Aditi twisted her neck to rest her cheek on the pillow, sliding her arms underneath and crossing them. She watched Rian as he turned to his side to face her, the cool air in his bedroom doing nothing to reduce the heat he was emanating. His fingers danced lightly along her spine and she resisted the urge to shiver.

"Good. I feel really good. You?"

"Wonderful," he murmured, enjoying the curvaceous profile of Aditi lying on her belly, in his bed, still in a post-coital daze.

Rian could not remember when he'd last enjoyed sex like this. He'd had his share of wild days during his teenage years, experimenting with women looking for a good time leading to random hook-ups, sometimes in a drunken stupor. He'd enjoyed it while it had lasted. But over the years, the lure of momentary sexual gratification had begun to fade. Sex had become dull and pointless.

Perhaps the women he'd tried to date had recognized this lifelessness in him, because none of them had stuck around for too long.

If the timeline of his life was woven into a tapestry, there would only be shades of black, white and grey for a long time. Meeting Aditi would have marked the change.

A hint of blood red.

From there, the dullness would have been banished.

The happiness she spread would have shown up as splashes of yellow. His growth under her sunshine would have been bursts of green, the peace she gave him a vast sea of blue.

But his love for her? That would have to be every shade imaginable. She was vibrant beyond his ability to explain.

She'd been open and willing in bed, eager even. But none of her actions had that layer of practised seduction which hid one's insecurities and faults. She made love like she lived life, giving all of herself, holding nothing back, and being honest in a way that only made him love her more.

Perhaps his thoughts showed on his face because she reached out, tracing his upper lip with the tip of her finger, resting it at his cupid's bow.

"You look like you have something to say," Aditi murmured, drawing a line down his nose, her touch gentle.

"It's nothing."

"Tell me."

He pressed a kiss onto her fingers, admitting quietly, "I find you incredible."

"I was thinking that too," she told him, causing him to raise a brow.

"You find yourself incredible?"

"No, silly! I'm talking about you."

"Explain," he muttered, stroking her back still.

"You're," she swallowed hard, biting her lower lip when he caressed the rounded globe of her bottom. "You're phenomenal in bed."

If Rian had a shit-eating grin on his face after hearing that, he wouldn't have been surprised.

"So, I earned a passing grade?"

"I think you earned a PhD."

His nostrils flared as he choked his laughter back.

"Doc, my Sunshine, my sweetheart, you do realise that PhD also stands for 'pretty huge dick'?" He snorted, laughing out loud when she looked horrified.

"Stop! You're the worst!" She groaned into her pillow, her stomach tickling with subdued mirth.

"But you liked what we did, yeah?"

She caught his eye and nodded, smiling shyly, and his silly heart fluttered at the sight. He might never be able to reconcile this juxtaposition of shame and sensuality in her, he thought, enchanted by the dusting of pink over her skin.

But nothing about her was fake or planned. Which meant he felt more addicted and intrigued by her than ever before. Unable to accept even the few inches of distance between them, he rolled over, lying half on top of her, his leg tangling with hers.

"What did you like?" he asked, surprising himself by wanting to know more of her enjoyment. He'd brought her pleasure but hearing her admit to it was a major turn on. He wanted to know how to make her feel like he did. Like being without him was torture.

"I liked it all, Bugs. It was intense, but amazing. I. . ." She shook her head like it was silly.

"What?" He nuzzled her cheek and brushed her hair away from her face, placing nibbling kisses along her exposed shoulder until he reached her neck.

"Your words," Aditi breathed, already feeling affected by Rian's kisses, the ever simmering desire for him slowly fanning into a bigger flame. "How I reacted to them. I didn't expect that."

His brows shot up, and he made a mental note.

"What about my words, Doc?" he teased when she hid her face in the pillow. "Is it when I said you were sexy with clothes but even sexier, naked, in my bed, begging me to fuck you?"

"Hmm."

He leaned in and tickled the back of her ear with his tongue, drawing his hands down the sides of her body, moulding her like she was made of clay.

"Or was it when I said I could lose myself in your sweet pussy for days?"

She gasped, his dirty words arousing her, causing her hips to hitch up automatically. Rian kneaded her ass, his fingers dipping between them, trailing down the inside of her thigh, close to her rapidly dampening core. Despite her shamelessly trying to shift so he would touch her there, he seemed intent on playing a cruel game of denial.

His stubble scraped her back when he moved lower, placing hot, wet kisses down her spine and under her shoulder blades. "Maybe," he supposed, settling his stiff length against the crease of her buttocks, "it was when I called you a good girl for taking my cock so well?"

Good girl it is, he smiled against her skin, her shudder telling him exactly what he'd needed to know.

She was going to die, she decided. This man, his filthy mouth and his sweet touch were going to drive her stark raving mad. He'd turned her into a sex-crazed wanton and that was before he'd given her an orgasm. Now that he'd begun to learn what affected her, she knew she stood no chance against his prowess. How had she ever thought she would survive a casual fling with him? She was addicted already and only expected this symptom to worsen.

"Do you like it when I touch you, Doc?"

"Yes," she whined, trying to twist her body to face him but he was too strong.

"Tell me more. What else do you like?" He held her shoulder so that she would stay belly down. He used the pad of his thumb and applied pressure at her lower back, massaging her in a spot that had her melting into his touch.

"I like how you make me feel. Like I'm desirable."

"You are," came his emphatic response. "So much. You're my own personal fantasy come to life. Your gorgeous breasts fill my hands perfectly, your pretty lips fit mine like they were made for me, and your luscious ass—work of art. I want to bite it every time I see you walk in those short pyjamas." He spanked her, the suddenness of it startling her. It barely stung but left a clear result in how wet she got.

Aditi was certain she was dripping onto the sheets at this point. She threw a look back at him, surprised with herself. There was so much she was learning about her own body and Rian had barely begun.

"Was that too hard?" he asked, watching her with that deeply contemplative look. His thumbs pressed into her flesh, working them, loosening them for him.

"No. Just sudden."

"Do you want me to do it again?"

The throbbing between her legs intensified at the thought.

"I. . .yes," she gulped. "But not too rough."

"I don't want to cause you pain, Sunshine," she heard him say, spanking each butt-cheek for demonstration. He rubbed over the same spots with gentle, circular motions that soothed the sting away. "I want to know what drives you mad with lust."

Another spank.

"I will learn every little thing that turns you on," he promised, dipping his tongue into her mouth just as his palm landed on her ass once more, the vibration twisting the coil of need within her even more.

"Such a beautiful body. So responsive." His praise had her wanting to preen. He trailed his fingers along her waist chain before flicking her nipple at the same time as slapping the rounded flesh of her ass. Hard.

She jolted, the momentary pain making her body ache for the promise of pleasure.

"Rian," she whimpered, feeling like she'd been teased into a crescendo that only led to insanity.

"You're ready for me, aren't you?" he asked, biting down on the spot that connected her neck and shoulder.

"Yes."

"Yes, what?"

"Yes, Chef!" she exclaimed, hoping he'd give her what she wanted now that he'd gotten her to say the words he wanted to hear.

"Do you want it fast or slow?"

"Fast, please."

The chuckle in her ear warmed her blood.

"So fucking polite. No wonder you like being called a good girl," he hummed, deliberately taunting her. "Are you going to be polite when you come all over my cock?"

She nearly orgasmed at the thought.

"Tell me what else you like," he whispered, tugging at her earlobe, his hand slipping between her thighs to find her soaking and swollen.

"Your fingers. Oh my god." She shuddered, trying to push her hips down so that his fingers would sink in.

"Keep talking or I'll stop."

"Long fingers." Her eyes shut, she tried to focus on the tip of his thumb circling her opening. She rocked back, tears of frustration pricking her eyes when his touch receded. Her mind wouldn't form words and he was using that against her.

"And?" he gruffed, making it clear that he would wait as long as necessary for her answer.

She released a ragged breath, trying to string together a sentence.

"I like your weight on me, holding me down."

"You like to be held down?" he asked, sliding his hand up to cup her breast, stroking the pebbled tip.

"By you," she mewled, her breath scattering when his hold turned possessive and rough.

With her laying prone, he slid a pillow under her belly for support. Raising her arms over her head, he kept her wrists trapped against the mattress with one large hand before settling behind her, his body stretched along hers. His fingers flirted with her as teasing touches turned into heavy petting, eventually reaching up to curve around her throat. Her pulse pounded against his palm when he tightened his hold just barely, using the pressure of his thumb to turn her face towards him.

Despite the dominance in his gesture, all he saw in her eyes was a glaze of desire.

"Does this scare you?" he asked, rubbing himself on her, the tip of his engorged cock sliding along her wet folds.

"No."

"Do you want to use your safe word?"

"No."

He gave her a bruising kiss that left her panting.

"Are you sure?" he asked, even as he angled one knee up and adjusted her hips, lining himself against her core.

"Yes. I like. . ."

"Sunshine, tell me."

Their gazes met. Her irises were blown, the ring of brown around them looking like it was molten gold in comparison. In a sultry voice that caused his belly to tighten, she whispered, "I like how you fit in me. Like you were made to fill me up."

Holy fuck, if she kept talking like this, he was going to embarrass himself by finishing too quickly. He was already rock hard from simply having teased her body into readiness. Seeing her get desperate for him had the most potent effect imaginable. Knowing that this desperation was unfiltered made the lust claw itself into his skin, demanding fulfilment.

His lips covered hers just as he thrust in, causing her to let out a cry against his mouth at the sudden weight within her, stretching her wide. Almost instantly, she orgasmed, the feeling of his rigid cock sliding into her more delicious than she remembered.

He held her hips to him, savouring their connection. She was right. They fit so perfectly together, it was hard for him to breathe.

"The way your pussy grips me when I'm inside you—you're going to kill me, fuck!"

She involuntarily clenched harder. "Don't stop. I need more."

Ready to oblige, Rian pulled all the way out and back into her in a single stroke, her words having driven him past his breaking point. He moved at a quick pace, needing her with a ferocity that astounded him. Her body thrummed once more, his lack of control stoking her pride and her own ardour.

"Harder," she gasped when he surged in, the sound of their bodies slapping against the other filling the room. The furious chatter of the chimes on her waist chain announced every thrust and pump, adding to the symphony of their movements.

Her body arched into his with each move, pulling against her outstretched arms, her fingers clawing at the sheets underneath for support. Using his palm to grip the underside of her thigh, he spread her wider apart, before resuming the bruising pace with which he claimed her.

His firm hold would leave a handprint, she was certain. But Aditi was beyond caring. She joined him move for move as best she could, turning her face to the side, kissing and urging him even when he might have paused to try and be gentle.

"Make me come again, Rian. I can't hold on." She moaned, needing his touch on her clit to push her over the edge when she felt his blunt fingers part her lips.

"Suck," he commanded, groaning at the feel of her tongue swirling against his skin. He let her suck on his fingers, fucking her mouth in tandem with her pussy, before popping it out.

Sure fingers found her swollen clit within seconds, massaging it, circling it in tiny arcs. The force with which he drove his hips into her had her thrashing and twisting, muffling her sobs into the pillow beneath her head.

He never got a chance to reconsider the roughness of their mating, and eventually, she went lax, giving up all power, letting him drive their desire to a searing completion that left her shaking. She let out a helpless scream at the height of it, a swarm of explosions overwhelming her, leaving her teetering on the edge of consciousness. Rian followed closely behind, groaning into her shoulder, having no ability to hold on as he jerked and pulsated until he was drained, finally coming to a slow and languid stop.

The only thought Aditi had by the time she drifted off to sleep, curled against one solid body, was that Rian Shetty had indelibly etched himself into her heart. And there was no escaping that.

31

An Uninvited Guest

ADITI

*R*IAN WOULD KNOW HOW *to fix this mess*, Aditi thought, staring desolately at the roti she'd tried to roll out.

She held it up straight in her line of vision, lips twisted as she mused how to make it better. The oddly distributed weight pulled the flattened dough down, contorting itself to look like the mask from the Scream movies. She tried to replicate the same scary face, grimacing when it plopped onto the counter, leaving her clasping two scraggly pieces in her hands instead of one beautiful flatbread.

Her medical prowess had not extended into the kitchen, much to her consternation.

No matter where they were in the world, every Indian household boasted one thing in common.

The cleaning cloth that once began as someone's shirt.

Once deemed not nice enough to wear outside, it would become a pyjama top. At the first sign of a hole or a tear, instead of being thrown out, it would be used for wiping down surfaces around the house.

Finally, after months of abuse, those scruffy pieces would get demoted to cleaning the floor or the toilets.

Her roti, regrettably, looked exactly like a cleaning cloth in its last stage of life.

When the bell to the apartment door rang, Aditi almost cried in relief.

She washed her hands, scraping the drying dough off her fingers before wiping her hands on her apron, too much in a hurry to care about using a towel.

Dinner today was a big deal and she'd already destroyed Rian's kitchen in an attempt to make a kickass meal that would win Nanamma over when she returned.

The plan, as she'd explained to an amused Rian, was to lull Nanamma into a food-induced stupor, and gently inform her that they were together and wanting to get married. She'd be too happy because of the good meal to have any concerns, she had supposed.

Despite Rian assuring her that Nanamma would be ecstatic with the news, Aditi's nerves had gotten the best of her. Thirteen failed matrimonial matches had not bothered her quite this much. This date, however, was more important than all of them combined. She needed Chitra Shetty's unconditional approval. Family was far too important a piece of her personality to take this casually.

Even the tiniest possibility that Nanamma might not want Aditi as her family terrified her.

Which is why, when she'd begun to have a meltdown because they didn't have enough yoghurt for curd rice (and let's be honest, the way to a South Indian's heart is tempered curd rice), Rian had crushed her to him, ordering her to breathe and calm down. At her attempt to argue, he'd given her a smouldering kiss, leading to a frantic interlude on their couch that melted her entire system and rendered her incapable of organised thought. He'd left shortly after, promising to return before their grandmother came home with all the extra yoghurt she'd demanded.

She gulped, trying not to jog to the front door like an overly dramatic heroine from an old Bollywood movie about to be reunited with her saviour hero. He was back, dinner would be fixed. And then, she'd show him how appreciative she really was.

She wrenched the door open. "Bugs, you're. . ."

She trailed off, the smile on her face dimming to a polite, confused one.

"Sorry, may I help you?" Aditi's gaze swept over the older lady standing there, who looked very much like she'd come to the wrong side of town. *She belongs in one of those fancy country clubs,* Aditi thought, taking in the obviously expensive clothing, the branded bag, and the air of wealth that emanated from her. "Are you lost, perhaps?"

Manicured nails curved over the edge of oversized sunglasses as the lady slowly slipped them off.

"I'm not lost. Where is Rian?"

Aditi peered into the unfamiliar face, shocked when the lady shoved past her and into the apartment.

"Excuse me, who are you? How dare you enter without asking?" She ran ahead of the lady and stood in her way, arms outstretched.

"Who am I? I am Leela Shetty, you stupid girl!"

Aditi's arms fell to the side with a whack.

"You're the girl from that party, aren't you?" the older lady barked.

Aditi's brows furrowed, unsure which party Leela was referring to.

"What are you doing in Rian's house?" Leela demanded, looking like she'd decided she would dislike Aditi irrespective of the answer.

"I live here."

Oddly enough, the response caused Leela's lips to twist cruelly. "You moved fast. How long have you lived with him? How did you convince him?"

"I...Nanamma brought me here."

"That bitch. I should have known she'd meddle in my plans for him. I don't care. You need to pack up and leave. I order it."

Aditi blinked, slowly recovering from the shock of realising who it was she was speaking to. She'd thought Leela was a sophisticated and beautiful lady when she'd first opened the door. A few minutes of staring into the eyes of someone she'd never wanted to meet, combined with the knowledge of the terrible things she'd done to Rian, and Aditi saw clearly that the elegance was just skin deep. The unblemished face that glared at her, though wiped of wrinkles, was also wiped of humanity. There was no graciousness in her tone, no distinction in her bearing.

Aditi couldn't help but compare her to Nanamma, whose intelligent grey eyes and kind personality, so much like her grandson, spoke of a strength that belied her age.

The woman in front of her was cruel. And cruelty was a crutch for the weak.

"Did you hear me or are you deaf?" Leela snarked, snapping her fingers rudely in Aditi's face. "I said I order you to leave my son. Immediately."

"You *order* me?" Aditi huffed out a sarcastic laugh.

Leela, having said her part, had already stopped paying attention. Clearly, she did not believe in extending the courtesy of listening to the opposite party. Aditi saw her rake a critical gaze over the apartment, stilling at the sight of the mess in the kitchen.

She scoffed. "I see what he is doing."

"And what is that?"

Leela turned to her, a superior look on her face. "Rian always does this to get my attention. Act out in extremes. Pick unsuitable women and unworthy pursuits just to make me angry." She pointed to Aditi before letting out a single, derisive *ha*. "I will not allow the two of you to be together. Do you think you can live easily without my approval? He will listen to me in the end. Because he craves my acceptance."

"If it makes you happy to think so, you're welcome." She shrugged, conceding to the older lady's delusion if that meant she would leave soon. Leela Shetty was a narcissist. Her behaviour confirmed it. There would be no point in Aditi engaging in a war of words with this woman.

"I don't just think so," Leela said, eyes narrowed. "I know him." She pulled out her phone, flicking it open.

Aditi peered at the picture of a model that was presented to her, unsure what the purpose of this was. Tall, with immaculate makeup and wearing a skintight dress that required the kind of perfect body Aditi had once dreamed of, she was forced to accept that whoever this lady was, she was stunning. There was not a hair out of place, not an additional ounce of fat on her hips. Her bearing and looks screamed money and confidence, clearly not misplaced.

"This is Sonia Dasavi," Leela announced. "She is the only daughter of the CEO of Dasavi Constructions. Sonia is the perfect choice to be my daughter-in-law. Beautiful, educated, with a family that matches ours in status. You don't compare."

Lips firm, Aditi crossed her arms, trying to stave off her irritation from the continued insults. "I'm not in competition with whoever this Sonia is."

"Are you sure?" Leela swiped to the next picture, one that Aditi was unprepared for.

In the cosy setting of a restaurant she only recognized all too well was Sonia, bodily draped over a handsome man.

Her handsome man.

Rian and Sonia resembled a pair of Greek gods when together. The power of their combined physicality was staggering and Aditi, to her chagrin, found that she was not immune.

"This picture," Leela continued, "is from when the two families met to discuss Sonia and Rian's engagement."

Aditi's stomach flipped, anxiety gurgling within her. The three cups of coffee she'd consumed threatened to make a reappearance. Her eyes fell on the expensive shoes Leela had not bothered to remove at the door, the flash of red on its underside—a dead giveaway for the brand. If she was going to upchuck the contents of her stomach, those shoes were precisely where she would aim.

"If you don't believe me," Leela added slyly, her shrewd eyes locking in on Aditi's wan face. "You can ask Rian."

"I don't have to. Pictures don't always show everything. If what you said is true, Rian would have told me."

His mother's clear annoyance at her response confirmed Aditi's suspicion. It didn't take much for her to understand that Leela was deriving some sort of sick pleasure from hurting her. Which was why, despite the absolute misery of seeing Rian with a woman she would never measure against, she was not foolish enough to believe this terrible woman. She may only have known Rian for a few months, but she knew him well. He was not a liar. He was not a dishonest man. She would bet her life on it.

"You must be an idiot," Leela snidely remarked. "Or desperate. Do you really think he'd pick you when he could have someone like her?"

Done with being demeaned, Aditi wiped all traces of emotion from her face. She squared her shoulders and looked the older lady straight in the eye. "Whether or not you like it," she bit out, the chill in her tone matched only by the expression she maintained, "he *has* picked me."

"For how long?"

"Forever. And now, you need to leave."

Leela's face turned purple. "How dare you say that to me? This is my son's house!"

"Then come back when your son is in residence," Aditi shot back, thoroughly fed up. "Right now, you're annoying me and I have no wish to put up with your presence."

"How disrespectful!" Leela screeched, her claws gripping her leather bag like she was about to throw it at Aditi.

She pinned Mrs. Shetty with a warning look, knowing that she was prone to physical violence.

"You have done nothing to earn my respect."

"This attitude doesn't befit you," Leela spat, her face contorting in fury. "You are pretending to be a good, well-cultured girl, aren't you? Do you think I don't know what happens with a young man and woman in the same house? Spreading your legs to entrap a rich boy is an old trick. What next? An unplanned pregnancy?"

"Mind your tongue!"

"That hickey on your neck tells me I am right."

"What I do with my private life is none of your concern," Aditi calmly replied, refusing to be shamed by a woman she didn't know.

"You're sleeping with my son to trap him!" Leela agitatedly shouted.

"Leave before I call security."

"Class always shows," she hissed. "Rian will realise he's making a mistake with you. Once the novelty in the bedroom wears off, you will be discarded just like his other girlfriends."

Before Aditi could respond, a familiar voice cut in, shocking both ladies into turning around.

"Years have gone by, Leela," Chitra began, dropping her bag on the ground next to her as she walked toward them both. "But your tongue remains as venomous as the most destructive poison. You drove my son away from me, and now you try to drive Aditi away from Rian."

She reached out for Aditi's hand, patting it reassuringly.

Leela turned to Chitra, her anger now finding a new target.

"I should have known you would be here too. Have you no shame, living off the money my son makes?"

"Have you no shame, calling him your son when you have not been a mother at all?"

"You have always driven a wedge between us!" Leela cried. "That's why he doesn't listen to me."

Aditi glanced towards Nanamma, wondering if such an accusation hurt her. To her surprise, Chitra seemed borderline bored. As if she'd witnessed this drama in the past and had judged it subpar.

"Rian is an adult," Nanamma snapped. "If he listens to me, it is because he wants to. Not because I forced him."

"I don't believe you."

"I don't care if you do. You have always seen problems and conspiracies where there have been none. You are a sad and dissatisfied person, Leela. Your soul is rotten," Chitra declared, making no attempt to hide her distaste for her daughter-in-law. "You think everyone is like you. When you are not happy, you make sure no one else is. But my Rian? He is happy with this girl here. I will not let you take that from him."

"Hah, the threats of an old, powerless woman are meant to scare me?"

"No," Aditi cut in, her patience at an end. "But the right hook of an angry doctor who knows which bone to break should terrify you. Now leave!"

32

Crescendo

ADITI

Aditi had rarely felt this level of shame before.

Standing in front of Nanamma, after she'd just witnessed her throwing Leela out of their apartment, made her feel like she was an ant who was being burnt beneath a magnifying glass in the desert sun.

This evening couldn't have turned out worse.

"I'm sorry, Nanamma," she offered, the silence starting to grate on her nerves. "I know I was being rude but I couldn't hear anything more from her."

Nanamma shot an indecipherable look. "Kanna, is there anything you wish to share with me?"

"About?"

"You and Rian."

Aditi startled, glancing up guiltily. She swallowed hard, hating the tense environment in which she was revealing this truth, that too, without Rian by her side.

"I'm sorry you had to find out like this. We were going to tell you tonight. It is all very recent, barely a few days now. We're still learning to wrap our head around it ourselves. I don't know how Mrs. Shetty found out."

"Leela has a big circle of gossip mongers. I wouldn't be surprised if someone she knows noticed how Rian is with you and connected the dots." Unsure, Aditi's forehead creased when she saw Nanamma's lips curve up. "My eyes are old, but my eyesight is perfectly normal. Anyone at that Diwali party would have come to the same conclusion. Your absence was noticed."

Aditi reddened. "You knew?"

"I had my doubts," Chitra admitted. "Kaya and Arjun's insistence that I stay with them for the weekend, and Rian not complaining when I called to let him know, definitely confirmed it. I walked in just in time to hear Leela's accusations. You didn't deny it."

Aditi clasped her hands together, looking away.

"I assume things progressed quite quickly since that party?" Chitra asked delicately.

"I'm sorry," Aditi apologised once more. She felt like she'd lost count of how many times she'd said 'sorry' today, and she feared she'd be repeating herself often given what Nanamma was asking her. "I didn't mean to disrespect you in your home."

Old, feathered hands brushed over her bent head, requesting her to look up. When Aditi's gaze met Chitra's, she was relieved to note no disappointment in her expression.

"I'm not angry with you, Adi," Nanamma explained. "It would be hypocritical if I blame you when Rian is a part of it too. I'm also too glad to be annoyed when seeing you two together is what I have prayed for for months."

Aditi knew she'd failed to hide her surprise when Nanamma guffawed at her gobsmacked expression.

"I know that the way things used to be in my time is not how the world is now. I have seen too much of life to judge you for your choice to be with Rian without matrimonial commitment first. I hope I am not embarrassing you by speaking my mind."

Aditi shook her head, the tightness in her chest curiously very much present. Nanamma's acceptance should have relieved her. Her logical mind acknowledged how very lucky she'd gotten in this scenario, but was unable to hone in on the reason for why she felt like she was hanging off the ledge of a multi-storey building. Perhaps the adrenaline from her argument with Leela hadn't worn off.

"I was afraid you'd dislike me," she softly confessed.

"Oh, kanna, I could never dislike you." Chitra patted Aditi's cheek in a motherly gesture. "I have seen your heart, and I have received your love. You are as precious to me as my grandson, and I am glad he has found you."

Aditi's lips curved tremulously. Leela's words still swirled within her like a poisonous fog, slithering in and out, nudging and poking at different areas, searching for the weakest parts of her psyche. Though she had been staunch in her support of Rian and his choice to be with her, old insecurities had been raked to life. The part of her that still struggled with the need for validation felt like it had been exposed once more, and she hated it.

"Are you happy?" Chitra asked.

She opened her mouth to answer. To her great surprise, she burst into big blubbering sobs instead. Immediately, she felt Nanamma's arms go around her, manoeuvring her towards the couch. When Aditi still didn't quieten, the old grandmother drew her into a warm hug, patting her back like she was a young child.

The overnight change in Rian's decision regarding marriage, her acceptance, the complete and utter surrender of her body and mind to him since then, now bookended with an explosive confrontation with his hateful mother, had forced her stress up a summit. Her breakdown was inevitable. She just hadn't expected that it would be over such a simple question.

"My child, are you not happy to be with Rian?"

"I am," she wailed, unable to stop, tears trailing down her cheeks. She sniffled, blowing noisily into the sheet of tissue that was handed to her.

"Then what is it?" Nanamma asked, using the edge of her saree's pallu to dry one cheek, her efforts wasted when the deluge of tears did not abate.

"I . . . Nanamma. . .I. . ." She hiccuped, allowing the concerned older lady to hold both her hands.

"I love him," she croaked, her nose burning anew as a fresh wave of anxiety swelled within her. Giving up, she slumped into Nanamma's lap, burying her face in the soft folds of her cotton saree and succumbed to the dismay that had come with the acceptance of this fact.

She loved Rian Shetty.

She had thought she was so smart, that she could separate the part of her that lusted after him from the part that desired more than a short-term fling. She'd believed that her mind negating impractical dreams of a relationship with him would stop her heart from doing so as well.

She'd told herself over and over again that she could not fall in love with him because Rian did not want marriage. He had made it clear that he didn't want to fall in love or give any space to it.

Even now, despite proposing to her, he had not promised anything other than a partnership. One that Aditi was certain would be filled with camaraderie, support, mind-blowing sex, and a very real chance of a happy life together.

She had refused to ask for more because this was already more than she had expected.

She had refused to want more because she was afraid to lose even this.

With Leela's unannounced visit however, Aditi's old misgivings had come to the fore.

Once more, she was with someone whose mother disapproved of her. Once again, she was deeply in love with a man without any clarity on whether or not he'd love her too.

And that would have been okay.

She'd reconciled herself with the idea of marrying someone on the basis of friendship and basic compatibility. After all, many marriages boasted far less.

With Rian though, she didn't know when her practical side stopped being quite so practical.

Every dream, every wish, and each day held a hope of him and his love, and she'd been powerless to stop that love from growing in her.

She had lied to herself. She'd pretended that fulfilling her desire to make a memory that held Rian's essence before she married elsewhere was possible.

Her life would have continued, she was sure. But today, she understood something critical.

Rian would have owned not just her memories— he would have owned her entirely.

She was the best version of herself with him. She would have missed him every day for the rest of her life because she would have missed the version of Aditi she most loved also. The version that Rian, with his unshakeable belief and unwavering support, brought out.

Imagining a life with someone other than him felt wrong now. No, it felt impossible.

He was supposed to have been a once-in-a-lifetime experience that she could look back on with fondness, but he'd somehow morphed into something else altogether.

A once-in-a-lifetime kind of love.

"Kanna, get up, please," Chitra pleaded. "Talk to me. Why is loving Rian so upsetting for you?"

"I'm scared."

"Does he know?"

"No." She turned to face Nanamma, anguish colouring her tone. "He told me he doesn't want to love anyone. He wants to marry me, but that's not the same as love."

Chitra sighed tiredly.

"Some people are simply better at asking for what they need. Rian is not one of them, but never doubt that that boy wants to love and be loved in return more than anything else."

"Of course you'd say that. He is your grandson, after all."

"You have met his mother now," she said, deciding that revealing the many ways in which Leela had scarred Rian might make Aditi understand him better. "You cannot imagine what Rian had to deal with growing up."

"I don't have to imagine," Aditi sniffed, still wiping her red nose. "He told me everything."

"Everything?" Chitra gasped, shocked by this revelation. More and more, it became clear to her that Aditi and Rian had formed a bond that was deeper than anyone realised.

"If he has told you this, he trusts you. Has he ever flinched from your touch?"

Aditi shook her head.

"Because of Leela," she continued, "he stopped wanting physical contact for a long time. Even now, on occasion, it takes him a moment to relax and respond when I initiate a hug. I can count on one hand the number of people he is comfortable with to not find their touch offensive. Believe me, none of them got there in just a few months like you have."

Aditi would have never guessed that. Apart from the first couple weeks when he avoided her like she was disease ridden, he had never behaved like her touch was troublesome. Sure, he'd been a little hesitant and stiff, careful even. But she'd chalked it up to the newness of their friendship.

Through their late-night street food dates to their tense arguments to now, the intensity and frequency of their touch had only increased.

"Please, give him time," Chitra earnestly requested. "He is capable of deep love. As he has shown you trust, please trust him, too."

33

Trust

RIAN

Hands shoved within the pockets of his sweatpants, Rian walked along the edges of his large balcony. He spun on his heel without thinking when he reached one end, continuing his stroll to the other side. Anyone observing him would have thought he was simply winding down after a long day. In reality, his mind was occupied with an unexplainable worry.

Raking a hand through his hair, his gaze travelled upwards to catch sight of the clouds shifting across indigo skies. The heat of the day had slowly abated, yet the atmosphere felt stuffy. He took a deep breath in, releasing it in a slow stream through pursed lips. With his elbows resting against the top of his railing, he looked out. The glittering skyline of Mumbai that formed his view did not offer him the same comfort that it previously did.

Yet again, he glanced behind at the loveseat that Aditi usually occupied. Without her tawny legs dangling over the edge of the seat, her floral scent in the air and her chatter to make him laugh, this otherwise restful space only felt empty. He knew why. His comfort was with Aditi now, not with places.

The old Rian would have smacked him for being so mortifyingly pathetic. He may as well put himself on a leash because he was no different than a canine tethered to his owner when it came to the woman he loved.

He sighed, his hand unconsciously massaging the centre of his chest, trying hard to let go of this anxiety that had taken root in him.

The day had begun well enough. After an entire weekend filled with glorious lovemaking and in-depth discussions of their future, they'd been ready to face the world together. Though Aditi had been nervous, Rian had had no doubts whatsoever that Nanamma would be happy for them. Which is why, when he'd returned home with the yoghurt Aditi had insisted he purchase for dinner, he'd not expected to find her distraught and crying in his grandmother's arms.

Nanamma, as he'd expected, had not only been ecstatic about their relationship status, but also emotional. Aditi had cried in relief, she'd explained. He'd given both the ladies the benefit of doubt, trying to turn their mood around to celebrate the occasion instead.

Throughout the evening however, he'd had the unsettling feeling that something was amiss.

Knowing he would find no relief if he didn't check in on her, Rian made his way to Aditi's room, knocking gently on the door. He waited, aware that she'd been tired and had most likely slept already. His fingers curled around the door handle, hesitating for a moment before he turned it, glad when he found it unlocked.

Quietly, he slipped into her room, shutting the door behind him with a small click. His eyes alighted upon a lumpy form under the comforter. He treaded lightly, the soft lights diffusing through the sheer curtains guiding him until he was kneeling beside her. He noted that she was rolled up into her blanket like a caterpillar, her cheek squished against the pillow, causing her mouth to settle into a pout. Automatically, he felt the edge of his lips tug up. Even asleep,

Aditi was the most adorable woman he'd ever laid eyes on. The sweet innocence of her soul kept him enthralled and in this moment, unaware of the world, her vulnerability seemed to reflect on her face.

It was perhaps because he knew this side of her that he found it so heartbreaking to see her upset. Maybe this is why he felt like he'd hurt the world to keep her safe.

He unthinkingly traced a heart on the apple of one cheek, her skin warm to the touch.

His mind flashed back to her tear-stained face and immediately, the pressure within his chest grew. She'd assured him it had been just her nerves acting up. He hoped that truly was it.

Maybe his thoughts had been too loud because a moment later, Aditi stirred.

"Bugs?" she murmured, surprising him when her eyes opened slowly before fluttering shut. He waited, wondering for a second if she'd gone back to sleep. Ever so slowly, her lips curved. "You're here."

Her eyelids swept open and shut a few more times as she drowsily watched him.

"Good night, pretty girl," he whispered, bending over to press his lips against her temple.

He felt a small hand clutch his pinky when he got up to leave.

"Don't go," she requested, her voice laden with sleep. "Come here."

The idea crossed his mind that the gentlemanly thing to do would be to let her rest. But when she pulled the blanket off and reached both arms out, inviting him so beguilingly, he couldn't resist.

For a while, they lay quietly with Aditi spooned into him until she sighed loudly. "I can almost hear you think."

"Sorry."

She turned towards him, snuggling closer, her palm landing on his chest. "Your heart is racing."

"Hmm."

"Talk to me."

Rian didn't know what to say. He would sound foolish and overly dramatic if he said he had a lingering sense of doom and it had him worried. So, he told her about something more tangible.

"Remember I mentioned wanting to build a school?" He heard her hmm in response. "I got the drawn plans for it today." He pulled out his phone from his pocket, swiping through the screen to show her the initial mock-ups from the architect.

"These designs look beautiful!" Aditi exclaimed.

"I've been working on them for a long time. It's my dream. I need to make this happen."

"You will."

Her inexorable belief in his capacity touched him.

"I wish the investing board was as easy to convince as you," he complained, turning his phone off to place it on the nightstand.

"Did someone indicate an issue?"

Rian lay back, absentmindedly stroking her hair, now truly dwelling on this part of his life. "Not to me directly. Most of the board members are supportive but I've heard the feedback that my proposal lacked heart, whatever that means."

"Maybe," Aditi supposed after a while, "they need to understand your reason for building the institute."

"My reasons are selfish, Doc. I wanted to leave something good for people to remember me by when I die. I don't think anyone is going to give me money for that."

"Brushing aside the very morbid thought of you dying, if you're in it for just a good name, why not create a shelter for abused animals instead? Why a school, specifically?" Aditi questioned, her fingers drumming a gentle pattern on his chest.

Rian had never sat down and thought about it. He had felt strongly about this project when the idea had first occurred, but he'd never probed into his reasons. Aditi's question made him feel nervous. Like he was being asked to admit to something that he'd gotten too used to hiding, even from himself. Before he could say anything else, he heard Aditi's sleepy voice murmur her theory.

"It's obvious, Bugs. I know it isn't easy to talk about it but you should. You suffered with school. You were made to feel lesser because you learnt things differently. It's no surprise to me that you want to build a place for safe learning to break that cycle of trauma."

She turned her head in to place a kiss on his chest, resting her chin so she could glance at his face.

"You can say it's selfish. I always believe it takes strength to create something beautiful from painful experiences. And you, sweetheart, are a wonderfully strong man."

Rian could hear his pulse drumming in his ears by the time Aditi finished speaking. Every word had etched itself into his skin, like a tattoo he would wear forever.

He hadn't been able to voice it, but Aditi, with her uncanny ability to see him in a way that no one else ever had, including himself, had reached into him, past the facade of his confidence, glimpsing into his very soul with an ease that felt otherworldly.

He cradled her cheek tenderly, his sights flickering over her features, too afraid to blink in case she was a figment of his imagination. Because how was she real? How had he gotten lucky enough to have her in his life, and in his arms? The fierceness of his need for her, like she was his saviour, ripped through him. At that moment, Rian knew without a doubt that if Aditi ever left him, he would be reduced to a shadow of who he wanted to be. The notion was terrifying.

Maybe she sensed a change in him because the sleep in her eyes receded, replaced by an alertness that wasn't there before.

Aditi saw Rian's eyes drop to her lips, watching her with a look she had come to recognize well. What confused her was that he wasn't doing anything else. Not touching her, not kissing her. Just looking.

A split second later, she wiggled out of his embrace.

"Doc?" he asked, sitting up, wondering if she needed something.

"Can't sleep anymore."

"Do you want me to leave? I can give you some space."

Instead of answering him, she swung a leg over his thighs, bracing her palms on his chest. If he wouldn't make his move, she decided, straddling him, then she would.

His hands naturally came to rest at her waist, steadying her. The moonlight filtering through the windows lit his face, his surprise evident.

"W. . .what are you doing?" he asked, trying to get his excitable body under control. "I didn't come here for sex."

She cocked her head to the left, looking at him like he'd just said the silliest thing. "I know."

"You were tired. You need to rest," he tried again.

In a sleep roughened voice, she husked, "I need you more."

She held his gaze as she reached for the buttons on her nightshirt, slowly popping one open before moving down.

"Should I continue?" she asked, her voice low but clear.

Rian gulped, nodding his assent, riveted as she slid another button through its hole, and then another, all the way until the two edges of her nightshirt were parted down the middle, revealing silken brown skin unbroken by the strip of a bra. Even in the dull light he could tell her nipples had hardened, straining clearly against the soft cotton. His eyes canvassed her, lingering at her navel, a thin golden chain glinting above her waistband.

Aditi reveled in the power that surged within her at being able to hold his attention. If the flush on his skin and his shallow breath weren't evidence enough, the growing stiffness under her thigh that had become prominent during the course of her deliberate strip show made it clear how much she affected him. And she hadn't even removed her clothes yet. She slipped a finger under his chin, lifting his face towards her.

"Take off your shirt."

Her order was soft, but the response was immediate.

Rian didn't care where he threw his T-shirt, whether it ripped, tore, or burnt to char. He simply wanted to feel Aditi's skin against his. He reached for her, frowning when she leaned away with a shake of her head.

"Put your hands on the bed and sit back against the headboard. You won't touch me until I say it's okay."

"What?"

With a firm hand, she pushed him until his back was supported by her pillows.

"I was having a nice dream before you woke me," she confessed, her nose tracking the curve of his face, down the sharp edge of his jaw. "Hmmm," she purred, rubbing her cheek against his lightly, feeling his roughened stubble scrape against her soft skin. "You smell so good. That's how I knew you were here."

She dipped lower to press her lips on his collarbone and heard him swallow audibly. Her fingers fluttered down his neck, over his pecs, drawing curvy lines and tiny circles that had him feeling dizzy. She sat back, watching her hands move across the landscape of his chest, down his abdomen, tracing the perfect lines of his abs, the shadows making it seem like he was made of stone.

"You're so beautiful," she told him, watching his stomach clench when she scraped a nail along his waist.

"Beautiful?" His voice was hoarse. Letting Aditi touch him, her eyes devouring his body while her fingers stroked him like he was made of glass, was as arousing as it was tortuous.

"Hmm. Handsome isn't adequate. You're beautiful." She leaned in to press her mouth against the pulse at the base of his neck.

She kissed her way down slowly, hearing the change in his breath as she licked the salt off his chest. She swirled her tongue around the edges of his small nipple, causing him to moan. When she raked it lightly with her teeth, his hand automatically sought her.

"Play by my rules," she ordered him, forcing his hands off her and back onto the sheets, "and I will let you do whatever you want later."

"Anything?" He watched her crouch lower, giving him the perfect view of her breasts, her shirt having slid open with her movement.

"Anything," she promised, looking up at him through her lashes. At his nod, her fingers dug into his waistband and she tugged them down.

The feel of her soft hands stroking his cock had him panting. She worked him gently, never increasing the pressure of her hold for too long. She bent low, cupping her breasts and pressed them in, trapping his arousal between them.

The feel of her warm flesh moving up against his rigid length, pillowing him on either side had Rian gripping into the sheets with deathly force.

"Sunshine, you feel incredible. Pinch your nipples for me," he ordered, amending it when she raised a sassy brow. "Please."

Aditi lifted herself just enough to give him a view of her fingers tightening around her puckered nipples, her mouth falling open in a gasp as she rolled them gently. Rian's eyes went dark, his hips hitching up at the sight of her touching herself for him. She moved her breasts over his cock, dipping her head eventually to lick the tip of his crown every time she got close, humming her appreciation at the taste of his precum.

"Take me into your mouth," he instructed her, watching as her berry lips enveloped him, tongue swirling at his tip over and over until he was close to emptying himself down her throat. He saw her hand disappear between their bodies, her soft whimper telling him exactly what she was up to.

"Fuck, yes, rub yourself." His hips jerked up and he pushed himself farther into her mouth. She moaned, feeling her body respond to his demand as she grew slick against her own hand. She brought her wet fingers out and painted his cock with her scent, taking time to trace his thick girth and the vein that bulged, leading up to his pulsating head.

Watching Aditi like this was just enough to whip up his urgency but not enough to satiate the beastly desire raging within him.

"Stop teasing me! Do you want to drive me mad?" he rasped when she sucked his tip for a bare second before popping off of him.

With a husky chuckle, she sat up, her grin telling him how proud she was to reduce him to this state. "I thought you said you'd make me beg."

"Taking revenge?"

"Are you telling me you don't like it?"

"I'd like it more if I could touch you."

"Ask nicely," she tutted, shaking her head teasingly at him, her hands working up and down his rock-hard cock.

"Please, Sunshine," he begged. "Let me touch you."

She bit her lower lip, thinking for a second, and then nodded.

The next instant, Rian pulled her towards him in a kiss that had her hanging on for support. He devoured her, his lips trapping hers, his hot tongue possessing her mouth and drinking her sounds. Aditi felt his hands tug her nightshirt off and push at her shorts, urging her to lift onto her knees so he could help remove them. The few seconds it took for them to disrobe and find a condom felt too long for their heated bodies, both aching for each other.

Aditi had never thought that teasing Rian would in turn feed her desires too. But that is exactly what had happened. Holding that power over him, seeing him get desperate for her, begging her to touch herself for his sake—it had brought a sense of urgency to feel him inside her again. To feel closer to him than anyone else.

"Rian?" she questioned, straddling him, her mouth twisting into a frown when he pulled the flat string out of the waistband of her shorts.

"I'm going to restrain your hands. I won't last with your hands on me tonight. Hold this part," he instructed, wrapping a length of the string over her wrists and drawing it through her palm, pinning both hands at the small of her back.

She arched her neck to see his handiwork when she tested the tightness of the knots he had used. She had very little range of motion. The wrap was firm, but not uncomfortable. Her chin came down and she found him looking at her, gauging her reaction.

"I'm going to keep you on top this time. I might tighten the slack for control," he told her. "You can stop me anytime with your safe word. Is this okay?"

She nodded, her heart thumping nervously when his eyes darkened at her acceptance. His fingers curled about her nape, pulling her closer.

"As much as I love making you scream," he whispered, pressing a kiss under her ear, "you're going to have to be good and quiet today."

"Why?"

"Don't want to get caught bouncing you on my cock."

With a gasp, she tried to move back, finding that his grip was too strong. "Shameless man!" she scolded him, biting down on her lip when he suckled her skin hard enough to leave a mark.

"You wouldn't like it if I stopped doing shameless things to you."

She could barely think of a retort when he trailed his fingers up one arm and along her rounded shoulder, slowly bringing them to her heated flesh. His knuckles dragged over the underside of one breast, one finger languorously circling her aureola, denying her the pleasure of his caress at the peak. He caught her eye, watching her deliberately when he closed a warm hand around her breast. Aditi couldn't look away, fascinated by the hunger she saw in him. He squeezed, and she let out a short huff of air, knowing there would be more. He petted her, gently at first. He got progressively bolder in his caress, satisfied only when he saw her mouth fall open in an effort to breathe, her eyes glazing over in need.

He pulled at her restraint, making her arch back so that he could kiss her throat. Her chest tightened, heaving at being unable to relax due to his grip but needing his touch more than her freedom. His mouth hovered over one dusky peak, teasing it with a single lick and blowing cool air on it until it hardened even more.

"Are you sure?" he asked her again, tugging at the thick string.

"I trust you," she replied, her mind screaming words of love, her lips substituting it with terms that he could accept. Even in her most vulnerable state, she felt safe with Rian. Time and again, he'd shown her that her comfort and consent were a priority to him. He clearly cared deeply about her. He wouldn't have snuck into her room to check on her otherwise.

Perhaps Nanamma was right.

Perhaps all he needed was some time to feel as she did. Yes, she would wait for him to catch up with her feelings and trust that he wouldn't break that hope.

"I trust you," she said again, using his surprise at her unexpected answer to bend forward and kiss him, drawing his lower lip between hers and suckling it so sweetly, he shuddered.

He groaned into her mouth when her hips moved invitingly against him. Without waiting, he lined himself with her entrance pulsed up, claiming her in a single thrust just as he tightened the reins. The pleasure of it caused her to tear up.

"Mine," she heard him growl; his teeth marking her chest, his tongue soothing the bite. "All of you is mine. This body, your moans, your jokes, your laughter, your mind. It's mine."

My heart too, Aditi thought, her insides clenching harder when his wet mouth found her nipple, suckling her, causing her to cry softly.

He groaned into her skin, his hands helping her slide back and forth in tiny nudges that only stoked the flames of their mutual need.

"You have me addicted to the way you fit around me," he confessed, his gaze trapping hers. "This feeling, when I'm buried so far in you that I think I can touch your soul—this is my heaven."

"Stay with me, then," she said, her eyes fluttering shut as he pulsed upwards into her, seating himself as deeply within her as his words. "And don't let go."

He didn't. Not when she fell apart on his lap, a choked scream erupting from her at the height of glory. Not when he untied her wrists and lay her down beneath him, kissing every precious part of her body until she was trembling with need once more, coming apart on his tongue with a tortured cry.

When he finally slid into her again, truly making love, their worlds collided, splintering with the heat of their combined passion. And as they slept that night, arms wrapped around the other, they both knew that without a doubt, they were forever changed.

34

Envy

ADITI

Wearing all the facets of one's nature with confidence was like having the perfect bra. It was not always a comfortable process to get there, and the damn sizes kept changing as you grew. But with enough effort, one could understand what suited them and find that they were uplifted in the best ways.

Aditi had believed she'd undergone this transformation already and had become self-aware. She thought she'd learnt to find a balance between the good and bad. She always tried to be kind, she tried not to covet that which wasn't hers. She tried to let go of bad experiences, forgive and move on.

Today however, she was neck deep in a feeling she had thought she wouldn't have cause to experience.

Envy.

Even with Harish, she'd only felt sad or disappointed when his behaviour had worsened. With Rian, she wanted to growl at any woman looking at him and hide him away.

She had to bite back a frown when the lady Rian was speaking to wouldn't quit staring at him. It was natural. Not only was he easy on the eyes, he was also an attentive listener, a polite companion, and a perfect gentleman.

She just wished he was being that way with her instead of someone else.

Not that this distance was his fault, her conscience chided her. He'd been more than ready to announce their engagement to their friends. It was Aditi who had stopped him.

It was neither the time nor the place for it, she had explained to a disappointed Rian. She wanted to tell her parents first, before everyone else found out. And she would get that chance later tonight, she thought, checking her phone for her flight details.

"All okay?"

Aditi glanced up to see Kaya returning to their little hideaway at the edge of the ballroom. She handed her a glass of some sparkling pink drink.

"Just checked in to make sure the flight is on time."

Kaya nodded, coming to stand right beside her. "Thank you, Aditi," she said after a moment, looking almost shy.

"What for?"

"For attending this party despite having to travel tonight. Being around so many people gets overwhelming for me," Kaya admitted sheepishly, gesturing to the crowded ballroom around them. "I don't make friends too easily either so events like this tend to be a lonely and trying affair. Having you here means I have one more person I'm not awkward with."

Aditi placed a gentle hand on Kaya's arm, squeezing it in support. "I wouldn't have missed your success party! Besides, I get to flex knowing a real-life author now. Do you know how jealous my sister is going to be when I tell her?"

"Tell her what?" a deep voice interrupted them. Immediately, Kaya's face cleared. Her entire body relaxed and a blinding smile lit up her features as her husband joined their conversation.

Aditi took a sip of her drink, watching Kaya's confidence grow under Arjun's undivided attention as he showered her with genuine praise regarding her work. Her face softened at the couple she was observing. They truly seemed to need no one else when they were together. Their affection for each other was obvious and their love—palpable.

She'd only heard bits and pieces of their story. That they had been separated for a long time. That they had only recently found each other again. Given the newness of their friendship, Aditi had not probed. As beautiful as she found them, she also felt envious.

They had the kind of love she hoped fervently to share with Rian.

Every day since her war of words with Leela, she had tried to not let her insecurities grow and get in the way of her relationship. More often than not, she succeeded. Rian made it easy to remain in the moment with him. He was loving, generous, and showed his care in a multitude of little ways. From staying up with her in the evenings to sending her packed meals at the hospital, checking on her via messages or simply dropping by with flowers to cheer her up during her night shifts, Rian had been everything she'd never dared to dream of.

Being in love with him was exciting, but it scared her all the same. The fear of losing him troubled her in the distant periphery of her mind.

Knowing she'd be away from him had unfortunately amped up all her negative emotions. It hadn't helped that in the week leading up to today, they'd both been so busy that they'd only managed to intermittently catch little moments of togetherness. She wished she could steal away time with him before she left, but being here to share in Kaya's achievements was important.

Inevitably, she found herself sweeping the ballroom to catch sight of her man. What she saw only made the tightness in her chest double.

Rian was standing with Sonia Dasavi and her family, his mother grinning approvingly as she hailed a photographer to take a picture of all of them together.

Aditi's gut twisted when Sonia hooked her arm with his, leaning her head on his shoulder like it was natural. The flash of the camera went off and when the haze cleared, Aditi's eyes met Leela's. The older woman raised a brow, her smile turning smug.

Aditi glanced away, knowing that Rian wasn't at fault. Leela was clearly trying to get under her skin. Unfortunately, she was succeeding. Her hands firmed over the flute she was holding. She threw her head back and chugged the rest of her drink, the bitterness in her mouth overwhelming her despite the sweetness of the liquid.

Excusing herself, she stalked off in search of a quiet spot to cool down in. So in her own head was she that she didn't hear the approach of footsteps behind her.

A warm hand curled about her upper arm, spinning her around.

"Rian?" she questioned, confused when his hand slid down to lace their fingers together. Wordlessly, he tugged her, nodding towards the winding stairs that led up to the hotel terrace. Her heels clicked on the marble floor, her dress swishing about her ankles as she let him guide them to an unknown destination.

Rian stopped beside a door and knocked, leading her in a moment later. Aditi cast a glance about the fancy washroom—the kind that people flaunted in their social media posts. This was less so a washroom and more a place for the ladies to rest their feet, touch up their cosmetics, and pout for the perfect behind-the-scenes pictures. Velvet loveseats with plush cushions, scented vanilla candles on the side, gleaming countertops, and muted gold sconces throwing light everywhere. It screamed opulence and glamour.

She spun slowly on her heels, awed by the details in the room. She came to a stop in front of the ornate wall mirror, realising finally that she was under observation.

The click of the lock sounded louder in the closed space than she would have expected.

Aditi said nothing as Rian came to stand behind her, his hands resting on either side of her hips. With her heels on, their height difference was reduced.

"Why'd you bring me here?"

The enigmatic look on his face revealed little of his thoughts.

"You've been somewhere else all evening."

"I've been at the same party as you," she said, tilting her head to the side when he dropped a delicate kiss at the edge of her exposed shoulder.

"But not with me," he complained, his voice low. "I don't like not having your attention."

Her lips twisted. "I don't like not having yours."

"You think I'd look anywhere else, especially when you're in a dress like this?" he muttered, his eyes trailing down towards her ankle before lifting up, lingering on every curve he adored. "Tease."

"You bought me this dress, Bugs. You insisted on it." Her stomach clenched when his hands slithered up and down her sides and pulled her into him, the ample curve of her bottom set firmly against his front.

"Because I thought I'd have you on my arm all night. Instead, I had to watch other men make eyes at you."

She scoffed disbelievingly, shaking her head.

"You have no idea how sexy you are," he insisted, running the tip of his nose along the elegant line of her neck and appreciating the mild scent of the floral perfume she used.

"As sexy as the woman you were taking pictures with?"

The moment the question left her lips, she regretted it. Insecurity was not attractive, after all. But it was too late. Rian's head lifted, eyes narrowed. He leaned in, caging her between his arms. His warmth at her back was a marked contrast to the cold stone counter in front of her.

"You didn't like it?"

She shook her head.

"It won't happen again."

The promise, so easily made, mollified her.

"You were jealous?"

She nodded, feeling embarrassed at having to admit this.

Aditi couldn't explain what it was she saw in Rian's expression. For a moment, he'd looked almost glad. Whatever it was, she was unprepared for his response.

"Next time you feel this way, claim me. No matter where we are or who is watching, walk up to me and mark your claim."

She blinked, goosebumps rushing across her skin when he dropped a whisper of a kiss on the hollows of her cheek. "I'm yours," he told her firmly, his chin resting on her shoulder. Their gazes were locked on each other's reflection. "Tell anyone you want, however you want to. But do it with a smile."

Her chin tipped up, questioning him.

"You haven't smiled much at this party. I know, because I've been watching you. I need you to smile, Doc, especially when I'm around." His hand cradled her throat from the front. A rough thumb traced the edge of her jaw, sending her pulse fluttering with the look in his eyes.

"And if your lips are not smiling when they are with me," he added, his voice dropping to deep rumble, "they better be busy moaning my name."

Her heart rate picked up when his hold tightened and he angled her face up towards his.

"What will it be, Doc?" he asked, his breath flirting with her lips. "A smile, or a moan?"

Her fingers clenched into the counter in front of her, feeling his arousal press into her back. Her gaze flickered between his mouth and eyes.

"Do it," she whispered. "Make me moan your name."

Clearly, she could still surprise him because his hand dropped.

"Here?" he asked, needing to be sure.

"Here," she repeated, maintaining eye contact despite the furious blush that was beginning to spread across her skin.

He had wanted her to claim him. She found that she felt no differently. She needed his closeness to dismiss the unwelcome fear that had struck her, watching his mother push Sonia towards him.

"Now," she instructed him, facing the mirror as she began to lift her skirt slowly, knowing that this action would entice him to listen.

He watched, riveted as inch after inch of her pretty legs were revealed for his view, his body tightening in response when she leaned forward, ass jutting back, her invitation clear.

Warm hands stroked up the backs of her thighs, cupping her at the apex between them. She grew damp against his hand, biting down on the inside of her cheek when she felt her thong being moved aside. The blunt top of one finger circled her entrance, collecting evidence of her arousal.

"Fuck, you really want this," he said, his voice thick with desire.

"I want you in me. No foreplay."

"I don't have a condom," he told her, giving her a chance to change her mind.

"I don't care," she panted, the mere feel of his index dipping into her pussy causing her mind to go blank with pleasure. "There's only you, Rian."

The vein in his head throbbed as he physically reacted to her words, growing immeasurably harder. "Then spread your legs wider, Sunshine. Show me what's mine." His pride deepened when she obeyed instantly.

He curled his finger into her, stroking her slowly to prepare her for him. Aditi would have complained, except she was too busy watching him release himself from the confines of his slacks. Their eyes locked as he held the base of his shaft, pumping himself a few times and moaning her name with each move. Her mouth dried at the sensuality of this view, her core wetting in anticipation of what would come next.

Her eyes fluttered to a close at the feel of his wide head nudging her opening. When he slid into her, she couldn't hold back a heartfelt sigh, focused on the pleasure of stretching around him when he was bare. "Holy fuck," Rian groaned as he hunched over her, one arm slipping around her waist to hold her to him. "So fucking good."

He shifted her hair over one shoulder, dropping a kiss at the exposed crook of her neck. Greedy hands cupped her bosom, kneading her, making her ache to feel his fingers on her skin. Impatiently, she grabbed both his hands and directed him to grip her hips.

"I need you to move," she commanded, pushing back onto him. "Or I will."

Chuckling at her bossiness, he pulled out leaving just the tip in.

"Rian!" she moaned, a warning and an entreaty in a single word. He pulsed into her without warning, making her gasp out loud at the force of his entry.

"Is this what you wanted, Sunshine?" he rasped, out of his mind with the beauty of her abandon.

"Yes," she whimpered as she fell forward, her palms slapping against the marble countertop when he drove into her with a particularly hard thrust.

To witness Aditi want him without any reservations drove him crazy with lust. He loved being desired without thought to the world around them. He exulted in her possessiveness because it told him she felt about him the way he felt about her.

His thrusts turned more forceful, pushing her chest onto the cold counter, her cheek resting sideways as he fucked her from behind. At his mercy, Aditi gave herself up for his possession, his passion consuming her. A finger slicked in between her legs, pressing at her bundle of nerves while his deep-seated movements nudged against that part inside that whipped her into a furious crescendo. A scorching flush spread across her being as she reached completion, waves of icy fire licking her skin, making her toes curl in pleasure.

The tight clenching of her body milking him stirred the beginning of his orgasm. His powerfully muscled arm clutched her, lifting her into him. One hand held the inside of her thigh, forcing her to remain spread until he pumped every last drop of his release into her quivering womb.

For a long minute after that, the only sounds around them were the rough and staggered breaths they took as their bodies relaxed, trying to come down from the high they'd both achieved.

Without slipping out of her, Rian leaned over to grab a soft washcloth, dampening one edge of it.

He held it between her legs while he pulled out and tucked himself back into his pants, manoeuvring her to face him.

"I can clean myself, Rian."

Aditi adjusted her top and tried to take the cloth from him, scrunching her nose when he pushed her hand away.

"Let me," Rian murmured. He kissed the side of her lips softly before kneeling in front of her, bunching her skirt up and holding it by her waist. "At least this way," he added, sliding the damp cloth up the inside of her thigh, "I can see what you look like if I could leave you marked with my come."

Her brows shot up. "What?" she asked with a breathy laugh that was part shock, part interest.

"Every time you feel me drip down your thighs, you'll remember what I did to you. What I have done before, and what else I will do in the future." Silver eyes pinned her in place, holding her attention when he spoke, each word sending a shiver down her spine.

Aditi thought she might faint a little. Rian was revealing bit by bit every desire he had for her and instead of scaring her, it felt thrilling. He was sweet and indulgent outside their bedroom, but incredibly outgoing, experimental, and as she had found in the last couple weeks, utterly insatiable in bed.

"What do you say, Doc?" he asked with a little smirk, pecking her thigh before standing up. His hand remained firmly wedged between her legs.

"About?"

The damp cloth swirled around her other thigh, slowly moving up. She didn't know if cleaning up after sex was meant to feel so damn sensual but she'd given up trying to understand her body's reactions to Rian altogether.

"Will you let me do it?"

"Hmm?" she swayed, her eyes struggling to focus.

With a silent laugh, Rian leaned in to place nibbling kisses on the side of her neck as he pushed the cloth against her clit. The coolness of the towel and the gentle rubs against her oversensitized skin made her gasp and moan at once. Reacting to this, she tried to close her legs, finding that one knee was held captive by his hip.

He pressed up against her, pushing gently as he whispered into her ear. "Should I fill you up again? When you try to talk to someone else, you'd do it with me on your mind, and me inside your body, my essence sliding down your perfect thighs, colouring that pretty little cunt."

She trembled, his words sending little bolts of current through her that collected at the tips of her breasts. Her clothes felt like torture devices, binding her, separating her from his touch.

"Will you wear my scent like I am wearing yours, Sunshine?" He rubbed her softly, dragging the edge of the cloth along her folds as his thumb pressed on her clit through the cool material.

"Yes," she cried softly, not sure if she was saying yes to his finger or his question.

"That's what I thought," he husked, scraping the lobe of her ear with his teeth.

He pressed the towel harder, then softer, circling exactly where she needed the pressure until she was panting against his shoulder.

"So lovely, spread out, ready to take my cock inside this sweet pussy, my good girl." Rian felt her body go taut before her fingers dug into him. His mouth covered hers, drinking in her cries as she barrelled off the cliff once more, her nerves tingling in rapture.

"You made me come again," she told him breathlessly, sounding awed.

His eyes twinkled, revealing to her that he'd done it deliberately. He had known exactly what to say and how to touch her to distract her spent body from the demand of another orgasm until it was too late for her to deny it.

He tossed the damp cloth into the bin, adjusting her skirt around her legs, looking supremely pleased with himself.

She checked the mirror once the aftershocks had dwindled enough to let her move, patting her hair in a wasted effort to look presentable. Her skirt was rumpled, her lips swollen, and the beginnings of a hickey marked the side of her neck. She spun towards him, drawing some of her hair to the front, hoping it would be enough to cover evidence of what they'd done.

"How do I look?"

With a smirk, he ran a finger down the side of her temple, leaving behind tingles.

"Like I made you come twice."

She smacked his chest playfully, giggling at his answer, feeling the hot flush of a blush come on again.

"Fuck," he cursed softly, gulping like he'd just seen a magical being.

"What?"

He drew the same finger across her cheek. "You're pink." Then, he groaned.

"What's wrong?" she asked, concerned with the sudden change in his mood.

"I just remembered where else you get pink and then I realised you're leaving, so I can't see your gorgeous body get pink for me for a while." He dropped his head against her shoulder, his hair tickling her collarbone. "Why do you have to go again?"

"Because it's my parent's anniversary." She laughed, pulling him out of the washroom in case he was tempted to keep them there longer. "I can't miss it."

"I should come with you," he suggested as they made their way down the stairs, back towards the ballroom. "I need to meet your family anyway."

"You can't miss your meeting with the investing board."

"That's two whole days away. I can drop you off in Bangalore, tell your folks about us, then pop back before the meeting."

Aditi was not convinced. "You need to focus on the meeting first. This is the dream project. Besides, I need a little time to lay the groundwork with my family."

"You think they won't like me?" Rian asked, worried. He knew how important it was for her to have her family's acceptance. Thankfully, Aditi didn't seem to share his concern.

"Have you met you?" She chuckled, coming to a stop a few feet away from the open hall doors. She brushed the lapels of his jacket, pretending to adjust them simply to have an excuse to touch him in public. "You could charm a cactus if you wanted to."

"Then why not tell them?"

"My parents were really hoping I'd agree to marry Pratik. I want to let them down easy."

"You better not listen to someone there and say yes to that perfect NRI."

She tapped his nose fondly to stop him from grumbling. "I think I'll stick with you." She gave him a sultry look that made him want to take her right back up for privacy. "Besides, that perfect NRI would probably not know how to sex me up in a fancy hotel washroom."

That made Rian grin so hard, he was sure his face was going to split.

She glanced around to check if anyone was watching before leaning up to kiss the side of his jaw.

"Go, socialise." She bashfully waved him off. "I'll find you when it's time to leave."

35

Bunny

RIAN

Rian stood outside the ballroom tapping his foot to the beat of the rhythm inside. He hummed silently, the tiny uptilt of his lips a constant.

He pushed his hands inside his pocket, curbing the urge to begin whistling like a young boy.

It was natural, he thought to himself, to feel this level of happiness. Anyone who was lucky enough to have landed a woman like Aditi would feel like he was floating on clouds.

He shook his head, having completely given up any pretence of control when it came to her. This only made it that much harder to acknowledge that she'd be leaving for Bangalore in a couple hours and he wouldn't be going with her.

He checked the time on his watch, waiting patiently for Aditi to finish saying her goodbyes. Keeping his distance all evening had been tough enough. He was not looking forward to the emptiness of his home with Aditi's departure.

He'd be taking her to the apartment to pick up her luggage before heading to the airport, which would give him enough time to confess the full extent of his feelings for her. He was confident that she felt the same way. Her possessiveness was proof enough of that.

Perhaps it was the impending separation that had had them both so tense. Their encounter in the bathroom upstairs was certainly one way to take the edge off, he acknowledged, chuckling to himself.

He tried to assume a sober mien when he received an odd look from a passing couple. He had heard once that only insanity or love would cause a person to laugh by himself. He could now attest that it was true. He was in love with Aditi, insanely so, and the ebullience he experienced because of that was hard to hide.

"Where the hell did you disappear?"

Rian shut his eyes, resisting the urge to groan. Almost immediately, the bubbles of delight that had kept him company burst. He turned just as Leela came to stand in front of him, her features drawn in a severe frown.

"We were in the middle of pictures with the Dasavis. How could you have been so rude? Sonia was so upset after you left."

"That's your problem. I had a date to return to."

Leela clenched her teeth, her nostrils flaring as her temper rose.

"Why her?" she asked, the displeasure in her tone making it clear to him that she was referring to Aditi. "I can find you girls that are far more beautiful than her, fair and. . ."

"And rich?" he interrupted, having heard this spiel before.

"Pick someone who will match our status," she said, her chin rising haughtily. "Whatever you are doing with that girl, break it off."

"No." His nonchalance increased her ire.

"Rian! Your rebellion needs to end now. I have put up with you dating one unsuitable girl after another but this is enough!"

His jaw tightened at those words. He clenched his fists within his pockets, trying to concentrate on taking slow and consistent breaths. A moment later, he let a veneer of calm settle upon his features once more. Getting angry would only make his mother recognize his weakness for Aditi and worse, she would sharpen her claws on the woman he wanted to protect.

"Your opinion is worthless to me," he muttered, sounding bored. "You've been wanting me to get married. I plan on doing exactly that. I would tell you to be happy for me but I don't think you know how."

"I wanted you to marry one of the girls from the country club! Not this loud, ungraceful goat." She looked like she was a hair's breadth away from stomping her foot.

Ungraceful? Rian was reminded of the spirited and happy dance Aditi had taken part in, her hairdo falling apart, her face red with exertion, her smile reaching her eyes. Unlike his mother's expectations of a graceful girl who was too engrossed in making sure her perfect makeup did not run, Aditi was messy and fun. That was what he wanted. She was so full of life, it ached to be away from her. Everything was so dull without her. Fuck, how was he going to pass two weeks of her being away?

"You cannot marry her!" Leela's shrill voice broke into his thoughts. "I will not allow it. The Dasavis are an impressive and wealthy family. Sonia is a better match in every way. She's my choice."

"Then *you* marry her," he insolently advised, irritation growing within him despite his best efforts.

For Leela to think he would still listen to her had to be the result of a delusion he didn't care to investigate the reason for. He knew her well enough to guess that a tantrum would be forthcoming. He didn't care much if she made a spectacle of herself, but he hated that he would be a part of it. It didn't, however, insulate him from being petty enough to want to return the frustration she had doled out to him over the years.

"I don't care about your choice," he finally told her, shrugging impertinently in a manner he knew would send her into a spiral. For all the times she had thrust him into negativity, this was a small payback.

"You have always wanted my attention and acknowledgement," he heard her say, causing him to guffaw at her ability to make everything about herself, yet again. "I'm giving you a chance, as my son, to finally make me proud. I have been embarrassed enough by you."

He stiffened instantly, his shield of indifference cracking as her words pierced through. She had managed to puncture the scabs of old wounds borne by his younger self. Hurt and rage formed a sickening concoction that drowned his ability to reason with himself.

"You've always said I'm a curse to you. That I've always disappointed you." He choked the words out, uncaring of his surroundings. The need to infuriate his mother so that she could experience just a portion of the pain she'd caused him overtook his sensibilities.

"That is precisely why I will pick Aditi," he informed her, his mouth twisting cruelly at seeing Leela grow visibly angry. "That you dislike her is more than enough reason for me to marry her. The more unsuitable the girl in your eyes, the better because embarrassing you has become a source of amusement for me."

"You will never be happy with her," Leela hissed, her eyes narrowing to slits.

"Making you unhappy would be worth it."

"You did not heed my warning with that girl, Kaveri or Kaya, whatever she is called these days. Are you sure you want to ignore me again?"

The small thread of reason holding him back, broke. He rushed up to her, spitting in her face. "Don't you dare threaten me. Stay away from my friend."

He recognized a second too late that his reaction was a mistake.

"Ah," she snickered, honing in on the same weakness she'd exploited in the past. "I know about your friendship well. I saw evidence of it when she was standing half naked next to you."

"Shut your vile mouth or I will make sure you get thrown out of here."

Leela threw her head back and cackled, deriving a perverted sort of joy from having torn him down. Whatever happiness he'd been experiencing ten minutes ago was lost beneath the darkness of the ominous clouds she'd drawn over him, surrounding him in a storm that he feared would leave some kind of wreckage in its wake.

"Sure," she taunted him. "Call someone to throw me out. I will ask my question louder, in a bigger crowd then. This friendship you have with Kaveri—is it the same kind of friendship you have with that girl living in your house, too? Does she know how friendly you are with Kaveri Rathore?"

His hands shook. "Shut up."

"Does Kaveri's husband know, too?"

"You disgust me."

Unwilling to witness more of her nastiness, Rian turned, his heart plummeting when he realised Aditi and Kaya had overheard his argument with Leela.

His gaze rested upon Aditi's ashen face.

"Doc," he started, about to walk towards her when she stepped back, stopping him with a single shake of her head. The moment stretched, his feet aching to cover the space between them, his mind in a turmoil. Dread seeped into him as her eyes grew red, watching him like he had betrayed her.

Just when he thought she would finally call for him, allowing him to go to her, to explain himself and make this better, she threw him into an abyss of anxiety and guilt with a single word.

"Bunny."

36

Respect

ADITI

SHE HAD TO KEEP going.

She had to keep moving, stay busy and do *something*, whether or not it was useful, she decided, throwing a random scarf into her suitcase. She turned, brushing past the man who'd been standing silently in her room for well over a half hour, waiting for her to give him a chance.

Waiting for her to acknowledge him.

But doing so would mean having to stop, and stopping would mean that the feelings she was running from would catch up to her.

She knew it was inevitable. After all, how could she escape a tidal wave that had been growing at her shore, the warning for which she had not heeded?

She pulled out two shirts from her closet, stepping around Rian, who'd followed her yet again.

"Can we please talk now?" she heard him request, possibly for the fifth time since they'd gotten home. Her response would be no different.

"No."

The ferociousness with which she zipped her bag made Rian flinch.

"I don't want you to leave Mumbai with this hanging over us, Aditi. I'll follow you to Bangalore if I have to."

"Then talk."

"I can explain everything, but will you believe me? You can't even look at my face."

At that, Aditi thwacked her bag on the ground, her anger driving her sadness and vice-versa. She moved to the dresser, grabbing items at random.

"I have done nothing but believe you, Rian. Since the day I met you until today, I believed you. When you told me that you didn't want a traditional relationship, I believed you. When you said you'd changed your mind and asked me to marry you, I believed you. I never inquired why because I thought it didn't matter. But it does." She stopped, feeling exhausted already, her voice trembling. "Why are you with me?"

It was a question as much to herself as it was to him. With everything she'd heard today, she no longer knew if she understood Rian as well as she'd once believed.

"I guess I really know how to pick guys," she scoffed, shaking her head. "First Harish, then you."

His lips thinned, knowing that Aditi was justified in her anger. He had been willing to let her speak her piece; lay her thoughts out so that her fury would abate. But he couldn't remain silent at this.

"Don't compare me to him. I never disrespected you."

When she finally turned around, it was with a look Rian couldn't read.

"Choosing me only because I'm useful to piss off your mother is giving me respect?" she asked emotionlessly. The lack of inflection in her tone spread a chill in the air.

The sinking feeling within him deepened when he realised that Aditi had been subjected to much more than just the end of his argument with Leela. He was horrified.

"You heard that?"

"Yes. I heard it. Along with anyone who was within earshot of you."

He raised both palms up in a gesture of surrender, approaching her as slowly as one would a wild animal who lay injured in the woods.

"I said that to make my mother unhappy. You have to believe me. It meant nothing."

He reached for her, stilling when she backed away quickly, rejecting his touch.

"You don't get it, do you?" she asked, her features contorted with grief. Her eyes filled rapidly with tears she wished she could have hidden.

"Can you even imagine what it must've been like for me to hear you say those words?" she whispered, her throat closing as emotions flooded her. "I thought you accepted me for who I am. I loved that I never had to feel like I had to be someone different when I was with you. But, you made me sound like an idiot." Hot tears spilled out of her, her features contorting in grief. "You made me feel like you'd have never picked me under different circumstances. All for what? To win an argument with your mother?"

With every broken question, Rian felt like he'd become unworthy of her. With every tremble of her lip or shaky breath she took, telling him without words that she was devastated, he felt like he'd somehow repeated his mistakes of the past.

He had done to Aditi what he had done to Kaya.

Unlike Kaya, however, he couldn't let Aditi go. Not without a fight.

"I made a terrible mistake," he admitted, trying to close the gap between them. He hated that he felt like he'd lost the right to touch her. "I know an explanation or a reason won't make this okay, but please, you *know* how I feel about you."

"Do I?" Aditi shook her head, resignation etched upon her features. Fear gripped him.

"You do!"

"What about Kaya?"

"What about her?" he repeated, confused with the unexpected detour in their conversation.

"I remembered meeting you in Velas earlier this year but I couldn't recollect the woman I'd tended to that night. It only occurred to me today when I heard you with your mother."

"Aditi..."

"That night," she continued, as if he'd never spoken. "It was Kaya who'd been ill. She was the patient I'd attended to. You'd been so worried about her because you were in love with her. I thought I'd made it all up in my head after the way you'd gotten angry when I told you to move on, but I was right. Wasn't I?"

Rian was at a loss for words. Giving her any answer right now felt like it would backfire on him.

"I met Kaya so many times and I never knew who she really was," she accused, feeling deceived. "Why didn't you tell me?"

"It wasn't relevant to us."

"Finding out that the man I've agreed to marry was previously in love with his best friend is not relevant?" she spat, her incredulity at his justification turning her voice shrill. "You know everything about my past. Did you not think I deserved the same consideration?"

"It was unintentional. I never meant to hide anything."

"Do you love her?"

He shook his head immediately. "No! And, she is married."

"That doesn't stop people," she scornfully accused, her envy cloaking her capacity to be fair.

Rian's lips tightened in a firm line. "Be careful of what you imply," he chided her, soft but stern. "Kaya loves Arjun. She's not a cheater and neither am I."

Shame swelled in her and she turned away, walking up to the window nearby. "You're right. This isn't about her at all, it's about you. Be honest with me. Did you love Kaya before?"

"Yes."

"For how long?"

"A long time."

"Years?" she asked, glancing at him. A single look was enough to confirm her suspicions.

A bone deep sadness took root in her at this realisation, feeling like her heart was being cut open with a scalpel.

Rian had loved Kaya. Not for a few days or weeks. For years.

He had loved her up until just a few months ago. How did one move on from that, especially when they were still very much a part of each other's lives?

It had taken her quite a while to get over Harish, and he was a horrible man. Kaya, on the other hand, was wonderful. It would have been a momentous task to fall out of love with someone like her.

Then what was Rian doing with Aditi? Was she...god forbid, was she a rebound? Was Rian redirecting his need for companionship, something he had wanted from Kaya, into Aditi instead? What did that mean for their relationship and its longevity?

The noise in her brain grew louder, weighing her down and making it hard to breathe.

"Aditi? Speak to me."

What could she say? With everything she'd just learned, she was afraid that if she told him to really delve deep and confirm his feelings for her, she'd lose him.

After Nanamma's entreaty for her to give Rian time, Aditi had chosen deliberately to focus on how he made her feel. How well he treated her. She had felt wanted, and cherished. Though he had not said it, she *had* felt loved. Had she just fooled herself into believing something because she wanted it to be true?

What if Nanamma was wrong? What if Rian really couldn't come around to loving her like she loved him? She would always want more from him. And if he was unable to give her that, then what would become of her? A lifetime of compromise would rip her heart to shreds.

"Doc?"

Aditi stared at him with a heartbreakingly blank expression. The innumerable thoughts in her head created a furor of doubts that left her crippled with fear.

"I need to go to the airport," she muttered, her feet carrying her aimlessly out of her room.

Alarmed, he gripped her by her wrist when she tried to pass him by.

"Stop!" she cried, angrily fighting his hold.

They stood facing each other, the air heavy with longing, fear, and disappointment. Her distress, her usually smiling face now twisted in pain, felt like a kick in the guts.

He took a careful step towards her, keeping his arms open, a request that was as much for him as it was for her. Little by little, he covered the space between them, giving her every opportunity to deny his touch, praying with everything he had that she wouldn't.

As his arms closed about her, gentle still, it was as though Rian took his first breath since Aditi had uttered her safe word. It gave him hope that he'd be able to correct what had gone wrong.

"Let me go," she sniffled, letting out a tiny whimper.

"Let me hold you. Please."

He bent low, breathing in her scent. If she pushed him away now, he may not recover with any grace.

"Why are you with me, Rian?" Her question was interrupted by her soft sobs and gasping breaths.

"Because," he answered, his voice cracking with emotion, "I love you."

She shook her head against his chest, hating that what she had so wanted to hear had come now, in a moment that was not one she would want to remember.

"You can't say that after saying hurtful things about me," she choked out.

That she remained in his embrace and allowed him to comfort her did very little to reduce the intensity of his guilt. Self-loathing gripped him in a chokehold, each shuddering breath she drew tormenting him beyond any wound inflicted by his mother.

"This is not how I wanted to tell you. The timing leaves a lot to be desired, but it doesn't change how I feel. I love you." He drew back, gently wiping her tears. "I know I said some fucked up things today. Please don't let that stop you from acknowledging my reality."

Watery brown eyes met his, her anguish palpable.

"What *is* your reality?" she asked, her chin wobbling.

"You," he breathed, devastated that he had made her question this. "I am not myself without you." He brushed her hair back and held her face in both hands, gazing at her with such deep yearning that Aditi had to close her eyes to not feel affected.

He gathered her in his arms, holding her closer as his palm curved over the back of her skull. "I'm not telling you to forgive me now, or easily," he said, his voice low enough to crack. "But don't break up with me. Please. Don't give up on me. I want you. I want a lifetime of us together. Give me a chance to fix my mistake."

His request made her want to wail louder. She was torn between wanting to protect herself versus protecting him. The wretched reality of loving a good man was that it didn't make him infallible. It didn't preclude him from causing her pain. It simply limited how long she was able to remain genuinely furious, especially when his vulnerability was as heartbreaking as his request.

"We're having a fight. One fight doesn't mean a break up. It just means we have things to work through," she finally answered, knowing that letting him believe differently would be cruel. She may be angry with him, but she did not want to wound him.

Rian released a trapped breath, one massive worry put to rest.

"I'm sorry," he apologised again, the words sounding hollow even to his own ears. "I'm sorry I didn't tell you about Kaya. And for whatever I said to my mother. Hurting you is the farthest thing from my mind."

She believed his apology. She even believed his confession. She simply couldn't subdue the shred of resentment that his choices had left in their wake. She felt let down, and it was clear that he didn't fully understand why. How could he, when she hadn't been able to explain her biggest point of contention?

"What about next time?" she asked, gently drawing away. Rian didn't let go of her hand however, and she didn't ask him to.

"What do you mean?"

Aditi took a deep breath in, fortifying herself for what she had to say.

"Your mother came to visit a couple weeks ago, just after we'd gotten together. I didn't tell you because I didn't want to lose you to whatever anger she generates in you. She told me that you can't disregard her. That she'd never make it easy for us to be together. I didn't believe her until I heard you today. Every time she's in the picture, you change into someone I can't recognise."

"Please," Rian begged, squeezing her hand. "Don't let my mother come between us. She does this. She poisons things around me."

"She's only between us because you've given her the power," Aditi announced, unwilling to mince words any more. "I wish I could fix this for you, but I can't. I can't force you to move on. Not this time."

"I know I hurt you today. It won't happen again. I prom—"

"Don't make promises you cannot keep," she interrupted, her disappointment clear. "When you don't respect yourself enough to ignore someone who is toxic for you, how will you remember to respect me enough to keep your promises? Last time, at the club, you took your anger out on me. This time, you insulted our relationship. Next time you face your mother, you might hurt me in a different way. How long before you break out of this cycle? Will I be expected to forgive you every time?"

Rian wondered how to respond to these questions, or if he had a solution to the problem she'd pointed out. He'd always wanted to cut his mother out of his life. For reasons unknown, he'd not succeeded. His failure had in turn damaged Aditi's trust in him. How could he give her an answer when he didn't understand it himself?

Throughout the drive to the airport, both Rian and Aditi remained immersed in their own thoughts. For two people who had never felt the slightest hesitation with each other before, neither one could find it in them to breach the disconcerting silence between them.

Rian parked in the busy drop off zone, stepping out to grab her suitcase. He clicked the button on the handle and extended it for her, needing to feel useful somehow. She accepted his help, stilling when his hand closed over hers. A warm finger slid under her chin, turning her face towards him. For a breathless moment, he said nothing. Remorse and regret had dampened his confidence.

"I'll fix this, Aditi," he promised her anyway.

"Okay," she whispered, but the tension on her face remained.

"Okay?" he asked again, cupping her cheek. Before she could pull away, he leaned in and pressed a brief kiss onto her lips. "Come back to me," he requested, his forehead resting on hers before he straightened. "I'll be waiting here."

She nodded quietly.

"I love you," he confessed yet again, hoping she would say it back. She watched him with an indeterminable look, eventually stepping closer for a hug. His arms wrapped around her immediately, his chest tight with the fear that if he let go, she wouldn't return. If he could, he would have taken her back home and held her until they both felt better. Until he figured out how to give her whatever it was that would make her trust him again.

That would make her look at him like she used to.

As though she'd heard his silent plea, she leaned back to glance up at him.

"Love me enough to heal yourself," she told him, her tone muted in sadness. "There is a part of you your mother still controls. That's not okay."

She cupped his jaw, a gloomy tilt to her lips.

"I want *all* of you, Rian. I don't think I can accept less."

Without another word, Aditi walked away, leaving him stunned with her request. She'd told him, in no uncertain terms, what it would take to gain her forgiveness.

A complete and clear step in severing whatever hold his mother had on him.

He watched her approach the entrance, the stiffness in her movements a dead giveaway for her stress.

"Turn," he whispered, observing her handing her ID card over for the guard to check.

"Turn." He almost raised his hand partway to wave to her.

"Turn," he wished quietly, his eyes glued on her person. He readied himself to smile at her, his gut twisting in disappointment when she walked through the guarded doors and faded into the crowds.

Aditi, the girl who never missed an opportunity to romanticise her life, had not turned back to wave at him.

He stood there, waiting, just in case she changed her mind, uncaring that the ushers around him were yelling at him to move his car. His feet remained grounded, wishing that she would come running out the doors, rush into his arms, and allow him to show her how much he loved her. That she would allow him to prove to her how sorry he was for having caused her smile to wane.

He waited, hoping that she would show.

She didn't.

37

Distance

Bugs4life (10:07 p.m.)

Did you reach Bangalore? I saw your flight landed.

Sunshine Doc (10:10 p.m.)

Yes, I'm with my family.

Bugs4life (10:12 p.m.)

Are you okay?

Sunshine Doc (10:17 p.m.)

Yes.

Bugs4life (10:18 p.m.)

Are *we* okay?

Sunshine Doc (10:20 p.m.)

Yes.

Bugs4life (10:20 p.m.)

missed call

Are you still angry?

Sunshine Doc (10:21 p.m.)

Yes.

Bugs4life (10:21 p.m.)

missed call

Can we talk?

Sunshine Doc (10:23 p.m.)

Later.

Bugs4life (10:24 p.m.)

Doc, I thought we cleared things up.

Sunshine Doc (10:24 p.m.)

Doesn't mean I stopped being hurt.

Bugs4life (10:28 p.m.)

Just promise me one thing.

Sunshine Doc (10:28 p.m.)

What?

Bugs4life (10:29 p.m.)

Don't let your anger with me affect your eating habits. Don't get anxious and skip meals.

And. . .don't cry. No one is worth your tears.

Sunshine Doc (10:30 p.m.)

I wish you wouldn't say things like that.

It makes it harder to be mad at you.

Bugs4life (10:30 p.m.)

Then don't be mad at me.

Sunshine Doc (10:30 p.m.)

I don't want to be. I just. . .

We'll talk in a couple days.

I need to focus on my family.

Bugs4life (10:31 p.m.)

I love you, Doc.

I miss you.

Sunshine Doc (10:33 p.m.)

. . .I miss you, too.

38

Catharsis

RIAN

Rian leaned against the cold metal railing of his balcony, his sights pinned at random at the highest point of the sea-link bridge that he could see from his apartment. The clear skies brushed in hues of pale pink and purple formed a delicate backdrop for the imposing concrete structure.

Had his mind been at peace, he would have taken the opportunity to appreciate this view. Amongst the cacophony of thoughts today were two additional voices that troubled him with their concern.

"Do you want to go to the new club that opened near the Queen's Palace?" Kaya offered.

"No."

"How about laser tag?"

"No."

"How about Arjun holds you down and I hit you with my shoe?"

"No...what?"

"I'm game," Arjun responded, his voice bored.

"You're driving me insane, Rian," Kaya grumbled while lowering into the loveseat near him. She gave him the stink eye at the subtle twitch in his jaw, shifting to the larger couch immediately. She'd made the mistake of trying to sit in Aditi's spot once already, leading Rian to throw a small hissy fit, much to Arjun and Kaya's amusement.

"Now I know why Aditi dumped his ass," Arjun muttered, throwing an arm around the back of the lounge to make space for his wife.

"Hey, go easy on the judgement," Kaya tapped his thigh.

"Love, I went easy on you when you kept running from me. I have no reason to go easy on this fool," Arjun pointed, catching the balled up napkin Rian launched at him in irritation.

"She didn't dump me," Rian snarked, frustrated by the nagging. "Nothing is wrong with us. And if you both plan to discuss me like I'm not here, then I'll leave."

"Sit!" Kaya hissed, pulling him into the seat beside her as he passed them by while Arjun rolled his eyes, very much unimpressed with his tantrum. "Aditi is too good for him."

Unfortunately, Rian agreed.

Kaya and Arjun had shown up to check in on him after days of not getting a response to their messages. A conversation with Nanamma had confirmed that he was sulking alone.

"Did you two fight?" Kaya asked, shushing her husband before he taunted her friend some more. "Adi was quite disturbed when she left the event last week, and I don't blame her."

Rian couldn't meet her eyes.

"If you argued, just make it up to her and apologise."

He glanced away, stubbornly silent.

Kaya turned to her husband, gesturing towards the inside. Understanding that she wanted a minute alone, he stood up.

"I'm going to go try to figure out Rian's coffee machine," Arjun announced, bending down to swipe a kiss on his wife's cheek. "Or break it. I haven't decided."

Rian noticed the silly, lovestruck smile on Kaya's face as she watched her husband walk away, and it only made him miss Aditi more. She would have made him smile like that as well.

Unable to help himself, he pulled out his phone and unlocked it to reveal a picture of the two of them making silly faces. He sighed, catching Kaya watching him with an exasperated look.

"What?" he asked defensively.

"What's the problem?" She turned sideways and sat with one leg folded under her, the other on the ground. "Explain it to me so I can understand, because Arjun offered to punch you on Aditi's behalf and I am tempted to let him."

"You're supposed to be my friend, not Aditi's."

"And that is the only reason why I am giving you a chance to explain why you are trying to run from a woman who loves you."

"I'm not," he insisted, indignation rising.

"Then why are you sulking?"

"She brought up some things that I am trying to figure out the answer to, without much success."

"Like?"

He sighed, rubbing the back of his neck. He had thought about Aditi's parting words constantly over the last couple days. But having to explain it felt like a Herculean task. At least Hercules had a road map for what he was required to do. Rian felt like a shipwrecked sailor floating in choppy Pacific waters, trying to grasp pieces of driftwood to stay alive.

"I don't know where to begin. She found out I loved you once."

Kaya's brows met in the middle, her lips twisting as she contemplated that.

"Okay," she drawled. "That's an easy fix. Did you tell her that we're like family? It was never really serious between us."

"I never got that far. I don't know how to fix this fucking mess that I've created." He pressed two fingers into his temple as he felt the slow indications of a migraine coming on once again. The existing strain between Aditi and him had kept him in the doldrums. Sure, she hadn't yelled and tried to guilt him for days on end, but her silence disturbed him even more. He would rather face her anger than feel like she was shutting him out.

Her teary accusations troubled him. To have his words make her feel ridiculed for who she was, when it was her beautiful personality that had drawn him to her in the first place, felt like a cruel prank. He rubbed his lips absentmindedly, the ghost of their last kiss taunting him, her dispiritedness hindering his own ability to function normally.

"Maybe I should let her go, for her sake," he supposed, his gaze pinned upon the moving cars on the bridge. "She deserves someone who knows what the fuck he's doing."

"That might be the most ridiculous thing I've ever heard you say."

"I don't know. I'm not cut out for love and relationships. I didn't like the heartache that came with it the first time around either. I didn't get over you for a long time and I didn't want to put myself through that again. But here I am. Making that same mistake. And it feels like hell."

Instead of sympathy, Rian received a smack with the pillow Kaya held.

"The hell?" he griped, rubbing the back of his head where she'd landed her hit.

Unapologetic about her actions, Kaya defiantly lifted her chin. "In Arjun's words, that's a flaming pile of bullshit."

"What?"

"Oh, come on!" she scoffed, throwing the pillow across from them at the empty loveseat. "You stopped having romantic feelings for me eons ago."

"That's not patronising at all."

Her eyes threw daggers at him.

"Sarcasm doesn't suit you, Rian Shetty."

He grumbled under his breath, the stubborn set of his jaw telling Kaya that she was in for a long tug of war. She was unused to obstinacy in him, but she was no less tenacious.

"Humour me," she proposed, praying for patience. "How does what you feel for Aditi compare with how you felt about me?"

"It doesn't. You were sad and angry for so long, unwilling to let anyone close. I didn't know how to help you. It was worrisome—no offence."

"None taken. What about Aditi?"

Rian sat back, his mind automatically recalling the times he spent with her. Almost instantly, the stress lines on his face relaxed.

"She said once that she's the sunshine to my grumpiness and I believe her. She makes me laugh with her ridiculous puns and positive outlook. She's uncomplicated and uninhibited. She makes me want to be like her. Free."

Kaya nodded, seemingly following him. "And how do you feel without her now?"

"Suffocated." The ache of not having her with him returned. "Fuck, I miss her so much. How did you stay away from Arjun for so long?"

Kaya shot him a small smile, one that spoke of a long journey, and possible regrets.

"I didn't love him then," she confessed frankly. "I can't imagine being separated from him now. I was also very afraid. Don't be like me, please."

He sighed.

"Do you not love her?" she asked.

"Of course I love her. I even told her as much. I doubt she believed me. Hell, after the shit I was spewing, I wouldn't believe me either. I hurt whoever I love. This just proved it. I'm cursed."

"Cursed?"

Insecurities and doubts that he'd successfully concealed within him for years were too close to the surface today to remain hidden. Perhaps he was simply exhausted, because he heard himself say, "My dad, Nanamma, you. I bring the blight of my twisted relationship with my mother upon whoever I love."

"I don't understand," Kaya frowned.

"I was responsible for what my mother did to you."

"No, you weren't." The immediate denial was laced with a flippancy that spoke of her utter belief that Rian was simply being dramatic. When the seriousness on his face didn't fade, she sobered up, the hair on her nape rising.

"She was cheating on my father," he revealed, swallowing the bile that arose when he recalled memories he wished he could erase. "Maybe I was too young to understand the impact, maybe I thought it would get her in trouble, but I told my dad. He died a few months later, heartbroken. I could have saved him the misery if I'd just kept my mouth shut. Nanamma was sent away because I wouldn't listen to my mother. She was forced to live away from her true home, with an ailing husband who she lost in the same year as her son. That was my fault."

"What does any of that have to do with me?" Kaya wondered out loud. "You were eight years old when you lost your father. We didn't meet until you were, what? Sixteen or seventeen?"

Rian felt her gaze land upon him with unexpected weight. A fog of fear clouded him, momentarily making him wonder if he should remain silent. He stood to lose not just Kaya now, but the friendships she'd brought with her. He would lose Arjun and Vihaan too if Kaya turned him away.

"Rian?"

Move on from the past, he heard Aditi's voice urge him. This was one way to do it.

"It was one of those shitty parties she had with her equally bitchy friends," he began, trying to find the words in him to explain this important part of their shared past. "They were talking about this new family who was joining their prestigious ranks. Not old money, so Leela of course thought they were beneath our notice."

"My family?"

He nodded.

"I knew if I dated you, it would piss her off. Hurt her pride. I wanted to embarrass her." He couldn't say more. Her expressions made it obvious that she understood the implications of what he'd confessed. The silence between them seemed to stretch endlessly as Kaya stared outwards, possibly reliving old memories. The fact that he was too ashamed to continue looking at her had him expecting the worst.

"That's why you befriended me?" she questioned him, her voice strained.

His nostrils flared, old regrets clawing at him.

"She'd warned me to stay away from you and I didn't listen. I told her I'd be happy to see her sad. That's why she reacted so harshly when she found us together. I'm so sorry. If I hadn't been such a self-centred asshole, she would have never insulted your parents in public and you wouldn't have suffered. I never thought that my actions would affect your life like that."

Though Rian tried to stick to the facts, recalling the negative impact he had left on this person he so cared for had him awash in guilt. Elbows on his knees, he leaned forward as he knit his fingers together. The muscles in his back remained tight with tension as he rested his chin against his crossed thumbs, his lower lip pressed into his fist to stop it from trembling.

"This is why you searched for me when I went to the US?" she clarified, still sounding like she was trying to piece all the information together. "This is why you continued to look out for me when I came back? Why Nanamma helped me when I left Mumbai?"

His shame deprived him of his ability to answer her with words.

"Why did you never tell me this before?"

He drew in a breath, releasing it with a shudder when the burn climbing up his nose abruptly settled behind his eyes. His vision grew blurry.

"I didn't want to lose my friend."

When he finally risked a glance at her, he was met with equally teary eyes. With no hesitation whatsoever, Kaya launched herself at him, struggling to hold him fully given the disparity in their sizes.

"You're the biggest idiot I've ever known," she mumbled, her tears dampening his shoulder.

"Sorry," Rian gruffed, flicking away an errant tear and giving up any attempt at trying to hold them back when she hugged him harder. How long they sat together like that, they didn't know. But when she pulled away, Rian knew both their faces bore similar blotchy marks and red noses.

"I'm glad you told me." Kaya sniffled, reaching towards the box of tissues. "I can't imagine how hard this must have been for you."

"Hard for me? Kaya, you should hate me."

"For what?" She dabbed at her eyes. "For being my friend through all this? For having had a moment of rebellion?" She blew her nose, irritated that her tirade had to be cut in the middle. No sooner was she done, she turned to face him fully. "Why are you taking responsibility for the whole incident when you were a minor part? You did more than enough to make up for it, Rian. I wouldn't have gotten through so many years alone if it hadn't been for you."

"Kaya..."

"We were kids. Arjun and I have spoken about this so much. I've dissected it with my therapist seven ways to Sunday. I used to think I was to blame for what happened to me. You think you are. But the truth is we had adults around us who failed us in different ways. Let go of this guilt. It's not yours to bear."

Her earnestness found a way to break through his misery.

"This curse nonsense you were spouting before," she continued, agitatedly waving her hand in the air. "There is no curse. You are punishing yourself, and you need to stop."

You need to stop.
You need to let go.
You need to move on.

The people who cared for him seemed to have the same thing to say. Why had he never listened before?

He'd been terrified that someday Kaya would come to know of his part in the drama that had upended her life, and that she would despise him for it. Instead, she was trying to release him from the guilt he'd carried within him for thirteen years.

If he'd actively tried to loosen the hold his past had on him, if he'd tried harder to move on, would he have been able to avoid causing Aditi pain?

"If I hurt Aditi, it'll destroy me. I let Leela Shetty get under my skin and the collateral was, once again, someone I love."

"Did you mean it when you said you were marrying Aditi to get back at your mother?" Kaya inquired after a moment.

"Of course not! I don't give a damn about my mother. I haven't for years."

"Your reaction was momentary, wasn't it?"

"I. . .yeah."

"Then what makes you think you'll let Aditi down again, especially because of Mrs. Shetty?"

Her pointed question brought him up short, the chaos in his mind suddenly calming.

Would he disappoint Aditi again because of his mother? No. This had been the final straw. He didn't care about anything related to Leela. All he'd thought about since the moment he'd left the airport was Aditi and how much he missed her. The glimpse he'd gotten of life without her was not one he ever wanted to see come to fruition.

Maybe Kaya read that in his face. She grasped his hand, bestowing him with a kind look, the sort filled with frustration and affection for the same person. "You're not that child who needed to hurt his parent anymore. And you did not ruin my life. Let go of the things that have held you back. You've been running from your past, like I did. I think it's time to stop. Just don't wait too long. Aditi told me about the suitor that her family wants her to meet."

"Did she say she's going to marry him?!" Rian sat up, eyes wide, taking his hand back to reach for his phone.

"Wow. Overreact much? That was nowhere close to what I said."

But Rian was lost to his worries, furiously scrolling through Aditi's Instagram posts.

"Are you stalking her right now?" Kaya's mouth fell open at his possessive behaviour.

"She isn't responding to my texts. She won't pick up my calls. I don't know what else to do."

"Oh my god," she gasped, her lips tugging upwards when recognition hit. "You're jealous."

"Of course I'm jealous," Rian shot back, still neck deep in his online stalking efforts and getting increasingly frustrated when her sister's profile was locked as private. "Some stupid fucker thinks he's going to get a chance with her. Not while I'm alive." He contemplated how many missed calls it would take for Aditi to speak with him without making him seem like an obsessive psychopath.

Kaya burst out laughing, wondering if Rian even realised that he'd proven her point. She believed that Rian did love her once, but those feelings had been a product of guilt. It wasn't the way she ought to have been loved. It wasn't anywhere close to the way he loved Aditi now. Love and guilt should never occupy the same space.

He had learned to live with the distance Kaya had placed between them after their short dating stint. Years later, when she'd finally reconciled with Arjun, Rian had turned around and become fast friends with her husband as well. She didn't think he would be a tenth as generous if he had to do the same with Aditi.

She caught sight of Arjun, who had been patiently waiting a distance away, concerned when she'd cried. She'd had to wave him away so that he wouldn't interrupt them. She smiled at Arjun now to let him know that he could come back to her. Within a few seconds, she was being pulled into her husband's embrace.

"All okay, love?" he murmured in her ear.

"Yes. I'll tell you later," she promised.

Arjun raised a brow, but accepted it with grace. "So, what're the plans now? Are we going bowling or to a movie?" he asked.

"Neither," Rian answered. "I'm calling my lawyer."

Arjun gasped dramatically. "Are you divorcing us? Who else will suffer in your company?"

Kaya unfortunately couldn't hold back a snort. She cast Rian an apologetic look, giggling when he rolled his eyes in pure exasperation.

"As much as I am going to regret this," he grumbled, checking his calendar on his phone, "are you both free in two days?"

"We could be," Kaya said, cautious and confused. Rian's sudden energy shift made her nervous, but he seemed less distraught than before. "Why?"

"I'm going to Bangalore to talk to the woman I love," he informed them, determination giving his voice strength. "And I would like some back up."

A massive grin split Kaya's face in half.

Arjun punched something into his phone with a nod of approval before raising his head. "I can have my plane ready for Saturday morning," he offered when loud buzz interrupted him. With a gremlin-esque grin, he flashed his screen towards Rian. "I texted Vihaan. He said he's coming and can't wait to see you grovel."

"Fantastic," Rian groaned. But, for the first time since Aditi had left him, he felt like he could see the light again.

39

Love Song

RIAN

R IAN STOOD IN FRONT of the bungalow he'd driven up to, forehead creased.

He didn't have to look next to him to know that his friends and grandmother probably wore the same look of confusion that he did.

His expectations of coming to Aditi's home in Bangalore were simple.

He would walk up to the front door and ring the bell. Hopefully, she would answer and he'd get to see her before having to meet her family. Knowing that she might be angry, he was fully prepared to use Nanamma as an excuse for having shown up without notice. Maybe he'd even be able to steal a few minutes with her in private to apologise and think of the next steps.

What was before him would afford him no space to think much less the privacy he had hoped for. People were teeming around the modest home, the front yard filled with tittering ladies in pretty sarees, men laughing raucously with friends and young children running about, playing games no one knew the names of. Near the outer edge where they stood was a group of people singing old songs, nearly three adults holding the same mic as they bellowed out the lyrics with no effort made to match tone or rhythm.

In one word, it was chaos.

"She's not picking up her phone," Vihaan informed him. They'd all tried to call her in turns, hoping she'd come find them.

"Quite the crowd," Arjun muttered, declining the server who'd come to offer them refreshments.

"Is it the 20th?"

"Yeah."

Rian grimaced.

"I forgot about the anniversary party. It's her parent's anniversary today."

A hand landed on his arm, drawing his attention. He twisted his neck to see Kaya.

"Want to return to the hotel and come back later?"

He almost agreed, but that's when he caught sight of Aditi.

A cloud of gauzy silver-grey material, the colour of his eyes, covered her upper body and curved over her like fluffy frosting on a cupcake. Her hair was slicked up in a high ponytail, swishing about as she moved, drawing attention to her long neck and the sleek lines of her exposed shoulder. The hint of skin at her waist had him staring at her like a creep, wondering if he could glimpse her waist chain from this distance. The flaring white silk skirt seemed simple, and he almost questioned if someone else had picked her dress. How was it that his Aditi was wearing such plain clothes with no hint of bright colour?

As he thought this, the crowds moved and she walked across the lawn. That's when he saw it.

The entire bottom of her skirt was covered in a profusion of multi-coloured floral prints, creeping up towards her thighs.

Till the end of his days, this would be the dress he would remember Aditi in. She looked like a woodland fairy who'd mistakenly entered the real world.

The desire to rush up to her and embrace her engulfed him like a gale, hitting him with unexpected force. He didn't want to wait anymore. He didn't care if the entire population of Bangalore was present, and then some. He needed to speak with Aditi, time and propriety be damned.

She had asked him not to embarrass her again in public. He'd broken his promise, though unknowingly, when she'd heard him with his mother. Maybe apologising in public would help his case. If it wiped that lost look from her face and brought the smile he loved back, then his embarrassment would be a price he was willing to pay multiple times over.

His eyes scanned the yard, finally alighting on the DJ table right near him, an idea striking him almost immediately.

"Wish me luck," Rian muttered, squaring his shoulders as though he was about to head into battle.

"What are you going to do?" Kaya asked.

"Something I never thought I'd do again." He marched up to the DJ and hailed him, leaning over to whisper his request. Seeing a new member join their ranks, especially one they didn't recognize, the group of jolly singers quieted and graciously handed their microphone to him.

Nodding his thanks, he tapped on the head, wincing at the feedback that pealed through the sound system. The abrupt noise caused most of the conversation around him to simmer down, the crowd throwing an annoyed look in the general direction of the DJ. Aditi, however, remained in her own world, seated at her table and flicking imaginary kernels off the table cloth.

"Doc," he called out, watching her head whip up in shock. Her mouth fell open when their eyes met, and his vision honed in on her. The music trickling through the speakers diffused in the air around them. He took a deep breath in, letting everything in his periphery fade, focusing on her to keep his nerves from taking over.

"This one's for you." With that, he began to hum, leading into the lyrics of a song he hoped would convey what he wished to say. Her look of shock was constant, but as he hit each note in time to the beat, his voice grew stronger. Singing too, he realised, was like riding a bike. He may not have done it for a long time, but he hadn't forgotten how.

He'd simply not had enough motivation to try again.

Cradling the bouquet of flowers he'd brought for her in one arm and the mic in the other, he strolled up to her, never letting his sights stray from her sitting figure.

She was so still, he wondered momentarily if she'd stopped breathing.

Aditi couldn't glance away. She was certain she'd blink and this would turn out to be a mirage. How could it be anything else? How was it that Rian, looking indescribably gorgeous in that bottle-green cable knit sweater, the dark wash of his jeans complimenting his long legs, was here, at her house, SINGING FOR HER?

She watched him, hearing him sing her a song with her name in it. An upbeat tune that lifted her spirits, through the lyrics of which he begged and cajoled her to smile again. He donned a sheepish grin at the part where the singer admitted to not knowing how to sing, yet doing it for the sake of the person they wanted to make happy.

Though it was a song well known to many, when Rian was crooning it, watching her the way he was, it felt like every word was written for her.

She was dreaming with her eyes wide open.

But what a beautiful dream this was, she accepted, gulping as he got closer.

"Hey Aditi," he finished melodiously, sighing as if the rest of the lines were too heartfelt to repeat anymore. He kneeled at her feet.

He dropped the mic on the table next to him before presenting the bouquet to her.

The music faded to a close, the refrain from the song still playing in her mind. The air around them was silent, gentle murmurs rising from interested spectators.

Neither Rian nor Aditi could find it in themselves to acknowledge anyone else at this time.

"Hey, Doc," he whispered.

She had to suppress the shiver that travelled down her spine at his husky voice.

"Hi. What are you doing here?"

His lips tipped up gently. "I missed you. You look exquisite."

Her expression softened, and Rian was hard pressed to stop himself from reaching out and touching her.

"You sang in public."

A statement and a question, rolled into one.

"Yeah. It's the big gesture," he explained. "Like in those books you read. Took me a while to get through one but I did."

Her brows shot up.

"You read for me?" she asked, knowing that if she hadn't been already sitting down, this would have done it. Her insides felt like jelly.

"There was no audiobook. I had to read."

"Why?"

He shrugged, a look of discomfort rushing across his handsome face. "I didn't want you to change your mind about marrying me."

"Rian."

"You can," he interrupted quickly, looking like it took a lot out of him to say that. His lips thinned, brows drawing low. "I deserve it for the crap I said. You can one hundred percent reject me in public, in front of your family and friends." He slowed down with each word as realisation hit. "Wow. I didn't plan this well at all, did I?"

She shook her head, biting the inside of her lips to stop herself from smiling.

"The anniversary party date slipped my mind," he admitted, looking like a little boy caught having forgotten his homework. "I did not imagine doing this in front of an audience."

"Why didn't you wait?"

"Because," he stressed, unable to stop himself from clasping her hands in his. He shifted closer so that her knees were against his chest. "I don't know how to live without you anymore. I probably can't get more pathetic than this, but I don't care. I'd crawl through broken glass if that means you'll forgive me."

Her lips trembled, torn between wanting to throw herself at him and staying firm. "I want you to stop hurting yourself."

"I understand, Sunshine. Sometimes, I might need a reminder. Just another reason why I need you. But you need me too."

"I do?"

He nodded, the glint in his eye familiar and soothing, like a balm over her wounds. "You need me because I will always laugh at your puns—even the bad ones. I constantly dream about your perfect eyes. I am obsessed with your radiant smile and in awe of your wild and untamed heart. I will never want you to be anything other than who you are."

White teeth trapped her plump lower lip, a fleeting shadow of hurt marring her face.

"Even if it embarrasses your family?" she finally asked, her voice low.

His grip on her firmed, his thumb rubbing soothing circles on the back of her hand.

"My only family is Nanamma and my friends. And they adore you. They're here too, by the way."

Aditi's eyes slipped past his ear, only now sighting Kaya, Arjun, Vihaan and Nanamma. From the edge of her vision, she noted her grandmother wave at her friend, hurrying over to greet her.

"Your mother—," she began, only to be shushed.

"Does not matter. You were right to call me out on not having let go of the past. You've always known I needed to learn to move on. I've started to. I hope you'll give me the chance to prove that to you also."

"You made me cry," she complained.

"I know. I'll accept a lifetime of punishment at your hands for that."

She glanced down where their hands were joined, shaking her head lightly.

"I don't like thinking that you want me for reasons other than love."

One warm palm cupped her cheek, tenderly raising her face up. "You weren't part of any of my plans, Doc. If tonight is any indication, you know you've changed me. What I thought I knew about love was very different until you came into my life and taught me how to be better."

"Meaning?"

"Meaning," he said, dropping the softest kiss on her knuckles before glancing up at her, his heart in his eyes. "I am drowning with how deeply I'm in love with you. Without you, I exist. With you, I'm alive. You have become the reason for my smiles, the peace in my soul. My heart, my body, my entire being—you own me. A lifetime wouldn't be enough to figure out how much I love you but I will try everyday to show you in words, in actions, in every way you need that you, and *only you*, complete me."

Aditi let out a soft sob, overwhelmed by his admission.

"I need you so much more than you could need me and I know I'm being selfish. But come back to me," he begged. "Save me, Doc. As part of your Hippocratic oath, save me, or. . .I'll die."

"Ayappa satyam, if she doesn't marry him, I will," they heard someone declare. "Hell, I would too after that speech," a man concurred. "Is this a skit?" someone else asked, multiple voices shushing them when Aditi spoke again.

"You're being very dramatic, Bugs," she teased, a tremulous smile on her lips, her eyes glimmering with happiness. "You'll die without me?"

The grin he bore was as much in response to her joy as it was in relief that she'd smiled again. "Don't make me prove it. I'd rather live with you."

"Did you rehearse that?"

He chuckled, sheepishly scratching above one thick eyebrow. "A little. Kaya wanted to write me a script on the flight here. She thought I'd mess this up."

"Was this from the script?"

"No. She uses too many big words."

Aditi let out a soft laugh. "The Hippocratic oath was a nice touch."

"I have something better," he said, before reaching into his pocket and producing a velvet box. Her eyes grew round when he opened the lid to reveal a flawless solitaire ring about the size of the nail on her index finger. Round, cut brilliantly, sitting on six high prongs—it was a stunning piece of jewellery that caught the light and bounced it off so perfectly, she couldn't hold back a gasp.

"It's a yellow diamond?" she asked, staring.

"To match the sunshine you spread in my life," he explained. The utter devotion written upon his face had her raising one hand to her chest, afraid of her heart bursting within.

"Will you. . ."

"Yes!"

He laughed delightedly. "Let me finish, Sunshine."

She nodded, her smile widening, her watery eyes shimmering like a million little stars had been trapped within her irises.

"Aditi Krishnan, will you make me the happiest man ever and please marry me?" he asked sweetly, causing her to take a deep breath in, trying valiantly to hold back her tears.

"Yes," she sniffed, feeling a joy that made her entire being glow from the inside. She'd never thought she would ever be loved like this. So openly, so thoroughly and so unabashedly.

Rian's trembling fingers grasped her equally shaky hand as he slid the ring on, the fit absolutely perfect.

"It's beautiful," she whispered.

"Not more than you."

"Shut up and kiss already!" they heard a lady yell, belatedly realising that the mic nearby was still on.

"Sorry," Aditi grimaced, her face red. "That's my rowdy cousin."

"I like this cousin," he murmured, the tip of one finger tracing her skin where her blush spread. "I don't know her but she's my favourite."

Aditi would have laughed except Rian actually did lean forward to kiss her in front of all her family and friends.

Her fingers speared his luscious hair, the glint of her ring shining brightly against his dark head. She sighed as his mouth moved over hers, enveloped by his love.

And truly, it was glorious.

40

The Krishnan Clan

RIAN

THE INSIDE OF ADITI'S house was laid out in a style reminiscent of older Indian homes. Tall ceilings, white paint on the walls accented with warm wood and red oxide flooring. The large, central living space was comfortably furnished. On one side was a shallow pond that caught the moonlight from the skylight above it, sounds of the ongoing party outside trickling through.

Rian glanced upwards, catching sight of red roof shingles under the waterfall of lush creepers that had been strategically grown to act like a privacy screen for the dining space on the other side.

The dining room was blessedly empty compared to where he was.

Seated on a couch, with nothing but the wall behind him and a room full of people he'd never met in front, their expressions ranging from curiosity to displeasure, he felt uncharacteristically nervous.

The only consolation he had was that Aditi was beside him, her shoulder touching his arm. He tilted his head to the side, eyes sweeping the crowd that had gathered within the living room.

"All of these people are related to you?"

"Yep."

"How big is your family?"

"Big enough to populate an island," she whispered back.

"Will you be okay living with just me and Nanamma, full-time?" She glanced up to find his eyes on her.

"Perfectly. Will you be okay with having my family members visiting us often?"

"We'll move to a bigger place to accommodate more visitors," he immediately offered.

"You'd do that for me?" Aditi asked, seconds away from leaping into his arms.

His dimple deepened. "I'd do anything for you."

"Okay, you two," someone clapped, drawing their attention. "Stop whispering to each other."

Aditi and Rian straightened, looking quite like a pair of detainees who were waiting for judgement. Mr. and Mrs. Krishnan sat directly across from them on the opposite side of the room, the entire force of their family backing them as they raked a critical gaze over their daughter and her lover.

"Before we begin," an old lady in a yellow saree spoke up, "I would like to say I approve of this boy and I wanted this to happen."

Aditi beamed at her, and Rian surmised that this was her paati.

"Amma, you knew about them?" Mr. Krishnan asked.

"He's Chitra's grandson. Chitra, you were right. They make a very good-looking couple."

"Nanamma?" Rian threw a surprised glance at his smug grandmother. "Did you plan this?"

Chitra laughed, shaking her head.

"God, no. I merely took notice of what was obvious every time you two were in the same room and pushed things along at the right time." She turned to her friend, pointing towards Rian. "His face was worth seeing every time I asked him to book a table for Aditi to meet other men."

Aditi smirked.

"Aditi, kanna," Nanamma teased, her tone causing her Cheshire grin to falter. "Don't think I didn't see you getting jealous when I pretended to set your colleague up with Rian also."

It was his turn to raise a brow while Aditi avoided all eye contact.

"I simply gave you the opportunity to get to know each other without my presence whenever possible," Nanamma continued, making them feel rather foolish for not having questioned why she'd always been too busy to spend time with them or why she constantly retired to bed early. "The fact that the two of you were living in the same house just made it easy for me."

"They're living together?" Mr. Krishnan held his heart as though it would give out.

"You go, girl," another cousin yelled out, someone else adding, "are we allowed to do this now? I want to move out, too!"

"Oh, grow up, kanna. Even I know the way of the world right now." Paati rolled her eyes, and Rian immediately knew whom Aditi had inherited her sass from.

"So, I guess you two are in. . . a relationship?" Mrs. Krishnan inquired carefully, eyes big behind her glasses.

Aditi nodded.

"This is why you refused to marry Pratik?"

Rian couldn't control himself, turning to look at Aditi in surprise. She smiled at him. "I learnt to say no, after all. I was never going to marry the perfect NRI."

"That's my girl," he whispered, his eyes hot on her, enough to make colour rush up her neck. Multiple people cleared their throats and he looked away, determinedly focusing on her parents now.

"Hello, Mr. and Mrs. Krishnan. I am Rian Shetty," he introduced himself politely. "Please ask me whatever you need to know."

"What do you do?"

"I'm a chef."

"Huh," Mr. Krishnan huffed. "Is it a steady income?"

"Why does it matter?" Aditi interrupted, her lower lip jutting out in a pout. "I make my own money."

As surreptitiously as possible, Rian linked his pinky finger with hers, the volume of her skirt hiding their hands. With his touch, he felt her relax, the tightness in her expression fading.

"It is somewhat variable depending on the market," he answered honestly, meeting Mr. Krishnan's gaze without flinching. "But I make a comfortable living. Aditi will not go without anything she wants."

She turned to look at him, wondering why he was downplaying his assets. It didn't matter because an uncle stepped in.

"Don't you own a restaurant?" he asked. "I've seen you in a magazine somewhere."

Before Rian could stop her, Aditi proudly added, "He owns several. He is a very hard worker and he did it all by himself. And he's going to get his second Michelin star this year."

Warmth suffused him. Undoubtedly, she would be his fiercest cheerleader.

"It's still under review," he mumbled, trying to control this surge of adoration he felt for her every time he so much as looked her way. "It isn't guaranteed."

"You'll get it. I'm certain."

Mr. and Mrs. Krishnan didn't seem to care about the material wealth he owned. "I guess Aditi wouldn't have to cook. She'd be tired after her shifts at the hospital," her mother explained to her father, who was nodding along.

"Okay. Chef is fine," he announced. "What about your family?"

"My grandmother is the only close family I have. And my friends who are standing with her." Kaya, Arjun and Vihaan politely nodded to everyone, smiling as some of the cousins waved their hellos.

"Your mother and father?"

Aditi's hand squeezed his, her look telling him that he need not reveal everything.

"My father is deceased," he answered, taking a moment before he continued, "and my mother is not in the picture."

He saw Aditi's parents exchange an indecipherable look.

"The family I will make with your daughter is my only priority. With your permission, I would like to marry her and gain a family."

Her mother melted instantly.

"And if we don't give permission?" Mr. Krishnan asked before being swatted on the arm by his wife. "What?" he grunted, his moustache twitching in annoyance. "He kissed my daughter in front of my eyes. I'm going to need to soak my balls in bleach."

Aditi groaned, and Rian was too shocked to laugh. Some of the family members sniggered, their whispers increasing in volume.

"What?" Mr. Krishnan looked around, frowning. "Did I say something wrong?" He turned to a young boy standing near him, presumably his nephew, and tipped his chin up. "Did I not say it right?"

The boy, barely a teen, pushed his spectacles up with a single finger. "It's *'wash your eyeballs in bleach'*, uncle, not your actual balls."

Rian saw Arjun turn away, an odd choking noise erupting from him. Kaya had hidden her face against her husband's bicep, her body shuddering silently.

"I would have thought that was obvious," Mr. Krishnan blustered. "Why would I soak my balls in bleach? But I guess I have had all the children I need so it doesn't matter which set of balls I soak."

Vihaan lost the battle to be polite and went into a violent coughing fit, half his face covered by his arm and his eyes glimmering with an unholy mirth.

His friends had deserted him, Rian realised. Completely useless, the whole lot of them. He didn't know why he bothered to bring them along. He was going to dump them all the minute he figured a way to escape this conversation.

"Please stop talking," Aditi begged.

"About balls or about you?"

The earnestness with which Mr. Krishnan asked this question only made Rian pinch himself on his thigh, curbing the urge to chortle. He was not going to have his future father-in-law dismiss him as a disrespectful brat. His eyes teared up when he pinched himself hard enough to leave a bruise.

"Appa, porum!" Aditi cried, having turned a brilliant shade of red. Fascinated, Rian noted this down for the future, curious to see if he could generate this colour on her in passion.

"Oh, you're embarrassed about your Appa talking about his balls but not about kissing your boyfriend in front of us all?" her mother calmly asked in defence of her husband.

"Amma!"

"Aunty," he interrupted, ready to shield Aditi if needed. "I'm her fiancé, not boyfriend. And the kissing was entirely my fault. I'm sorry. I didn't mean to embarrass anyone."

"You're sorry for kissing my daughter? Why? Do you not love her?" Mr. Krishnan snarked immediately, skewering him with a look that made Rian realise that there was no correct answer. He simply had to subject himself to this torment and let their annoyance run its course.

"Kanna, are you sure about this guy? He seems flaky," one of her aunts commented.

"We won't give our daughter away if you don't treat her right," an uncle grumbled.

"He could sing another song to convince you," Arjun piped up. The glare Rian threw his way had Kaya stepping in front to protect her husband.

"That's a great idea," someone else said and suddenly, everyone was throwing out suggestions for songs. Rian couldn't keep track of who was speaking anymore. This was not a family, it was an army.

Finally, Aditi jumped up, stomping her foot like a little girl with a major grievance.

"Stop it!" she yelled, wagging a finger threateningly at them all. "Stop bothering him or I swear I will elope and not a single one of you will be invited to the birth of my child."

"Are you pregnant?" one cousin screeched. Aditi shook her head, but her denial was drowned out in a chorus of new questions and sassy comments.

Her father seemed torn between rejoicing the possibility of becoming a grandfather and the discomfort of realising that his first born had a sex life. "I'll have to bleach my ears too, now," he dejectedly moaned, turning to his wife for support.

"If it helps reduce the hair growth on them, then it's a good idea," Mrs. Krishnan tartly responded.

"I'm going to be an aunt? So cool!" another cousin wailed in the back.

Aditi kept trying to explain that it was a misunderstanding, but no one was listening.

"How is that possible? She's not married yet," an older aunt mumbled. "That's not a criteria anymore," someone else said.

"How far along are you?"

"Can I plan the baby shower?"

"Can we draw names for the baby?"

"Enough!" Rian roared, surprising even himself. Thirty-seven sets of eyes turned to look at him. He stood up and tucked Aditi into his side. "She is not pregnant," he announced, glancing at her for confirmation once before continuing. "But that is a distinct possibility in the future so if you all want to see the baby, you will listen to Aditi when she speaks and not interrupt her until she allows you to do so!"

Proverbial crickets sounded in the background, the entire room still because of his outburst. He glared unrepentantly at them all, daring even one of them to pipe out of turn. Satisfied that they would behave, he looked at the woman beside him. Almost immediately, his frown softened into a smile.

"Go ahead, Doc."

"Thank you," Aditi whispered, looking at him like he'd won a war for her.

"Anytime, Sunshine," he winked.

She took a deep breath and turned to face her family. "Amma, Appa, Paati, and everyone here. I love you all. You are very important to me and I would very much like you to accept Rian as my future husband because," she gulped, reaching to the side to hold his hand for strength, "I love him. And I want to marry him."

There was a severe silence and it stretched and stretched.

"Guys?" she prompted, on the verge of tears.

Her mother was the only one brave enough to venture a question.

"Are we allowed to talk now?" she asked, eyes darting between Rian and Aditi. When her daughter nodded, Mrs. Krishnan stood up and marched over to them, throwing her hands about them in a bear hug.

"Welcome to the family, Rian. Any man who can stand up so my daughter is heard in a crowd is one hundred percent okay by me."

Aditi almost sagged against him in relief.

Her father came up to them next.

"Appa?"

"No further questions," he said, patting his daughter lovingly on her cheek. "Your mother is correct. Welcome, son."

Rian accepted the hand Mr. Krishnan held out, shaking it once.

"Thank you, sir."

"I saw you brought a bottle of scotch."

Rian's lips twitched at the surreptitious glance Mr. Krishnan sent his wife before saying this.

"Yes, sir. Fifteen-year-old, single malt. Aditi mentioned you like it."

"Good choice. Aditi's amma will not get angry if I have some with you. To get to know you better." His palm landed with an approving thump on Rian's shoulder. "Tomorrow evening then? Come for dinner. Bring your friends."

"Thank you, I will."

"We will have to talk about the details of the marriage soon. I assume that will be with you?"

"Aditi and I, together, sir."

"Yes, yes, I know," Mr. Krishnan grumbled, rolling his eyes. "Boys these days, totally whipped. In my time, we used to be real men."

"What did you say?" Mrs. Krishnan asked sharply.

"Nothing, my dear. Come, let me get you some dessert before the guests take it all. I heard the payasam is delicious."

For the rest of the evening, they were surrounded by family. As much as he wanted to have Aditi all to himself, Rian finally understood the attraction of the love she received from them. And by extension, what he too would get.

For a boy who'd been lonely much of his life, he was overwhelmed with the ease with which the Krishnan clan enveloped him in their fold. As if they'd been waiting all along for him to come to them.

For him to come home.

41

& Then They Wed

Rian & Aditi

One Year Later.

Dog, My Sunshine,

I could not imagine our ~~webing~~ wedding day without you ~~vwearing~~ the flowers I picked. I hope Vhaan didn't crush them. I hate that he gets to see you before I do.

Though I cannot be ~~theit~~ there to help you put them ~~no~~ on, this will be the only time I'll let it happen. I have tried to fight it but Nanamma is scary & will ~~nut~~ not let me out of her sight before the ~~web~~ wedding is complete. I'll be glad to be ~~dun~~ done with these rituals and finally have you in ~~are~~ our home again.

Every day hereafter, I will be present to pin flowers on you. Every day, I will be ~~ther tehir~~ there to feed you the ~~feebs~~ foods you love, but more importantly the ~~be~~ foods you need. Every day, I will love you. I wouldn't know ~~who~~ how to alive otherwise.

When you come down that aisle today, I'll be there. Waiting. Planning for the ~~teri test~~ rest of my life with you.

Yours, and only yours,

Bugs

PS: Can we please revisit this nickname? Bugs is weird.

No, Chota Bheem is not a valid option. Neither is ~~Baba~~ Bada Bheem! Don't even suggest it.

Chef is fine, but we both no know what happens when you say it.

PPS: I ALSO HAVE A NEW NICKNAME FOR YOU. TELL YOU LATER.

Aditi chuckled warmly, reading through the letter as the stylist put the final touches on her hair. Her thumb swiped over the edge of a sentence where it looked like Rian had irritatedly smudged it in an attempt to correct the spelling. The little errors, crossed out words and mildly illegible writing did not lessen the impact of his message. She picked up the thickly strung garlands of closed jasmine that Rian had sent with a handwritten note that left her sniffling back happy tears.

For a person who'd once told him that she rarely cried, Aditi found that Rian had a penchant for making her emotional. In the year and a bit since they'd gotten together, his ability to render her speechless with his thoughtfulness, a reflection of his selfless love, had only increased.

True to his word, he had done what he could to leave the past behind so that it never again hindered their future together.

"Careful with this." Aditi handed the lengthy gajra to the stylist, letting her sister step in to finish sliding bangles on both her hands. Anika's happy face beamed at her, clearly excited that her two favourite people were getting married today.

Rian had quickly endeared himself to her entire family. Where she'd once been worried that he'd find it overwhelming to accept her large family, he'd turned around and effortlessly slipped into the role of a big brother for her siblings and cousins. His patient and calm demeanour made him their go-to person for problem solving.

To her never-ending amusement, he took this responsibility very seriously, which is why he was also privy to every school crush and romantic problems of her teenaged cousins.

The drama was better than his Korean sitcoms, he'd once told her.

At one point, she'd returned after multiple weeks away at medical camp, only to find that he'd coerced her parents to come to Mumbai to spend time with him, citing that he was lonely. Her mother doted upon him, her father trusted him like he would a son, and Rian soaked up every bit of their attention with a hunger she knew was a result of the loss of his own parental relations.

With his hesitancy fading in time, Rian had taken over as the darling of the house and her family members had unequivocally declared him their favourite.

She'd have been jealous, but seeing his efforts to establish familial relationships given his past made her heart swell with love and respect for the man she'd claim today as her husband.

Aditi took a moment in front of the mirror to sweep her gaze over her bridal outfit. The dark mehendi designs adorning her hands bore evidence of being deeply loved by one's spouse as per an old wives tale. Ancestral jewellery graced her forehead and neck along with the waist chain that Rian had gifted her with express instructions that he'd be the one to remove it on their wedding night. Her diamond ring glinted every time she wiggled her fingers to reduce her nerves.

Every part of her today represented an amalgamation of her past and present, as she stepped into a future she'd once prayed for. With one last look, she turned and walked towards the door where her sisters and friends waited patiently to escort her to him.

Her love.

Rian sat on his groom's throne, offering prayers directly into the holy fire as directed by the priest. Every so often, his eyes would travel across the open gardens in front of him. It had been transformed completely with chairs laid out in neat rows for attendees to sit in, white tents in the back where the party would shift to later. Gauzy curtains wrapped the trunks of the tall trees that shaded them, creating an almost mystical greenwood feel around them.

Long ribbons with crystals and pearls formed a glittering archway above the carpet of flowers that led from the back of the mansion to where the wedding dais was.

The crash of ocean waves behind him added to the enchantment of the venue.

That his wedding was taking place on the grounds of his childhood home felt surreal. When Aditi had suggested it, it had made perfect sense. This place had held only bad memories for him. Step by step, little by little, he'd replace them all with good ones. He would fill every nook and cranny within this manor with laughter for the family he would have with Aditi.

His lips curved softly, recalling her surprise when he'd brought up accepting his inheritance.

"You told the investing board you're dyslexic?" She'd stared at him like he'd grown a third eye.

"Yes," he'd sheepishly admitted, lying down on their couch with his head in her lap. He nudged her belly with his nose, annoyed that she'd stopped massaging his scalp in shock.

"I'm recovering all of myself that I hid before," he told her, grabbing her wrist to direct her to keep stroking his hair, sighing in happiness when she did. *"I had a hard time talking about it, but I'm in a position where I can affect change. We've come a long way as a society to accept that disabilities exist, but we can be better. I want to make conversation around it normal whenever I can."*

"That's. . .I'm proud of you, sweetheart," Aditi had murmured, bending down to brush a kiss across his lips. *"There truly is nothing to be ashamed of."*

"Hmm. I've put into motion changes on hiring practices at my restaurants already. I've given instructions to open up employment for differently abled individuals in Singapore as well."

"And the school?"

"I have money."

"I know, but. . ."

"No, Sunshine," he'd interrupted her. "I mean, I have a lot of money. My inheritance—I'm claiming it."

At her blank stare, he'd shown her the papers he'd been sent by his lawyers.

"My father left all his assets to me," he'd revealed to a bewildered Aditi. "He changed his will before his death. I've known since I turned twenty-one but I thought leaving everything behind would let me escape my mother and help me forget my past. It didn't. So, I'm facing it now. Whatever weird connection I still held with her, I'm severing it. I meant it when I said you'll never have to come in contact with her again."

"What did you do?"

His look of innocence had not fooled her one bit.

"I didn't do anything. My lawyers did. She'll be moved to a different home and will subsist on what I allow for her living expenses."

He'd chuckled at the way her jaw had dropped open, chucking her under her chin playfully.

"She agreed to that?" Aditi had questioned immediately.

"I am certain my lawyers heard every curse word in the book. But I didn't give her a choice." He slid his hand down to hold hers, his thumb drawing lazy circles on her warm skin. "She had to accept my conditions and stay away from us, or she would have nothing. I will no longer allow Leela Shetty to take the things I rightfully deserve. Whether that is my name, my father's legacy, or my happiness with you."

"So, you're rich?"

"Yep."

Aditi had leaned in, hesitating before asking, "Like, seafront-mansion-rich?"

"I'm afraid so." He'd grinned at her stunned expression. "We can pick the smallest one to live in if you want."

"*You have more than one?*" *she'd gasped, eyes widening as the truth slowly set in.*

"*We do. It's not just mine— it's ours.*"

"*Uh-huh. What about the school? Does this mean you don't need to rely on investors for the school anymore?*"

Rian had shrugged, drawing her into his arms.

"*I still want investors. It is good to have big names involved if I want it to be accepted as a formal institute. But I am not limited by them. I can build a bigger facility, have a larger scholarship pool, pay for better instructors, and figure out a way to use the money my dad left me to do good.*"

"*Sounds like a plan.*" *Aditi's approval of his decision had relieved him.* "*Between your restaurants and my earnings once I'm through specialisation, we won't need your inheritance at all.*"

Rian had nodded, saying nothing else. The truth was that there were portions of his estate that would always remain his, bound to pass from him to his children. Entailments that were substantial enough that he could spend like a madman, and still leave wealth behind for the next few generations to live in comfort.

To his amusement, Aditi still seemed to be adjusting to the idea that he was as rich as Croesus, and by default, so was she. The fact that her ideal date was still a nighttime bike ride and a plate of pav bhaji at Chandan's stall only endeared her more to him.

Excited whispers and tittering had him breaking out of his musings. The wavering sound of flutes filled the atmosphere, an indication of the bride's entry.

Rian stood up, running a hand down his front and nervously straightening his kurta. He blew out a quick breath, his eyes stuck at the bend around which she would arrive. The sound of anklets and the clinking of bangles accompanied the group of ladies who slowly came into view as they sang verses that spoke of two beloveds tying the knot, of the heavens witnessing their union and blessing them with untold joy. He observed them, as mesmerised with their coordination as the other attendees. Surrounded by her sisters and girlfriends, all swathed in various colours of rich Kanjeevaram sarees, he couldn't catch sight of Aditi. He noted Kaya in the procession at one time, and Vera beside her, even Nina—but not the woman he was desperate to see.

Anxious and excited, he leaned slightly to the side, waiting with bated breath for that first special glimpse of his bride.

A heartfelt prayer of thanks escaped his lips when the bridesmaids parted. Aditi emerged, looking resplendent, a true goddess today. All the gold on her didn't shine as much as her eyes did when they met his. Her radiance was unmatched when her smile widened at his besotted expression, and his heart damn near exploded with happiness.

The prickle behind his eyes increased when she accepted his hand to step up on the dais, her unwavering gaze upon him, the subtle tightening of her fingers in his palm anchoring him to her.

He'd never thought he would be here. That he would find someone to love and commit to for a lifetime, who felt the same for him. The world around him faded as he drew her closer, knowing that what he found so clearly reflected in her eyes was all her love, and the promise of forever.

It was hours before Rian and Aditi caught a moment together alone. Through every part of the ceremony, especially the vows, they had found ways to acknowledge each other silently. Their absolute incandescence was not hidden from any of the guests, and the entire atmosphere was one of revelry and jubilation.

Now, standing in the guest cottage that was serving as their temporary resting spot, they'd been afforded a brief respite to freshen up before joining everyone once more for the post-wedding rituals.

"Our family seems happy," Aditi said, dabbing at the edge of her eye to wipe the kohl that had smudged. She'd shed a few tears when her father had given her away. Her emotions, though mostly happy, had certainly oscillated today. "Our friends, too," she added, accepting the bottle of water Rian held out for her.

"Hmm."

"Kaya is glowing and Arjun was being extra annoying while checking in on her. And did you see Vera and Vihaan?" she asked, gasping when firm hands settled on her hips and pulled her back into him.

"I don't want to talk about our friends, Sunshine," Rian murmured against her ear, tickling it. "I want to talk about us. Our friendship."

She laughed, shaking her head.

"What?"

"I just remembered those days when you kept saying we weren't friends."

He dragged his lips along the delicate arch of her neck, pecking her intermittently.

"There was nothing remotely friendly about the way I felt for you. But you wormed your way into my life and became my friend anyway."

She turned towards him, sliding her arms up to loop about his neck, leaning up to kiss him softly.

"I'm pretty irresistible, aren't I, Mr. Shetty?"

"You're my Kryptonite, Mrs. Shetty," he muttered against her lips, making her giggle.

"Sweet talking to me using superhero terminology *and* the Mrs. tag? You're going to make me swoon."

When they drew back to look at each other, they wore matching expressions of devotion, a sense of profound contentment connecting them in that moment.

"If my life were a story," Aditi whispered, drawing her mehendi laden fingers against the edge of his jaw, "meeting you would be my favourite plot twist."

Rian gulped, taking in a deep breath. Not that Aditi had not seen him cry before. During frustrating therapy sessions where he worked through his remnant anger and fears, during sad movies, during happy times as well. He simply didn't want to go through the rest of his wedding day with red eyes. "Is this how you plan to tell me you love me today?" he teased, needing to stave off the rush of emotions he'd been experiencing on and off.

She huffed out a small laugh, happy to confess as many times as he wanted to hear it.

"I love you, Rian Shetty." Her abject adoration of him spread through him like the effervescent fragrance of the jasmine she wore. "I love your dimples, and your stunning eyes. I love your possessiveness for me, and your ability to apologise in the sweetest ways. I love that you laugh with me instead of at me, that you think my opinionated self is to be admired instead of hidden. I love that you feel so deeply for those who struggle, that you want to do good in the world. You have the softest and most beautiful heart under those rock-hard abs. While I suggested something temporary, my heart broke every plan I'd made and I fell permanently in love with you. Thank you for being mine. For giving me *all* of you, and accepting *all* of me."

His forehead dropped to hers, their noses nestled against each other.

"You're not supposed to be this good at confessions," he rasped, his throat tight, engulfing her in his embrace.

"Must be all the romance novels I read," she smiled, snuggling into him.

For a while, they held each other thus, exhilarating in the knowledge that today would be the first day of the rest of their lives as man and wife, savouring this newfound feeling of togetherness.

"You once told me you aren't perfect," he started, his voice muffled against her crown.

She pulled back to look at him, tilting her head curiously.

"That might be the only thing you've been wrong about."

"Think so?"

"I know so. I love you, Dr. Mrs. Aditi Shetty, the most perfect woman for Rian Shetty."

"Dr. Mrs.?" She frowned, scrunching her nose in distaste. "That is not the new nickname you mentioned in your letter, is it? I thought 'Doc' suffered from lack of creativity but this is pushing it."

He chuckled, nipping the tip of her nose in an affectionate move.

"Trust your husband, Doc. I have a whole list of new names, but one in particular that is the absolute best."

"Oh?" She tilted her chin imperiously. "And how will you be addressing me henceforth, Mr. Husband?"

With a flirtatious grin, he grasped her hand and lifted it to his lips. He kissed her knuckles, his eyes warming to a smoky grey as he beheld the woman who'd torpedoed his life so unexpectedly and swept him off his feet.

"My love." He dropped a peck on her cheek.

"My life." A kiss on her forehead.

"My blessing," he added, bending down to capture her lips under his before whispering her soon-to-be favourite moniker against the smile that started it all.

"My wife."

& THEN THEY WED

Before You Go...

Please take a moment to leave a review on Goodreads and Amazon. Every rating helps an indie author like me reach potential new readers, and I'd be so grateful for the support.

***

If you liked this book, you may also like:
& Then They Met – Ampersand Love Book 1, Arjun and Kaya's story.

***

Stay tuned for Ampersand Love Book 3, Vihaan and Vera's story, expected to be released early-Spring 2025.

About the Author

Riya Iyer is an Indo-Canadian author of contemporary romances, featuring South Asian characters and happily-ever-afters.

Her enchantment with books and Bollywood has kept her entertained for years, and she draws upon that enjoyment to create dramatic love stories full of fated connections, missed opportunities and desi drama.

When she's not writing, she's busy being a science nerd, making futile attempts to understand social media, cracking puns that make her life-partner roll his eyes and losing every argument with her young kiddo.

If you'd like to connect with her, you can email her at riyaiyerwrites@gmail.com, or follow her on Instagram @authorriyai.

Printed by Libri Plureos GmbH in Hamburg, Germany